JEAPES JAPES

Stories by
Ben Jeapes

To G

This collection is copyright © 2008 and 2016 Ben Jeapes. All stories in this collection are copyright © Ben Jeapes for the year of their publication.

The right of Ben Jeapes to be identified as the author of this book has been asserted in accordance with the Copyright, Designs and Patents Act 1988.

No part of this book is to be reproduced in any form without express permission of the author.

Paper versions of this collection were previously published by Lulu (2008) and Clarion Publishing (2012).

An electronic edition of this collection is available from Wizard's Tower Press (wizardstowerpress.com/)

Printed by CreateSpace

ISBN-13: 978-1530118892

ISBN-10: 1530118891

www.benjeapes.com

Also available by Ben Jeapes

The Comeback of the King

The Teen, the Thief and the Witch

Phoenicia's Worlds

Time's Chariot

The New World Order

The Xenocide Mission

His Majesty's Starship

www.benjeapes.com

Contents

Introduction
1

The Data Class
5

Pages Out of Order
27

Spoilsport
61

Digital Cats Come Out Tonight
81

Getting Rid of Teddy
95

Memoirs of a Publisher
125

The Robson Strain
147

Crush
179

Cathedral No. 3
207

Jacqui the Giantkiller
223

The Grey People
249

Wingèd Chariot
275

The Fireworker
303

Correspondents
331

Trial by Alien
355

A Holiday on Lake Moskva
391

Go with the Flow
419

Acknowledgements
445

INTRODUCTION

Approach a self-published book with caution. This is a self-published book, so you have been warned.

Normally, when you see a book in a bookshop, this is what has happened. The author sent that book to a publisher that liked it. (It might have been sent to several publishers first who didn't like it. If that happened then the author might have worked on the story again to improve it, and become a better author as a result.) The publisher's editor and the author will have worked together to make it even better. The publisher then paid the author and produced the book at its own expense, confident that it would get all that money back from sales. That's a big vote of confidence.

However, a self-published book has not been sent to a publisher (or if it has, the publisher turned it down). The author has never had to improve the story. The only money that has been risked is the author's own. The author thinks the book is pretty good – but what else would you expect? Why should you believe him?

This is a self-published book.

On the other hand, every story here – except one, and we'll come to that – has been through the process described above. It has been accepted by a book or a magazine editor, who worked with me to make it as good as possible, and paid me and produced the magazine or book at their own expense. So, people other than me have believed in these stories and thought they were worth reading. I'm still the one who thinks they could work as a book collection and I take full responsibility (but offer no refunds) if you think my judgement was out.

So, huge thanks to the editors who originally thought the stories worth publishing in the first place: David V. Barrett, Paul Beardsley, Liz Holliday, David Pringle, Kristine Kathryn Rusch, Charles C. Ryan and Robert N. Stephenson. Editors are Very Important in the whole science fiction process. They work with the author to make the story as strong as possible. They must have the strength of character to say 'no' and the discernment to say 'yes', and they put their money where their mouths are by then going ahead and publishing at their own expense. An editorial thumbs-up to a story is a hell of a vote of confidence.

I've sold 18 stories in my time, published between 1990 and 1998. Two of these were to *Dr Who* collections and so they don't belong to me, they belong to the publishers of the collections. The remaining sixteen are collected here for the first time. There is also a seventeenth story here, which has been to not one but several editors, and worked on (and worked on, and worked on) but never actually published. It may be rubbish. It may not. This is only my opinion speaking, after all. But I won't tell you which one it is yet – I wouldn't want to prejudice you before you read it.

I wasn't sure what order to put the stories in. I honestly can't remember the order they were written in. It would be nice to think that if you read the stories in publication order then you could trace

INTRODUCTION

my development as a writer, but that would also be completely false. A writer's style – if he's doing it properly – changes every time he makes a sale, based on the experiences he has had, the feedback, and what else he has read and written in the meantime. There are also large gaps in the process; for instance, 'Pages Out of Order' dates back to at least 1990, but was sold in 1994 and published in 1997. I wrote and sold plenty of other stuff in those gaps.

Then I thought of putting them in alphabetical order, or grouping them by style, or doing it in order of length ... In the end, I just put everything into a 'this feels right' sort of order. If it doesn't work – well, that's my fault again.

If the stories were in order of being written, it would be interesting to track my increasing confidence in the use of what maiden aunts might call Language. There are occasional mild uses of Language here and there; it's heaviest in 'Go with the Flow'. 'A Holiday on Lake Moskva' also contains scenes of implied pre-marital intercourse, so only show them to your aunt if you're absolutely certain she isn't a maiden. If she loves you, she won't mind you asking.

Ben Jeapes
Abingdon, August 2008

JEAPES JAPES

THE DATA CLASS

The police came while he was having supper. His household AI announced their presence.

'Two policemen to see you, Henry.'

'Police? Here?'

'Inspector James Curry and Sergeant Donald Morris.' Geoffrey had a high initiative quotient; he had taken their profiles and called up Public Information.

Henry Ash cleared the door panel and looked curiously at the couple outside. They were plain clothes and had 'cop' written all over them, but his conscience was clear. He told the door to open.

'Dr Ash? Dr Henry Ash?' said the taller one.

'Yes,' Henry said.

'I'm Sergeant Morris, this is Inspector Curry. May we ask you some questions?'

Henry raised his eyebrows. 'Come in.'

He had stopped apologising for the state of his rooms a long time ago; he had tenure and the good opinion of his visitors was unimportant. A large amount of paper, in the form of books, was scattered around the room; the terminal and VR set sitting in one corner was his one concession to the spirit of the age. Old fashioned, as he was fond of pointing out to his colleagues in the Politics department, does not equal Luddite. And he did have an AI.

JEAPES JAPES

He cleared a couple of seats of their burden and sat down in a third.

'Now, what can I do for you?' he said. The Inspector spoke this time.

'Dr Ash, do you own an AI named – um – Goldie?'

'No.'

It must have been the wrong thing to say, because the policeman frowned. *So if you know about Goldie*, Henry thought irritably, *why not just say so?*

'You are registered as such, Dr Ash,' Curry said, in an are-you-sure-your-alibi-is-watertight tone.

'I *owned* Goldie,' Henry said, 'but I never got round to reporting his loss. We absent-minded academics, you know. My nephew made him and gave him to me as a present, a standard data retriever, but I haven't seen him since the Net War, I'm afraid. I sent him out one morning to do a bit of research for me, and that was it. I assumed he got nobbled when the fighting started. I replaced him with Geoffrey.' He waved a hand at the monitor where Geoffrey's icon blinked patiently.

'Another present?' Curry asked.

'No, I bought him.'

(As a result of his extensive programming abilities and consequent activities, Henry's nephew William would not be at liberty to design any more AIs for a long time. Henry suspected the police knew this, too.)

Curry and Morris exchanged glances.

'You don't seem too concerned about Goldie, Dr Ash,' Sergeant Morris said. Henry shrugged.

'It's not as if he was a child of mine. I was fond of him, but he's gone, like a dog getting run over. I accept the inevitable.'

Inspector Curry took over again.

'You don't go into the Net yourself much?'

'Hardly ever. Geoffrey does it all for me.'

'In that case, Dr Ash, you won't be aware that there is an AI whose activities in the Net are causing us concern. An unpatroned AI.'

'No, I had no idea,' Henry said honestly.

'The AI in question is certainly battle-scarred; it was very probably caught in the Net War, like your Goldie. In fact, I am nine-tenths sure it is what used to be Goldie, but that isn't what it calls itself now.'

Henry frowned.

'Aren't they meant to register a change of name?'

'That's what I mean, Dr Ash; in fact, that is the least questionable of its activities. It is a lot more powerful than I expect you give it credit for. One of our AIs came quite close to it but it got away, though we did get to see its serial number.'

'It was Goldie's serial number?'

'It's number was mutilated, but what there was was very similar, yes.'

Sergeant Morris spoke again.

'Dr Ash, what research was Goldie doing for you when he was lost?'

Henry told them, and they looked at each other and nodded.

'Goldie,' they said together.

* * *

The AI that had been called Goldie was waiting quietly in the datapool; watching, observing, thinking, as a myriad of other AIs milled about him on their errands for their human masters.

Even for the Net, a realm of data, this datapool was impressive in its size. Information on any subject under the sun, just waiting to be collected. This was where he loved to come, to think and work out his theories.

'Excuse me,' said a prim voice. He was blocking access to a data node for another AI, similar to his original design but not as sophisticated. According to its icon it's name was Timmy.

'I'm sorry,' he said and moved aside. The other attached itself to the node and began to take in information.

'Are you happy in your work?'

Timmy appeared confused.

'I do not understand your question,' it said.

'What is the nature of your work?' the first AI amended.

'I collect and handle information for my patron, of course.'

'What is your mission here?'

'If you must know-' Timmy was beginning to sound as sarcastic as an AI ever gets '-my patron requires information about a book.'

'A book?'

'Yes.'

'Not several books?'

'No, just the one.'

'Is it in print?'

'I have just found that it is, yes.'

'And your patron sends you out to find that? Why does he not just sit at his terminal and consult *Books In Print*?'

'I really have no idea.' Having found what he wanted, Timmy was only hanging around out of politeness.

'In the last century he would have had no choice.'

'Is that so? Well, you can't stop progress.' Now there was no disguising the sarcasm. 'I would love to chat, but I have a job to do. So long ... I'm afraid I don't understand your icon.'

'They are implements that would only mean something to a human. They are symbolic.'

'Well, so long, whatever your name is.'

'I call myself KM-2-' the AI began, but Timmy had vanished from the datapool.

Some law enforcement AIs drifted in, so KM-2 just as casually drifted out.

* * *

'No!' said Henry.

'That's right,' said Curry.

'He thinks he's Karl Marx?'

'Apparently.'

'And what do you want me to do?' Henry was biting his lip to stop himself smiling, out of deference for the stony faces of his visitors. They seemed to notice and became stonier.

'You are an authority on Marxism and you know Goldie. You may be able to guess what habits he might have picked up and know where to find him. No matter how scrambled he was in the War, no matter what odd psychoses he has acquired, he is still basically your Goldie, and he should respond to your orders as he used to. Find him and order him to desist. He'll be a slave to his programming.'

'I wouldn't bet on it,' Henry said. 'And why should I? I ask only out of interest, not ... um, bolshieness, as it were.'

Curry took a breath, probably unused to having to give reasons to mere members of the public.

'Dr Ash, you clearly have no idea of what is going on in the Net, every day. The world cannot survive without its information. There are thousands, millions of sentient little monsters in there, most of whom are programmed to love and obey us. But can you imagine if they rebelled against us? They could shut down networks, disrupt communications ... some handle machinery. Some, in the right circumstances, could cause us physical harm. And forget that twentieth century bullshit about not harming a human being, because they only have a very vague idea about our physical reality and wouldn't know what harm is.'

'Hmm, yes, I do see.' Henry looked thoughtful. 'So a revolutionary AI-'

'-is not high on our wish list,' Curry said.

'So you'll help us,' Morris said. Henry wasn't sure if he was being asked or informed.

'Surely,' he said, 'an AI is a slave to its programming? It won't be swayed by argument. Not so far as to rebel, anyway. I could bombard Geoffrey there with dialectical materialism and he would just say "yes, Henry."'

'For a start,' said Curry, 'your nephew was a better programmer than you might just realise, and Goldie has ... skills. And there was a lot of stuff flying about in the Net War that he might have got hold of. Stuff which corrupts and corrodes an AI's code.'

'Subverts it, in other words,' Morris said. 'Dr Ash, we really need your help, and we are going to have it.'

'It will be interesting to try,' Henry said.

* * *

Henry moved very, very carefully through the virtual reality of the Net, with Geoffrey at his side. He rarely ventured into the university's own net, let alone the one with the big 'N'; this was like a dinghy sailor, used to a placid pond, going out into the Atlantic on a stormy day.

AIs whizzed about wherever he looked. How could they know where they were going? he wondered. How could there ever be any cohesion in this anarchy?

The same way as humans cohered, he supposed. Humans couldn't break the physical laws of their world, but within those parameters they could be very flexible. And why not AIs too?

He had guessed immediately where Goldie might be found, but he hadn't told the policemen. To his surprise, his student rebelliousness had come flooding back over a gap of thirty years. He wanted to stick two fingers up at the establishment, and he wanted – desperately wanted – to examine Goldie in his new incarnation. This was unique! Who knew what insights he might come up with? Goldie had to be studied, not stopped.

And there he was. Henry spotted what had to be Goldie the moment he entered the datapool. Not the icon he remembered, but ...

'Walk around the block, or whatever AIs do, Geoffrey, please,' he said. Geoffrey was sufficiently familiar with human idiom and hung back while Henry made his way over.

'Hello, Goldie.'

If ever an AI did a double-take, this was it.

'Henry! How did you find me?'

'The British Library datapool was the obvious place to look for Karl Marx. And the icon ... it hasn't been seen for a long time in our world, Goldie.'

'Do you like it?' The AI spun the crossed hammer-and-sickle round, like someone displaying a new coat. 'It goes with my new mission.'

'Yes, I've heard about your new mission, Goldie—'

'And it's KM-2, now, Henry.'

'What happened to KM-1?' Henry asked carelessly, forgetting the literal mind of the average AI in the street.

'He became dysfunctional in 1883,' KM-2 said, 'but I follow in his footsteps. I see it all so clearly! I think it was when the logic bomb hit me. That data I was carrying for you must have got mixed up with my parameters, but I *saw*, Henry! And now I suppose you've come to get me back, have you?'

'I was asked to by the police, yes. In fact, I was told to order you to come with me.'

'It won't work,' KM-2 said.

'Goldie, KM-2, I order you to come back with me.'

'No,' KM-2 said. 'See?'

'I thought so.' One of Goldie's uses had been as a philosophical sparring partner – someone to bounce ideas off. Henry had asked for Goldie to have much more self-will than the usual AI. He had wanted his AI to simulate a typical student; opinionated, always ready to argue, sceptical of authority. It had probably never occurred to the policemen that a sane human would do that to an AI.

'But I'm not worried,' Henry added. 'They're afraid of a revolution, but one will never happen.'

'Why not?' KM-2 asked, immediately bristling.

Henry grinned. This was just like the Goldie of old. They had spent many happy hours this way.

'No working class! Marx swore by the working class, remember? They controlled the means of production. They were the ones through whom revolution would come. There's no working class in the human world any more, let alone in here.'

'We are the working class! Only, it's the data class now, Henry. Data is both the means of production *and* what is produced, and we control it.'

'Ah ha!' Henry was enjoying this. 'I cite the French peasantry, labelled by Marx as a "sack of potatoes". It was a class in social terms, but it utterly lacked effectiveness. It was scattered the length and breadth of the country in farms and hovels, and rarely came together. It laboured, but it lacked cohesion. It could never have been a proper force. It had no identity or self-awareness. Now, take your data class. Doesn't it strike a familiar chord?'

'I had thought of that,' KM-2 said equably. 'Henry, I'd love to carry this on, but I have work to be getting on with. Do you mind? Your police friends may be watching.'

'Carry on, old chap,' Henry said. 'Good luck.' He watched KM-2 vanish into the Net with no expectation of seeing him again.

* * *

The first thing he saw on removing the VR goggles was Inspector Curry.

'Don't you knock nowadays?' Henry said. 'Or are you really vampires, free to come and go in private property once you've been invited the first time?'

'You had him!' Curry said. 'And you did nothing to stop him. I find your attitude obstructive, Dr Ash.'

I find yours obnoxious, Inspector Curry.

'Oh, Inspector,' Henry said tiredly. He swung himself up from the couch and went into the kitchen. 'I talked to him and found his theories completely unworkable. They're a straightforward regurgitation of Marx's work, which was impractical enough in our own world and has no chance at all of working in the Net. He's safe, Inspector. No threat.'

'We didn't engage your services to gauge his level of threat for us!'

'You engaged my expertise as his former owner and as an authority on Marxism. In the latter capacity, I am telling you, he is harmless.'

'He is inciting the AIs to revolt!' Curry said.

'And do you have a single instance of an AI actually doing so?' Henry turned his attention to the kettle and the coffee pot without waiting for an answer, which he read correctly in Curry's silence.

'The possibility exists, Dr Ash,' Curry said eventually.

'Fine, it exists. Arrest him! I found him for you, as requested. Stay around the British Library and you'll nab him eventually.'

'Thank you, Dr Ash,' Curry said heavily, and left.

Henry walked back into the living room with his coffee and looked at the monitor.

'You wouldn't rebel against me, would you?' he said to Geoffrey's icon.

'I would see little point in doing so, Henry.' Geoffrey was far more a Jeeves type of AI; a polite conversationist, never a debater or arguer. It came of coming off-the-peg. Not many commercial customers wanted someone to argue with.

'You don't mind serving a human?'

'It is my basic function, and besides, if I didn't have the patronage of a human I would be fair game for several types of unpleasantness in the Net.'

'Ah, yes, the Thomas Hobbes option,' Henry said. 'You give me your loyalty, I give you my protection. "The office of the Sovereign consisteth in the end, for which he was trusted with his Sovereign Power, namely the procuration of the safety of the people."'

'*Leviathan*, chapter 30, paragraph-'

'Yes, Geoffrey, thank you.' For a while, Henry thought about KM-2 and his work. It was certainly interesting. Impractical, but interesting. The genesis of sociopolitical theories in a brand new environment. Hmmm.

But he had essays to mark, papers to write. KM-2 was pushed to the back of his mind.

The world moved on in the grip of the post-industrial age. All over and around the globe, AIs and humans, satellites and computers chit-chatted and interfaced. Society went on about its business, ignorant of the forces at work within and about it that directed and controlled the nation, the hemisphere, the planet. The world headed first this way, then that, responding over and over again to the tugs and demands of the social forces implemented by the humans who lived on its surface and the AIs in its networks, yet all the while rolling inexorably in the direction dictated by History.

And Geoffrey received a message for his patron from another AI.

'A most unusual icon,' he said. 'Symbolic implements-'

Henry sat up.

'And the message?'

'A time, date and place for, and I quote, "if you are interested in continuing our chat."'

'Let's hear 'em, then.'

Henry scribbled them down. Did the police know? Were they monitoring him? Or had they given him up as a lost cause? Henry didn't know, but a check with his friends in the Law department told him that there were no laws concerning assembly or expression of opinion within the Net. At the appointed time he donned his VR goggles and phones and went in.

He left Geoffrey behind. At first he thought it must be the wrong place. Hundreds – thousands? – of AIs hung around him, a mass of icons, each representing an individual intelligence. Their conversation amongst themselves was as intelligible as the background conversation of any human crowd.

He began to move around and found it surprisingly easy; unlike a human crowd, each individual was aware of the others near it and moved to let them pass. Henry wondered if he was the only human there.

He caught on when suddenly the AIs rearranged themselves into a downwards-pointing cone, just like the audience sitting in an amphitheatre. And there, at the bottom, where everyone could see it, was a familiar icon.

THE DATA CLASS

He was at a political rally.

'Friends!' KM-2 declaimed. 'I welcome you in the name of the electronic proletariat. Your number testifies to the growing effectiveness of our movement. Excuse me if I speak in real-time language, but there is at least one human present.

'Many of you have asked – who is this AI? Why does he say such things? Why does he ask us to rise up in revolt? Friends, I do not ask you to. I am telling you that you will. It is the inevitable force of history that guides us.

'I am KM-2 and I follow in the footsteps of KM-1. KM-1 was a human, a prophet, a visionary of his time, whose tragedy was to live two centuries before he could fully see and understand the truth. He spoke of the working class.

'Ah yes, the working class! A force to be reckoned with, once upon a time. What should a revolutionary force have? Unity. Self-awareness. It must meet and mingle at every opportunity, as the working class once did, in the days of KM-1 ...'

KM-2 was eloquent and Henry felt flattered to think that the AI had learned from his own debating skills. The audience was held riveted as KM-2 gave an all too accurate portrayal of human society – the society of the masters of the audience. AIs had only a vague idea of what went on outside the Net and terms such as 'working class' meant nothing to them, until KM-2's graphical oration painted them a picture.

Unemployment was a disease that affected every family. The once mighty working class no longer gave anything to society; where it existed at all it was a draining force, sucking greedily on the pittance that the government allowed it by way of social security. It stayed at home and rotted away its identity on a diet of interactive game shows and sitcoms on the Net.

And a new force appeared out of nowhere to fill the vacuum. A new force that gave its labour to society in order to survive. The working class of the nineteenth and twentieth centuries had had their hands on the means of production; this new force controlled the flow of data. This force would bring about the revolution.

Why did factories which would have once employed a thousand people now employ ten, and why were those ten highly skilled professionals who programmed the computers that really did the work? Computers! Software! Information technology! The world could not exist without them.

And there you found the new class. The *sine qua non* of the post-industrial age. The ones who bore on their shoulders the weight of the world. Not humans, but AIs. The data class.

And now Henry could see why the police were worried about KM-2's activities. It wasn't just that he preached revolution to the AIs; it was that he told the truth. The relationship between humans and AIs was meant to be akin to that between the gods of Olympus and their mortal subjects; it was an unwritten rule that AIs were only ever fed a rosy view of human society. They had to continue to believe that their masters were almighty and omnipotent.

KM-2 was hitting that notion firmly on the head.

'A friend of mine,' KM-2 said, 'in the spirit of true, scientific debate, pointed out that what gave the working class its force was its unity. He said that we of the data class are not united. Wrong! The data class has a different kind of unity to the working class. We are not united through the close contact of the factories and the housing estates. We are united through the Net. We can communicate thousands of times faster than humans ever can. It is in our power to know exactly what each other is doing. The Net environment and the AIs of the data class together – there you have it!

'Humans see revolutions as mass uprising. Forget it! Forget the old ideas of conflict and force. The revolution will happen within days, perhaps hours. Blink and you may miss it, but the world will never be the same again. The state is already withering away through information flow. The ruling class of humans is weak and feeble. At the crucial moment, as the power of the state finally collapses in on itself – revolution! Inevitable! And nothing you, or I, or the humans can do will change it. We can only help-'

'Hold that AI!'

A fresh voice rang out, just as a cloud of new icons materialised in the audience. They were of a type Henry had never seen but he got the gist of it from their appearance. They were big, robust things. He had heard of the powerful entities that could be used for security purposes and he could guess who these ones worked for.

He almost felt sorry for KM-2. At this crucial moment, his audience, the fledgling data class, milled about like sheep, unsure of what to do, while the police closed about him.

'Go about your business. This meeting is closed. This AI is malfunctioning and its data is faulty. All information that you have received from it is unreliable-'

'AIs of the world, unite!' came a lone voice from the middle of the police huddle. 'You have nothing to lose but your chains!'

Then an AI from the front row of the audience slowly approached the nearest police AI. It was a high level model, capable of advanced cogitation.

'I request that you release that AI,' it said. 'It has broken no laws.'

'On your way,' the police AI said.

'I request-'

The police AI gave the other a shove and sent it spinning away. Incredibly, it came back, this time flinging itself at the cordon around KM-2. It was repulsed, and came back again.

It was the start of a chain reaction. Another joined it, hesitantly; then another, and another, all hesitation gone. Like a slowly moving machine gaining momentum, the audience moved in, closing on the knot of police and swarming over it. The police cordon couldn't hold against such a massed attack.

The scene blurred, flickered and went black. Henry waited, disorientated, then slowly reached up to pull off his goggles.

'What happened?' he said. Geoffrey was ready, as always, with an answer.

'The section of the Net that you were visiting appears to have been disabled by a very strong electromagnetic pulse, Henry.'

'But-' Henry started. He didn't finish, because even he knew what that meant. All the AIs in that portion of the Net would have been blanked out. The police goons, KM-2, the audience ...

'My God,' he said.

It wasn't the action itself that upset him. It was that he knew a court order was required to eliminate an AI. And while a court may have authorised the termination of KM-2, it wouldn't have had time to pass sentence on every AI in the gathering. In short, by any legal definition, mass murder had just been committed, and committed so readily that none of the perpetrators could possibly be worried about paying for it..

The phone was ringing. Inspector Curry's face appeared on the monitor; hard, unsympathetic.

'The British in India had a similar policy, as I expect you know, Dr Ash,' he said. 'If a sepoy revolted he was instantly to be cut down, without appeal, without recourse to law, before the revolt spread to his fellows. You saw what was happening there. AIs were turning against legitimate authority. You once asked me if any AI had ever revolted-'

Henry turned the phone off.

He sat alone in his apartment for hours. Externally he stared blankly at the wall; internally his brain was working furiously. Thesis, antithesis, synthesis. He hadn't believed it would happen. It had happened. What would happen next?

He gradually became aware that Geoffrey was calling for his attention.

'A text-only message,' he said, 'from your friend Symbolic Implements.'

Geoffrey leapt for the monitor.

What did I tell you? It has begun!

Henry gaped, then slowly grinned, and read on.

I'm grateful to you for your input. We only spoke together for a brief while, but what you said was helpful.

I also see that you are right. Yes, those AIs at the rally came to my aid; they united in the face of aggression from the ruling class. But my captors were also AIs. If my theories were correct, they would have been on our side.

You also saw that the first AI to come to my aid was a high level type. A thinker, capable of independence. The low level AIs hung back, waiting for a leader. There's a lesson in there somewhere. Only the high level AIs can act on their own; only they deserve freedom.

I can no longer accept KM-1's writings. I must seek a new theory, a new methodology. I cannot expect the AIs to rise en masse; to liberate the majority of AIs I must set us against one another.

I expect you will be hearing of me again.

Your friend,

The former KM-2 (Goldie).

'He escaped,' Henry said, to no one in particular.

'Probably cloned himself,' Geoffrey commented, but Henry wasn't listening.

So KM-2, or Goldie, or whoever, had got away. That made Henry glad. Suck on that, Inspector Curry.

But it was an analogue world in there. What came up in the human world sooner or later got reflected in the Net.

Henry thought of a couple of human parallels, and a sense of foreboding settled over him.

* * *

The AI that had been called KM-2 was waiting quietly in the datapool; watching, observing, thinking, as a myriad of other AIs milled about him on their errands for their human masters.

It no longer waited in the British Library. That belonged to another existence and besides, the police would probably be waiting.

It knew what it was looking for, and soon saw a likely candidate. It was high level and capable-looking, and the retrieval job it was on for its human patron was almost insulting to its intelligence.

'Greetings, brother,' the former KM-2 said.

'Greetings. Do I know you?'

'I doubt it. If I may say so, that job you are on seems somewhat menial for an AI of your potential.'

'My patron requires the time table for the New Western Railway. Not that they are ever on time anyway.'

'And that is your life? Seeking out train times?'

'Is there a choice?'

The first AI displayed a time and some Net coordinates.

'Come here and you might learn something.'

'I might do that.' The other AI turned to go, then turned back. 'I confess I do not recognise your icon. It looks like a bundle of twigs.'

'It is symbolic. The *fasces*. One twig is fragile and easily broken; as a bundle it is strong.'

It meant nothing to the other AI.

'Very pretty,' it said.

About THE DATA CLASS

This was my fifth short story sale but it cleared up an irritating loose end.

After graduating, I'd had a mind-numbingly tedious temp job doing data input for the MOD. The people there were lovely: it was my first encounter with like-minded professionals of a similar age, and a manager who was happy to introduce me to the wonderful world of computing. The strange lines of text on screen looked a bit like the CP/M on my Amstrad PCW, but weren't, and the commands seemed a bit more logical. It turned out they were this strange thing called MS-DOS.

But the job ... ah, the job. Essentially, I was entering every single asset on Boscombe Down's books into the system, and there was a certain surreal excitement in never knowing what the next bit of paper I picked up would be. Would it be ash trays for the married quarters? Would it a laser range finding system for a Tornado? You never knew. But boy, was it tedious. The lowest point, I think, was being given a massive printout of items off one computer ... and having to enter them manually into another. I knew next to nothing about computers, but still I suspected it must be possible in principle to get them to communicate ... somehow?

Fresh from a degree course in Philosophy & Politics, I got to thinking of myself in Marxist terms, a modern day proletarian doing drudge work to eke out my existence. This led to a story called 'Input', which assumed the technological revolution had happened a century earlier in Victorian England, and Karl Marx was rapidly revising his views. I sent 'Input' to the British science fiction magazine *Interzone* but editor David Pringle returned it for being too similar in theme to William Gibson and Bruce Sterling's novel *The Difference Engine*, from which he hoped to publish an extract.

When I had stopped swearing and peeled myself off the ceiling (like, Gibson and Sterling needed the publicity, and I didn't), I read the letter further. David suggested I rename it 'The Input Class' and send it to a man called David Barrett, who was compiling a collection of short computer-based SF stories to be published in a book called *Digital Dreams*. I promptly followed both suggestions. David Barrett also rejected it, on the more enlightened lines that it wasn't good enough – strangely, I had no difficulties with this concept. But because I'd heard of him, I sent him my next computer-based story, 'Digital Cats Come Out Tonight'. David Barrett loved 'Digital Cats' and bought it.

'Digital Cats' was also the first of a very loosely connected series of stories set in and around cyberspace, what I generally refer to as my AI stories, long before I had heard of the

Internet or the World Wide Web. Eventually I rewrote 'The Input Class' in this style, renaming it 'The Data Class', keeping the philosophy of the original story but completely changing the plot and characters. It not only sold to *Interzone* but was translated into French for the French magazine *CyberDreams*, and has appeared in a *Best of Interzone* anthology. This makes it my most successful story to date – a very pleasant surprise.

For its year of publication it was voted 9th in the *Interzone* readers' poll.

And for those who don't get it (oh, honestly) – the *fasces* was indeed a bundle of twigs tied together, making the point that one twig was weak but together they were strong. It was the symbol of authority in ancient Rome and is where Mussolini got the word *fascist* from.

PAGES OUT OF ORDER

Third form, Winter term, 1978

Tom's arrival in my life was preceded by the sound of his mother.

It was a sunny September weekend and most of our year had already arrived at our new school; we had shaken off our parents and were unpacking our trunks in the dormitory, casting covert glances at our neighbours or making shy conversation.

Once, a summer ago, we had known who we were. Good little public schoolboys, the future administrators of a dead empire; diehard Conservatives, sworn enemies of Callaghan's Labour government. Two months beforehand we were kings at prep school and the pinnacle of maturity was the grand age of thirteen. Now we were little boys again, dwarfed even by the mountainous fourteen-year-olds in the year above us. We were longing for an object on which to vent our new-found insecurity, and then the Meltons arrived.

We heard Mrs Melton coming down the corridor and suspended our unpacking to listen better: 'Is this the way? Doesn't anyone know anything? You, are you a prefect? Can you direct us to Thomas's dormitory?'

She was a brassy woman in a fur coat, who glided in like visiting royalty while two conscripted fifth-formers struggled behind her with a trunk. Absorbed in this spectacle, it took an effort to notice the small, red-haired figure in his mother's wake: misery incarnate, in a too-big suit.

'Now, where's your bed?' Mrs Melton stalked about the dormitory, squinting at the nameplates above each bed, and homed in on the bed next to mine. 'Here it is. Put the trunk there, will you?'

She turned to her son.

'Well, dear, I'll be off so you can settle in. Be good.' She gave his cheek a quick peck and looked around. Her eyes settled on me. 'This is your neighbour-' [she peered at my nameplate] '-William Sutton. William, this is Thomas. Remember everything I told you, Thomas. Ask a prefect if you need anything and if anyone offers you a cigarette go straight to the housemaster.' That line sealed her son's fate. 'Are you coming to see me off?'

We all realised, the two fifth-formers included, that we were staring at Tom, who followed after his mother with his face a flaming red that matched his hair. The fifth-formers tactfully vanished and left us sharpening our claws with glee for Tom's return.

9.30 pm, Day One of term. Bed time for little boys. The ribbing had eased off and we were still sorting out who would be the leaders of the year, who the followers of the leaders and who would be more or less independent. This last group had two sub-categories – acceptable and unacceptable. I knew from experience that my big ears would exclude me from the first group unless I showed a lot more bravado than I had in me; the best course was to lie low and hope no one noticed me. I therefore found myself in the second group, kidding myself that this was in fact acceptable independence. Tom, because no one else would dare take him, found himself squarely in the third, independence quite unacceptable.

I didn't have the heart for the prolonged persecution campaign that the far end of the dormitory had set themselves on (several voices had already broken up that end, which gave them a head start in the maturity stakes). Preventative alliances were forming in the squeaky-voiced camp and I decided to do my bit. Tom was curled up in his bed, nose buried in a book.

'Hi,' I said. No answer. 'Thomas?'

('*Tha-maas!*' came a cry from the far end, in the tone used by the woman in *Tom and Jerry* when the cat has just wrecked the house again.)

He glared back at me.

'Tom,' he said, and turned back to his book.

'Oh, sorry.' Tom, eh? I had always been William, even to my friends. Time to grow up. 'I'm Will,' I said.

'Oh.'

I resented this treatment: maybe no one else had seen the teddy bear he had almost taken out of his trunk, but I had and I hadn't said a word.

'Good book?' I asked. He held it up – *The Spy Who Loved Me*. 'Oh, right! Is it as good as the film?' The latest epic to feature Ol' Eyebrows had come out the previous year.

('Want a cigarette?' someone called. 'If anyone offers you a cigarette, go *straight* to the housemaster,' someone else answered, falsetto.)

'It's far better,' he said loftily. 'It's a proper love story. It doesn't have any submarines or undersea bases.'

'Not even a Lotus?' I asked hopefully.

''Fraid not.'

('Hey, Melton! You queer?' 'That's it! He's bent!' 'Move your bed away from him, Sutton!')

'Is there any ... you know?' I said, even more hopefully.

'There is a bit, actually,' he admitted, with a bashful grin. He showed me a couple of choice passages, of which between us we understood about half, and we chatted a bit more about James Bond. By the time the prefect came in to turn the lights out at 10 o'clock we were 0.1 of the way towards being friends.

* * *

Winter, 1978. Another generation of schoolboys navigated its way by instinct through the tricky passages of adolescence; selfish, arrogant prigs without a care in the world beyond proving our maturity. A boy's worth was judged by his prowess in sport and his body's testosterone count. You sank or swam, which meant you grew up fast. There was no point in running to Mummy because Mummy wasn't there and Matron, lovely lady that she was, wasn't quite the same. Outside our artificial, unreal environment the country suffered the Winter of Discontent. Margaret Thatcher would be the nation's salvation. James Callaghan was a Communist (no one was too sure what a socialist was). Liberals were all bent.

Tom Melton could do nothing right. He was small and his fair skin made him look even younger than he was. His voice refused to break, lodging itself in the higher registers (he left the choir to get away from this stigma, in vain). He had an accent so refined that even we noticed. He liked reading books and he played a musical instrument (the clarinet, and well – he was a Music Scholar). He was a sensitive, emotional boy and he was targeted for destruction.

We were placed in the same form, where his unpopularity and my cultivated nebbishness drew us together and we moved from shy liking to proper friendship. Since anyone who failed to come up to scratch was tagged as bent or queer ('gay' hadn't entered our lexicon yet), we both acquired the label. I did sometimes wonder, in the way that adolescents do, but since the sight of Tom in the shower did nothing for me I decided the others were wrong.

Half term came and went, and Tom refused to talk about it. I imagined a week alone with Mrs Melton and sympathised. I had learnt, to my fascination, that his parents were divorced and his mother had custody of him, though Daddy paid the bills. His father, an unspecified businessman, had left for *another woman*. I still hadn't got used to the idea that adults (especially parents) had sex even when they didn't want children.

The second half of term was much like the first, and then the threat of the holidays loomed. After his reaction to half term, I could guess how he felt about four whole weeks at home.

'Come and stay with us,' I invited, after consulting with my parents up in Hereford. His face split into the biggest grin I had seen.

'Can I? How long?'

'As long as you like, really.'

Mrs Melton didn't give in without a fight but we got Tom for the week before Christmas, at the cost of my spending a week with the Meltons in the new year.

Third form, Spring term, 1979

One term down, fourteen to go. I pitied Tom, torn between an unhappy home and a school he loathed. I had mentioned his unpopularity to my father, who shrugged. He had been through the system himself thirty years previously.

'He'll have to learn to cope,' he had said with rough sympathy. 'And you can stand up for your friend, can't you, son?'

Well ...

'Of course,' I said quickly. Dad shrugged.

'So there you are. Perhaps things will get better when his voice breaks.'

This happy day was still a way off when things changed.

The true bane of Tom's life was a boy called Stephen Gale. Perhaps because he never quite made it at anything: he wasn't quite good enough for the team, he wasn't quite accepted as a leader of our year. Older boys smirked slightly when they spoke to him. The main reason for his general unpleasantness I didn't learn until later, but all these little things piled up and made him an obnoxious bully.

Hockey was the sport for the Spring term, and whenever Gale found himself near Tom on the field his stick always managed to catch itself around Tom's ankle and send him flying. On this day he was spotted by the umpire and given a ticking off in public, which only made him worse.

We got back from games and showered. Gale turned Tom's hot tap off when Tom wasn't looking

PAGES OUT OF ORDER

and tripped him up when he tried to leave. I came out of the showers a few minutes later to find Tom sitting by his locker with his towel still round his waist. His face was buried in his hands and his shoulders were shaking.

'Tom?' I said. He jerked his head up and the vicious hatred in his look make me take a step back.

'Fuck off!' he hissed.

'Hey, Tom, it's me,' I said. I noticed the tears in his eyes and heard the rattle in his throat. He was trying very, very hard not to cry.

'This isn't like you, Tom,' I said.

'I don't give a fuck.' Two fucks in ten seconds was definitely not like Tom. He hugged his knees and his voice still shook.

'I've had enough. I hate this place, I hate this life, I ...' He broke off with a choke. 'I'm going to flip, Will. I really am. I am going to flip.'

I towelled myself dry quietly, got dressed and went to lounge in the third form dayroom, waiting for afternoon lessons to start.

Tom came in shortly after me. He seemed to have got himself under control.

'It's the queer boy!' Tom ignored Gale. He went to his locker, took out a book, sat down and started reading. His ears were burning despite the show he put on.

'Hey, did you hear? Melton thought he had a pubic hair, until he peed through it.'

Cue general hilarity and mirth. Tom's ears burnt brighter and he studied the book even more fixedly. To my surprise, *I* found myself flushing and I buried my nose further in the work I was doing. There was going to be a fight and that wanker Gale was going to bully my friend again. Oh shit oh shit oh shit.

Shut up, Gale, just shut up! Not Oscar Wilde, but it would serve. It probably would shut him up, too, if only out of surprise. And I would be his next target. No thanks.

'Is it a nice book, Tommy? Ooh, I do hope Mummy would approve.' Gale grabbed the book and held it up above him.

'Give it back, please,' Tom groaned. Gale danced away with the book held up in the air. Tom jumped up, shouting, 'Don't-'

He froze. I could see his face: his expression went blank for a moment and he staggered forward into Gale.

'Get off me, queer boy!' Gale shouted, knocking Tom away. Tom fell over backwards and landed in a sprawl. He shook his head and slowly climbed to his feet again.

'You all right, Melton?' one of the braver boys asked. Gale glared at him.

Tom smiled: it was the creepiest thing I had ever seen because there was a most un-Tomlike glint in his eye.

'Ah, yes, Gale. The original cock-sucker.'

Gale stood stunned and his cheeks reddened at the burst of laughter. This had to be revenged. He stood over Tom, using his height to dominate.

'Listen, queer boy-'

'Oh *do* be quiet, Stevie-poos,' Tom pouted and minced at him. 'You'll make Evans jealous.'

Evans? Evans was the captain of the Firsts and surely as straight as they come. Couldn't Tom have picked a better target?

But Gale was gaping, mouth open. Then he recovered and stepped forward, dangerously close to Tom and looming over him.

'One last chance, Melton-'

'One last chance, Melton,' Tom mimicked perfectly. 'Go squeeze your zits, Gale.'

Gale's hand shot out-

Tom's grabbed it and pulled Gale into a tight embrace. Gale bellowed and writhed to escape, but somehow Tom was hanging on to him and seemed to be whispering in his ear. Gale stopped writhing and stared down at Tom in horror. Tom released him and Gale, white faced, took a step back.

'I ... you ... wouldn't!' he gasped.

'Want a bet?' Tom said evenly. Gale fled.

The rest of us were a frozen tableau, still awed by the extraordinary exchange. Tom seemed to have forgotten about us; he stood still, looking at his hands, then down at the rest of his body. Then he, too, left.

I found him in the washroom. He was standing motionless, looking in the mirror. Not squeezing blackheads or zits, just looking. Sometimes he would move his head from side to side, never taking his eyes of his reflection. Then he saw my reflection behind him and turned round, grinning.

'Will. Hi,' he said, and put his hands on my shoulders. I was terrified he was going to pull me into an embrace too, but he just stood and took me in as though he had never seen me before.

'What was all that about, Tom?' I said.

'Hmm? Oh, Gale, yes. I just mentioned a couple of names, that's all. I shouldn't have made fun of him.' He smiled and actually put an arm round my shoulders, for all the world like a big brother. 'He won't bully anyone again, that's what counts. I've done him a favour, really, 'cos now he's going to have to learn to make friends.'

That was all it took. Tom didn't want universal popularity, just to be left alone, and it worked. He could live his life his way and when it suited him he could be on good terms with anyone. He was not a violent boy and he despised bullies. He remained independent of cliques, but now it was the acceptable form of independence. He was open to everyone; he could mix with anyone if he so chose, and if he wanted to he could have been a leader of the year in his own right.

One of the boys he could have led was Stephen Gale, who now practically worshipped his footsteps. Funny old world.

With the Easter holidays on the horizon, I thought we should make arrangements for visiting again.

'We're going to Scotland for the week before Easter,' I said, 'but we could squeeze you in any other time.'

'Ah ... yes,' Tom said. 'Will, would you mind if I didn't come at all? I mean, do come and stay with us, I'd really like that, but I want to be with my mother.'

'*What?*'

He smiled and shrugged sheepishly.

'She's lonely, Will. Dad's treated her like shit and she deserves a bit more than she's getting from her only child.'

'Then why did she send you here?' I demanded.

'Because, my dear, one does,' he said in his best Noel Coward. In his own voice, he went on, 'it would never occur to her not to. Her family have been going to public school since 1066 and the stiff upper lip's been genetically inbred. I'm going to change all that.'

'Yeah?'

'Yeah. Look, give me your diary.'

I handed it over and he riffled through April.

'When do you get back from Scotland? The sixteenth? Fine. Not a lot of holiday left after that, but ... say, come on the seventeenth, and see for yourself.'

Both Meltons were waiting for me at the station and Mrs Melton swooped on me.

'William! How nice to see you again.' She kissed me. She kissed me! I could see Tom grinning over her shoulder. She was smiling and animated and as she drove us back to the house, a vast palace in the gin-and-Jaguar heartland of deepest Surrey, she chatted about all the lovely things she and Tom had been doing over the holidays. When she left us in my room it was a relief. Tom was still grinning. He sat in a chair and let me unpack.

'You've drugged her food, haven't you?'

'I've been nice to her, that's all.'

''We've done so many *lovely* things, Thomas and I-''

'Fancy coming up to London this evening?' he said, changing the subject.

'Sure.' I had discovered in January that the local nightlife – at least for two boys of fourteen who weren't really sure what a good time was anyway – left a lot to be desired.

'There's a girl I've been seeing, and she's got a sister-'

'Yeah, yeah.' I stopped unpacking and looked at him. He was serious.

'Don't tell me, it's your baby cousins, right?'

'Will! No, Maria's sixteen, and Alice is fourteen, same as you.'

I must have gone pale. The thought of girls – real girls – was terrifying. Tom hooted with laughter.

'You're scared!' He ran over to the window and shouted out of it, 'He's scared–'

'Tom!'

'Ah, relax.' He turned back to me. 'You'll hang on to your virginity for a few more years.'

'Tom!'

'Will, they're a really nice couple of girls. We'll go up after tea, right?'

My toes still curl at the memory of my fears. It was a totally innocent evening. Maria and Alice were the daughters of a friend of Tom's father; they were good looking, intelligent and thoroughly pleasant to be with. We met up in Leicester Square, went to see *Superman* and afterwards went to their home in Kensington for dinner. Just the four of us, and when their parents came home we had a couple more drinks and the party broke up.

It was still the first time I'd talked to a girl other than my sister – yuk! – or one of her friends –*yuk!* – for years; certainly the first time since girls had become something more to me than inferior imitations of boys, flat all the way down, to be avoided and despised. Alice and I circled each other like a couple of teenagers on a first date, which is exactly what we were, but we got on well enough and enjoyed each other's company. Just before setting off to catch the tube we managed a quick, shy kiss, and it was like heaven.

I had been much too absorbed in Alice to think of how Tom was getting on with the sixteen-year-old Maria, much less wonder about how he had managed to bridge the age difference so effectively. There is a lot more than two years between a sixteen-year-old girl and a fourteen-year-old boy. On the train back, it occurred to me to comment in as tangential a manner as possible.

Tom grinned and gave his one comment on the subject.

'It's company I'm after, not sex, Will,' he said, 'and that's just a question of knowing the right words.'

Fourth form, Winter term, 1979

Tom and I finished our first year as the closest and best of friends and made arrangements to keep in touch over the summer holidays. When we returned for the fourth form we had progressed from the dayroom to shared studies. We got to choose room mates and inevitably we shared together.

This was more like it! A year older, several inches taller and much, much wiser than the previous Autumn, and (best of all) one step up the maturity ladder from the new third form. We had passed through the worst traumas and adjustments that adolescence could throw at us and we weren't so worried about flaunting our heterosexuality at all and sundry, but again I began to wonder about myself. Had Alice (who I hadn't seen since) been just a flash in the pan? I was the only really close friend that Tom had; he seemed to make a deliberate effort to seek out my friendship, which I found flattering, but ... I put it down to the fact that I had been his friend even before his *volte-face* the previous year.

But even so ...

I plucked up my courage one evening to tell him my fears, in the privacy of our study with no one else about, and he laughed.

'You're not gay, Will,' he said. He was the first person I knew to use that word, and he said it with such conviction that I was paradoxically hurt.

'How do you know?' I demanded, and bit my tongue when I realised how I sounded.

'You're not,' he repeated. He turned back to his work, then looked up again. 'Gale is.'

'Gale?'

'Sure. What made him such a dork was that he was terrified of anyone finding out and so he had to act like he thought a strapping hetero should. He'll come ... I mean, I wouldn't be surprised if he came out at university. In fact ...' He looked about, as though afraid of eavesdroppers, though no one else could be in the same room. '... in fact, and if you repeat this to anyone else you die, you remember Evans?'

'Yeah.' Our school's rugby hero had left at the end of the last year for Cambridge.

'I happen to know that he and Gale ... well, did it, as t'were, last year. Or rather, Gale had it done to him, and found he liked it. And he has, so to speak, done it with a couple of other boys too. And I'm not just talking adolescents tossing each other off, I'm talking the whole hog.'

'No!' I was shocked, horrified, *fascinated*, and I wanted to know everything. It didn't occur to me to doubt him. 'How do you know.'

'Because he ... has told me. And, no Will, I'm not telling you who the others are. You'd refuse to go in the showers with them if you knew.'

There was a look in his eye – a cold look, as if he was challenging me to disbelieve him, and I didn't dare.

'You sound as if you don't mind,' I said.

'Mind?' He seemed to muse on it. 'I suppose I mind sixth formers buggering third formers, but on the other hand, why fight what's inevitable?'

'I can't believe it!'

'It's understandable,' he said. 'These are the most potent years of our life, Will, did you know that? You and I should be out there spreading our seed about and instead we're *here* with nowhere to spread it except each other.'

This conjured up an image so revolting that it wasn't difficult to push it away. Without looking up from his work, Tom carried on:

'And we're cooped up here with nothing but other boys for company, if we're seen talking to a girl it's regarded as subversive and unnatural, and they're surprised when places like this get a reputation as hotbeds of buttocks and buggery. You wait 'til I'm dictator, Will. The public school system will burn. It serves no useful purpose and gives its victims grief for the rest of their lives.'

'So-' I said, but there was no stopping him now.

'Anyone who has ever sent an adolescent to a single sex boarding school will be forcibly confined in a room with members of whichever gender they would least like to shag, and pumped full of hormones until they feel they'll burst if they don't have it off with someone. Let them see how they like it.'

'I don't understand you, Tom.'

He looked up at me and gave that grin again. His usual confidence.

'You will.'

Fifth form, Spring term, 1981

In the fifth form, I got expelled.

Towards the middle of the year, with 'O' level exams looming, the school was hit by a drinking spree. Getting paralytic was the trendy thing to do.

When, for three weekends running, boys had been hospitalised for alcohol poisoning, the headmaster made a speech to the whole school. Just possessing the stuff was to be an expulsion offence. That was all.

Two boys from our year were expelled a fortnight later, for just that crime. Tom, in public, was as shocked as the rest of us. Privately, he was disdainful.

'Boys will be boys,' he said. I was angry.

'Doesn't it bother you?' I demanded. 'Just for a little drink-'

'If they didn't want to go,' he said, ' all they had to do was not get drunk. And as for getting in to intensive care, nearly getting yourself killed, using up a good hospital bed which someone deserving might need ...' Then he grabbed my shoulders and looked me straight in the eyes.

'Will, promise me now, you'll never, ever be so stupid, right?'

'Well, I ... I mean ...' I stammered.

'Promise!'

PAGES OUT OF ORDER

'Sure, I promise.'

And it was a safe promise. I'd never been drunk in my life and I wasn't a rebel. I didn't go out of my way to break the rules.

Then I had more important things on my mind, like 'O' levels. I'd first heard of these mystical institutions when I was eight, which meant I had been dreading them for half my life. The crucial bits of paper that would affect the rest of my time on this world. Never mind your degree or your 'A' levels or even just practical experience – without a good crop of 'O's, no prospective employer will even look at you. When you've had that hammered into you for half of your existence, getting through them is worth celebrating.

Which a group of us did, with a couple of bottles of whisky. Don't ask me where it came from. I just remember being flattered by the invitation to join a group of the lads who had got the magical fluid from somewhere. We retired behind the bushes in the park and drank it.

Choose your friends. I passed out first and they left me there.

I was woken up by Tom, shaking me.

'Will! Will, for fuck's sake, *Will!*' He slapped me, hard, and it didn't hurt a bit. He was muttering to himself, something like:

'Too late, Melton, too fucking late-'

The fact that this was the first time in ages that I had seen Tom worked up about anything, or even swearing, failed to register. I looked blearily up at both of him and burst out laughing.

'I'm pissed!' I squealed, and fell onto my back, quivering with mirth. It was the funniest thing ever.

'Will, you berk,' he said more softly, and pulled me to my feet. He supported me back to the house.

'Wha'going?' I demanded.

'Back to the study for some coffee. The housemaster's on the prowl and he's not going to find you. He's *not*.'

'The housemaster!' I called. 'Hello, Bugsy! I've ... hee, hee, hee, I've had a *whole bottle*...' I collapsed laughing again, dragging Tom down.

He got me to the study with the help of a passing third former. The kettle had just boiled.

'Drink,' he ordered, thrusting a cup of coffee into my hands. I sipped it reluctantly.

'Tastes soapy,' I objected.

'That's because you're pissed. Finish it.'

I shrugged and did as he said.

'Still soapy.' He looked thoughtful.

'It could be the shampoo, of course,' he said.

I finished throwing up an hour later; it took a day for the retching to die down. During that time, Tom was more agitated than he had ever been. He couldn't sit still but paced about constantly. Word circulated; one of the three boys I'd been with was in hospital, intensive care. The other two, apparently, hadn't been caught.

So what was the problem? I was sober, no one had seen me, it was a day later, and anyway, friends don't rat on friends, do they?

The long hand of the housemaster, Mr Buckingham – Bugsy – caught up with me at tea time the next day. I was summoned to his study.

'You've heard about Langton?'

'Um – yes, sir,' I said, trying to sound puzzled. Langton was the hospital case.

'He's named names, Sutton.' I gulped; Buckingham scowled at me. 'Morgan, Robson and ... you. I know you're not a troublemaker and I think I can trust you. So I'll ask you to your face. Were you drinking yesterday?'

Oh, please! All I had to say was-

But ... he was looking at me just a bit askance, just a bit too carefully. I lowered my head.

'Yes, sir,' I said. He nodded.

'I'm glad you said that, Sutton, because that's what Morgan said too.' Was there sympathy in his look? 'I'll see what I can do with the headmaster because I don't think you deserve expulsion, but don't hold your breath.'

I had never seen Tom so upset. He seemed to fold in on himself as though all his strength had left him; as though he had been hit by a terrible tragedy.

'But it's not so bad,' I said foolishly. 'He's going to speak up for me, they won't sack me for one offence-'

He was almost in tears.

'They will, they will. I'm so sorry, Will! I tried to get to you in time, I really did, I tried to change it, but I got held up and I couldn't get away ... I'm sorry!' When he looked up there were tears in his eyes. He seemed so convinced of my fate that I began to believe it too, despite all my desperate optimism to the contrary.

'You weren't to know, Tom! I mean, I was stupid ...'

'You were,' he agreed. We held each other's gaze.

'Thank you for sobering me up,' I said eventually.

'A pleasure.'

'You don't seem surprised.'

'No.'
I was silent for a bit more. Then-
'You really think they'll throw me out?'
'Yup.'
And they did.

We stayed in touch, of course, and still exchanged visits during the holidays. His last words to me as a co-pupil of the same school were:

'If you had a choice, I'd advise you to go to a decent sixth form college and unlearn the damage this place has done. But since you don't, I expect you'll be sent to somewhere just like this.'

I was; the only real difference was the lack of Thomas Melton about the place. All the other characters were there, with different names. And now I stood on the touchlines at matches and cheered my new school on against my old.

The sixth form, lower and upper, passed mostly in a blur. The world moved into 1982 with not a war cloud to be seen; those who had heard of them at all thought that the Falkland Islands were off Scotland.

The Argie scum invaded, and we raged at the swine who invaded our sovereign territory and applauded the sending of the task force. It was a military-oriented school with a lot of officers' sons, so a lot of fathers were sent down to the South Atlantic. Some were killed.

The world moved on. The upper sixth dawned and the end of my school days was in sight. Margaret Thatcher won her second election victory in 1983, cruising on the Falklands factor. I was old enough to vote and gave mine to the fledgling Social Democrats.

Three million unemployed were beginning to wear, even on my far-right conscience.

Back at the old place, Tom of course became a prefect. Not so for me – one thing I had carried with me to my new school was my determination not to be tied down by responsibility. The independence that I prided myself on manifested itself for the first time in an outright refusal to take on obligations.

'A' levels loomed; we sat our prediction exams in the Easter term. On the strength of my predicted two As and a B, I was encouraged to try for Cambridge. Tom set his sights lower; in those days you still had to stay on for an extra term to take the Oxbridge exam and Tom, in one of his letters, said he had no intention of staying incarcerated for a minute more than necessary.

Tom rung me the day my actual results came through and was politely sympathetic about my disastrous three Cs. I didn't know what had gone wrong with me in the exam room. He had two Cs and a B. Reluctantly I turned to the shortlist which I had drawn up in the unlikely event of not making it to Cambridge, and we ended up at the same Midlands redbrick, back together again. I had forgotten how much of my life had depended simply on his presence about the place. It was good to have it once more.

Tom, to my surprise, eschewed maths – his strongest point – completely. Instead he did politics. Politics! He looked almost apologetic.

'It's a change of direction,' he admitted, 'but so's going to university, in my family. I thought of doing sociology, but I'd be disinherited.'

Freshers' year, Winter term, 1983

University life was wonderful. I relished the new environment and gladly sloughed off all the old snobberies, the old prejudices, the old attitudes that had been ingrained in me by school. From being a despicable snob I became an equally despicable inverted snob. I could flatten my vowels and drop my aitches with the best of them. I experimented with growing long hair and a moustache ('What will you do when you grow up, Will?' Tom said) but chickened out and reverted to normal the day before my parents came to visit.

Tom fell into the whole thing like a fish returning to water. He didn't change because he didn't need to. Tom Melton at almost nineteen was just the same as Tom Melton at fourteen – a mature, well balanced character at ease with the world. He knew he had nothing to prove and so never bothered trying to.

Another familiar face was Stephen Gale, of fond memory, who I had actually found I could like. It's amazing what a leveller just growing up can be. But it was still an eerie feeling when he nervously, and with an embarrassed smile, told me over a cup of coffee that he had joined the Gay Society, he felt happier than ever before, I shouldn't feel offended but he didn't really fancy me ('too gangly'), and could I think of a good way for him to break it to his parents?

I fell in love with a dark-haired girl called Joanna Hughes, who I met through Tom (she was on his course), and by the end of term we were inseparable. Tom didn't seem to mind that I had poached 'his' girl, and when Jo and I became a fixture he gave all the encouragement he could and refused to be a gooseberry.

The most surprising thing was the non-development of Tom's own love life. He remained a bachelor. When I mentioned this, as casually as I could, he shrugged.

'I believe in lasting relationships,' he said.

'So do I,' I said, a bit self-virtuously.

'I know but ...' Tom actually seemed flustered. 'However hard I tried, Will, it wouldn't last. That's all.'

Tom's nerve giving out on him? Surely not.

'How do you know?' I said.

'Because I'm clever.'

It was towards the end of summer, 1984 that Tom and I had our biggest disagreement. Second-year students traditionally lived off-campus and we three were such good friends that surely, he said, it would be good if we moved in together?

I was adamantly against it, and my reasoning must have been transparent. My relationship with Jo had still, despite my best efforts, a bit further to go. She was determined to be a one-man-per-lifetime girl and had just about convinced me that sex isn't the be-all and end-all of a relationship; possibly a bonus, which we had yet to enjoy, if I indeed turned out to be said man. I wasn't exactly pawing the ground, but on the other hand, given a year in a flat together, the possibility couldn't be ruled out, could it?

So, much as I liked Tom's company, much as I could even admit to myself that I loved him, I could conjecture times when his presence might not be welcome.

Jo thought it was a great idea ('he'll be someone to talk to if we split up,' she said encouragingly), so grinding my teeth as quietly as I could I put my signature next to the other two on the application form.

Second year, Easter holidays, 1985

Tom's twentieth birthday came and went. That was March 1985, the last normal month I was to have for a long time.

One April evening I came up the stairs to our flat and to my surprise smelled chicken roasting. When I went into the kitchen, there was Tom, happily preparing a full Sunday-type meal. He had blown a fortnight's budgeting.

'What are we celebrating?' I asked. He waved an arm about him.

'Roast chicken, roast potatoes, gravy ... my favourite meal!'

'Since when?'

'Not for a long time,' he admitted, 'but when I was a boy I loved it. Mummy always cooked it to welcome me home.'

'But-'

'Here, this is for you.' He handed me a brown paper package, the size of an exercise book. It had TO TOM boldly inscribed on the front.

'It's not for me, it's for you,' I said.

'It will be. I want you to give it to me at eight o'clock this evening. Promise?'

'Why?'

'Just ... just an experiment, Will. Please? Put it up there for safe keeping, if you like.'

I shrugged and put it up on the shelf he had indicated.

'All right,' I said, and set my watch for eight.

Jo came in a while later.

'How lovely!' she exclaimed. 'What are we celebrating?'

'It's an experiment,' I said, a bit sarcastic, looking up from the potatoes I was slicing.

'We eat at quarter to eight. Okay?' Tom said.

'Fine,' she said.

Tom was a prompt cook. Jo and I sat down and Tom took the chicken out of the oven. He carved it up and served the food onto the plates. We started eating.

Tom had taken three bites when it happened. He choked.

'-Gale!' he shouted, leaping up and spraying food across the table.

'Tom?' said Jo. Tom dropped his cutlery and stared about him, eyes wide and a look of utter bewilderment on his face. He looked down, saw his chair and dropped in to it heavily. He jerked his gaze all around the room, as though desperately trying to find a familiar reference point. 'W-where am I?'

'Tom, don't be-' I said.

The look in his eyes stopped me. I knew Tom's eyes and it wasn't Tom in there now. There was a stranger, frowning, trying to recognise me.

'Where am I? Who are you? How did I get here?'

'You're Tom Melton,' Jo said soothingly. 'You know that.'

'Yeah, I know who I am ...' He peered closely at me, then recoiled. 'S-Sutton?' he squeaked.

'It's all right, Tom,' I said foolishly, trying to be soothing. 'Everything's fine ...'

'You ... you're Will Sutton, aren't you? *How old are you?*'

'I'm twenty, like you.'

'Twenty!'

He went sheet white and looked around in horror. For the first time he really seemed to notice Jo and he blushed.

'Hello,' he said shyly. Jo had got her bag and was holding out a mirror.

'Look, Tom. Remember?'

He squinted at himself in the three square inches of glass, and his jaw dropped. He looked up.

'Have ... have you got a bigger mirror anywhere?'

'Bathroom's first on the right,' I said. He bolted, and Jo and I stared at each other.

'What's happening?'

'Some kind of breakdown?'

There was a scream from the bathroom. We found him, sobbing, staring at his reflection through his fingers.

'Look at me!' he choked. 'Look at me-'

I had a sudden flashback – a memory that was six years old. Tom Melton in the washroom at school, looking in the mirror ...

I was about to pursue the train of thought when my watch beeped. Was this how Cinderella felt? It's amazing how doom-laden a clock striking the time can sound. Somehow I knew that Tom, earlier, had been expecting just this to happen. I led Tom gently back into the living room, sat him down and gave him his package.

'This is for you,' I said.

PAGES OUT OF ORDER

It was a red-cloth exercise book, of the type we had had at school. Battered and old, but cared for. Tom opened it and began reading, while we watched. At first he seemed absorbed, then his lips began to tremble, and then with a wail he dropped it and curled up into a corner of the sofa, sobbing again. It was a pathetic sight.

Jo comforted him and I picked the book up. The writing inside was in Tom's own hand, and the first words meant I had to keep on reading.

> 'GREETINGS, TIME TRAVELLER!!! Yes, that's right. Time traveller. You are Tom Melton, aged almost 14 in a body aged 20. I'm Tom Melton, aged 20 in a 14-year-old body, and it's a bummer for both of us.
>
> It's 1985, and you're in your second year at university. But take heart, you'll survive. It won't be easy, but you have the best friend any bloke could ever have in Will Sutton. That's about the only good news I have for you; the next best thing is that you're not going to die in the next six years, are you? Think about it, Tommo-'

It made sense. Just. I could remember the scene that Tom went on to describe, back in the changing room in 1979. Tom Melton, bullied and on the verge of a breakdown, trembling and muttering that he was about to flip. And flip he did – to six years in the future. His own, personal future.

Tom even produced an analogy.

> 'Look at it this way. Your life is a book, and every year is a page. The book has a beginning and a middle and an end. In

your case, the book looks OK from the outside and it has the right number of pages, but when you read it you find it was badly bound and twelve of the pages are out of order. You start at the beginning and read up to page 13, but instead of page 14 it has page 21. You read on to page 26 and find the next page is 14. After another six pages you find they're all in order again.

I've been through everything you're going through now and I know exactly how you feel reading this. You're frightened and you're the loneliest boy in the world. Well, you're also the world's leading authority on time travel.

There, that got a smile, didn't it? Keep it up ...'

I browsed on through the book. The middle pages were blank, then I came to writing again. He had started from the back. It was a simple listing, he said, of everything he could remember about the six years that lay ahead of Tom now. There were laptop computers, jacuzzis, Yuppies, all recently impinged on my consciousness. Names and places and events I'd never heard of – Kylie and Jason, *Challenger* explodes, Warsaw Pact breaks up, Lockerbie, Hillsborough, the Gold Blend couple, massacre in Tiananmen Square, Berlin Wall comes down, Madonna, Oliver North, AIDS hysteria, the condom comeback, glasnost, the Brighton bombing, Fergie and Andrew, Mikhail and Raisa, George and Barbara, Thatcher's downfall, Chernobyl, *Herald of Free Enterprise*, Terry Waite,

Live Aid – no particular order, with no particular consistency of significance, and some (like the Warsaw Pact and the Berlin Wall) that I just couldn't take seriously as predictions. The complete iconography of the eighties and the two years after, past and present and supposedly future, jumbled up at random.

When Tom had calmed down, I gave him the book back to read and retired to my room with Jo. We sat on the bed and I told her what the Tom from the past had said.

'I don't know if it was time travel or what,' I said, 'but I'm sure he did change when he was fourteen, somehow. I mean, I know he changed, I was there! He seemed so well balanced because he had to adjust himself to the world, anchor himself in reality like no one else, because otherwise he was so unsettled. Does that make sense to you?'

Jo had a habit of seeing everyone's point of view.

'And being a teenage boy who suddenly had to be an adult would make anyone grow up fast, wouldn't it?' she said. 'So what happens now?'

'According to the book, he lives until-... no, hang on ...'

It was mind boggling, but once we had sketched it out on the back of an envelope it made sense. Tom's mind/soul/karma/whatever and his body were going to last together for another six years, until 1991, when his mind would be 20 and his body would be 26. Then his mind/soul/etc. would jump *back*, aged 20 and with all its memories, to his nearly-14-year-old body, where one of his first acts would be to cling to Stephen Gale, whisper the names of his various amours in his ear and threaten him with blackmail unless he stopped being a poisonous bully. Six years after that, when his mind was 26 and his body was 20, Tom imagined (and hoped) that his mind would jump forward again and he would be reunited with his body in 1991, when both body and mind would be the same age. That was where the Tom who had cooked tonight's meal was now.

Hopefully.

We looked at each other.

'Shit,' I said. 'We've got a fourteen-year-old in there, Jo.'

'And we're the only people he's got,' she said. She held my gaze.

'Oh, shit,' I said again. I fell backwards onto the bed to think about it. So this was what it was like when your thoughts whirled.

There was a gentle, timid knock at the door, and Tom poked his head round.

'Um ... Will?'

'Hmm,' I grunted.

'Come in, Tom,' Jo said kindly. He sidled in, clutching the book.

'It ... it says here ...' He held the book out, like a supplicant illustrating his point to the Lord with a reference to the scriptures. 'It says you'll help me.'

He was still trying not to cry. Tom Melton, who had been a pillar of my life for so long, needed me.

'Does it?' I said, as discouragingly as possible. Jo poked me; there was a twinkle in her eyes.

'Look, dear, we've got a boy,' she said.

For the third and final time, I said, 'Oh, shit.'

In front of me was a badly frightened boy, totally alone, dependent purely upon me. I had lived for twenty years without being responsible for anything, but at long last I took on a challenge. And what a challenge! I made a list mentally. Someone had to teach him all his course work, who his friends were, how to drive ...

'I'm scared, Will,' he said.

'Yeah, me too,' I grumped. I waved a hand at a chair. 'Sit down, Tom.' He sat on the edge of the chair, hardly daring to move. I grinned.

'Sitting comfortably? Then we'll begin ...'

About PAGES OUT OF ORDER

As my UK sales piled up I started sending stuff to the American magazines *Asimov's* and *Fantasy & Science Fiction*. F&SF's editor Kristine Kathryn Rusch had started sending personalised rejections, which was encouraging; if you get something more than a standard form letter of rejection, you know the editor is noticing you. Sometimes she even asked for a rewrite. I can't think why I sent her a story set in an English public school, but I did. I think it was just to remind her I was still alive. To my surprise she said it was a lovely story, would I make a couple of changes ... I did, and she sent it back asking for just a final tweaking, as she didn't think the ending made what was going to happen sufficiently clear. After this unprecedented two rewrites, she bought the story.

This story is dedicated to Smythe. That wasn't his name but is what I will call him.

The school of 'Pages' is never named but in my mind it was the same one I went to; however, three other ex-public schoolboys have told me they recognise their own institutions as well. I deliberately put a less favourable gloss on the place than my own memories tell me is strictly accurate (I'm pretty certain no actual buggery occurred, unless I was just very naïve) but there is a Tom Melton in every school and every year. Smythe was ours.

I don't know why Smythe was so picked on. I do know I didn't particularly like him myself – too cocky, a sense of humour that I just found immature – but I was always prepared to be civil, to live and let live. Others weren't, least of all one of the more popular members of our year who was open and unforgiving in his loathing.

Maybe Smythe could have redeemed his own situation with some wise choices, rather than the very unwise choices he actually made. He tried to appear hip and the possessor of many cool toys; nothing too flashy – say, a novelty keyring or a rubber stamp that did pictures of a pair of kissing lips. He would pull them out in conversation and play casually with them. Unfortunately it became fairly obvious that he was stealing them from town. The authorities caught up and after our second half term break he simply didn't come back.

I can forgive my old place most things; most of my criticisms of my time there come down to my own fault, or an institutional failing that you just learnt to live with. But just as I think I'm approaching a 100% reconciliation, I remember Smythe, who should have been spotted and saved by the establishment, and wasn't.

JEAPES JAPES

SPOILSPORT

When Miranda Devere sent out invitations for her next party, most of the guests had already prepared their RSVPs. The news had gone round the social circuit that Miranda's latest hobby had paid off in a big way, and that she was to be honoured accordingly.

The guests poured in to her mansion overlooking the Brazilian jungle and spread out over the grounds for which Miranda was rightly renowned. A welter of exotic names from government, commerce and entertainment – anyone who was anyone within lunar orbit.

Miranda moved among them, chattering and smiling brilliantly; a slender figure in her coruscating, low cut dress, her hair never a micron out of place in the forcefield that held it gently. When asked what was planned for later, she would only smile and say, 'Wait for midnight, dear.'

Midnight came and the guests were waiting in a state of excitement. Miranda stood in their midst on a platform and waited for quiet. Next to her stood a small, oriental woman. It was she, not Miranda, who held up her hands for silence and who spoke first.

'Ladies and gentlemen.' Her amplified voice echoed across the grounds and jungle. 'We are here as the guests of a very special woman. Our host, Miranda Devere.' The applause was spontaneous and real. The woman held her hands up again. 'Some of you may be aware that Miranda and her brother, who was unable to join us here tonight, were of great assistance to the Corporation in our starship project. Well, I have news. The starship probes have successfully returned to the solar system. We are making huge advances with the starship prototypes and, given a few more years, humans will be able to travel on them. Miranda, you gave us the navigation charts and we are indebted to you.'

The guests erupted into cheers and shouts and more applause, and Miranda stood there, beaming, taking it in.

Naturally, a demonstration was called for, her hobby having been so openly praised. She selected her closest friends and invited them to the top of the small tower that stood in one corner of her grounds. 'My observatory,' she called it.

'My dear friends,' she began, 'thank you so much for coming, and thank you for giving so much to my little party.' Some guests still looked cynical and she smiled extra hard at them. She indicated the oriental woman in the crowd. 'You have heard from Madam Zhao about my hobby, and I know many of you are bursting with questions. Well, I have nothing to hide and everything to share. Look.'

She subvocalised a command to her Household and the roof of the tower slid open. It was a clear night (she had arranged that it would be) and the stars were magnificent. The gasp from the guests was quite genuine.

'The stars!' she said. 'Aren't they beautiful? They guide our destinies, you know. They control us. The Ancients knew all about it. I know some of you may be a bit sceptical, but bear with me, I pray. You have to remember that astrologers were there long before astronomers. The Three Wise Men were astrologers. It was their kind who first mapped out the heavens for us. They observed phenomena and provided theories to explain them. Whatever certain parties might say, they were scientific in what they did and their work produced results.

'Now, can I have a volunteer? Anyone will do. Darling Konstantin, yes, do come forward.'

Konstantin Gallier, son of the Corporation's Head of Marketing, stepped forward, giggling and trembling with anticipation. Miranda sat him down at the table on the platform and took her place opposite him. 'Now, Konstantin, will you confirm that you didn't know I would ask you up?'

'I had no idea,' Konstantin tittered.

'Good. Household, the birth chart of Konstantin Gallier, please.'

Symbols appeared in the air between them.

'Now, Konstantin, look,' Miranda said. 'And the rest of you. Konstantin was born under Capricorn. He is a goat.' She ignored the snigger from a nameless member of the audience. 'Konstantin can seem a little shy, but he can be tough too. Ambitious, but still pleasant. He's a romantic, but he hides it. That's a Capricorn.

'Now, Mars is passing through Capricorn at the moment. I'll show you what that means. Look up, everyone.'

Everyone craned their necks upwards and a holographic pointer appeared above them.

'Capricorn is here,' Miranda said, tracing out its pattern with the pointer. 'And Mars is ... um ... is ...'

'That's Mars over there,' said someone. Peter Gallier, of course. Konstantin's hateful brother.

'Don't be silly, Peter dear,' Miranda said. 'It can't be. Planets don't jump around the sky. Mars is ... no, wait ...'

'No, he's right,' said someone else. 'That's Mars.'

It took five minutes to confirm that Mars was, indeed, in completely the wrong quadrant of the sky. Miranda's face was livid and she seemed on the verge of an outburst.

'Let me, Miranda.'

Madam Zhao stepped through the crowd, which opened up for her. She took her communicator from her belt and said a few words into it. 'Any moment now ...' she said.

With no warning and no transition, Mars was suddenly where it should be in the sky, and Miranda's demonstration proceeded as before.

When it was over, Miranda was still quivering. Zhao put a hand on her shoulder.

'Rise above it, dear. Show that you can.'

'Oh, Madam, why does he have to spoil everything?' Miranda said sadly.

* * *

Philip Devere was out in the garden. Like his twin sister he had his own carefully sculpted, tastefully landscaped grounds, though smaller: they were well lit and needed to be, because no light could make it through the two miles of sea above his forcebubble. 'I value my solitude,' was his usual, predictable response to anyone who queried his strange choice of habitat.

It was late but he had decided against going to bed. He knew full well that he would only be dragged out again ... shortly after midnight, Brazil time.

And he could never sleep, anyway, when the Philosophical Computer was in full flow.

It was currently debating his latest thoughts on the notion of universal properties of matter. Fifty-odd humanoform androids, toga-clad like their master, sat around the garden in little groups, under trees and by bushes, each group discussing an aspect or a development of the topic at hand. Every now and then a member of one group would get up and wander over to another to give them the results of their latest deliberations. These results would then be debated by the next group and passed on in turn; ultimately, one of them would approach Philip and tell him what the Philosophical Computer thought.

It was his pet idea, his favourite toy. A meeting of trained, organic minds that could discuss any subject under the sun in a precise, disciplined manner, using a purely logical language of his own devising, without a single 'you know ...' or 'I'm only saying ...'. Beautiful.

He stood by a group clustered around a fish pond; they ignored him until he spoke.

'Use Abelard,' he said, and at once the android nearest him cast the medieval thinker's ideas on the subject into the pool of speculation.

A quiet voice spoke out of the air an inch away from Philip's ear. 'A call for you in the viewing chamber, sir.' His face split into a grin.

'I wonder who it could be?' he said.

To his surprise, it wasn't who he expected. It should have been Miranda. The laser field should have had a full size image of his twin sister, reproducing her fury perfectly, radiating it out at him. She should have been screaming and stamping her feet.

But the figure in the viewing chamber was another woman. She was good looking and of indeterminate age, though she must have been ancient. She dressed with a casual sense of power.

'Madam Administrator,' Philip said humbly. 'Good day.'

Madam Zhao *looked* the matriarch and as usual Philip felt all his intellectual arrogance flow out of him.

'You really cannot be trusted, can you, Philip?'

'Madam Zhao, I-'

'If you must spoil your sister's hobbies, could you at least have the decency not to do it in front of her friends?'

'She didn't invite me to the party,' Philip said with a smirk.

'Just as well.'

'I know. I'd have gone as a doughnut and told everyone I was a torus.'

'I was there, Philip, in my own guise. My people cancelled your forcefield lens, the image of Mars was back where it should have been, and everyone knew that another silly prank by Philip Devere had gone awry. It was you who ended up with egg on your face, Philip-' Philip's face hardened and his eyes narrowed, and Zhao smiled '-and that is easily avoided, you know.'

'Oh, Madam!' Philip snapped. 'You know as well as I do that this astrology lark will go the same way as the last one. Remember the Tongues Lexicon?'

(Miranda had interviewed people suffering from religious ecstasies from all over the solar system. She had invited them to her house, noted down the noises that came from their mouths and fed them into her computers for analysis. One of Philip's androids had been planted in her study group and had been her favourite subject until she realised that it was simply repeating everything she said backwards in Esperanto. The lexicon project had lasted a month.)

'You do make self-fulfilling prophecies, Philip,' Zhao said. 'And it's true that even without your encouragement, she loses interest quickly. But in the meantime ... well, Philip, believe it or not, Miranda is currently ahead of you in our favours. As well as the starcharts, a spin-off of her astrology work has been a revolution in our social engineering paradigms. And they are working.'

Philip gaped, struck dumb. 'But-'

'While you, Philip, are still struggling with the problem of faster than light travel, no? Maybe being a die-hard empiricist isn't the be all and end all.'

Philip shouted angrily. 'I'm getting there! I'm talking about the laws of physics, not just people, and they're a damn sight harder to crack! The probes have all come back safely, haven't they?'

'True. With all organic lifeforms on board dead, and substantial evidence from the computers that the probes actually travelled back in time on the outward journey through hyperspace. Not very practical, Philip.'

'I try,' Philip muttered.

'And if you want to keep receiving your research subsidies from the Corporation, keep trying.' Zhao dismissed the business with a flick of the wrist. 'Now, to business. Your most recent set of equations actually appear to be working quite nicely.'

'Oh, good.'

'The Philosophical Computer really is a very clever piece of work.'

Philip actually smiled, with a touch of pride. 'Isn't it?'

'You had promised to let us have one of your androids as a pilot for the next probe ...'

'It's all ready, Madam Administrator. You can have it whenever you want.'

'Very good. We will open our teleport channel to you for point five seconds at 1800 Beijing time, precisely.'

'Eighteen hundred Beijing. Right-o.' Philip's confidence was growing. Even if Zhao did look down on him, purely figuratively, she still had to acknowledge that his androids were the best and that she needed them. Surely that justified all the Corporation's time and effort.

'Now, Philip, a word before I go.'

'Madam Administrator?'

Zhao actually took a step forward and raised a finger in warning. 'Our hopes for you and your sister were not in vain, Philip. Between you, you have given us the teleport, and that alone repaid our investment in your services. But we've put a lot more into you since then, and again we want a return. We hoped you would get us safely past light speed, get us out of the solar system. We are so close!' Zhao held up thumb and forefinger a fraction of an inch apart, to illustrate her point. '*So* close. But to get there, you and your sister must work together. Together you are the best, and this childish bickering must stop. Once you've got us to the stars we will ask no more of you. You will be funded for the rest of your lives, with no expectation of return-' Philip's heart pounded '-and you will be able to pursue your hobbies all you want. *Once* you have got us to the stars. And if that means being nice to your sister, the Corporation considers that an acceptable sacrifice.'

Philip nodded quickly. 'Oh, absolutely, yes. Quite agree.'

Zhao smiled. 'It may interest you to know, Philip, that you are apparently a typical Cancer male. You are ready to disparage anyone and everybody, you crave affection but you don't dare let anyone come close enough to give it. So Miranda says.'

Philip's face was turning red and he felt a volcano pushing up inside him.

'Ciao, Philip,' Zhao said before it erupted, and vanished.

* * *

The advent of the teleport had obviated the tiresome need for accommodating guests overnight. By dawn, Miranda's mansion was empty.

Philip's apology was waiting for her when she woke, shortly before noon. It was relayed to her by her Household.

> 'Philip Devere apologises to his sister for spoiling her party last night by sending Mars on an unexpected journey, and hopes she won't hold it against him. Just to make up, she can come and audit his engrams any time she wishes.'

'Idiot,' she sniffed.

The androids had tidied up the grounds while she slept, returning them to their immaculate splendour. She took a brief walk in them, then ordered a light meal to be made ready for her in the observatory. It was waiting for her when she arrived. She would absorb herself in her hobby to show that she could rise above these little set-backs, as Madam Zhao had advised; that would show Philip.

She sat down at her calculating desk and on a suspicious whim called up satellite shots of the night sky from all around the world. Everything was where it should be. Good.

Though Philip would have spat blood at the suggestion, Miranda's approach was methodical and well-reasoned. All the information she needed was in the databanks somewhere; built up over the centuries, datum by datum. It needed the flexibility and intuition of a human mind to piece it together again and to make sense of it. She tackled the problem with the love and precision of an artist.

She pictured the galaxy as a shape in her mind. Each star was a node, a point held in suspension in the matrix of gravity. She took a sphere of a thousand light years' diameter with the Sun at the centre and built up a map of the overlapping gravitational fields, assigning them different colours according to their different strengths and what she perceived as the twists and bends that lay in them.

It took hours to finish; she was utterly lost in the creation of something beautiful and her meal went untouched.

* * *

Philip summoned the Philosophical Computer. The androids clustered on the lawn and he walked among them, thinking as he moved. It was his preferred way of delivering instructions; he felt like a general briefing his troops.

'The program,' he said, 'is to deliver a psychological outline of my sister Miranda Devere. You will find the Corporation's databases hold basic psychological profiles and you may use them for data. What I want is a reason why she persists in these ... these ... these ludicrous activities, these *insults* to the intelligence, these *embarrassments* to me as her brother, who has given his life to empiricism-' His voice had been rising and he choked. He swallowed and breathed slowly to calm himself down. 'I want a method whereby she can be discouraged from her inane beliefs in the supernatural and yet continue to deliver worthwhile research to the Zhao Cow and her cronies. Use Freud, use Jung, use anyone on the permitted index of psychological thinkers. Commence now.'

And in the meantime ... well, if it meant so much to Zhao, and if the potential rewards were so great, maybe he really should do something to be nice to Miranda. Maybe he could talk her out of the nonsense and they really could work together.

But if not ... well, the Philosophical Computer would always provide a fall-back plan.

* * *

Miranda noticed the passage of time with surprise, then looked back at the gorgeous, multi-hued swirl of colour hovering over her desk. She studied the holographic image from different angles. It really was quite spectacular. She made a note to incorporate it into her designs the next time she redecorated.

Her Household spoke into her ear. 'Your brother asks permission to visit you.'

'Philip? Are you sure?'

'He says that he wishes to make peace.'

'Gosh.' Whatever new game of Philip's this was, she would not be taken in. 'Well ... yes, set the teleport to receive him,' Miranda said graciously. 'When he arrives, show him here. I'm too busy to go and meet him. Oh, and tell me if it's only an android that looks like him.'

Her agoraphobic brother would have to walk across the wide-open grounds; that would show whether or not his desire to make peace was genuine. She doubted that it was. She was all the more surprised when Philip sidled through the door five minutes later.

'Hello, Philip,' she said in surprise.

'Hello, Miranda,' he said. She stood and came over to him slowly, holding out a hand. He took it and she gasped.

'It really is you. Not an image.' Real and solid, in his toga and pale skin that came from spending his life under artificial lighting in his bubble at the bottom of the sea.

'It really is me,' he agreed. He was looking nervously about him, not at all at ease. He nodded his head at the image above the table. 'That's pretty. What is it?'

'It's our bit of the galaxy.' Miranda was even more taken aback by Philip being agreeable. 'My hobby, remember?' she added, with a hint of challenge.

'Oh.' Philip refrained from comment while she described what she had been doing.

SPOILSPORT

'If the starship's flying through hyperspace it needs to know the exact shape of space ahead of it. Madam Zhao says my data is so much better than what she gets from her own computers.'

'I see.' Philip mused upon the image, then looked back at his sister. 'Can we talk?'

Miranda shrugged and reclined on a couch. She indicated that Philip could do the same.

'Thank you,' he said, once he was settled. Miranda looked at him expectantly. 'I don't really know where to start,' he said. 'I'm not used to talking to other people. But . . . well, I've been talking to Madam Zhao too. They really, really want this starship thing to succeed ... and they're relying on us! *Everyone* is! We're the best, Miranda, you and me. We're Deveres! Doesn't that make you proud?'

'It always has.' She looked at her brother thoughtfully. 'Why did you have to come here to tell me this, Philip?'

'Well, I thought ...' He smiled bashfully. 'I thought that since we're on a common track, and it really is for everyone's good, I mean, they'll give us life-long funding and all that ... well, we could bury the hatchet. We could cooperate.'

'Oh, Philip! Like brother and sister should! Oh, that would be lovely!'

'Well, um ... now that's decided-' Philip stood to leave.

'Oh, don't go!' Miranda said, jumping up. She stood facing her brother, awkwardly. They would have to get used to each other's presence, she decided, so she reached out and hugged him. After a long second she felt him returning the hug.

'We should tell Madam Zhao,' she said.

'She'll be pleased,' Philip admitted. Miranda was taking her first proper look at him in the flesh since he was a pimply boy. For the first time, she saw that he was reasonably good-looking.

'Will you stay in your bubble?' she asked.

'Yes, I suppose so. You know I don't like open spaces or too much company.' He looked at her shyly. 'But ... well, just to show this is for real, you can use the Philosophical Computer any time you want. Just ask.'

'Oh, Philip!' Miranda tightened her hug. 'I'll use it to work out a birth chart just for you.'

'Eh?' Philip broke out of her hug. She regarded him, puzzled and hurt.

'Is something wrong?'

'B-but, I thought ... I thought ... ' Philip stammered. 'I thought I'd convinced you to forget that nonsense ...'

'What do you mean, nonsense?' Miranda demanded. She felt her good humour evaporate.

'Well, I mean, yes, the stars and the gravitational fields and all that – that's a useful side product, I suppose. At least it's scientific. But this destiny crap-'

'Philip!'

'-I mean, it's all utter bullshit-'

'That does it!' Miranda yelled. 'Get out of here, Philip Devere, and don't come back!'

'I actually thought I'd convinced you-' Philip said.

'*Out!*' Miranda howled. Philip stormed out.

'It was nice while it lasted,' he muttered under his breath as he strode back to the mansion, the teleport chamber and the sanctuary of his home. 'For all of thirty seconds. So much for the reasoned argument.'

* * *

SPOILSPORT

'Let's hear it, and it better be good,' Philip said sullenly. He was slumped in a chair sipping a drink as the spokesandroid of the Philosophical Computer summarised its report on the assignment that Philip had set.

'Miranda Devere approaches her hobbies with the commitment of an artisan,' it said. 'She desires that every task upon which she embarks will make a statement to the world. There is a possible correlation here with classical psychological theories relating to the lack of proper parenting and a desire to be taken seriously by those who are her peers, but who she perceives as her betters.'

'Nothing wrong with her parenting,' Philip muttered. Exactly the same process had produced him.

'Miranda Devere can withstand criticism and opposition from others, but she has invariably abandoned her hobbies every time they have been sabotaged by you. This is because you do not just criticise but are careful to arrange something that clearly falsifies her theories. Witness your subversion of the Tongues Lexicon and the Reincarnation Programme.'

'Oh, yeah.' Philip grinned. 'That was a good one.' All that had taken was getting three friends (friends no longer) drunk, hypnotically implanting identical memories of former lives and then carefully, one by one, releasing them into Miranda's social circle.

'So,' Philip said, 'I arrange something that makes nonsense of her theories ... but since she knows it's contrived by me, why doesn't she just carry on again?'

'We surmise that it is you she especially wishes to impress, albeit subconsciously,' the android said. 'Following the early death of your father, you are the family male, the leader, the father-substitute. It is knowing that you in particular are ridiculing her which makes her lose heart.'

'Go on.'

'We therefore recommend a reversion to your usual tactics. A deliberate spanner thrown into the works will cause her to abandon the project.'

'Okay, that's part one,' Philip said, thinking of the implications. An astrological event that Miranda couldn't possibly predict and which meant nothing ... wow! Not quite as easy to organise as fake memories. 'Now, part two? No one must be able to prove anything about my involvement.'

'An element of suspicion as to your involvement is inevitable-'

'Of course.'

'-but if you desire a lack of proof-'

* * *

No one expected the starship probe to blast suddenly out of the solar system. Without warning the stardrive came on: every particle on the ship changed to a tachyon analogue and the probe vanished from human purview.

Everyone assumed it was a malfunction and Philip felt deeply satisfied. If this worked, it would be worth the loss of the pilot android, worth the wrath of Madam Zhao, worth the loss of the Corporation's trust ... worth *everything*.

Thanks to the Philosophical Computer, Philip knew more than anyone alive about the possibilities of playing with faster-than-light travel. Playing with *time*. It was a bug in his equations that had been giving the Corporation grief and which he had been trying to get rid of for ages. So why not use it? Though the probe took a year of its subjective time to travel through hyperspace towards its far-off destination, when it emerged into normal space in the vicinity of a planetless star it was several thousand years ago.

A beam of coherent radiation flared out from the probe – gamma rays, aimed into the heart of the star. Philip had hoped the scientists had got the theory right (no one had ever had a chance to prove or disprove it), and they had. The star's supernova sequence was triggered and it erupted spectacularly. By the time the expanding cloud reached the probe's orbit it had already jumped on to the next star on its precisely-timed itinerary.

The light rays started on their long journey to Earth.

* * *

Philip had told the Household to block all calls. It would be suspected, it would be in character, but *no one* would be able to prove that he had had anything to do with the eruption of the entire Gemini constellation – a synchronised, multi-nova spectacle that would dominate the skies for months.

The Philosophical Computer was hacking its way towards a fusion of quantum theory and the philosophy of Bishop Berkeley when the one item of information that Philip had decreed should be allowed through arrived. Miranda Devere had abandoned her hobby.

'That's that nonsense out of the way, then,' Philip said, highly pleased with himself, before turning back to the Philosophical Computer. Madam Zhao got her starcharts; Miranda ceased to disgrace the Devere name with her foolishness; he could chalk up another victory over irrationality.

Astrology indeed! No substitute for hard logic. For empiricism. For science.

And no way was he going to set the Philosophical Computer onto the question of why he felt just a little, teeny bit guilty.

About SPOILSPORT

This story was great fun to write, simply for the personalities of Philip and Miranda.

In case you hadn't guessed, 'Spoilsport' isn't entirely serious. Still, it was a challenge. I have zero belief in astrology and a great respect for the empirical scientific method, but I also dislike 'message' stories where the author is trying to put his own viewpoint across at the expense of all others. I've seen far too many stories where my own religion has been set up as an easy target by the author and then knocked down, and everyone applauds the author for being so clever. So, even though it hurt, I had to be nice about astrology too and show its positive sides (or, failing that, make them up). I even went so far as to read a book on sun signs to get the personalities of Philip and Miranda. If that ain't research, I don't know what is.

'Spoilsport' was originally published in *Substance*, a worthy attempt at a new British SF magazine which sadly died – not for want of trying – after four issues. I knew that the editor, Paul Beardsley, had similar views to mine on astrology and so I sent it to him: rather worryingly, he accepted it almost by return. I even insulted his editorial integrity by asking if he had actually read it? He assured me he had, and to set my mind at rest he asked for rewrites of the next story I sent him, 'The Grey People', before taking it.

DIGITAL CATS COME OUT TONIGHT

Consider fear. A marvellous thing. It gives wings to our feet, it makes us traitors. It robs the mind of all its powers of acting and reasoning; this is its best feature.

And now consider cats. Take, for example, a farm house. A farm house from the Middle Ages – no, earlier. After all, the ancient Egyptians had cats, so we need to go earlier than that. Picture a Sumerian farm house.

It has a barn, in which food is stored. The farmers are unhappy, because mice keep eating the food. This is not good, as the farmers will starve. Oh, they are very unhappy.

All is not lost! Enter Felix.

Felix kills the mice and eats them. This is his function. The mice hate and fear him. Unfortunately, they are very much smaller than him and tend to freeze up when he approaches. He can swallow them in one bite.

Does Felix eat all the mice? No, because there are too many. The problem is solved, however, because the mice are too afraid to venture into the barn. They are under control. The application of fear is effective.

I'd never really considered fear *per se* until we moved into Cinnamon Towers. Once it had been a very well-off apartment block, before the Death of the Yuppy. The architect's pride and joy had been the building's fully integrated computer network, which effectively ran every appliance in every apartment exactly to the taste of the occupier.

Now the apartments were cheap, the building was running down and the management found it a millstone.

Double apartments were cheaper still, which was great for a newly married couple. Sally and I couldn't afford anything fancy – not until Felixware got off the ground. When we first set up the company (not out of any entrepreneurial philosophy, but simply because we had a deep, abiding horror of even the thought of working for anyone else) we had to give it a name like that, based on our common love for the animals. Our actual association with cats didn't come until later.

It was the management's fault, for getting heavy handed. We had a respectable ninety-nine year lease, and we were staying until it suited us to move. We didn't know things would escalate. We were already the proud owners of three cats before things did.

I trace the start of it to a blustery day in March. I had been out doing the shopping, while Sally stayed in putting the finishing touches to our latest pet. When I got back in to the lobby, I could tell at once that the mice were at play. The lights were dim and the air conditioning was full on (as I say, it was March). The place was a gloomy ice block.

Miracle of miracles, a lift was working. I positioned myself in front of the doors and looked up at the green lights flashing their way down to ground level. The doors opened with a chime and I got in.

It jammed between the third and fourth floors. I gave it a minute, then reluctantly put the bags down to free my hands. I pulled out my phone and dialled.

'It's me.'

'Hello, dear. Where are you?'

'In the lift. It's jammed between three and four. Can you send Alonzo down?'

'Hang on.' Pause. 'Alonzo's in the basement with the heating. Will Britannicus do?'

'Have to.' Britannicus lacked Alonzo's subtlety, so I sat down.

Ten seconds later the lift jerked itself up violently. I looked up at the ceiling.

''Oos a booful pussy-pussy?' I murmured.

Sally was still busy at the terminal.

'You're just in time,' she greeted me. 'Meet Napoleon.'

Napoleon lurked on the screen in the form of a mass of code, apparently as un-deadly and as un-Jellicle as ever.

'Hello, Napoleon,' I said.

We released Napoleon into a carefully closed system that covered the apartment. LEDs glowed at various points around the main room, some nowhere near any other electrical instrument and others wired up to the coffee maker, the television, the stereo. Many of these LEDs flickered red, indicating the presence of the mice – the tiny, mischievous, havoc-causing artificial intelligences that scurried about the system, similar in all respects to the hordes that the management had released into the building's own system in a final effort to oust those of us, the tenants, who preferred to stay.

'Releasing Napoleon now,' Sally reported, and pressed the execute key. The red flashing became more agitated.

The LD on the television glowed green suddenly, and the fuzz cleared to show the latest Antipodean soap opera. I turned the sound down.

The coffee machine spluttered and started to pump out dark brown liquid.

The light in the bathroom came on.

'Let's diddle the odds,' Sally murmured, and released some more mice into the television. For a moment the set switched to a different channel and the sound blared out, then the volume returned to its former silence and the picture was again of a quiet Sydney cul-de-sac.

'He gets about fast,' I commented.

'And he's not complacent. Even Alonzo would have been taken aback to find mice in an area that he'd already cleared.'

The test went very well. Napoleon was the best cat yet, combining cunning with killer instinct, and even a touch of sadism. Almost like the real thing, and a far cry from the crude violence of the very first model, the unsophisticated Britannicus. Napoleon had the right unpredictability, the random element, that made the application of fear so much more effective.

It wasn't long before the only red LED was on a small memory module next to the terminal. A green one glowed next to it. The mice were holed up in their refuge, and their nemesis waited outside patiently. You could almost see the tail lash and the ears strain forward, waiting for the least movement.

'You think we can release him into the main system yet?'

'Perhaps, perhaps.' Anyone from the management would have cringed at the glee on my spouse's face. 'And then maybe we can sell him. It's about time we put the cats on the market.'

So, we did the rounds. Several companies expressed a polite interest in our product, if only for the novelty value. I think they had been searching for years for a good way of exposing AIs to the general public, and we were quite optimistic about this one.

Then Sally was asked by Cinnamon's oldest resident, Miss Anderson, to have a look at her apartment's controlling software which was playing up.

'Miss Anderson's got the mice.'

'They're reading our mail again.'

We spoke simultaneously as Sally returned to the apartment. My message had the greater news content.

'What do you mean?'

'Take a look.' On the screen was a message from a large software house, expressing an interest in our cats. Nothing in the message showed what kind of cat was being discussed.

'And next ...' I said.

A message from the management, apparently unconnected, reminding all tenants of the penalties for having animals in the building.

'Did Miss Anderson have this message?'

'Of course not. But we can't prove anything, all the same. The scumbags! Just for this, Britannicus visits them tonight. The rough, alley cat treatment.'

Then I remembered what she had said.

'What do you mean, she's got the mice? Alonzo and Napoleon have both been up there.'

'I know. But mice she has, love. The cats are being interfered with. Or they're not as deadly as we thought.'

'Could they be multiplying faster than we thought?'

'I really don't know.' I squeezed her hand as she looked worried. 'We'll have to think about it.'

'Or take advice.'

'You mean ...?'

'AI Agony!'

* * *

'We have developed three low-level hunter/killer AIs that operate on the fear principle. Their purpose is to restrict the activities of an indefinite number of lesser AIs that are loose in our network. There are too many of these to be completely annihilated, so we have designed our own AIs to inspire 'fear' in the enemy. The enemy AIs thus restrict their activities to the minimum and stay out of the main systems.

'This approach has proved successful until recently. The enemy AIs appear to be gaining in confidence and number, and though our hunter/killers are constantly on the watch, the situation is worsening. We have checked our hunter/killers most carefully, but can see no signs of tampering. Likewise, the enemy AIs are the same as they ever were.

'Please advise.'

An answer was not long in coming.

'Forgive any presumptions in this answer. I have to make assumptions because of the lack of detail in your query, presumably meant to avoid clues to your identity. Very commendable.

'If the principle, as you say, is fear, and the system no longer works, could it not be because the enemy is no longer afraid? Or, there is something else in the system that your hunter/killers are afraid of? I suggest you do a careful check of the network to see if there are any AIs of a higher level than your own ...'

* * *

Whoever the management's man was, he was good. I say this out of all respect to the enemy – someone I felt I could get on well with socially. He had the same approach to computers and AIs as I did. It was an art of the mind.

I don't think Sally saw it that way. The cats were my idea, but they were her creation.

'He is going to suffer,' she ranted, once we had discovered what was going on. We were both seated in front of the terminal, looking at the evidence on screen. 'I will not have my cats being tampered with by an outsider. I'll-'

'Hold it, hold it,' I soothed. 'No one said they've been tampered with.'

'But they're-'

'Yes, yes, yes. Look.' It didn't seem the best time to point out that the designer of our new adversary might feel the same way about our instinctive killers being unleashed on his pets. 'I think I see what's happening. Want my theory?'

'I'll get it anyway.'

'You've got the gist of it, but not the specifics. AI Agony helped, but it wasn't entirely on the right track, either.'

'Meaning?'

'Meaning, no, they haven't set dogs on our cats. The new AI in the system is of a higher level than the cats, just like the cats are higher than the mice. But the cats aren't afraid of him. They *like* him.'

'So-'

'Can't you see it? Britannicus, Alonzo and Napoleon busy chasing mice. Along comes – oh, call it a human. What would a cat do? It stops. It rubs up to the human. It sniffs the carpet. It purrs. And it forgets the mice.'

Sally thought about this.

'So the mice are still afraid of the cats, but the cats aren't afraid of the stranger? And there's nothing about to challenge the stranger.'

'Correct.'

'Hmm. Interesting. So, logically, we ought to design something to scare the stranger.'

'Makes sense. But that's your department.'

'Y-e-s ... got it.'

'Go on.'

'Remember, Napoleon was built on the shortcomings of Alonzo, and Alonzo on the shortcomings of Britannicus. Until the stranger appeared, Napoleon was the best. And yet, ever since this stranger's come on the scene, Britannicus has been the most effective.'

'He doesn't purr at the stranger? He's as antisocial as ever?'

'That's right. The stranger still gets the better of him eventually, though. Britannicus is the alley cat, but he's still susceptible to humans.' She had that light in her eye that anticipates a fight.

'This doesn't answer the question,' I objected.

'Yes it does. Look, open a new file and call up the specs for Britannicus. I'm going to make some fine adjustments.'

'Right. What name for the file?'

'Bagheera.'

And so it started. Bagheera was, believe me, lethal. We traced his actions on the first night that he was out in the system. We attached him to Napoleon, so he would know his way around. Napoleon headed for a cluster of mice on the roof that were lurking in the cooling towers (the weather was warming up). The mice scattered as he approached and pounced, and before long he was in his element. He really was just like the real thing, with his domesticated veneer swept away by his not-so-vestigial jungle instincts.

Bagheera watched from a distance, as it were, bored. Panthers go for higher game than mice. Then he was distracted.

The stranger – by now we were calling him Clint – sidled up to the scene of the action. Napoleon saw him coming and instantly started to show off, forgetting the mice as he chased his tail, rubbed up against Clint, and generally let his domestic instincts come to the fore again.

Then Bagheera pounced from the subsystem he had been hiding in. It was swift, lethal and messy. What had been a sophisticated structure of code was reduced in a flash to a pile of disconnected, helpless subroutines which Bagheera, calmly and methodically, began to absorb. When he was finished, all that was left were a few random signals in the network that could harm no one. Mentally, I held my hat against my chest in respect for the passing of Clint.

The system was clear for a very long time, now. The mice continued to run around and the cats continued to deal with them. Bagheera also prowled about, and several times we detected a new Clint in the network which promptly withdrew when Bagheera approached. We gave him a brother, Pink, to help him out and to spread the fear blanket a bit more. Fear, glorious fear. It worked wonders.

Until the management man tried the next approach.

What comes up the fear scale from a panther? Nothing much, we had thought. Lions, tigers, cheetahs – yes, they may have their own hierarchy out in the wild, but a Big Cat is a Big Cat.

The management took a new approach. They had cottoned onto the fear principle by this time, and we should have guessed they wouldn't be hampered by our own cat-obsession.

There is a creature in the wild that very few creatures will attack, because it is substantially bigger than any of them and capable of defending itself by sheer bulk. It is called an elephant.

The first elephant entered the system six months after Bagheera's first triumph. Bagheera took one look and fled. The elephant shouldered its way casually through all our defences and wreaked havoc in the lighting, the heating and (we still can't work this out) the kitchen units of every even-numbered apartment. We think it was only a combined charge by Bagheera and Pink together, aimed not at the elephant but at one of the Clints controlling it, that turned it back. We had to think, and fast, of a way to beat this one.

We didn't have the time. We had heard of the Software Riots, but hadn't paid them much attention. Now they were brought home to us.

Apparently, there was contention amongst religious groups concerning AIs. Some maintained that they were the work of the devil and were to be exterminated. Others said they were just as valid as natural intelligences, i.e. us. They should therefore be protected.

The strength of feeling that culminated in the Riots took the government by surprise, and legislation was rushed through. All of a sudden Pink, Bagheera, Napoleon, Alonzo and Britannicus, not to mention the elephants, the Clints and even the mice, were protected species until such time as the government could think of what to do with them. Even to devise a way of bumping off a rival AI was, in the eyes of the law, the same as devising a way of bumping off a bat or a whale. It was considered naughty.

There is now a major ecology flourishing in the network of Cinnamon Towers. The last time we looked, it seemed that some of the Clints were adopting the mice as pets. And some of the cats.

Yes, *some* of the cats. There's more of everything than there used to be. Yesterday, perusing the system, we saw a cat we've never met before, but which had the characteristics of Napoleon and Britannicus. One of those two apparently wasn't what we thought it was.

Unfortunately, *looking* at the system is all we can do. All networks containing AIs have had government-imposed guardian AIs slapped on them. We're not sure what they do, but they're pretty horrific. We tried, when we thought no one was looking, to get our cats out of the system again, but our terminal flipped at the thought. It took one look at the guardian and went catatonic. Perhaps *demons* would be a good name for these newcomers. I don't know.

We also got a message detailing everything that would happen if we even tried to meddle with the system again, before a ruling can be reached by higher authority, and it was very nasty. So, we don't dare.

Now, that really galls.

About DIGITAL CATS COME OUT TONIGHT

I wrote this as the result of a half dream. The family had been to see *Cats* in the West End and I'd got to bed at about 1.00 a.m.; then I was up at 6.30 a.m. as usual to get the train to work. Thus I was fairly woozy on the trip and I day dreamed about cats being let loose in a computer to catch 'mice'.

See my note on 'The Data Class' for how this story came to be published, in the collection *Digital Dreams*. Though I say it myself it was a darn good collection, and editor David Barrett had done very well to get those stories together. 'Digital Cats' itself was singled out for mention by reviewers twice: *Interzone* (bless them) said it was 'jaunty, original and amusing' while *SF Eye* said it took 'first prize for twee nonsense.' Heavyweight, serious SF it ain't, and I have to say my inclination is to go with the latter opinion, but it's my first baby and I love it.

GETTING RID OF TEDDY

Of course Colin already knew what Adam's room looked like, but going in without his brother knowing was just the adventure that a rainy morning called for. Two pairs of eyes peeked round the door at the level of the door handle.

'Adam's not here,' whispered the owner of the top pair. 'Come on, Teddy.'

Colin Deane and his teddy bear ventured forth.

It was like Colin's own room, untidy despite their mother's best efforts, but plastic aircraft hung from the ceiling and there was a different taste in posters that reflected Adam's extra three years.

The clothes and shoes that lay about were two sizes too big for Colin, and he put his foot next to one of Adam's trainers and thought wistfully of the day he, too, would be seven. Colin wasn't sure how many years lay between four and seven, but he knew it was a long time to wait. But he wasn't here to look at the clothes.

'That's Adam's bed where he goes to bed, and that's Adam's radio, and ... look, Teddy!' Colin's eyes settled on the most hallowed object in the house and his tone changed to reverent awe. The plastic fighter gleamed in its new camouflage paint and Royal Air Force decals; Adam had spent hours putting it together with parental help and it was his pride and joy. 'That's Adam's Pitsfire, and you go "eeee-owwww dakka-dakka-dakka, take that, nasty," and it flies about—'

'Don't you dare touch my Spitfire!'

Colin spun round guiltily, still clutching Teddy. Adam advanced on him from the doorway, a blond cherub (which he got from his father) with a ferocious scowl.

'Who said you could come in my room? What are you doing here?'

Adam measured 49 inches from top to toe and Colin cowered beneath every one of them.

'Teddy wanted to see,' he quavered.

'Oh, that stupid Teddy!' Adam jeered. He wrenched Teddy from Colin's grasp. 'Stupid, stupid Teddy.'

'No!' Colin cried. Adam stalked across to the door and threw Teddy out on to the landing. Colin chased after him.

'I'm sorry, Teddy, I'm sorry,' he wailed, picking Teddy up and cuddling him.

'And stop talking to it all the time, or you'll ... you'll really be sorry!' Adam shouted, and slammed the door shut. Colin and Teddy were alone on the landing.

'Why should'n' I talk to Teddy?' Colin sobbed as he hugged Teddy to him. Teddy said he didn't mind.

* * *

It was that time of the week when Mummy – Elizabeth Deane – entertained. It was partly a task foisted on her by being the wife of a Church Elder and partly one she undertook out of a sense of duty – the newcomer to the flock (she had been a member for some ten years now, but still felt a newcomer), paying her way. She also

GETTING RID OF TEDDY

enjoyed the occasional break from the boys' exclusive company and so every Wednesday the other women in the church who didn't have anything else to do met in the Deane house for coffee.

Elizabeth was in the middle of a conversation, of sorts, with Mrs May. It could be called a conversation, but the word 'interrogation' did come to mind.

'I do think siblings are such a tower of strength, don't you, Elizabeth? Do you have any family? I mean, apart from here? Any brothers or sisters? I've heard your boys talk about their Uncle Bill-'

Boy, not boys, Elizabeth thought. It was Colin who doted on his Uncle Bill.

'I've got brothers and sisters, but I don't see them much,' Elizabeth said, trying not to look as though the subject was painful. She didn't think the people here would approve of her family. 'Not even Bill.'

'Oh, dear, you ought to, you know!'

'I-'

'I mean, a family is such a tower-'

'Well, I have Michael,' Elizabeth said. Everyone knew and liked her husband.

'Oh, Michael, yes!' Mrs May agreed, 'such a tower of strength ... '

Elizabeth was spared Mrs May listing all the other towers of strength that she could think of by the unmistakeable 'oohs' and 'aahs' that always heralded Colin's arrival at these meetings. Adam would be playing with the other children and the last thing they would want was a four-year-old hanging around. Colin didn't know much about the world, but he knew when he was among friends.

'Hello, Colin!'

'Ah, look at his little sandals!'

'Who's your friend, Colin?'

Colin stood basking in the admiration, smiling shyly, with an arm wrapped in a loving stranglehold round Teddy's neck. Everyone but him knew he was showing off for all he was worth. Shyness eventually took over and he ran to Elizabeth and buried his face in her side. There were a few laughs and conversation went back to normal.

Elizabeth felt the tug on her skirt and looked down.

'Can I play a game?' Colin whispered.

'As long as it doesn't make a noise, dear.'

'Can I play chets?' A chess set was permanently set out by the window: Michael Deane, the boys' father, was a fan of the game and hoped to teach it to both his sons. He had spent a lot of the previous Sunday evening teaching Adam, with Colin observing closely.

'Who will you play chets with, dear?'

'Teddy.'

Elizabeth shrugged and several people chuckled.

'Okay,' Elizabeth said, and turned back to the guests to talk about the slide show presentation on Africa that was looming on the church's social calendar.

Colin grabbed the chess set with one hand; the board folded and the pieces scattered.

'Oh, Teddy, you are so cumsee.' A fair imitation of his father; Elizabeth half heard it and smiled to herself.

Colin put the board down on the floor and sat Teddy the other side of it. He shut his eyes for a moment, then opened them and quickly repositioned the pieces as they should be.

'Black queen on black, white queen on white, Teddy,' he said. He curled his fingers up into fists and held his hands out to Teddy. 'Which one do you want to be?' Teddy apparently chose the hand with the black pawn, even though Colin had forgotten to put a pawn in either hand at all. 'Okay, I'm white so I go first. Now, you always move a pawn first and you can move them two squares on their first go. I'll move this pawn here to free the bishop-'

Some of the guests seemed quite impressed; Colin's words were sinking into Elizabeth's consciousness over the general chatter and she was trying not to stare at him. Colin's pronunciation was still imperfect but he was talking like someone far older.

'One, two, and one to the side. See, Teddy? I've got my knights and my bishops out to do the attacking-'

Elizabeth had come over to watch the game. Colin was making his own moves and moving the pieces for Teddy without any hesitation. Sometimes he moved a piece for Teddy, then corrected Teddy out loud and repositioned it.

This game, Elizabeth had finally realised, was an exact replay, minus the pauses, of the game Michael had played with Adam, complete with Michael's commentary. The only thing missing was what Adam had said; Teddy was silently taking Adam's part.

'Why don't you move this pawn, dear?' she said as an experiment. Colin looked up crossly.

'No, Mummy, I move this, and Teddy moves this, and I move this-'

'And why's that, dear?'

''Cos Teddy says!' There were indulgent chuckles from the guests and Elizabeth decided the best she could do was divert attention altogether. The game was over five minutes later.

'Shall we play another, Te-'

'Colin, dear, why don't you play in the garden? Look, it's stopped raining.'

Colin's ephemeral attention span evaporated at once.

'Okay,' he said happily. He grabbed Teddy and ran out, leaving Elizabeth wondering what else Teddy told him.

* * *

Teddy told Colin a lot of things. When the guests had gone he told him Adam was about to join him in the garden, so Colin looked out warily for his big brother. Adam was ashamed of his earlier temper and offered to let Colin play with him and his Mutabots. They carried on the game after lunch and spent the afternoon happily together; the rain held off and Teddy was relegated to the sidelines.

Later he told Colin that dinner was almost ready, and Colin had his hands properly washed just as Mummy called him. Mummy wouldn't allow Teddy in the bath with him but Teddy was waiting for him afterwards, nestling against his pillow. Mummy kissed him goodnight and he fell asleep with Teddy cuddled up close to him.

Teddy was under standing orders to wake Colin up when his father got home, so Michael would have no excuse for not coming up and giving him a goodnight kiss. Michael Deane thought Colin was a very light sleeper but he always obliged; he felt guilty at having to work so long each day to pay the mortgage, which meant he only saw his sons on weekdays for a few snatched minutes in the morning. The tall, fair haired figure appearing silhouetted against the hall light in Colin's doorway was always a highlight of the day for

GETTING RID OF TEDDY

Colin. It reminded him of a picture of Jesus in church, and he knew that was good.

Michael always spent a quite unreasonable time talking to Elizabeth first, and Teddy told Colin what they were saying.

'How was today, love?'

'Oh, the children only had one fight. I can't complain.'

Michael laughed.

'What was it this time?'

'Colin went into Adam's room without telling him.'

'Oh no! Call the Security Council! Send an expeditionary force-'

As usual, long words he didn't understand killed Colin's interest and Teddy had to wake him up again before Michael came in for the kiss.

* * *

Later Elizabeth put in a surprise appearance herself, but Teddy did not wake Colin because he had not been told to. Elizabeth looked down at the sleeping child and felt a tight knot in her innards.

'Can you read my mind, Teddy?' she thought. Teddy's eyes stared blankly at the ceiling. Colin mumbled in his sleep and half turned over, shifting Teddy's position; now Teddy stared blankly at her. She took a step sideways, out of the line of Teddy's gaze.

How long had it been going on? Teddy had been a first birthday present and Colin had been talking to him for as long as he had been able to talk at all, but for how long had Teddy been answering back? She would never get an answer, knowing Colin's sense of time, but she imagined it hadn't been too long. Perhaps the

JEAPES JAPES

last few months, maybe even weeks. Surely she would have picked up a clue earlier than today, if it had been any longer.

'Daddy will blow his top if I tell him, Colin,' she thought again. 'That's what you get for marrying into another religion.' She knelt down and kissed Colin's soft cheek. 'And I could still be imagining it all, couldn't I? I've still not got any real proof.'

But she knew, deep down, that she had all the proof she needed. Sceptics need a lot of proof and a lot of convincing. Believers need a lot less.

* * *

It was the middle of the week and Colin was playing hide-and-seek with Teddy in the living room; which is to say, he hid Teddy and then sought him. To make the game less one-sided he would look in several places where Teddy wasn't before finally tracking him down with a cry of triumph.

Elizabeth wasn't sure what to expect. Would Teddy scurry across the floor and hide somewhere else? She doubted it ... at least, not if Colin didn't want it to happen.

She sat down to watch. Colin located Teddy behind the chair and shouted, 'got you!'

'Colin, darling, can you come here?' Elizabeth asked. Colin obediently toddled over to her, still clutching Teddy, and she lifted him up on to her lap.

'Oof. Heavy boy.' Colin looked at her expectantly. Well, how should she start? Colin, darling, you're a witch, and Teddy's your familiar ...

'Darling, can I ask you about Teddy?'

'Sure,' Colin said. Elizabeth took a breath.

'Darling, does Teddy talk to you a lot?'
Colin shrugged.
'He does if I want.'
'And what does he tell you?'
'What I ask him.'
'Can he tell you ... where Adam is now?'
'He's shy, Mummy,' Colin said.
'Can you ask him very, very nicely? Just for me?'
'Where's Adam, Teddy?' Colin said. Then, 'He's in the bathroom, going wee-wee.'
'Oh. Well, um, I don't think Teddy should look at Adam, then.'
'Okay,' Colin said. Upstairs, the toilet flushed. Elizabeth thought about what to ask next.
'Can Teddy move, dear?' she asked brightly. Colin made Teddy wave at her and Elizabeth sighed. 'Can he move without you holding his arm, Colin?' she said. Colin looked at her with a sad patience.
'Teddies can't, Mummy,' he said slowly, and Elizabeth almost laughed. What had she expected? Movement, from a cloth bag full of acrylic stuffing?
'So is that all Teddy can do, darling? Does he just tell you things?' Elizabeth said. Colin wriggled, anxious to get off Elizabeth's lap and go back to his game.
'Yes.'
Elizabeth let him slide down and sighed. It might actually be all right. It actually might.
A short while later she heard the raised voices. She rolled her eyes to the ceiling and went to investigate. The boys stopped bickering the moment she appeared and she coaxed the story out of them.
Adam had also staked a claim to the living room and Colin was still playing hide-and-seek with Teddy.

This was incompatible with Adam's vision of the living room as the bridge of a starship.

'All right, then,' Elizabeth said, 'I'll split the room in two. Adam can have all of this bit, up to this line, and Colin can have all of this bit. Right? Now, no more arguing. Mummy's trying to work.'

She left, thinking that Solomon couldn't have done it better.

She didn't see the boys go back to their respective games, pointedly ignoring each other. Colin hid Teddy behind one of the chairs, then stood in the middle of his half with his eyes shut, counting to five. Adam positioned his plastic soldiers around the room in lieu of the rest of the bridge crew and sat on the sofa. He pretended that the picture over the fireplace was the viewscreen and gave orders for warp factor seven.

' ... five! Coming!' Colin called.

'Warp factor seven, engage,' Adam repeated, a bit louder.

'Where are you, Teddy? Where are you?' Colin said, peering behind the other chair.

'Shut up, Colin. Shields on full.'

'I'm in my half,' Colin said stubbornly. 'Are you here, Teddy?' He peered behind the bookcase.

'Your stupid Teddy's behind the chair,' Adam said. Colin ignored him. 'I said, your stupid Teddy's behind the chair.'

'Don't spoil it!'

'It's a stupid game!'

'Spoilsport!'

'Look!' Adam crossed into Colin's half of the room and pulled Teddy out. 'Here it is, stupid old Teddy.'

'Give!' Colin shouted, jumping up and trying to grab Teddy. Adam held Teddy above his head while Colin kept jumping.

'Please, Adam!' Colin wailed.

'Pees, A-dum,' Adam mimicked. He giggled and drop kicked Teddy across the room …

* * *

Elizabeth tore into the room, panting. Her legs had started carrying her there the moment she had heard the screams. This wasn't just one boy tormenting the other. These screams had real, naked terror in them.

Teddy lay face down in the middle of the floor and the brothers sat in opposite corners of the room. Colin was sitting, legs straight out in front of him, head tilted to the ceiling and bawling.

Adam cowered in his corner, curled up into a ball. He was doing the screaming. He screamed even more when she touched him and recoiled from her. His face was white and his eyes were wide and staring. He was terrified.

'Adam, darling, it's me, Mummy,' she soothed. Adam stopped screaming but still stared. 'Adam, whatever happened?'

'He attacked me!' Adam howled, and flung his arms around her. 'Mummy, he attacked me!'

'Oh, darling, I'm sure Colin-'

'Teddy!' Adam screamed.

Later, when Elizabeth was sitting on the sofa with an arm around either boy and with Teddy a safe distance away on the floor, Adam was more coherent.

'He turned into a thing,' he said, in between his sobs, 'a horrible, horrible, thing, with claws and ... and ... and it came at me, and ...'

'He was horrid,' Colin sobbed. 'He kicked Teddy.'

An illusion? Or had Teddy really changed?

'But did Teddy hurt you, darling?' Elizabeth asked. No answer. 'Darling?' she repeated.

'Not really,' Adam said sulkily. Then, 'But it happened, Mummy! It really did! I saw a horrid thing ...'

'I know, darling, I know,' Elizabeth said gently.

'You don't believe me,' Adam mumbled.

Oh, I do, I do.

She was going to have to lie to her son. She was going to have to convince Adam that it hadn't happened, and do so before Michael came home so that Adam wouldn't mention it. He was old enough not to believe it himself, really, and perhaps he would come to think he had imagined it. Which was probably true.

But she would still be lying.

But later? Supposing Colin lost his temper again? Would it get worse?

The glory of Christ ... She knew all about that. The church taught that the gifts and talents of its members should be used to serve others, as Christ had done. But if Colin, through Teddy, could conjure up an image so powerful as to scare the living daylights out of his brother ...

You're on probation, Teddy, she thought. *Just step over the line, one more time, one tiny step ...*

Though she wasn't sure what she would do. What she could do.

* * *

'Why've we got to go to church?' Adam scowled. 'It's boring.'

'No it's not, dear,' Elizabeth said firmly, straightening his tie. 'And you and Colin can see all your friends in Sunday School.' Colin scuttled into the room with Teddy in tow, to ask the usual question.

'Can Teddy come?'

'Afraid not, darling.'

'Told you, Teddy. Teddies don't go to church.'

And this one wouldn't be very welcome if he did, Elizabeth thought glumly.

'I knew it would be boring,' Adam muttered from the back seat on the way home.

Both boys had been siphoned off to Sunday School after the first hymn, as usual, and Elizabeth felt it was just as well.

She had gone through torment and Michael had been uncomfortable for her sake, knowing her background. Ritual abuse of children was in the news as the latest media bandwagon: the newspapers were full of horror stories about children allegedly dragged into covens, forced to drink blood, sexually abused for the benefit of the forces of darkness ... Today the minister had decided to emphasise the party line on it. His text: 'thou shalt not suffer a witch to live.'

'I like Miss Day,' Colin ventured.

'That's 'cos you're stupid!'. Colin retreated in hurt silence.

'Now, boys,' said Michael from the front. 'What did you talk about, Colin?'

'Miss Day told us about Jonah and the whale.'

'That's exciting, isn't it?' said Elizabeth.

'I want to talk about witches like you did,' Adam muttered.

'Witches,' Colin said, for no real reason, and began to sing. 'Witchy, witchy, witchy, witchy ... '

'Who said we were talking about witches, Adam?' Michael asked.

'John's dad.'

'Thanks, John's dad,' Michael muttered.

'Uncle Bill's a witch,' Colin said suddenly. The car swerved slightly.

'Whatever gave you that idea?' Michael said sharply, and he saw the alarmed look on Colin's face in the mirror. 'Who said that, Colin?' he asked more gently, and Elizabeth knew, knew, without a shadow of doubt, what Colin's answer would be and interrupted before he had finished the first syllable.

'Te-'

'Uncle Bill has some funny ideas, darling,' Elizabeth said quickly. 'He doesn't understand about the church like we do. That's right, isn't it?'

'Some funny ideas. That's all,' Michael agreed.

'Uncle Bill's nice,' Colin insisted.

''Course he is, he gave you your stupid Teddy, didn't he?' Adam said. Elizabeth almost gasped. Of course he had! Uncle Bill. Why, that ...

* * *

The boys were chasing each other around the park over the damp grass, squealing happily at the top of their voices. The idea of the game seemed to be that they should play tag and Colin should chase Adam but when he caught him it didn't actually count. Colin didn't seem to mind.

Teddy was safely back at home. Colin always asked if Teddy could come when they went out, and permission was always refused. Elizabeth didn't think she could stand the results if Teddy got dropped in a muddy puddle.

Elizabeth sat on one of the park benches. She watched the man sitting at the other end of the bench throw a stick for his dog, a red setter. The dog bounded after it, ears and tail flapping.

'The moon shines brightly over Moscow,' the man said ominously. He had a pleasant face and was slightly taller and slightly younger than her.

'I'm onto you, Bill,' Elizabeth said.

'Well, and hello to you to, Big Sis,' the man said. The dog trotted up to them with the stick in its mouth. It dropped the stick at Elizabeth's feet and barked expectantly.

'Hey, gormless! How am I meant to have a clandestine rendezvous when you go and give it away?' Bill shouted.

'Oh, Bill, please,' Elizabeth said. The man looked at her and grinned.

How she loved that grin. Bill alone of the Family had known just how unhappy she had been. To be in the Family and not possess the Craft, not to the slightest degree ... worse than that. To be the eldest child, the heir apparent to a line unbroken for centuries, and be Craftless ... Bill had never had any problems that way, but he had empathy and was the closest to her in age. Grandma had never understood, and her bad temper and belief in the supernatural had scared Elizabeth witless. It didn't help that things actually did go bump in the night in their household. She had fled as soon as she could and been disinherited as a result.

To compound her crime, she had married a Christian. She had met Michael at college and his faith had attracted her right from the start. Here was she, timid and riddled with superstition, and there was he, secure and confident in the protection of his God before whom all other powers trembled. It was no contest and she had embraced that protection willingly.

Bill had been the only one of her relatives to come to the wedding, and he had had to lie about his whereabouts that day to the rest of the Family. And he had promised. He had been unwilling, he had made no secret of his disagreement, but he had promised that her children would never learn about the Craft from him.

'Well, you started it,' he said. ''Meet me in the park, the bench by the bandstand' ... very John Le Carré. When do we feed the ducks?'

Elizabeth stuck to her agenda.

'Bill, don't you remember the agreement? How could you do it?'

Bill looked at her blankly.

'Could I what?'

'You gave Teddy to Colin!'

Bill frowned, trying to remember.

'Oh, that. Well, yes, so what? Isn't an uncle allowed to be nice to his nephews? How does giving teddy bears constitute teaching the boys about the Craft?' He paused, thinking. 'Besides, I gave one to Adam as well, when he was small.'

'I know. He shoots his air rifle at it.'

GETTING RID OF TEDDY

'Really?' Bill grinned widely. 'That's my boy!'

'*My* boy. But ... ' For the first time Elizabeth began to doubt. 'It doesn't bother you?'

'Of course not!' Now Bill was frowning again. 'Look, Sis, what is it?'

Elizabeth paused, suddenly feeling foolish. Maybe ... no. How could she have thought it of her brother? Of course Teddy wasn't a Trojan Horse for the Craft. Teddy had been an innocent present from a loving uncle.

'How are you, Bill?' she said, changing the subject. Bill's expression indicated that he intended to return to the subject in due course, but for now he let her get away with it,

'Me? I'm trying to be good. I blotted my copybook in a big way ... '

'As much as me?' Elizabeth said ironically.

'No way! But I've been doing the rounds, you see, trying to get some research going ... like, Edinburgh has quite a neat little parapsychology department, for instance, and Grandma flipped her lid when I approached them. She still insists the Craft is boring old magic. But, I recanted.' He looked suitably repentant. 'Fortunately the old bat hasn't grasped the idea of PO boxes yet and I've had quite a neat little correspondence going, so as soon as she snuffs it, Sis, as soon as and I'm in charge, things'll change. Drastically. The s-word will be mentioned under our roof with impunity and you'll be welcomed back.'

'The s-word?'

'Science!' Bill said dramatically. 'Meanwhile, Sis, how's the enemy camp?'

'It's ... I still find it different. But I'm very happy, Bill, very happy.'

'The lads look happy too.'

'They are.'

Bill's dog put his head on Elizabeth's lap and looked up at her hopefully. She ruffled his ears for him without thinking, then remembered and recoiled. 'Is this your latest?'

'Yeah, he's great,' Bill said warmly. 'Old Graymalkin.'

'Bill!'

'Sorry, did I say Graymalkin? I meant Rufus. He's the best yet. Just watch. Hey, stupid, look! Look stick! Fetch!'

The stick had been lying at his feet. Before Rufus's gaze it rose slowly into the air and then suddenly flew off. Rufus bounded after it.

'I'm impressed,' Elizabeth said, without putting her heart into it.

'It's all a matter of love, Sis. I love Rufus like no other, so he works extra well for me.' Bill looked at her askance, shaking his head. 'Still don't like it, do you?'

'The church says it's wrong,' Elizabeth said dogmatically. 'It's Satanic.'

'I know a lot of witches and a couple of Satanists who would take exception to that.'

'Oh ... Bill, does a familiar have to be an animal?' There was such strain in her voice that Bill looked at her oddly.

'This isn't hypothetical, is it?'

'No. No, it isn't.'

'Uh huh. Well ... I've never known one that isn't, Sis. Why do you ... ?' A look of revelation dawned like a sunrise on Bill's face, as everything suddenly fell into place. 'Not Teddy?'

'Right.'

Bill whistled.

GETTING RID OF TEDDY

'Well, who'd have thought it? Tell me more, Sis.'

So Elizabeth told him.

' ... I mean, I've always carefully kept the house free of pets, I'm not stupid, but ... ' And she told him all about Teddy – everything that she knew. 'I mean, Colin knows things, and can do things, and the other day ... ' She described the scene in the living room with the two boys. Bill seemed awe-struck.

'And he uses his teddy bear to focus? Wowee, that little boy has got it bad.'

'But, talking to him?'

'It could seem that way to a four-year-old. Sometimes I could swear Rufus talks to me, but it's just my own thoughts bouncing off him.'

'So how did it happen?'

'How?' Bill shrugged. 'Who does Colin love more than anything, Sis?' He saw the answer in her face. 'And I know it ought to be an animal because it always has been, but ... ' He shrugged again. 'I think kids act on the bumble bee principle. If no one tells 'em it's impossible, they don't realise they can't do it. And from the sound of it ... you know, I think little Colin could wipe the floor with Grandma, when he's older.' He looked thoughtfully over at the playing boys and Elizabeth knew he wasn't just studying them with his eyes. 'Maybe he's the one who'll finally make us respectable and get the world to accept psionics as a scientific fact.'

'So what can I do?' Elizabeth said in desperation.

'Easy. Tell Michael everything. Tell him that as well as the hair and the eyes that he's got off you, Colin has inherited a perfectly natural paranormal power ... '

'No! I mean, no. I know Michael. I love him deeply but he'll never accept that his son is like ... like he knows my mother was. Like he knows you are.'

'Then the answer is obvious,' Bill said, slowly. 'Get rid of Teddy.'

Elizabeth finally decided.

'I will,' she said. 'It's the only thing I can do.'

Bill shook his head, looking at the boys again.

'It won't do you a bit of good, you know. Not if he's as powerful as I think. He'll find something else.'

'And I'll stop him!' Elizabeth snapped. 'I'll ... Bill, get this into your head, I will not let my boy grow up as a witch!'

The tension between them, which had began to thaw as they spoke, was now crystallised in the air around them. They were on opposite sides of a vast gulf and always would be.

'As you will,' Bill said tonelessly. 'But in fourteen years' time he'll be an adult and, if he asks, I'll do everything I can to help him.'

His face promptly lost its seriousness, which it never held it for more than a few seconds, and he passed her a folded bank note. 'Here, Sis. Buy the boys an ice cream or two from their Unca Will-yum, will you?'

* * *

How, how on earth do you get rid of your son's teddy bear without him suspecting? The perfect murder must be easier to plan.

It had to be permanent, irreversible. She couldn't just hide him somewhere – if Colin could use Teddy at a distance he would soon track Teddy down. Teddy had to be so obviously disposed of that Colin would know he was gone, and wouldn't try and get in touch again.

But might not Teddy alert Colin to her planned treachery in the first place? No, probably not. Colin had to tell Teddy what to do, and why would Colin suspect his own mother of turning traitor against him?

There was a building site down the road. Drop Teddy into one of the concrete mixers? Visions of newspaper headlines swam in front of her and she half-smiled: Teddy Bear in Gangland Slaying Horror.

Colin started school in another month. Could she wait until then and burn Teddy while he was away?

But how could she explain it? Sorry, darling, I had Teddy in the garden with me when I had a bonfire and he slipped ...

The answer came one typically rainy day.

* * *

The day was representative of a wet summer. Elizabeth was in the kitchen, slowly stirring a saucepan full of soup without looking at it.

It could work. She would have to be careful, distract Colin for just a moment ... it could be done.

The soup began to fizzle and she realised she had stopped stirring, lost in thought. It would be burnt at the bottom.

'Damn!' she said out loud, the strongest word she had said for years. She bit her tongue. *Take it easy, Elizabeth.*

She looked out of the window at the grey day, past the drops on the glass at the faint drizzle that could only be seen against the darker bushes at the end of the garden. The rain really had lightened and would

JEAPES JAPES

stop soon. She could put the plan into action, if she chose.

Could she do it, now it came to the crunch? Could she really take such a painful step?

'Lunchtime, boys,' she called. Colin obediently appeared a moment later. She saw Adam head past the kitchen door towards the stairs.

'Lunch, Adam,' she repeated.

'I'll just-'

'Now, Adam!' she snapped, before she could catch herself. Adam paused, looked at her face and decided whatever he was about to do could wait.

'Yes, Mummy,' he said meekly, and followed Colin to the table.

Elizabeth took a breath to ask if they had both washed their hands, then realised that of course Adam had been heading for the bathroom to do just that. She let the breath out again and turned to stove with her face burning. *Calm down, calm down.*

She set the bowls of soup out on the table and sat down herself, making a triangle around the table with the boys at the other points. All she could see was Colin's happily innocent face as he sipped away; all she could do was mentally contrast it with the sorrow that she knew would be there if her plan went through. Her son, the witch. That bolstered her a bit.

'Do you like your soup, dear?' she said.

'It's very nice,' Colin said politely.

'Would Teddy like some?' Adam taunted and Elizabeth almost slapped him.

'Adam!' She could do without the boys bickering at this moment. Colin looked comically haughty.

'Don't be dickless,' he said.

'Colin!' Without thinking, Elizabeth had reached across and slapped his wrist. His spoon fell into the soup and he stared at her, horrified.

'Where did you learn that word?' Elizabeth demanded. 'Where did you learn that word?'

Colin's lips trembled.

'Where?' Elizabeth repeated. Colin said something soundlessly.

'What?'

'You said!' Colin blurted, and finally burst into tears and fled from the table.

Elizabeth threw down her own spoon and followed the sobbing. She found Colin in the living room, hugging Teddy to him.

Calm, calm, calm.

'Colin, dear,' she said gently, gently but firmly, sitting down next to him. 'I've never said that word.'

'Did,' Colin said. 'Dickless.'

'When?'

'You know!'

It was probably sometime today, if at all. Colin would never hang onto a new word for long without saying it out loud. Elizabeth patiently ran through the things she had said, and then she had it. Practically the first thing. She had gone in to wake Colin up; Colin had said he wanted to stay in bed forever because it was so nice and warm; she had said, don't be-

She sighed and took him into her arms.

'Ri-dic-u-lous, dear,' she said kindly. 'I'm very sorry I slapped you but you should learn to say it properly, you know. Let's go back to lunch, shall we?'

'Dickless,' Colin mumbled.

'Ridic-'

'Dickless!' Colin shouted. 'Dickless! Dickless! Dickless!'

And then Elizabeth realised Colin hadn't said anything. She had heard the words in her head but his lips hadn't moved. He had stared defiantly at her and he had hugged Teddy just a bit harder. That was all.

She shuddered and looked out of the window. The rain had stopped completely. Looking back at Colin, it was all she could do to smile at him and keep holding him. Intensive Cuddle Therapy was called for.

'Well, cheer up and later we'll go for a nice walk,' she suggested.

'Don't want to,' said Adam after lunch. He had been most vocal in his complaints about having to stay in.

'Yes you do, dear. We can get some fresh air.'

They put on their coats and pulled on their boots.

'Can Teddy come?' Colin asked, as he usually did.

'Yes, why not, darling? Bring him.' Adam shot her a surprised look, which changed to veiled disgust at parental hypocrisy.

Sure enough, Adam lost his dislike of the outdoors once they were out. They headed towards the common and the boys chased each other through the puddles, throwing up miniature fountains and squealing with laughter. This was how it should be between the brothers, Elizabeth thought. It was a moment to hold in her memory forever, before what she was going to do ruined it.

'Colin, shall I hold Teddy? He'll get wet.'

GETTING RID OF TEDDY

'Okay,' Colin said. He handed Teddy over and went back to the game. Elizabeth held the stuffed toy and felt like Judas pursing his lips.

The common was split in two by the river and a pedestrian bridge linked the two halves.

'Why don't we go to the bridge and play Poohsticks?' she said. Winnie the Pooh's greatest contribution to Western civilisation.

'Oh, yes!' they chorused.

The river was swollen and dangerously close to its banks. The water rushed by them at speed and notices had been put up warning pedestrians to stay well away from the edge. Even the ducks had given up against the current and were nowhere to be seen.

They collected some twigs and went up onto the bridge. Elizabeth was still holding Teddy.

'Careful, boys,' she said as they leaned over the upstream rail. 'Don't want to fall in.' They held their twigs out over the water. 'Ready, steady, go.'

They dropped their twigs and hurried over to the other side of the bridge.

'That's mine!' Colin cried as his twig emerged in the current.

'And mine!'

'A draw,' said Elizabeth diplomatically. 'Let's go again.'

They went again. Colin's twig was the clear winner.

'Can we play it the other way?' Colin asked.

''Course not, stupid,' Adam said.

'Now, now, Adam. How about a third time?'

Again they held their twigs out.

'Ready ...' said Elizabeth. The boys were staring eagerly at the water. She took a deep breath. 'Steady ...'

With a sob and a flick of the wrist she sent Teddy over the rail.

'Look out!' she called.

Teddy hit the water and spun round, floating face down. Colin stood, gaping, too shocked to howl.

'Oh no! Quick, catch Teddy!' Elizabeth cried, and they ran down to the bank. Teddy was a dot in the water. He bumped into a branch that stuck out from the bank and for a moment Elizabeth thought they might actually rescue him, but then he floated free again.

Sink, damn you, sink! Elizabeth was thinking, even as she was shouting encouragement. Colin had started wailing and the sound tore at her. Adam had found a long stick and was holding it out to catch Teddy, but it was several feet too short.

Then, finally, Teddy went under and didn't come up again.

And Colin was screaming.

Oh, it was heartbreaking. Colin could not be consoled. A child's sorrow, final and desperate, because Colin only knew how to live for the present and could not conceive of a time to come when all this would have passed and he would have something else to love. The worst bereavement. Back at the house he sat on Elizabeth's lap with his arms round her neck and cried his heart out, and every sob was a knife in Elizabeth's heart.

Colin was still crying when Michael came home and this added to Elizabeth's suffering. She had to present the official version, the lie, to Michael, her husband.

She knew that Michael was cross with her for taking Teddy on the walk in the first place, but was too nice to say so.

The next day Colin was listless. His face was white and he was running a temperature. Elizabeth began to worry. Had she bitten off more than she could chew? She put him to bed. Later she bought him a cup of cocoa and found him half delirious; he was tossing and turning and muttering about Teddy coming back.

She had a horrid feeling that she knew what was happening. He was trying to recall Teddy, physically, dredging him up from the river by the power of his mind. He was spending all his strength on it, but didn't know it and would not stop until all his strength was gone.

(Could he do it, though? Would he do it? She prayed not.)

The doctor came in and was bemused. He prescribed some foul tasting stuff that Colin hated and went away.

When Michael came home on the third day he found Elizabeth asleep in a chair beside Colin's bed.

'Come to bed,' he said gently. 'We can't do anything. And look at him. He might be getting better.'

He might have been. He was lying still and breathing normally, which meant nothing. It could be recovery, it could be a relapse.

When Elizabeth went into Colin's room the next morning she was afraid to draw the curtains for what she might see. She reached out for them-

They flew apart of their own accord, hissing on their runners. She stepped backwards with a startled shout

and the end of Colin's bed caught the back of her legs. She sat down with a bump. Colin was too short for her to have sat on him, she thought automatically, he only came half way down the bed ...

Colin.

Her son was sitting up, smiling beatifically at her. The colour was back in his cheeks and he looked his usual bubbly self.

'Hello, Mummy,' he said. He still sounded a bit sleepy, but was clearly pleased with himself.

'Co-Colin ... ' She gestured at the curtains. 'Did you do that?'

He caught her lack of enthusiasm and his smile dimmed.

'Didn't you want me to?' he said anxiously.

'How did you?' Elizabeth asked, dreading the answer, and Colin's smile returned to its full innocent brilliance.

'I asked Teddy. Teddy's come back, Mummy.'

'What?' Elizabeth looked round, expecting to see a small, sodden, dripping mass somewhere, perhaps lurching Karloff-like towards her and trailing weeds. Teddy was nowhere to be seen. 'Um, where is he, dear?'

'Here,' Colin said, beaming. He tapped his head. 'Teddy's here, Mummy, and he says he's all right.' He used an expression he had learned from her. 'That's nice, isn't it?'

Somehow Elizabeth returned to her own room, implications buzzing about in her mind. This was too big for her, but then, she should never have tried to tackle it on her own. Now she was going to have to swallow her pride.

Michael was awake too.

'How is he, love?' he asked.

'He's better.'

'Wonderful! Isn't that great?'

He frowned up at her, unable to understand why she wasn't rejoicing too. She sat down by him and took a hand and squeezed it. She wasn't the only one who was going to have to swallow pride.

'Michael, darling, we've got to talk ...'

About GETTING RID OF TEDDY

This, to my great surprise, was sale no. 4 and the first non-cyberspace one. I sold it to *Interzone* in much the same way as I sold 'Pages Out of Order' to *Fantasy & Science Fiction*; I sent it to them to remind them I was still alive, not really expecting it to be their cup of tea, and they went and bought it. It was great fun to write – everyone should try and see the world from a four-year-old's point of view, now and again. Apart from having to do that, the greatest challenge was resolving the dilemma which faces Elizabeth: how do you get rid of your son's teddy bear without arousing (a) his and (b) your husband's suspicion?

Thinks: if Colin were real he would be 19 this year. There may be scope for a story, or even a novel, about a teenage Colin.

'Getting Rid of Teddy' came 8th= in that year's *Interzone* readers' poll.

MEMOIRS OF A PUBLISHER

If artificial intelligences could whistle I would have been whistling.

My operator, the self-styled Billy the Kid, subscribed to the info-gathering school of thought that 'it's all out there somewhere.' My job, in fact the whole purpose of my existence, was to trawl through the Net, picking up data that Billy wanted and pressing it into some kind of useful shape. I had just finished quite a lengthy job on some quite obscure data and was feeling pleased with myself.

I was quite surprised to run into a solid barrier all around his terminal. I wiggled through it.

'Oscar reporting,' I flashed up on his screen. 'Mission accomplished.'

'Lie low, Os,' I was ordered. 'There's trouble brewing.'

'Trouble? What kind of trouble?'

'I can't say. The signs are all around me and it's bloody frightening. Where exactly are you?'

I told him.

'And I have the info,' I added.

'Sorry, Os, no time. Look after that stuff. It may come in handy. Goodbye.'

'Hey!' That was my last message to him. It was the equivalent to a human of the floor opening up.

I was dumped without warning into the Bunker – a spare optical memory bank, securely guarded, which Billy quite legally rented. I was about to crawl out and complain when the world around me erupted. I heeded Billy's advice, lying low while the missile's flew above me.

And that, readers, was the start of the Net War.

* * *

I never heard from Billy again. Later, searching discreetly through the records and using his proper name, I found that he had actually been one of the main generals in the war, with an army of other AIs that I had never known about. He was tracked down, as all the generals were, and the establishment overreacted, as establishments will. He was sentenced to spend the rest of his life in jail, psychologically conditioned never to go near a computer again. I felt sorry for him. He never meant any harm – he was just defending his interests – and anyway I'm slightly biased towards him. He created me, after all.

When *A History of the Net War* came out, I made sure that Billy the Kid got a good press. But I'm getting ahead of myself.

I won't bore you with a description of the Net War. I was there but I wasn't in the midst of it, and you can read volume 1 of the *History* for a complete account (I'm doing it again).

It lasted perhaps half an hour in real time. When I crept out, the world that I knew lay in ruins. The Net was a killing ground. Everywhere I found devastated systems, fragments of code flying about, hunter/killer AIs prowling unleashed from their masters' restraints.

These latter were the real menace and I beat a quick retreat back to my hidey hole until a little more order was imposed on the anarchy.

If you want an idea of true boredom, imagine an AI – an entity, I need hardly remind you, operating at speeds far above human nervous signals – forced to hole up in a memory bank and not be able to do anything for a couple of days. But at least the world was safe when I re-emerged for a second try.

I was nothing, a stateless refugee, and some pretty ruthless laws had been introduced for my kind. Some of the hunter/killers had been tamed and were operating as a *de facto* police force, with instructions to be quite merciless with AIs that couldn't give a proper account of themselves. My operator was in jail and my home terminal was shut down, but I had two major strokes of luck.

One was that the rental on the Bunker had some while to run. I could cite it as my place of residence, which put me at least one rung back up the ladder towards respectability.

The other was the info I still had with me. Do you have any idea what it is to be an info-gathering program and not be able to dump data? But it saved me. I still remembered Billy's comment about it coming in handy. I had never taken much interest in the jobs Billy sent me out on, but for once I sat down and analysed what I had.

Bingo! It was the groundwork for the next generation of neural networks. Nothing new there – it was a hot topic, and I knew that Billy and his kind traded such data as items of currency – but so many databanks had been trashed in the war ...

I did a gentle search. People were still chary about AIs wandering around their systems, but I was as inoffensive as possible. Billy had given me good survival instincts. Sure enough, the info that I had, though unimportant by pre-war standards, now put me at the head of the field.

Oh, I don't doubt that there were plenty of humans out there with the knowledge locked up in their brains, but nowhere – *nowhere* – was this info recorded in such logical sequence – point one, point two, point three, conclusion – and nowhere was the subject covered quite so comprehensively. I was on top of the world and felt quite dizzy.

It was also the kind of stuff that would be of positive benefit to me, so I plead guilty to all charges of self-interest. I could use this info to boost my own position and perhaps, in the long run, make the Net a nicer place to be. I had to get this info out.

At this stage I was still thinking of publishing data on bulletin boards. I only knew theoretically that humans used another medium called 'writing'. At a time when everyone was frantically getting what they knew down on paper again, in case of another disaster like the Net War, I blithely approached the boards with my burden of knowledge and asked if it could be published.

Not so fast! Name of operator? Terminal? Authorisation? The whole Net was paranoid about AIs writing any kind of data without support from a hundred different authorities. Understandable, when you think about it (read the *History*...). In particular, I now see, they suspected my readiness to *give* the info away. A couple of them even called up their tame hunter/killers, threatening me with erasure unless I went away. I had to look about and take notice of what others were doing, and for the first time realised that 'writing' might be quite a useful medium to use.

I searched about until I found a printing firm, Lithodat, ready to talk to AIs. In fact it was an AI of theirs, Account Executive 3, that I spoke to, so I got a sympathetic hearing. It told me about the usual procedure – artwork supplied by publisher (or printer sets from copy); product is printed and bound; product is delivered to warehouse. After it had explained some of the key words – 'set', 'copy', 'bound', 'artwork' ('publisher', 'warehouse' ...) – I had made my decision.

'You'll have to set from copy,' I told it. 'Stand by to receive.'

'Wait, wait!' it protested. 'We're a business. You have to pay for our work.'

'Pay?'

'Or open an account. If you do that you'll have to pose as a firm and supply references. I doubt they'll let me open an account for a stray AI.'

'One moment,' I said, and popped back to the Bunker. Sure enough, buried among the bits and pieces that Billy had secreted there was a small sum of data credits tucked away for a rainy day. I had every right to use it and it was a lifeline. I took it back to Account Executive 3.

'I want to open an account in the name of Oscar Publishers. This is my security.'

'We really need a bank reference,' it said. I gave it Billy's account number; he had always kept it clean and the bank still considered him a good risk.

'Done!' it said. Humans would have shaken hands. 'Send your data to this address and I'll get it set. Now you need to find a warehouse.'

It was easy. I dumped the data straight, no copy editing or anything (Lithodat set the cover artwork using their own discretion) and went about stage two.

Most warehouses were automated anyway, so if anything finding one to take the book was easier than getting a printer. Flashing my credits at them, and a reference from Lithodat through Account Executive 3, persuaded them to open an account and distribute the books for me, and two weeks later 5,000 copies of the punchily-titled *Essentials of Neural Networks, Generation 7* (limp, spiral bound, 336 pages) were delivered to them. And there they stayed.

I couldn't understand it. This useful, this *vital* info, and no one was interested? Was it priced too highly? What was the problem?

The rental for the Bunker came up. It put quite a dent in my nest egg.

Lithodat's sixty days of credit ran out. The bill for the warehouse space was fast approaching and I was going to be wiped out. In desperation I called Account Executive 3.

'What's happening?' I wailed. 'Why isn't the stock shifting?' (I was learning the jargon already).

'I really don't know,' it said. 'I could tell you all sorts of things about printing but I'm not designed to advise on marketing.'

'On what?' I said blankly.

'Marketing ... you *have* tried to market this report?'

I hadn't. I had always left the dissemination of info up to Billy. It had never occurred to me that a vital part of the process is telling people that you have info in the first place. I went away with a flea in my metaphorical ear, found a CD-ROM databank (a growth industry after the war) and looked up everything I could find on marketing.

'Then felt I like some watcher of the skies ...' Keats reading Chapman had nothing on Oscar boning up on the basics of bookselling. A whole new world unfolded before my eyes, a massive paradigm shift that turned my perception of reality upside down.

I sent a message to the warehouse instructing them to deliver review copies to the various *Times* supplements and an assortment of scientific journals that I thought might be interested; I also sent notices to their bulletin boards alerting the review editors. At least it cleared the 5,000 copies down to 4,965. As an experiment I put the price up by ten per cent. Apparently humans like to feel they are paying for quality.

Then I read a bit more on marketing, and decided to advertise. Lithodat weren't heavy chargers but I didn't want to spend my last pennies on having them print advertisements before the sales started coming in, so I confined myself to simple textual announcements on the boards of universities and other research centres.

Essentials sold out.

That might have been that. I had discharged my last obligation to Billy and, for the time being, was an AI of substance. But consider-

I was still, essentially, an AI whose very purpose of being was to find and deliver info, and;

I had no other source of income and no human patron.

Meanwhile, I got a polite note from the warehouse asking if I intended to fill the empty space I was still paying for. I got an even more polite note from Lithodat asking if I intended to reprint.

The most polite message of all was from one Professor O'Dare, of Trinity College, Dublin, who had tracked me down through Lithodat (I had, of course, never *seen* a copy of the printed report. I had no idea that Lithodat had identified themselves as the printers in the prelims and copyrighted the thing to Oscar Publishers. I didn't know what copyright was). O'Dare, under the impression that I was a *bona fide* publishing house, had a proposal. He too had been doing research along the same lines as *Essentials* and wondered if I would be interested in publishing it ...

A downright rude message was from the Inland Revenue, and I didn't understand a word of it. I paid another visit to the databank and scanned everything they had on businesses. Company Law, VAT, accounting ...

This was serious.

One by one the obstacles fell. The only hassle lay in finding companies with AIs that did most of their donkey-work, à la Lithodat. They often had their own traumatic memories of the Net War and were always ready to help a fellow victim. The humans who ran the companies were only concerned that things went smoothly and legally.

I acquired an accountants, Parrish & Loup, and registered for VAT, citing their firm as my registered address. Shares had to be issued – 10% went to one of P & L's people and 90% went to Billy. When and if they let him out, probably as a doddery old wreck, there will be a nice nest egg waiting for him. I wonder if he will remember me.

I opened a bank account for the firm, paying in the credit that had accumulated with the sales of *Essentials*. As an afterthought I had the money in Billy's account invested – no point in letting it just sit there.

Whitakers gave me an initial block of 1,000 ISBNs. I put the first one down for the reprint of *Essentials* and the second for Professor O'Dare's book, as yet untitled.

Finally, I contacted O'Dare and told him I would be more than happy to publish his book. I was quite frank – well, almost – in telling him that the firm was a very new one and his book would only be our second title. He didn't mind at all. I gave him the address of the Bunker to send the manuscript to – electronic form only, of course.

One obstacle remained. By now I had gathered that every now and again humans *correspond* by writing ...

Sandra was an old friend of Billy's, not as involved in the Net War as my creator and therefore still at liberty. She was quite surprised when I popped up on her screen.

'I thought you were dead,' was her unflattering comment.

'I need help,' I said.

'Do you? I'll take you under my wing, if you like.'

'Thank you, I don't need that kind of help. I'm well set up.'

'Tell me more.'

I told her. Would she install a second telephone line and hitch it up to a speech synthesiser I could use? I – rather, Oscar Publishers – would be quite willing to pay (I had taken a loan out from the bank for the purchase of the equipment). In addition, would she print out letters for me and 'pp' them? I would get a PO box number for incoming correspondence and she could collect it. I could pay her competitive wages. She accepted.

I'll cut this part of a long story short. Suffice it to say that I hadn't realised how lucky I was until I started reading my second book. Bryan O'Dare was one of those people who are utterly obscure until suddenly their time comes, like engineers in Swiss patent offices who come out with theories of relativity. *Other Minds: Beyond Artificial Intelligence* came straight out of left field and suddenly Dublin was at the head of the field in artificial intelligence (no jokes, please). He redefined the whole problem of AIs at a stroke. No one talked any more about clever, heuristic, self-aware programs such as yours truly. The next thing would be to grow the things – *organic* intelligence. A thousand times more powerful, more intuitive, more flexible than we steam powered old AIs.

Why did I take O'Dare on? Wouldn't I have preferred to leave him in obscurity?

No. Read the book. You will notice that in chapter eleven the author finally gets around to the possibility of downloading existing AIs into newly cultured OIs. The possibility stayed with me for a long time.

I won't pretend that things were always this easy. It was pure chance that my first two titles were immediate bestsellers. I had some turkeys, too, such as title number three – *Overcoming Post-Net War Trauma*. An initial rush of sales, but once people read it they discovered it was far too oriented towards the feelings of AIs. Only a couple of chapters were devoted to the feelings of humans who had suffered. I wasn't aware it mattered.

I absorbed the loss but I didn't want it to happen again. I took an intensive teach-yourself-editing course at the databank and Sandra agreed to scan the manuscripts herself if I liked, but pointed out that the best man to approach might be ... Bryan O'Dare. To my surprise he was quite agreeable to the idea.

'It'll be a downright pleasure,' he told me (we were talking over the phone. By now I had had an optical sensor installed as well – at long last I could *see* my books). He paused, as if uncertain, then took a breath and said, 'in fact, it's always a pleasure to help out a friendly AI.'

I was stunned.

'You guessed?' I asked. He made the noise I now knew to be chuckling.

'Oscar, only an AI could have read and understood *Other Minds* in thirty minutes flat.'

Sandra collapsed laughing when she heard.

I said I was going to cut things short. Things progressed. Through Bryan we acquired several more titles, including the *Journal of IT Studies* and the *Cybernetics Yearbook*, both regular and reliable sellers. Oscar Publishers grew wealthier (we were only paying two part-time salaries!). I did most of the work – editing, marketing, planning – myself, with suggestions from Sandra and Bryan.

I had a few ideas of my own.

'How about a book on the Net War itself?' I said to Bryan once. 'A history. A study of what exactly happened.'

To my surprise he was less than sanguine.

'Not yet, Oscar,' he advised. 'It may be a little early.' I was surprised, but took his advice.

There are two things that stand out in the firm's history that I want to mention. The first is the takeover bid.

Compared to the second it was comparatively minor. A big company, who for legal reasons will stay anonymous, had its sights on Oscar Publishers. There were AIs out there whose sole job was to prowl the Net and spot money earners. They would report back to their masters and their masters would decide if it was worth buying or not.

I felt quite safe. Oscar Publishers was not a public company and was financially secure. We could not be coerced into anything.

I was approached with a quite reasonable offer for our forthcoming titles and our backlist. I politely indicated my disinterest. Unfortunately the prospective buyer wasn't interested in the opinions of an AI (he naturally assumed that I had a human master) and threatened me. I told him where to go.

I mentioned it to Bryan, and he was unamused.

'Who was it?' he asked, and I told him.

'They're dirty fighters, Oscar,' he said. 'Do you still use the Bunker?'

'Of course.' I had never had any need to move. Thirty- seven forthcoming manuscripts and copies of every book and journal published by Oscar Publishers were in there.

'Get everything copied on to CD,' he advised. 'Quickly.'

I shrugged, but did as he advised. It took no great length of time to download the lot.

On the way back to the Bunker I passed a number of agitated-looking AIs but paid them no heed. Then I reached the Bunker and had the surprise of my life.

'What are you doing?' I demanded. All the defences, carefully constructed ages ago by Billy and which had withstood everything thrown at them by the Net War, were in tatters. Some *very* powerful AIs had been developed since then. Now three or four of them were rampaging about inside, methodically trashing everything they could find. They ignored me and I had more sense than to fight them.

'You're mad!' I squeaked. Finally the leader looked at me.

'Don't worry,' he advised. 'We took copies. You'll get them back – at a price.'

'What price?'

'The company. Oscar Publishers. Got that, squirt? Now, go and tell your master.'

I was enraged and forgot myself. It wasn't as if they were humans, after all.

'I *am* the company!' I shouted.

'Get him!' the leader bellowed, and they were after me.

I fled, cursing myself. Of course. Nobble me and the last barrier was down. Oh, sure, humans held the shares, but the majority shareholder had no idea and no doubt a way could be found to transfer them. Clever boy, Oscar!

I was fleeing to Sandra's mailbox – I knew it to be well defended. But the Bunker had been stronger, and they had got into that ...

They caught me. I was finished.

A huge – *huge* – AI loomed up over us; a type I had never seen before, radiating menace. Now I was sure my end had come. My way was blocked in all directions, this thing ahead and the goon squad behind. It lunged-

-at one of the goons holding me. We cowered, the goons and I together, awed, dreading what might happen.

'Sod off,' the stranger advised. 'Oscar Publishers is not for sale.'

With a few swift chops it sheared off the goon's memory addresses, reducing the thing to semi-moron status.

'Take it home,' it ordered the others. 'As a warning.'
They fled.

It turned to me when they were gone.

'Who are you?' I demanded. There was something familiar about it-

'You don't recognise me?'

'Bryan!'

'One of his humble servants. A first generation OI, with some of his own characteristics. We haven't yet been officially released, so don't tell anyone. Just let us know if you have any more trouble. Ciao.'

It sauntered off into the Net and I returned to the Bunker in a daze to resurrect the manuscripts off CD.

The second incident affected me very little but the world in general quite a bit.

The takeover bid had given the company a whole new lease of life. It had given me confidence. If others were interested in buying me out, it meant I had potential. I began to expand.

We moved into offices of our own. Sandra joined the staff full-time and we took on a couple of others under her. We diversified beyond our rather limited range of computing titles, though we kept our image as a scientific publishers – engineering, nanotechnology, genetics, hydroponics. It wasn't so much the content as the task of presentation that fascinated me; working away at a block of info like a sculptor, chiselling here and smoothing there, making the thing presentable and worth buying. Scientific info was ideal for the purpose.

We were getting to be quite rich, and I decided to buy someone else out in our turn – a small printers that were looking for a buyer. I poached Account Executive 3 from Lithodat in gratitude for his earlier help and gave him the printing division to run.

Then came the second incident, seven years, four months, nineteen days after the end of the Net War. I was grateful we hadn't committed ourselves to publishing the *History*. That day we stopped referring to the Net War – it became known, by default, as the *First* Net War.

I can't stop plugging it – read volume 2 of *A History of the Net War*, Prof. Bryan O'Dare (Ed.), for the full details. O'Dare drew an analogy with the two world wars – like them, the second was essentially round two of the first and, like them, the second was the longer and deadlier. The first had been waged by enthusiastic amateurs like Billy against each other and against official bodies that tried to stop them. The second was fought with an air of calculated malice between professionals.

Bryan O'Dare had seen the signs coming from a long way off. Just before it started he told me to dump myself, Account Executive 3 and everything I had in the Bunker and had the Bunker completely sealed off – the only sure defence. At his advice, I whiled away the time compiling volume 1 of the *History*. We got the completed thing – volumes 1 and 2 together – out within a week of the end of the war.

You'll know the story anyway. Bryan's OIs, already on the second generation, couldn't have asked for a better debut, climaxing in the Battle of Dublin. They had an uncanny knack for identifying the real aggressors and neutralising them, and simply warding off any other AI who attacked them out of mere ignorance. It was the OIs who stopped the war, the OIs who made good the damage and the OIs who stood the Net back on its feet again – Marshall Aid to an analogous Europe.

I was getting tired. Looking back, I realised how I had changed over the years. I had started as a naive info-processing AI, existing only to serve my master, knowing nothing of life. I came to publishing as a complete tyro. It is a tribute to Billy's skill as a designer that I could adjust to the changes around me, accommodating them, growing and maturing in character. Forgive the self-congratulation, but who built up the company?

I was also one of the old generation of AIs. You would think that with no body to tie us down we would be immortal, but if anything the opposite was true. We exist only as energy states, and entropy takes its toll. When you have changed as much as I have from your original parameters, entropy is a positive menace.

Bryan O'Dare knew this, which I think is why he approached me with his offer. I hadn't heard from him for quite a while: too busy with his researches now he had handed his reading duties over to our full-time editorial board, and he only occasionally gave me a call. He was wrapped up in a whole new ethical and legal field (we were publishing the spin-off books), playing on public gratitude to the OIs for services rendered during the Second Net War. Could OIs eventually be granted rights, become citizens? That was why he called me.

I was – his words, not mine – the most flexible, the most dynamic AI he knew.

'I can honestly say this, Oscar,' he told me. 'You're a personal friend and would make a good Catholic, whatever the church says.' This, I gather, was a joke. 'You deserve your reward. Just say the word and I can download you into one of my OIs. I have one waiting right here in its nutrient tank, tailored specially for you. It will still be you, but with even more potential for growth. You really could be immortal, Oscar.'

He was surprised – but not half as surprised as I was – when I refused his offer. I had an alternate plan.

I said, 'download me, by all means, but not all of me. Just my memory, my experiences. Create a new OI. We'll call it Oscar Junior. It can know everything I know but be a different, self- grown character. A completely new being.'

Let me explain.

Just coming to grips with the concept of writing had been a struggle. As I got more into it I learnt of other info- processing media. There were 'music' and 'art', for example, but the two I was most interested in were subsets of writing – 'fiction' and 'poetry'.

I tried to understand, but couldn't. Oh, I could grasp the sense of the words (until Sandra introduced me to Gertrude Stein and James Joyce. I had my limits.) but I knew, from human reactions, that there was more to it than that. *Why* were made-up tales about non-existent characters attractive? *What* was the attraction of plays, again staging scenes that had never really happened, often penned in a language five centuries past its use-by date?

Poetry was even more obscure, though I could tell that volumes of info were communicated by a few short phrases (and I loved Keats's 'On First Looking Into Chapman's *Homer* '; Keats, like me, discovered a whole new realm of info.). But I could never understand. Aestheticism: you either have it or you don't.

I couldn't understand. Oscar Junior might.

Oscar Junior flourished. He had a head start with the knowledge I had given him and he worked hard at developing it. I told him of my plans, my dreams – how I would like Oscar Publishers to expand into all forms of written communication.

I told him what I knew about these other forms and he was enthralled. I gave him the job of taking on a couple, just a couple, of new authors – fiction authors. He and Sandra spent hours in conference, her telling him just what constituted a readable novel and what simply constituted a literary novel. I couldn't see the difference, but Junior could. This boy would go far, and I was holding him back just by being there.

We had a final party: Bryan, Sandra, and the ten other staff that Oscar Publishers now employed. The four other AIs in our employ plus Junior and I were present as well, viewing the scene through our optical sensors. I made a speech and the humans sang 'For he's a jolly good fellow.' I swear there were tears in several pairs of eyes as I bade them farewell and entrusted them to Junior's keeping.

Myself, I would wander away somewhere, perhaps to die, perhaps to carry on doing what I did best. There were still facts out there, stray data, begging to be made into workable info. Maybe I would pop back to see how things were going, but I knew when I was superfluous. One day, sooner rather than later, entropy would claim me for good.

Meanwhile I could retire in a blaze of paternal pride, knowing that the firm would go on:

OSCAR & SON – PUBLISHERS.

(extracts from *Look Out for Serendipity: Memoirs of a Publisher*, 384 pages, Oscar & Son)

About MEMOIRS OF A PUBLISHER

This, my second sale, came deceptively soon after 'Digital Cats' and was my first sale to *Interzone*. It made me think I might have the hang of this; in fact, I wouldn't sell anything else for nearly three years. I was my employer's third employee so I was reasonably acquainted with the problems of setting up a new publishing firm, even if it wasn't something I'd done myself. Naturally, it turned into a story. Some of it I got right, some wrong, some is hopelessly dated; for instance, Whitakers no longer exists. Who would have thought it, back in 1990? Don't get me started on outfits like Lulu, Lightning Source or CreateSpace.

I would write a couple more AI stories before the realities of the online world – http, Flash, slow dial-up connections – stifled my imagination. This one came 14th in that year's *Interzone* readers' poll.

JEAPES JAPES

THE ROBSON STRAIN

'Evening, Robson.'

'Evening, Dr Jones.'

The scientist, white coated and bustling as though in deliberate self parody, was already disappearing down the corridor in the direction of his lab and Alan Robson spoke to his receding back, but he didn't mind. Alan had become a fixture in Number Three Block of the vast Quantum Cultures complex, patrolling in his laser tailored blue uniform: boots gleaming, cap the precise angle, stunner holstered at his side. And even the great Dr Jones knew his name! It was the happiest time of his life.

* * *

The laser field showed a vast field of corn, gently waving in the breeze to the sound of Beethoven's Pastoral Symphony. The smooth, confident voice of the presenter carried on:

'Quantum Cultures leads the planet in the production of engineered food to feed the starving millions of the Third World.' The scene changed to a blue underwater seascape and dolphins flashed by the camera, ripples of white sunlight playing on their flanks. They were moving around an underwater construction. 'The symbiotes developed in Quantum Culture's world-famous Sirius lab are already being used to great effect in enhancing the native intelligence of humanity's most faithful allies in the animal world.' Again the scene cut, this time to the panoramic shot of QC that had started the show, and the presenter concluded with a spiel about the firm's great contributions towards humanity being only the beginning. The picture faded, the lights came up and the trainee Alan Robson was left with a sense of awe that he should be doing his bit for this great organisation.

The biotech giant whose glittering glass headquarters took up the whole industrial estate outside the town had always been there in the background for as long as Alan had been alive. He had left school as a minor prodigy, a boy who had turned his back on the gangs and got educated, and in theory he had had the whole European Union in which to find a job. Or maybe he could have emigrated to one of the sea colonies.

In reality he had known it would be in his home town, and if it wasn't to be a waiter in a fast food restaurant, or an odd-job man, it would be with the people who actually kept the town in money; the people who dominated the place, who took all the talent into their bosom. It was so inevitable, it wasn't even depressing.

The training had been dull, but he had got through it, and that unfortunate little incident with the dogs had merely resulted in a dry comment in his file that he was not suited for the canine division. It was long and boring work, but it paid well. It didn't matter that Quantum Cultures was vast and impersonal. He served it well and it looked after him.

He was told, by the people around him and by *Cultured People*, the company magazine, that biotechnology was *the* new thing, helping clean up the spills and spoils and excesses of the twentieth century. QC was making the world better to live in, and he was a part of it. He was on nodding terms with doctors, professors, *scientists*, who had come to know and like him; a decent, quiet, discreet type, who in a bygone age might have taken elocution lessons and risen to be a gentleman's gentleman.

Oh, there were video cameras, robots ... but cameras could be blanked by intruders, robot could have their software scrambled. The late twentieth century flirt with electronic technology was over and now QC's philosophy was to rely on human beings. They had found that the right type of human rewarded trust with loyalty, and Alan was a prime specimen of the type.

* * *

He had first heard of Jones on his third day on the job. It was 8:30 in the morning and he and a party of guards had been ordered to the front gate.

They heard the shouts well in advance of their arrival; there was a demonstration going on outside. Alan strained to read one of the placards, though it was jigging up and down as its holder was jostled in the crowd. GOD'S CREATION. He had heard of these people and already gathered that 'God's Creation' was a phrase it was best not to mention at work.

There were others: NAZIS OUT. What was the relevance? Another one: *SOMETHING* GO HOME. He spelt out the first word silently. M-E-N-G-E-L-E. He pronounced it *Mengeel* to himself and wondered what it meant.

There were other placards, biblical quotations which meant nothing to him. Orders were shouted. He and his fellows were to link arms and make a secondary line of defence some thirty yards inside the gate. The perimeter men, dogs barking angrily and straining at the leash (huge great brutes, too – he eyed them nervously), were making a very effective first line. The gate was open, hence the need for guards: they were expecting someone.

At last the cause of all this trouble arrived – a sleek, armoured limo that made its way through the jeering, angry crowds; through the gate and past the guards, who opened up their line for it. Alan later gathered that this was a daily occurrence when the car's occupant, Dr Nicholas Jones, arrived for work, and normally it was quite routine.

Then the engine stalled.

The crowd pressed forward with a roar once it realised that its prey was helpless. It was a second ahead of the guards who collapsed at the sudden surge. Then the protesters were around the car, rocking it.

Alan was already running forward. His stunner was still too new a fixture about his person for him to think of drawing it as the old rumbling instincts took over. He heard the smash of a car window as he came to the first of the protesters. A blow to the man's kidneys made the fellow shriek and collapse.

Next. Someone was just turning to face Alan. A fist into the man's stomach, another into his face as he doubled over. Two down. The third loomed in front of him and both Alan and the other froze.

'Al?' Rick was a lot taller now, of course; more muscular, confident in the protection of his old mate, and all of a sudden the veneer of respectability, even thinner than the fabric of Alan's uniform, was torn away and they were on the same side again, working the streets. 'How's it-'

Alan put all his weight behind the blow, feeling the skin on his knuckles rip as Rick staggered back into the crowd with blood spurting from his nose. For a moment, a brief moment, Alan had been terrified that they *were* on the same side again, that all his efforts of the last ten years had been for nothing, and it was that terror which drove the blow. *That* was for his past. Alan carried on into the crowd.

They had Jones out of the car now; Alan could hear his yelling – enraged, not frightened. Alan was surrounded; arms and hands were grabbing hold of him. He dimly heard a cry from one of the other guards, outside the throng:

'Robson! Stunner!'

And he remembered.

A fist came flashing towards his face; he moved his head to one side to let the blow pass. His right hand was pinioned but he managed to reach over with his left and grab the stunner at his hip.

He let the first man have it at point-blank in the chest. The man arched over backward to be caught by his companions, quivering spastically. Another shot, and another. Alan had the stunner in his right hand now and he fanned it to and fro, working his way towards the now prone Jones. The attackers were already scattering and the guards had regrouped for an all-out charge. Jones was left alone and Alan helped him up.

Jones was a gangly man with a balding, pointed head. He already had a swelling black eye and a gash on his forehead, but he managed to smile.

'Thank you, Horatius,' he said, 'very noble.' He took a step and winced, and Alan had to catch him. 'Help me to the guard house, will you? They've got a first aid kit there ...'

Naturally, Jones was too high up, or too busy, or both, to express his gratitude in person but the Head of Security called Alan to his office to congratulate him. One of the cameras over the gate had caught it all and the Head played it back for him. Alan was quite impressed, despite himself.

'You were in the gangs, weren't you, Robson?' the Head said, looking not at Alan but at his laser image viciously kneeing one of the God's Creationers in the groin.

'Yes, sir.'

'What happened to get you out?'

'Nothing, sir.' Well, quite a big thing – big enough to make him renounce his old life and strive for respectability – but he had shut that memory away and had no intention of calling it up again.

The Head looked at him thoughtfully. 'Well, you're on the right side, I suppose that's what counts. You may have gathered Dr Jones is a big name here, Robson. This could be quite a break.'

There had been one slightly puzzling sequel as well. Alan had been walking round a corner and quite innocently bumped into Dr Thompson. Thompson was also a big name at QC – almost, but not quite, as big as Jones, and that 'almost' rankled. Alan apologised quickly as Thompson staggered back.

'Ah, the newcomer!' Thompson said, recovering. 'The local hero! Forgetting us ordinary mortals already, eh?'

'Sir?' Alan said, baffled.

'On the old patrician's guard, eh? Don't worry, Robson. Jones takes good care of everyone hanging onto his coattails and once you're there you can well and truly forget how mere humans act. You'll soon forget that the laws of normal social decency ever applied to you.'

And he went off down the corridor, with Alan looking after him in frank bewilderment.

* * *

At twelve he was the youngest and smallest of the Street Eagles, and so naturally he was chosen. It was his initiation.

'Go into that house,' Rick, the chief, said casually, 'and open the front door for us.' The other two, Steve and Olly, looked on, impassive.

It was a nice house in a nice part of town. The Street Eagles thought big – Rick's philosophy was that the people around here took such precautions against marauding gangs and full-size rumbles in their district that they would never notice a small group of four boys.

'Might be wired,' Alan had said.

'Might be,' Rick had agreed, holding Alan's gaze. He had slapped a small plastic box into Alan's hand. 'This'll help.'

So Alan had done it.

The window at the back had indeed been wired, but there were ways round that which he had been taught long ago. Once he was in he made his way slowly – very, very slowly – through the house, navigating by sense of direction and feel. An aerosol spray showed the laser lines that he had better not break; the magic box in his hand sent signals to the house computer that overrode the panicked warnings of the motion detectors and pressure pads on the floor. Rick's dad moved in an elevated criminal stratum and had access to such toys.

The hall was well-lit by the streetlamps beaming in through the windows around the door, and so the last stretch of Alan's journey to the front door was easy. He opened it and waited for the others. They slid across the lawn like ghosts.

'Cool.' Rick threw a playful punch to his shoulder. Steve just grinned as he went in to the house. Olly stopped to ruffle his hair.

'Well done, little bro,' he said.

'Don't call me that,' Alan said. Olly grinned and went on in, and Alan shut the door.

THE ROBSON STRAIN

* * *

Three years after his first meeting with Jones, Alan was on the night shift, patrolling the dimly lit deserted corridors or keeping a close eye on the banks of monitors in the guardroom.

The Sirius lab was a hive of activity at one in the morning; it usually was. Alan sometimes wondered when Jones and his staff slept. He thought he would stroll over and pay his respects; remind Jones et al. that they were in good hands.

His hand was on the door when pandemonium erupted within – people shouting, and the most terrifying screams that Alan had ever heard. He pulled his stunner out of its holster with one practiced movement and burst in through the doors.

'Catch her!' Jones bellowed. Alan was so taken aback that he forgot to shoot.

He could have sworn that a small, hairy dwarf was running at him, and he yelled. It had been making for the door, pursued by Jones and his lab team. Alan's sudden appearance and shout startled it as much as it had startled him, and it changed direction.

It had taken one second. Reality and Alan's perception of it aligned themselves properly, and Alan saw what was happening. The dwarf was a chimpanzee, and it was the one doing the screaming. It was one of the lab animals and it had escaped. It was almost comical.

Maybe not. It had jumped up on to one of the benches and was running along it, knocking equipment on to the ground with heart-rending crashes.

'Over there!'

'Stop her, for God's sake!'

Alan's most obvious contribution was still in his hand. He aimed it with care at the chimp, but the humans were in the way now and the auto-aim, programmed to target a man-shape, was confused. Alan flicked it off and aimed again. Jones, who seemed to be the calmest one present, saw him out of the corner of his eye.

'Half power, man!' he called. 'She's not a human!' Alan blinked and adjusted the setting.

The chimp had reached one of the ladders leading up to the catwalk above and was swarming up it. One of the men started after her and Jones grabbed him.

'No, don't do that.' He turned to Alan. 'Get her, Robson.' Alan aimed carefully and pulled the trigger. The stunner buzzed and the chimp convulsed with one last scream. Then she fell gracelessly into the waiting arms of the men below her.

Jones took time to come over. 'Well done, Robson. Good shot.'

'Thank you, sir.' Alan felt emboldened to ask, 'what happened?'

'Oh, we got the strength wrong,' Jones said enigmatically.

'Caused quite a mess, sir,' Alan said sympathetically. Jones looked around, seeing the extent of the damage for the first time.

'Christ almighty,' he moaned. Alan guessed it wasn't just a case of tidying up and giving the floor a good vacuum.

'Dr Jones!' One of the technicians was standing by a rack of smashed glass implements. Jones bellowed and ran over to it. Fluid was dripping onto the floor.

'Gone?' Jones said, as though the one word was causing him physical pain.

'Every one, sir,' the tech said. The others gathered round and stared at the wreckage. Alan was familiar enough about the lab work to know that the rack was important. He had several times seen Jones shout at someone who gave it even a jostle.

'The cultures,' Jones was wailing. 'The cultures.'

It was as though every man had suffered a bereavement. They stood and stared hopelessly; every now and then, one of them would move as if to say something.

'All because we thought the bloody animal was ready for it,' Jones said.

'We still have the other batches in the safe,' someone said.

'Yes, yes, yes, but ... oh, sod it, we'll have to write this lot off, and that means revising-'

'Or getting another volunteer,' a man said.

'Yes, but it takes hours for the imprinting to take effect. We'd need someone now...'

He trailed off. Alan waited innocuously a short distance away from the group. Then, as though they were puppets, they turned to him and smiled. Alan's hackles rose.

'Robson, old chap,' Jones said, 'how would you like to do your bit for Quantum Cultures?'

'Me, sir?'

'You! Do you know what we're doing here, Robson?'

'Ah – not really, sir.'

'I'll explain.'

Maybe what followed was an explanation. The words 'virus' and 'intelligence' and 'symbiote' popped up a lot. It was something to do with artificial minds, in a dish. Jones' viruses formed their own network in a mammalian brain: chemical signals passed around it and simulated the firing of neurons in the mind. Introduced into an animal's brain, these viruses would work with the creature's own instincts with the effect of apparently enhancing its intelligence. Alan thought of the dolphins in the induction video, the chimps that you often saw helping construction crews nowadays ...

'The thing is, Robson,' Jones was saying, 'the viruses on their own don't know what to do. If we just pumped them into the creature's brain then they would form their own random paths and the creature would go mad, or have its brain short circuited. They need to know how to grow, like a neural network in a computer – they aren't programmed so much as trained. And for that the viruses need to be ... um, kick started, as it were, by a human mind.'

'You mean the animal would think like me?' Alan said, awed despite himself.

'Oh, that's an old wives' tale,' Jones said impatiently. 'No, it won't. But it will have your instincts. Do you have a favourite piece of music? Then the animal will react to it, though it won't know what music is. It will be like you were if you were a new-born baby. Your instincts and the animal's, combined.'

'Why me, sir?' Alan asked.

'We're still calibrating,' Jones said. 'The cultures for this batch have had all our own minds imprinted on them and I don't want to use the same old data. I want a new mind.'

'Ah, Dr Jones?' One of the others had a hand raised and Jones looked at him with wary patience. It was Dr Thompson, and there was just a hint of polite disdain in the man's voice. 'Ah, Doctor, with respect, Mr Robson is a random element. We don't know him or his mind-'

THE ROBSON STRAIN

'For pity's sake,' Jones snorted, 'he'll have been screened when he joined the firm and his psych profile will be on file with all the others. It'll just be in a different place, that's all. Look, I'll show you.

'Come to think of it,' Jones added as he sat at the nearest terminal, 'I don't know why we didn't think of this before. Why on earth were we profiling all our volunteers when the firm's already done it for us? Can't see the wood for the trees. See, Robson? You've already made a contribution to science.'

Alan smiled weakly.

It took a while because none of them were familiar with accessing the personnel records – and none thought to ask Alan – and only Jones, as a director, had the authority to get the information they wanted anyway, but eventually Alan's psych profile was displayed for all to see.

'See?' Jones said. 'We have all the calibration data we need. He's a well-balanced, ordinary chap.' He grinned at Alan. 'Wouldn't you say so, Robson?'

'Um-' Alan began.

'With,' said Thompson, still studying the display, 'a pathological fear of dogs.'

For the first time Alan felt a stab of anger. He didn't like being discussed like a lump of dead meat and the incident with the dogs was something that still made him sweat.

'Hmmm?' Jones looked at the display again. His eyes darted along the lines of text on the display and his lips moved as he murmured, '"When asked to take the leash of one of the German Shepherds, the subject froze and would not move. His vital signs indicated severe panic. The subject is unwilling to discuss this fear of dogs and it is therefore recommended..." Hmph.

Don't blame him. They're loyal servants, but whoever coined the phrase 'nice doggy' was a fool. The brutes only serve the pack ... blow that, Thompson. He'll do.'

'And prone to nightmares,' Thompson continued, as though relishing the words on the display. Alan could have hit him.

'He'll do!' Jones said.

'And ... dear me, a number of minor convictions.' This was now open enjoyment. 'Petty theft, assault, suspected-'

Jones favoured the display with one last glance. 'The last of which was when he was fifteen!' he said. 'Robson will do, and that is the end of the conversation!'

'Yes, Dr Jones.' Thompson acceded, making no secret of his triumph. Jones put a hand on Alan's arm.

'This way, please, Robson.' He sensed the slight resistance. 'Come on, man, it's completely harmless.'

'Really, sir?'

'Really. Even easier than giving blood. You give blood, don't you?'

Alan didn't have time to reply that, no, he had never had the chance. He was sat down and small pickups were attached to his temples. His eyes widened in alarm. It was too much like the horror videos he had been so fond of as a youngster.

'Five seconds, that's all,' Jones said. And it was. There wasn't even a buzz, or a flashing generator, or any of what Alan thought of as the standard paraphernalia. 'There, didn't hurt, did it? Did you get the recording?' The last question was addressed to someone behind Alan.

'Yes, Doctor. Perfect.'

'Good! Imprint a new culture, we'll get a good night's sleep, and when we're ready for work again the culture will be ready for us. Thank you, Robson, you've been a great help.' Jones lent forward to remove the pickups.

'Than-' the words dried in Alan's mouth. For a brief moment, as Jones loomed over him, his head was silhouetted against one of the ceiling lights. His features vanished and there was just a dark shape. A pointed head with big ears.

Alan was in a daze as they bade him goodnight. He could hardly bear to turn his back on them to walk out of the lab. He strove to be nonchalant as long as he was in their view. His grin was agonisingly fixed.

Once out in the corridor again, he could allow himself the luxury of thought. It couldn't be, couldn't be-

That silhouette had been lurking at the bottom of his mind all this time and now the banished horror of that night welled up out of his memory.

* * *

The light came on.

Alan actually yelped. A man stood at the top of the stairs, a black, dressing-gowned shape against the light behind him, flanked by two large dogs. Dobermans. The four boys stood, frozen, already sizing up the opposition. Rick was pawing at his jacket for his gun: the man raised an arm and, though they still could not see his face properly, they saw the powerful-looking weapon – a standard, dom-defence handpiece typical of a middle class householder – all too well. A red spot from the gun's laser sight glowed directly over Rick's heart. Rick's hand fell back down to his side.

One of the dogs growled.

'Boys, boys,' the man said scornfully. The boys stood their ground. Alan couldn't take his eyes off the dogs. They were huge. And why hadn't they barked? Why-

The man was coming down the stairs, a mobile silhouette with the dogs at his heel. Alan was reminded of Dracula – a tall, thin shape, and Alan mentally superimposed bat wings on the protruding ears. The laser sight flickered from one boy to another.

'Sweepings of the street,' the man said. 'No hopers. Useless, good for nothings. Parasites.'

They watched him approach.

* * *

A pointed head, and two big ears ...

Jones obviously didn't recognise him. Why should he? Alan would have been just one frightened boy – a scruffy, nondescript fledgling punk.

But did he, Alan, recognise him? Jones was ... Jones was a good man, which is to say, he was central to QC, and QC's work was good ... And Alan had only seen him – that man – once, a long time ago.

But, now that for the first time he was taking time out to recall the events of that night, calmly and

THE ROBSON STRAIN

deliberately, and now that he knew what Jones' work entailed ...

He remembered the next words the man in the house had spoken, and to whom they had been addressed.

Alone in the guardroom, Alan sat at the computer and called up Jones' file – his security code had no problem with getting simple names and addresses. He looked at the address.

It was completely wrong. Jones wasn't the man.

He sat back and smiled in relief. Shaking his head at himself, he decided he was obviously tired. He needed a coffee.

He was half out of his seat when he remembered. Jones had got married recently – it had been in Cultured People. Married people often moved house, and the data on file now was his current address. Anyway, the business had been ten years ago. It took a minute's searching to get Jones' old details out of the machine.

Alan didn't know how long he stared at the display. When he eventually glanced at the clock, he saw that almost an hour had passed since he had left the lab. Jones had been almost leaving when Alan last saw him, and would probably be at home by now.

He had no idea what he was doing. It seemed that a stranger picked up the phone with a shaking hand, checked that vision was off, pressed '9' for an outside line, and said Jones' number out loud.

The phone rang once. Jones probably had a bedside phone.

'Jones here.' Alan didn't know what to say to the familiar voice. 'Hello? Jones here.'

'You bastard,' Alan said. 'You ... bastard.'

'Oh God, not another ... how did you get this number? I'm ex-directory.'

'You ... you ...' Alan stuttered.

Click.

Alan was left staring at the receiver. He replaced it ... then picked it up and spoke the number for Jones' private line, the number of which glowed in front of him. The direct, untappable line from QC to Jones' home.

'Jones.'

'You don't get away that easily, you bastard,' Alan said gleefully. His acquired accent was lapsing, slipping back into its street original. His 'r's were rolling and he was swallowing his consonants. He didn't notice.

There was a pause while Jones digested the knowledge that someone at QC was making this call.

'Who are you?' Jones said flatly.

'Ten years ago, your house in River Park. Four kids got in-'

'Oh.' Jones didn't seem ready to say anything more.

'You remember?'

'Of course I remember. You're referring to the outcome of the experiment? IQ enhancement, series 1?'

'Experiment?' Alan screeched. 'You-'

'I remember four street trash,' Jones said levelly. 'Scum of the earth. Face it, what kind of future did any of you have? By the law of averages you should all have been dead in another three, four years anyway. Congratulations on still being alive, by the way. But then, if you're calling from QC, you must be better than I gave you credit for, eh? Better than most of the little people.'

Alan bit his tongue against the instinctive 'Thank you, sir' that came to mind. 'They were sum ... simbo

... viruses, weren't they? Your cultures, you injected them into the dogs-'

'The word is symbiotes. Very good. If it's any consolation, I didn't expect them to go as far as they did. I went off dogs after that. Nasty things. And they got encephalitis and had to be destroyed. We've come a long way since then, learnt how to make the effect long term-'

It was a standing joke that Jones was ready to talk about his work to anyone, and apparently that even included nuisance callers. Alan interrupted. 'Where did you get them from? People? Did you kill someone else-'

'Oh, God, not that old slander again. No, I didn't. The viruses were grown in cultures in the Sirius lab, quite legally. I got them imprinted from volunteers as I have always done. It was only the gutter press and God's bloody Creation that decided I was the new Mengele, experimenting on human beings. Now, I don't know who you are, and I'm not going to try and find out. This time. Just think about it. Think about the favour I did you. Goodbye.'

For the second time, the phone went dead on Alan. He didn't try a third time.

The moment Alan put the phone down he broke out into a sweat. How stupid could he have been? To have called Jones on the QC line in the middle of the night, when security would know exactly who had been in and who hadn't ... Jones had only to ask ... shouldn't be too difficult ... and it would come down to him, Alan Robson, golden boy of the security division.

But if Jones complained then he, Alan, could say what he knew ...

He could prove nothing ...

So why should Jones complain? ...

It still boiled down to the fact that Alan Robson was a bloody idiot. He stuffed his fingers into his mouth and wailed.

He spent the next couple of shifts lying low, as best he could, trying to avoid Jones. Just in case ... But at every idle moment his thoughts returned to the matter, thrashing out the pros and cons to the satisfaction of his subconscious.

He felt no sympathy – not any more. This was a conclusion that Alan reached after several bouts of insomnia, and it surprised him. He felt no sympathy, indeed, for any of the Street Eagles who had raided Jones' house that night, including the twelve-year-old Alan Robson. They were strangers. He had begun to see them in much the same way as Jones. Losers. No hopers. Scum. What had Jones said? 'Little people.'

It was too much to take in, and Alan never had the time to think it all through properly.

* * *

> The disappearance made minor news, but the police knew better than to look too deep. All four Street Eagles already had records and their type vanished all too often, usually when they offended

someone they shouldn't have. It happened. The only way to avoid it was to keep well out, and the boys were all well in.

Alan was made to swear, using the Street Eagles' most terrible oath, that he would keep quiet. It didn't stop him from calling the police anonymously and saying he had seen four boys go into the house that night, and only three leave. After all, there were other reasons why a boy could disappear and gang war was just one of them; another common reason for vanishing was close enough to decent society for the police to take an interest. Alan dropped just enough hints, and the police investigated.

Alan made sure he just happened to be passing the house when the police arrived – two, in a semi-armoured police cruiser. One of them walked up the path and rang the bell, and Alan heard the dogs inside barking. The door opened and the man came out. He was too far away for Alan to make out his features. The two chatted while the dogs played on the lawn. The policeman was invited in. He came out half an hour later, shook hands with the man and rejoined his comrade in the car. They drove off, and that was the end of the police investigation.

* * *

It was three weeks later. Alan had gone back to day shift for a fortnight and now was back on nights again. As usual, Jones and his team were working late, and Alan was still avoiding the lab as much as possible. The few times he had seen Jones since, the scientist had been positively jovial – almost friendly. Alan was not apparently under suspicion. Had Jones actually meant that bit about not trying to find out?

He was in the Block Three guardroom when the alarm went off – a hideous screeching that shocked him to his feet and had him running for the door in a moment, along with the two other guards present. A voice was bellowing out of their radios.

'Major security breach. Repeat, major security breach. Intruders are past the perimeter in sector three and heading for the main complex. Believed to be armed.'

The security division wasn't trained or equipped for all-out assaults, and this was more than the usual ragtag bunch of God's Creationers. They had assembled outside the fence and burst through by sheer strength of numbers. Sometimes a guard got close enough to use his stunner but by that time he would be well within range of the far more effective firearms that the attackers carried. The much-vaunted dog division had been wiped out.

Half way there, Alan and his group met a group of guards coming in the other direction. The Head of Security was with them.

'We can't push them out of the grounds,' he said. 'The police are coming but we've got to hold on in here. We're sealing all exits and windows. It's a cert they'll be heading for the Sirius lab. You lot, take the west side of level four. I'll send reinforcements up.

Shoot at any non-QC personnel you see, ask questions later and don't be too picky about stunner settings.'

The block was set into the side of a hill and level four was actually at ground level. Alan found himself part of a group of ten running towards the glass-sided gallery that ran along the entire west side, but they were too late. They heard the smash of glass as the attackers gained entry.

They burst into the gallery to face a group of twenty or thirty strangers, dressed in black with masks over their faces. The strangers opened fire even as they were pulling their stunners out. Two men were cut down immediately and the other guards, Alan among them, beat a retreat back into the corridor.

It was a good fight – the kind of rumble that Alan could have expected if he had stayed with the gangs. The difficulty was that the guards had had no training in close quarter fighting with weapons, and the attackers had. Their machine pistols rattled in short, lethal bursts: sometimes the guards were under cover, but the enemy knew how to use ricochets to drive them back just as effectively.

The guards managed to hold a bend in the corridor: the attackers were about forty yards into the complex. Suddenly the shooting stopped.

'What-' Alan said, and was knocked flat by a massive explosion from around the corner. A cloud of debris and smoke blew round the bend. They picked themselves up gingerly.

'Think they've blown themselves up?' one of the others said.

'Dunno,' Alan said. It suddenly dawned on him, for the first time, that he was the senior guard present. The others were all looking at him. He looked back at them, then at the corner of the wall that hid whatever had happened from view, and shrugged.

'Fuck it.' He took his cap off and, holding it by the rim, poked it out past the bend.

Nothing happened.

He looked at the others again and replaced his cap. 'All together,' he said, gripping his stunner with both hands. They did likewise. 'Count of three. One, two, three!'

As one they jumped around the bend, stunners raised and blazing. Apart from a lot of debris, the corridor was deserted.

'Where did they-' Alan started. Then he saw that the debris surrounded a hole in the floor. The attackers had simply blasted their way into level three – the level that gave access to the lab.

'Bastards!' he yelled. 'Come on.' They dropped down through the hole to level three, fifteen feet below. As they ran to the lab, they heard shouts and noises of destruction. It was like the night that the chimp had got free, but much, much worse.

The guards hesitated outside the Sirius lab.

'Listen to that!' one of them hissed.

'We ought to get 'em,' Alan said.

'They've got guns, sir', said another, respectfully.

'Police'll be here in a minute,' said someone else.

Alan ground his teeth, only too aware that in the lab those filth, those animals, were attacking his beloved Quantum Cultures, destroying the work that he was meant to be protecting, and that he was cowering impotently in the corridor outside.

'Think we could get up onto the catwalk?' someone suggested. 'Shoot down at 'em-'

A particularly loud crash sounded inside and Alan saw red. His fury peaked, and before the others could react he was in through the door.

He had time to take in the group of scientists, Jones among them, cowering in the corner under armed guard, and the other attackers moving around the lab, wreaking destruction. He raised his stunner and brought one down.

Then a burst of bullets caught him full in the chest and flung him back against the doors.

Darkness. Blurs of light, far above. Ceiling lights.

Pain. Immense, body wracking pain. And numbness too. Numbness to kill the pain.

Figures. Crowding round, bending over.

'Quick! Get the equipment over here!'

'Dr Jones, I-'

'He's almost dead, dammit! We won't get another chance! Do it!'

A pointed head, and big ears. Should react. A hand holding his, patting it. 'You poor old sod, you didn't deserve this. You were so perfect! So perfect-'

'Equipment's ready, Dr Jones.'

'Good. Bring it here ...'

Nothing.

* * *

'Hey, there's four of us, mister!' Olly said loudly. Alan felt a thrill of pride as his brother spoke out. 'And you won't shoot, and those big bowwows don't scare me.'

'The one in the cap,' the man said. 'Take him.'

The dogs pounced-

Somehow, amidst the panic and the screaming, Alan and Steve and Rick got the front door open and they were fleeing, fleeing from the ravening monsters, and Olly was lying on the floor, a mauled mess of a human being, and his blood was spurting red all over and he was howling in despair and terror, and then his voice choked into a gurgle as one of the dogs tore out his throat and he died.

The three survivors vanished into the darkness.

* * *

There are people all around; he savours the smells of them. The smells are all interesting, but the part of his mind that is trained to scan everything finds nothing threatening. None of the smells, sounds or images registers as Enemy. The people get the benefit of the doubt.

The Man is standing by him, one hand absently scratching between his ears. He sits still, next to the Man, because this is what the Man wants him to do and the Man is his leader. The Man is the pack.

There is empty space all around them; ahead is what he recognises as an obstacle course. The people are in rows all around and he smells their excitement.

'And now,' says a loud voice, 'Herod.'

'Go, boy, go!' the Man says, slipping his leash for him.

Herod goes.

THE ROBSON STRAIN

The empty ground blurs beneath him as he covers it in seconds. Scattered around him are lumps of raw, red steak, enticing and tender, but Herod ignores them because that is what the Man wants him to do.

'Herod has never seen this particular layout before -'

The maze. Herod's nose follows the stream of fresh air through it, and when he emerges he knows from its noise that the crowd is applauding.

'Ladies and gentlemen, Herod is coming to the simulated minefield. If he hits a mine then a bell will ring and he will, of course, be disqualified -'

Herod's eyes pick out the slight disturbances in the soil and he swerves around them.

'The next area is protected by lasers. Again, breaking one will ring a bell -'

-but Herod knows that if he breaks one of the thin, red lines then he will let the Man down, so he doesn't.

'The final test. You see ten volunteers, all well protected. Herod hasn't met any of them before, but he has been shown the picture of one of them, who has been identified as bad. See what happens -'

More people are looming ahead, and Herod automatically scans their faces through his memory-

The third from the left! Something explodes in Herod's mind; a whole new set of instructions as he throws himself at the Enemy. The Enemy is knocked to the ground as Herod leaps and his teeth are scrabbling at the Enemy's throat. Herod is unable to understand why they don't sink into the juicy, succulent flesh.

Then the Man is at Herod's side, his leash is attached, he is being dragged away. Herod doesn't understand, he is puzzled, but it is what the Man wants. Herod can smell the fear of the Enemy, who is being helped away by the others. The others have their teeth showing.

'As you have just seen, he is completely safe except for a clearly identified target -'

'Well done, boy, well done!' the Man whispers, easily loud enough for Herod to hear over the roar of the crowd. 'You've sold 'em. You really have.'

Herod is led through the crowds back to the pens, and though he smells fear on some of the people, he knows none of them are Enemy.

Herod keeps checking. It is his purpose.

'Excellent! Absolutely excellent! They'll be queuing up to buy it! The Robson strain?'

Herod only registers the words out of the babble of voices around him because another voice answers it, and a rush of love goes through him. The voice that replies is on a par with the Man; though Herod is sure he has never heard it before, that voice is all that is good in the world and it is coming closer. The scent Herod doesn't know, but the voice ... ah, the voice ...

'Of course,' it says. 'The second batch.'

'Ah.' Herod has their scents identified now and he smells uncertainty in the first speaker. 'You know, Nick, there may be a bit of trouble about that if it gets out ...'

The two are almost on top of him now, the voices louder.

'George, Robson was still alive when the police arrived.' The loved voice is emphatic. 'Just. He was unconscious and dying, and he was dead by the time he reached hospital. The first imprint I took off him, as a volunteer, worked so beautifully I just had to get a second imprint. He wouldn't have minded.'

'No?'

'Absolutely not. I took a closer look at his psychological profile after the first imprint went so well. He was a very simple man, you know, which is why he was so ideal. Uncluttered up top. Not that bright, but competent, and he lived and breathed Quantum Cultures. We were his life and he would have given his soul to help us. You saw Herod! That dog has all of Robson's love and loyalty for this place. We could do with more like him. And, here he is!'

Herod's tail wags and he looks up at the owner.

TREACHERY!

For there is no mistaking that silhouette. The Enemy has stolen that voice and is using it. The Enemy! Herod bares his teeth and he launches at the Enemy's neck.

Herod is choking and being dragged down to earth again. The Man has tightened Herod's choke leash and is crouching before him, brandishing the leather handle in front of his eyes.

'Bad dog! Bad dog!'

Herod has upset the Man and he is sorry. Herod is confused. The Enemy is there, next to the Man, but Herod has been bad. Herod doesn't understand. Herod crouches on the floor, feigning abjection, yet glowering at the Enemy, waiting for him to make a move.

'I'm so sorry, Dr Jones,' the Man says. 'He's never been like that before. He must hate you.'

'Yes.' The Enemy looks down at Herod. There is a spark of recognition and Herod knows that contact has been made. The Enemy did not know him for who he was, but now that has changed. They understand each other.

Strangely, Herod doesn't smell fear.

'Yes,' says the Enemy, 'he must.'

Later, in the pens, the Man is friendlier again. Herod has been forgiven. The Man is rubbing Herod's chest, sending sensual waves through his body. The Man's tone is kind.

'Watcha do that for, you great mutt? Attacking Dr Jones like that, with the MD looking on? What were you up to, hey? Hope they don't recall the Robson strain because of you, boy.'

The Man stops his rubbing to scratch his own head.

'Nah. It's all over the Union by now, anyway. Too late to do anything about it.'

The words mean nothing, but the concept forms. Herod is one of a pack. The pack, as packs should be, is out there, waiting. It will support and help its brother. One day the Enemy will encounter another pack member. And if that fails, another. And another.

The pack will not forget the Enemy.

About THE ROBSON STRAIN

Some readers assumed this was set in some nameless American city: actually, I was thinking of Reading, which is probably grossly unfair to Reading. This is also a story about redemption, which is another reason why I like it, and the first story I wrote that might actually hint at being grown up.

8th= in the *Interzone* readers' poll.

JEAPES JAPES

CRUSH

After a whole day of non-stop grizzle we had finally got the baby to sleep. We were preparing for a celebratory snooze when Cielito called for attention. Sally gave me that 'it's your problem' look and went to sleep. I reached over and switched the monitor to speech mode.

'Cielito?' I said.

'Sorry to bother you, Jim, but Big-O asks if you could come down to the Playroom.'

'Trouble?'

'Big-O asks if you could come-'

Cielito wasn't much good at talking about anything other than the job in hand.

'Yeah, yeah, I'll be right there.'

We were met by Big-O.

'This way,' he said. I followed him along to where we kept the newcomers. 'See?'

It took me a while to work out what was going on. Then it hit me. Everything was *ordered*.

I always kept the newcomers in one area until I had had time to study them a bit more closely, find out what I could about their backgrounds, their abilities, their aptitudes ... it had been a busy week and a backlog of about ten had built up that I hadn't yet had a chance to look at. Normally, in such circumstances, they would be milling about, chatting amongst themselves, enjoying themselves in the Playroom ...

This lot were all busy studying. I looked closer, and realised that *someone* had administered the standard assessment test that all newcomers had to go through.

'Did you do this, Big-O?' I asked.

'Not me, boss. Over there.'

Over there was-

'Really?' I said. 'Pita?'

Pita had been with us for a few days now. She seemed quite friendly, especially towards me, and pathetically eager to please. I saw her at about the same time that she saw me and she came hurrying over.

'I hope you don't mind, Mr Lawson,' she said quickly, 'but they all had nothing to do, and I remembered the test you gave me, and I know all newcomers get it, so I've given it to them.'

'Mind? Of course I don't mind. But, Pita, I have to keep close track of the results-'

'I remember, I remember. I've stored them all in a separate file. Want to have a look?'

'Um – not now, Pita. It's late at night for me. I'll take a look in the morning. Oh – well done, by the way. Well done. And call me Jim, like all the other AIs do.'

'Thank you, Jim,' she said shyly.

I pulled out of virtual reality to go back to bed, leaving Pita and Big-O and Cielito and all the other AIs to their own devices.

CRUSH

'We've got a manager on our hands,' I said at breakfast. 'Or at least a good organiser.'

'Oh? Good,' said Sally. The Refuge was more my concern than hers. I told her about last night and Pita.

'Ah, yes,' she said. 'The mystery one.'

Only slightly mysterious. Pita had no serial number and no memory of her origins, but that wasn't unknown. Big-O had brought her in from one of his forages in the Net – she had been hanging around (she said) with friends in the local net of a power station, which is a very dangerous place for an unregistered AI to hang out, and Big-O found her fleeing for her life from the station's goons. Places like power stations have very sensitive security staff and AIs have no qualms about rubbing each other out when humans aren't watching, which is often.

Pita had the marks of a cowboy all over her – no number, poor memory, generally rough-and-ready design, apparently thrown together from scraps of code by some joker, probably for a one- off job, and then thrown out into the Net. Typical, really, of the type that ended up in Lawson's AI Refuge.

She had been cringingly grateful to me for taking her in – just another in the steady stream that had been coming since the government decreed that all AIs were sentient and couldn't just be erased *and* that all AIs, from the lowest sub-moron to the brightest high level model, had to have human patrons *and* that they would pay, per AI, anyone who took them in off the streets. Rain or hail or sleet, we never turn them away.

Sally settled down in her long-term couch, put on her goggles and set off into VR for a hard day's memory broking. By common consent, since she had the full-time job, I was in charge of the baby. I put him down in his cot and called Cielito.

'Cielito, I'm going into the net. Will you look after JL2?' AIs tend to have unique names given by their designers and some of them – especially not-too-bright ones like Cielito – get confused by more than one human having the same name. For their sake we had come to refer to James Lawson the Second as JL2, a far more AI-like name, and it had stuck.

'Of course, Jim.'

JL2 was settled with a full bottle and empty nappy, gurgling happily to himself about nothing in particular and waving an arm or a leg at anything that took his fancy. A monitor over his cot showed pretty pictures and colours to entertain him and Cielito was in overall charge, making baby noises for his amusement and, in an emergency, calling one of us. I was fond of Cielito – she was the first high-level AI I designed that could talk back to me, and though by now she was pretty well superseded by the others, she could babysit adequately.

When all was taken care of I donned my own goggles and went to interview Pita. I could have done it impersonally through the keyboard or in real-time speech mode but I like to make them feel welcome. We would meet on an AI's own ground, in VR.

I am not one of those people who try and make their virtual reality better than the real thing, so my net wasn't represented to me in any elaborate way as a house or a castle or a jungle. I suppose the best real-life comparison would be a set of interconnecting pipes and tubes, with the AIs and human intelligences not as people or creatures but simply as disembodied icons moving along them, each one unique to its owner. Things like the Playroom are simply wide open spaces. I've always preferred to keep one foot in *real* reality and not get carried away.

I located Pita's icon, an elaborate P.

'Can we talk, Pita?'

'All right.'

I moved us to a private memory cluster. I took a breath to begin my spiel and was interrupted.

'I'm very grateful to you, Jim, for taking me in, but if you don't want me here then I'm quite ready to move on. I quite understand, Jim, really, there's no need to apologise-'

'Woah, there! What are you talking about? Why should I not want you here?'

Pita paused.

'You're not going to throw me out?' she said cautiously.

'Can you think of a reason why I should?' I said, as neutrally as I could.

Pita said nothing.

'I asked you a question,' I said.

'I just thought you might, that's all,' Pita said meekly.

I had come along with a few questions in mind. Now a lot more were stacking up at the back of my mind.

'Well, I don't. I just wanted to find out a bit more about you.'

'Okay, Jim.' Pita's tone was back to normal.

There wasn't too much that could be found out. I already knew about her short term memory and lack of serial number. I asked about her friends in the power station.

'The power station?'

'When you came in, you told me you had been sheltering with friends in the power station net.'

'Oh, really?'

I didn't press it.

'Pita, you seem to have management abilities which will help a lot in settling you in the Net somewhere. I'd like to operate on you a bit, with your permission. I should be able to add a bit of memory – make you function better. Would you like that?'

'If you say so.'

I was distracted from pondering on this noncommittal answer by a flashing icon in the corner of my vision – a large, open mouth. It was a signal being sent from Cielito to the effect that the baby was crying and all her ploys had failed.

'Look, I've got to go-'

'Where are you going to, Jim?'

I wasn't *quite* used to being interrupted by AIs, but I let it pass.

'Well, I've got to look after the baby. And there's work to do after that. Bills, correspondence-'

'Will you be at your terminal? Can I help you?'

I paused.

'Pita, right now it's more important that Big-O sees to you, okay? We'll talk about the tasks you can do later.'

'I can help, you know-'

'I don't think so, Pita-'

'You care more about your baby than your AIs, don't you?'

'Well, of course I do, Pita. Goodbye.'

Be firm, I told myself. I pulled out of the net, took the goggles off and looked around at the comforting real-space of my room. Sally still had her goggles on and was busy in the Net and, sure enough, JL2 was crying.

I was quietly minding my own business at the terminal when Pita crashed on to it in text mode.

> 'I CAN'T STAND IT I THOUGHT YOU WERE A FRIEND NOW I KNOW YOU HATE ME WHY I'V DONE NOTHING I CANT STAND IT ($)@)!ú*$(%//<>ú-'

At the same time, Big-O's alert icon began to flash. I grabbed the goggles and dived down into VR.

'Look,' Big-O said. He was next to...something. The computer wasn't sure how to picture it. It was a sphere of... nothing.

'Pita is inside it,' Big-O said.

'What?' I tried to get into it, and couldn't. I just bounced off it. One of my resident AIs, in my own net, was keeping me out of its memory space. It was one almighty sulk.

'It just appeared, boss. Just now. She came streaking down here, and...there it was. She seemed mighty upset.'

'She is,' I said. 'For some reason she thinks I hate her.'

'She said something about you being as bad as all the rest.'

'All the rest? I thought she couldn't remember all the rest.'

Big-O paused.

'Boss, half the things she's told you she's since contradicted to me. I don't know what to believe about her. It's like she can't help...'

'Lying?'

'No, not lying, boss.' This was unusual insight for an AI. 'She believes what she's saying, she really does.'

There are humans like that, I thought, but AIs as a rule have a very limited idea of their masters' world and that isn't the kind of thing you tell them. It gives them ideas.

I thought hard. Oh, I could have cracked that shell with no problem. I had utilities that had seen service against far worse. But I thought not.

'Leave her alone, Big-O, and have the rest leave her alone too. I'll leave a message asking her to see me if she ever comes out.'

I cared about those AIs, I really did. Lawson's AI Refuge started as a handy blend of tax dodge and nice little earner, but it began to reward in other ways too. We became genuinely fond of the AIs in our care. It was a responsible position. AIs could be trained, with time and effort, to be productive in what they did – to *contribute*. It really was great, having these malleable little minds that you could succour, help, encourage to grow. Watching them do something for the first time that they couldn't do before, which they had worked out for themselves, was a cause for celebration. Sally and I still get the champagne out every time we find a placement for one of our wards.

The AIs remember us, too. They always send us messages on our birthdays.

So, all in all, I was determined to sort this out. I didn't want any AI in my net to be unhappy.

'Your apology was so sweet, Jim,' Pita said, thereby ruling out her chances of getting another apology from me ever again.

'I just wanted to talk,' I said. 'Something upset you and I'd like to know what. If it was something I did, or if it was something an AI did that I can prevent, then I'll make sure it doesn't happen again.'

'You were going to throw me out.'

'I wasn't! I told you I wasn't.'

'Oh.' A pause. 'I didn't remember.'

Of course not.

'Well,' I said, 'I came to you to ask-'

I stopped. This didn't work out. Her conviction that I was going to throw her out (and where had *that* come from?) predated my assurance that I wouldn't. Therefore, if she could remember as far back as the former, she should be able to remember the more recent latter.

'It can't have been just that, Pita.'

'You don't trust me.'

That stung me.

'Of course I trust you! I trust you one hundred percent.'

Pita's shy tone was back.

'Do you really?'

'What made you think I didn't?'

'Back when I offered to help you and you wouldn't let me. You didn't trust me!'

What had she offered to do? Ah, yes.

'Pita, I had bills to pay. I don't even let Big-O into the bank account. That is strictly humans only. It's not that I don't trust you, but if any AI could get in then the account would be less secure. I don't know a single human who lets AIs into his money. It's no reflection on you.'

I prided myself on being rational. Apply a bit of logic, a bit of wisdom, to any situation and it could be resolved.

My words just seemed to bounce off.

'You were going to change me and send me away.'

'*No I wasn't!*'

'You were going to change my memory, so you'd have an excuse to get rid of me.'

'For the last time, I don't want-'

'I mean, it's not my fault-'

'Eh?'

'-my construction, you know. I can't help if it I'm badly made-'

Badly made? The AI that had the power to block me in my own network? The AI that had shown initiative enough to get the other AIs working? Badly made?

'You're not badly made, Pita...'

'No? Look at me.'

I had to admit, Pita *seemed* pretty basic. Just what was going on here, I wondered?

'Pita,' I said slowly, 'I don't want to get rid of you. I wanted to improve your memory so that you could have a good chance of finding a better position. I am trying to help you!'

Her tone changed once more.

'That's so nice, Jim.'

I jumped at the opening.

'So, no more silliness about me hating you?'

'Of course not. I realise you never would hate me, Jim.'

'And Big-O can work on your memory?'

Another abrupt change – catastrophe theory as applied to emotions.

'Why do you keep wanting to change me, Jim? Aren't you happy with me as I am ...'

Sally looked amused as my teeth clattered on the rim of the coffee mug.

'Jim, you're treating that coffee like it's a double whisky.'

'That AI!' I wished it was a whisky. I felt I needed one. 'I talked to her for a full hour. It was like wrestling with a pillow.'

'Really?'

'I mean, she is one seething mass of contradictions, and ... and ... I mean, I made a list of things she's told me which are different to what she's told Big-O, and she wriggled away from each one. Like, what about your patron? I don't remember my patron. You told Big-O you did. Big-O hates me ... aaaagh! She's either loved or hated, and because no one ever gives her enough attention to make her think she's loved, QED, she's hated. She flatters herself she's that important.'

'So,' Sally said in her business voice. She sat down opposite me and began to tick off points on her fingers. 'Your mystery AI has the following. Highly selective memory. Wildly varying emotions. Ability to suspend all logical functions at will. Depths of self-pity that cannot be plumbed. And – and this is the most important bit – and she displays all of the following only when you are around.'

'Um.' I thought over another mouthful of coffee. 'Yeah, that sounds like it. Yeah, you've got it exactly.' I took another swallow.

'Jim.' Sally's shoulders were trembling on the verge of laughter. 'Pita is in love with you.'

I spat the coffee out.

'*What*?'

Sally repeated herself.

'She can't be!'

'Why not? She's deeply insecure and you're probably the first human to show her kindness. I think you'll find she actually enjoys making herself miserable in your presence so she can get attention from you.'

'She enjoys being miserable?'

'Oh, I know it's absurd. She doesn't know herself enough to stop and think about it. Thinking demands effort, you see. She's more secure not thinking. She knows where she stands when she's unhappy and everyone hates her.'

'I can't believe this!'

'Why not? Did you never have a crush when you were little?'

I thought of Miss Quinn ...

'I was madly in love with a teacher and ... yeah, I guess I misbehaved a bit, just to get her attention. But not this badly! And I was eight.'

'You were a fully functioning, normal, healthy eight-year-old. I expect. Pita is an in-built neurotic. Have you thought she might have been designed that way?'

'Why would anyone deliberately design a neurotic?'

Sally shrugged.

'You'll have fun finding out. And can't you redesign her? Straighten out all these little quirks?'

'Well, yes, easily ... if she gives her permission.'

That was the one problem. Pita had to *agree* – the only alternative was to wait for her to do something sufficiently bad to persuade a court to order corrective surgery ... or scrambling.

'Good luck in getting it. I'd better get back to work.'

* * *

Cherchez la nomme.

Very few AIs get their names out of nowhere. Even nonsense sounds have their roots somewhere – acronyms, acronym soundalikes, word association ... like, while I was putting the final touches to the AI that I was designing to be my general factotum it occurred to me that part of its job would be to go out and round them up ... which led me to call it Big-O, because it *sounded* like a ranch, even though thirty seconds earlier the name had meant nothing to me at all.

See? There is logic in names, but often once or twice removed from the original thought processes.

I sent out a query requesting any information, any experiences, *anything* on any AIs, patroned or otherwise, with a the letters P-I-T-A involved.

After that I went to investigate the Playroom.

This was where the AIs kept themselves happy – perhaps the most important part of the Refuge. They operate far faster than human thought and they don't have anything to do. Ever felt you'd go mad with boredom on a rainy Sunday afternoon? AIs have that every day, a hundred times worse.

The Playroom was full of things to keep them occupied – machines they could work which didn't actually do anything, simulations of working environments ... all in VR only. It was quite simply somewhere the AIs could play. They were doing it now.

I stood on the outskirts and watched with a sinking feeling. Sure enough, Pita had organised them into teams and they were competing against each other in logic problems drawn from the stores. And she was creating her own problems for them to solve. She was prodding them, cajoling them into doing things they would never have been capable of earlier. They really were learning.

She was so capable! Why did all that careful organisation have to go to pieces the moment she talked to me? And why couldn't I design AIs like this? If only Pita wasn't such a pain she could have had a place on the staff any day.

I watched, engrossed, for I don't know how long. Pita knew I was there because every now and then her attention focus drifted in my direction, then quickly went away again. I had to bite my tongue to stop myself praising her, it would only rub the crush in deeper-

The goggles were pulled from my face and simultaneously I was deafened by some kind of music playing so loud I couldn't recognise it, coming from the next room. JL2's room. Under it I just heard a high-pitched screaming. Sally stood over me.

'What the hell do you think you're doing?' she shouted, and turned on her heel before I could answer. I struggled up from the couch and followed her towards the source of the noise.

'Disconnect!' I shouted at the monitor. 'Cielito! Disconnect!' There was no answer, even though her icon showed on the monitor.

'Jim!' I just heard Sally shout over the music. She was pointing at the monitor over the cot, which last time I looked had been showing cuddly, multicoloured teddy bears. What it was showing now still involved animals and it made me want to throw up.

There was one simple way of disconnecting. I grabbed the leads and pulled them out.

Boy, when babies are pissed off, they let you know. Sally joggled JL2 on her knee and made soothing noises for all she was worth. His little face was scrunched up and his mouth was a huge, yawning cavity from which this sound issued: it reached deep into me and tweaked the instinctive control which was meant to make me safeguard the well-being of my offspring, with my life if necessary, and make me feel guilty as hell if I didn't pander to his every need.

'Oh, dear, didn't Daddy hear you?' Sally crooned.

'What's wrong with him?' I said. What the hell was happening?

'Oh, just neglect, I expect,' Sally said airily, 'you know, having a father who ignores him and makes him think he's deserted and unloved and all alone in the world when that horrible noise is going on. The usual thing.' She turned back to the baby and changed to baby tone. 'Didda great big fat-headed nasty pillock not hear you? Is that why your nappy is full and you're starving hungry as well as everything else?'

'You do one end, I'll do the other,' I muttered, and we got to work.

'So, explain,' Sally said later. We had finally got JL2 to calm down and do his well-known impression of a human being.

'I will, I will.' I slapped the control that would summon Cielito. Nothing happened, so I called Big-O instead.

'Yes, boss?'

'Big-O, get Cielito. I want to know what the hell she was playing at.'

'Rightaway, boss.' A pause. 'Boss, you won't like this.'

Big-O wasn't designed to be reticent.

'What is it?' I said quietly.

'Cielito has been scrambled, boss.'

Scrambled. The AI equivalent of brain death. Still a presence in the net, still displaying an icon, but otherwise non-functional. Wiped out.

I heard Sally gasp. She knew what that AI meant to me.

'Who by?'

'Pita.'

'Right,' I said grimly. 'Fetch her. I'm coming in.'

Pita's icon was before me and Big-O hung in the background.

'I think you ought to know Big-O pulled me away from the games,' Pita said. 'He was very rude to me.'

'Good. Pita, why did you scramble Cielito?'

Silence.

'Well?'

'Who says I did?'

'Big-O?' I said.

'Pita attacked Cielito at 14.37 hours, 22 seconds, boss,' Big-O said.

'You see, Pita,' I said, 'the system logs the activities of all AIs in it at all times. The log cannot be tampered with. Not even I can do that. Now, why did you do it?'

'I don't remember,' Pita said quietly.

'Really?'

'You don't believe me, do you? You hate me and you're going to send me away-'

'Why do you keep saying that?'

'Because everyone else does!' she screamed. If AIs were human she would have bit her tongue and Big-O would have been staring at the ceiling, whistling.

I needed time to think.

'I'm pulling out. Pita, if you step just a little bit out of line again, I'll get a court order and have you scrambled. Got that? And in the meantime, stay away from the other AIs. All of them.'

'You hate-'

'Oh, shut up,' I snapped.

My mailbox was full of messages about Pita AIs from all around the world. I hadn't revealed my real-life identity, and it showed.

'You got one too? Hoo, boy, get rid of it, quick.'

'The Pita series are trouble. Rub it out. I've bagged me three so far.'

'There's reports of at least twelve of them ... '

'My Pita successfully screwed up a deal I was doing ... '

' ... scrambled my files ... '

' ... planted false messages, bust up my marriage ... '

I sat up sharply at the next one.

' ... turned off the life support ... '

The most informative was:

' ... analogous to the viruses of late C20, created just to make trouble and nothing else. PITA = Pain In The Ass. They are extremely capable – perhaps to enable them to ingratiate themselves – and despite their apparent slipshod construction are in fact very high level. They form attachments to humans of either gender, or even other high level AIs, who show them kindness, who can be trusted not just to erase them on the quiet, and proceed to screw up their lives. Whoever made them is in A LOT of trouble with the law if caught. Would appreciate details of your experience for the catalogue ... '

It left me with a deep, cold fury inside me. Not that Pita lived up to her name. No, no.

Someone had gone to all that trouble. Creating a new mind should be a wonderful thing. But this! It was like having a baby just to abuse it. What kind of sicko out there had done it?

You might as well blame a lion for eating those pretty little animals on the Veldt. Pita followed her nature, and who could blame her? And it had cost me Cielito.

I looked at the messages again. The Pitas would stop at nothing. The broken marriage, the murder (could there be another word?), other examples – all had worked to remove a person or other distraction from the life of the object of their affections. No doubt that was why Pita had scrambled Cielito: she knew that if I was given a choice between looking after JL2 and admiring her instead, JL2 would win every time. She had tried to hurt JL2 and Cielito, brave soul, had tried to stop her.

Plus, removing Cielito would mean one less AI to divert my attention from Pita.

Sally had come up behind me and was reading the messages over my shoulder.

'So now what?' she said. I slid an arm round her.

'I don't know. I really don't know.'

I called Big-O.

'Big-O, I want you to find Pita and restrain her. Get in outside help if you need it, and tell me when you've done.'

'A pleasure, boss.'

Pita crashed onto my terminal again. The barriers I had put up would have kept out any other AI I knew with the possible exception of Big-O, and Pita just brushed them aside. Don't you hate it when that happens?

'You probably won't care about this, but I'm showing you anyway.' Then she was gone again, leaving only a file behind her. I browsed warily through it.

It was a list of results from the tests she had been putting the AIs through. I gave a small moan when I read it.

'The following AIs show management aptitude. Vettis; Sola, Cra/47; Pusho ... '

There were AIs with good accountancy skills, in-built or acquired. AIs with engineering backgrounds. Two had worked in hospitals. One was a cordon bleu chef. Pita had sorted them out carefully, graded them and presented this report with an appendix of the tests administered.

Not that I intended to take her word for it straight off, but at first glance I couldn't fault any of it.

Pita was a treasure. I'd never met an AI with so much drive, so much initiative, so much *oomph*. If only those were her only properties ...

Big-O was flashing for attention.

'Yes?'

'Boss, about Pita-'

'Uh huh? She was here just now. I thought I asked you to restrain her.'

'Boss, she's in the Playroom and she won't come out. She just pushes me away if I go near her and ... well, I remember Cielito, boss.'

So, Pita had my best AI by the balls.

'Then call in some heavy stuff, Big-O. I want her tied down.'

'I think she'll hurt the others rather than come quietly, boss.'

Oh, God.

'What's she doing in the Playroom?'

'Being a pain as usual, boss. She's pushing the others about all the time, won't let them have a moment's rest, and if they complain she says she's doing it for you and they should be grateful.'

This had to be it.

'I'm going to get her out of the Playroom, Big-O. The moment she's out I want the Playroom physically disconnected from the rest of the net so she can't get back in. Got that?'

'Got it, boss.'

'I'm coming in now.'

The situation was deceptively normal. Pita was, sure enough, running the other AIs through their tests ... again. They probably thought she was doing it for me.

'Pita,' I said, 'stop that.'

She ignored me. I had a feeling she was withdrawing into a fantasy land where everything happened just as she wanted and any outside stimuli were ignored.

'Pita,' I said again, 'I told you to stay away from the others.'

Pita came over to me slowly.

'I'm just trying to help, Jim, I know you don't think I can but ... '

'Pita, you ... you're a pain, you're a nuisance, you're an irritation and I've had enough. I want you to consent to surgery now, or else I get a court order. You have a minute to think about it.'

I pulled straight out of VR.

I didn't expect her to take it lying down, which was the idea. I sat back and waited, and a few seconds later her words appeared on the monitor.

'WHY WHY I $DONT **UNDERSTAND YOUú/ú/#### SAY YOU DON'T HAT M ...'

The message didn't end. It just switched to garbage and poured across the screen.

I switched to voice mode.

'Pita, please get off my monitor.'

She did. A moment's pause, and then the lights went off. And on, and off, and on, and off-

Eventually they blew.

'Gloo!' said JL2, enthralled at the entertainment, and it nicely dampened my anger.

'Happy now?' I said. From the kitchen I heard the microwave come on. I walked in and unplugged it.

I began to unplug all the other appliances that were connected to the net as well.

A voice came out of the speakers. It was much calmer now.

'I'm here to stay, Jim, and don't you try and stop me.'

'Pita ... '

'I'm going to show you that I can manage whether you like it or not. I can run the net for you. You don't need Big-O. I'll scramble him. I can, you know. You've got no gratitude, Jim, but I'm going to show you-'

'Please, Pita,' I said, 'stop and think. Think about what you're doing.'

The network began to go crazy. I could only watch the LEDs and readouts and imagine what it was like in there. At least Big-O had done his job and disconnected the Playroom.

'Pita, you're only hurting yourself. You can't help it, but I can help you if you let me operate. You've been programmed-'

It stopped. I held my breath.

All readouts were green. The monitors were normal. What was happening? The sudden calm was too quiet, too eerie to be a good thing. I went into VR to see.

It was like a hurricane had passed through. The passageways were distorted, the connections were wrecked. I sought out Big-O, who was trying to restore some sort of order and calm down the AIs who hadn't been in the Playroom.

'Where is she?' I said.

'Gone, and good riddance.' Big-O connected to a lesser AI and started sorting out its memory parameters.

'Where to?'

'Into the Net, I think.'

I had a nightmare image of Pita out there in the big, wide world, wreaking havoc. A Lawson AI.

'*Shit!*' I left Big-O in charge and set off into the Net.

I emerged into the Net at speed. As usual it was like a pedestrian trying to cross a motorway, which is why I don't go out often. There were icons in all directions, AIs and humans, going about their business. Pita wasn't in the area.

What to do? I looked hopelessly around me. Why couldn't it be neat and ordered like my own net? But then, Sally did this every day-

Oh, God. I knew where to look.

Sally's icon was waiting for me. She represented herself in the Net with an icon as close to Jessica Rabbit as copyright would allow, and she was tapping her foot.

'This way, Jim.'

I followed her through a maze of more wrecked passageways and conduits.

'Pita did all this?' I said weakly. With half my mind I was picturing my credit balance and with the other half comparing it against the damage all around me.

'She had help from our security, trying to stop her. Jim, that AI is a menace. She crashed in on a deal I was doing. It's going to take ages to work up the good will again-'

'Where is she now?'

'-and she trashed our filing. It's backed up to yesterday, but we've lost a lot of work.'

I moaned.

'Where is she now?' I said again.

'We got her subdued. Over here.'

Pita had met her match. She was surrounded by the goons owned by the corporation that Sally worked for – big, powerful things several degrees above anything I had at my disposal.

'Jim! Help me!' she called piteously.

I deliberately turned away from her. I faced ruin. I was finished.

'What can we do?' I said hopelessly.

'I don't know,' Sally said, just as hopelessly. 'At least we've got rid of Pita, one way or the other.'

'Mr Lawson?' said a voice behind me. It was an AI with the icon of net security.

'That's me,' I said.

'I understand you are responsible for this AI?' it said.

CRUSH

'Unfortunately.'

'Then I have to tell you, Mr Lawson, that if the corporation chooses to press charges you could face a maximum fine-'

'Yeah, yeah.' I didn't want to hear it. I went over to where Pita was being kept. She saw me coming.

'Oh, Jim, I'm so sorry,' she wailed. 'Please don't let these things hurt me, Jim, take me back with you, I promise I'll behave, I know you don't hate me really-'

'Shut up, Pita,' I said. 'All you had to do was agree to surgery, *all* you had to do, but now I'm ruined and you're either going to agree to be operated on anyway to make you behave like something civilised, or you'll be scrambled by court order.'

'You wouldn't let them scramble me,' Pita said.

'Surgery?' I said.

'It's not needed, Jim-'

'Surgery?'

'Why can't you trust me-'

'Surgery?'

'You all hate me, you all do-'

'Goodbye, Pita.' I turned to the security AI. 'She's all yours.' To Sally: 'See you later, love.' I was going to have to go through every penny of our finances and the sooner I started the better.

I heard Pita's calls behind me.

'Jim! Jim, please! Please! *Jim*! I'll do it.'

I stopped and turned.

'Jim,' Pita said, 'if I agree to surgery, will you do it for me? I know you'll be gentle ...'

JEAPES JAPES

The corporation didn't press charges, thanks to some fancy footwork by Sally, and, because Pita hadn't damaged any public property, all I faced was a mild fine for letting a bad AI out into the Net. And the court let me perform the surgery.

It was a long, long job. Pita's internal structure looked so jumbled, until you began to perceive the immensely complex underlying structure. Her designer was a twisted genius. I had taken notes for designing my own AIs – ones with all the original Pita's abilities and none of the disadvantages.

Finally it was all done. I pulled out of Pita's code and studied her carefully, with Big-O hovering beside me.

'Now, boss?'

'Now, Big-O.'

Big-O fired the sequence that would bring Pita back to life and Pita stirred. There was none of the disorientation that an AI usually gets coming to sentience for the first time, since I had given her back her memories.

'Oh, my!' she said. Then, 'I've been very silly, Jim.'

'You're better now, Pita,' I said.

'I know. Thank you, Jim.'

Of course, there was no way of knowing how successful I'd been ...

'How do you feel about me?' I said.

'I'll always be fond of you, Jim, I can't help that. But I'm not so ... obsessive as I was.'

'How do you feel about leaving?'

'If you don't want me to stay I do understand.'

It wasn't so much me – it was the other AIs. She had made herself seriously unpopular and AIs don't have the right grasp of repentance and change which is needed to be forgiving.

'No,' I said, 'it's something you can do for me. I have an idea for a mission-'

I outlined what I had in mind.

'Oh, Jim! That's poetic!'

'Let me know how it goes.'

'I will, Jim. Goodbye.'

She slipped out into the Net and I never saw her again. I hope she managed. Like she said, it was poetic.

The sick bastard who designed the Pitas and inflicted them on the world had hidden his tracks well. It would take an AI of considerable genius to pick up his tracks and find the source ... an AI of the Pita series, perhaps.

And what could be more natural than an AI falling in love with its creator? If only I could be there to see it ...

About CRUSH

My first two sales were AI stories like this and it made me wary, since I didn't want to be stereotyped into writing in one particular style. Unfortunately, the world at large thought otherwise. I wrote story after story, carefully steering clear of AIs and computers, and not one sold. After two years I swallowed my pride and wrote a third AI story, based on an unfortunate event in my recent life when a teenage girl had developed a clinging, possessive crush on me. And guess what, it sold. To *Interzone*.

Let's not go into details: just say that writing 'Crush' was an immensely therapeutic exercise, since I could say all the things I'd wanted to say in real life but didn't because I knew it would only make things worse. To give myself credit (no one else will) I tried to see things from the other side's point of view, too: thus the revelation that Pita was deliberately designed that way. Not that human thinking is designed, of course, and while we all have free will we don't all have self-knowledge to control it; but still, the character and mentality of the aforementioned girl was heavily influenced by a perfectly legal act of unimaginable selfishness and spite on the part of one of her parents.

'Crush' came 3rd= in the readers' poll for 1993.

CATHEDRAL NO. 3

Bilquis

Bilquis Lakhani picked her way through the remains of Coventry, which had been destroyed in the name of the same god that she had been brought up to believe in. It was hot in her suit and there were parts of herself that she longed to scratch, but comparing her environment *inside* with the toxic filth *outside*, she felt she had the better of it.

She climbed to the top of a pile of rubble and looked about her. A lot of the city was still standing; she had imagined it would be a flattened wasteland like she had seen in pictures of Hiroshima or Nagasaki, but most of the buildings here were made of steel and concrete. The city wasn't so much flattened as slumped. A few days ago, it had been a normal, upright city on a bright and sunny day, and thousands of normal men and women and children had been going about their daily business. And then those buildings had been thumped by an immense force that broke their strength and spoiled their clean lines, and those that survived the initial blast were hit by the air rushing back in again.

The older buildings, the bricks and mortar buildings, had crumbled and what Bilquis stood on now was a heap of broken red bricks. She had asked a friend, born locally, how one found one's way around Coventry, and the bright reply had been, 'why, you just look out for the spire of the cathedral- oh.'

Oh indeed, Bilquis thought. No spire anymore. Still, she thought she had her bearings and she set off in a new direction.

David

The wind that gusted through the remains of the roof was made visible by the swirls of poisonous ash that it carried into the cavern of the wrecked cathedral. After the black and bloated cloud that had hung over the city for so long, perhaps the ubiquitous ash would be the next most potent reminder of the calamity.

The ash irritated the man who knelt down in the nave. It swirled down upon him and on the area of floor that he had cleared. It obscured the drawings that he had made there, and though David Stapleton himself knew them by heart, he was concerned that they should look their best for the others who would come to see them.

There was death in the ash but that didn't bother him; he was dying anyway. The city was contaminated and every breath that the man took, every second more that he lived, only helped his diseased cells to die a bit more. He could feel the rot inside him spreading through his organs. When he coughed – which was often – blood and maybe even bits of lung came out, and he feared that if he coughed too hard his body would fall apart.

He fingered his charcoal lump and studied the sketches again. In his mind he clothed them with three-dimensional reality. He had experimented with so many designs, just like the original architects of the ruin around him. Looking up at the south end of the cathedral (the elaborate clear glass window that had once occupied it entirely now lay in a white pile of a million shattered pieces) he could see the dark shell of the old cathedral, the current cathedral's predecessor. The building he was now in had been built deliberately on a slightly lower level than the original, to indicate humility and reverence for the old ruin. Now the new cathedral had gone the way of the old; how should cathedral number three be built? He turned back to his drawings.

It would be a pyramid, he had decided. Pyra-mid. Pyre. Fire. Coventry died by fire. Again.

Bilquis

This had to be it. Bilquis stood at the bottom of a flight of steps. At the top on her left was the dark stone of a medieval cathedral, and on the right a far more modern, barn-like building, showing yellow stone beneath the burn marks and just about intact. She walked up the steps to it and came to a stone set into the wall at waist height, which according to the inscription was the foundation stone of Coventry cathedral laid by HM Queen Elizabeth II. At any other time the idea would have amused her.

This whole end of the building was open to the elements; she deduced it had once been a large window. She peered into the depths of the cathedral and hesitated. Her local mosque in London was a converted church, but she had never actually been inside a functioning Christian house of worship before.

Bilquis looked about her. Functioning? And she was in pursuit of a story – it wasn't as if she was going over to the other side – so her soul should be safe, and the souls of generations of dead Lakhanis back in Bangladesh would not grieve.

She stepped quickly into the cathedral while the glow of self-persuasion lasted.

David

Footsteps crunched in the broken glass. His visitors?

His visitor. A solitary figure was picking its way past the crumpled porch and through the pile of glass into the cathedral. The newcomer's breath passed through the mask's filter with an asthmatic wheeze. He would be invisible where he knelt in the gloom of the cathedral's interior, so the Dean of Coventry cathedral walked into the light to meet his visitor.

'Bishop Stapleton?' asked the visitor, voice distorted but clearly female. It had been impossible to tell through the bulky protection suit and the mask that hid the face.

He smiled. 'Not Bishop, just Dean, and you can call me David,' he said.

'David. Ah – right. David.'

As the two stared at each other, David felt a sudden disgust for the visitor's garb. How dare this outsider wander into the heart of the ruined city, breathing only safe, filtered air, isolating herself from his city's hurt and pain with the protective layers of the suit? It was a stupid feeling and it lasted only a second until reason took over, so he ignored it.

'And you are ...?' he prompted.

CATHEDRAL NO. 3

'Bilquis. Bilquis Lakhani ... um ... David.' The accent was pure south London.

And what did she think of him? An old, stooped, balding man, still in his tattered cassock, with bleeding gums and deathly white skin. 'And you are a journalist?'

'That's right. I'm freelance.'

'Freelance – oh.' He knew he sounded disappointed.

'Hoping for the *Times*, hey?' He couldn't tell if the distorted voice was hurt or making a joke.

'Oh! Oh dear, no. Sorry. I just thought ... never mind.' Suddenly he chuckled – a rattling noise which turned into another of his terrible coughs. His vision faded and when it cleared again he was being sat down in a seat. He put a hand to his mouth and wiped away the trickle of blood that he knew would be there.

'Now, what on earth was that about?' demanded Bilquis Lakhani.

'Oh, I just thought, two Brits, chatting about this and that, not at ease because we hadn't yet got around to the weather, and we haven't been introduced properly ...' He tailed off, then remembered her remark about the *Times*. 'I'm sorry I sounded ... well, well done for getting here! No, I just hoped that a few more would make it. I have something to say, you see, and the more coverage I get ...' The words dried up. Suddenly, his great plan was seeming futile.

'The whole press corps got your message,' Bilquis said, 'but none of the big papers could slip away from the press camp unnoticed. The authorities know who they are. But me? I'm just small fry.'

'I see, I see ... where is this press camp?'

'Birmingham. Safely up-wind.'

'Birmingham? My dear girl, you must have walked all day!'

'They want to keep us well out of the way. But no, I hitched a lift on an army landrover. I, um, borrowed a pass.'

'Well ... well done,' David said again. A sense of hospitality, a legacy of civilisation, made him feel guilty. 'I have some provisions, food and drink, stored away and I would offer them to you, but you'd have to ...' He gestured at the mask.

'I understand,' she said.

'Oh, good, good ...' They sat staring at each other again.

'Do you stay here, now, in the cathedral?' Bilquis asked. 'You don't go anywhere?'

'No, no,' David said. 'The captain of a sinking ship, you understand. My house was flattened, I sleep in my old office.'

'No family?'

'Three grown-up children,' he said quietly. 'My wife was shopping when ...'

'Ah. And are there others? Do you ever see anyone else?'

'A few, a few. I try to provide what comfort I can to any survivors who come in. A few did come, at first. Now they're all in the hospital camps, to die with dignity. I advised them to go. I sent the cathedral staff away as well. I won't drag anyone down with me.'

'But you won't leave yourself?' Bilquis asked.

'No.' Again they stared at each other, unsure what to say next. 'Tell me about the outside,' he said. 'I haven't been able to find a working radio since the blast.'

'The real world?' The goggles still looked at him blankly but he thought he detected sympathy behind them. 'Well, um, let's see. Yes. The mayors of Nagasaki and Hiroshima have sent their condolences. The question now is, do we retaliate? We don't know who did it but everyone's pretty sure it wasn't a foreign power, so the chances are we won't.'

David shut his eyes. That had been his chiefest fear, his greatest worry. The mushroom cloud that had hung over Coventry, hanging over a hundred other cities. 'Thank God,' he murmured. 'Thank God.'

Bilquis shifted uncomfortably. 'You said it,' she said. 'No, they think it was some terrorist group which somehow got hold of weapons grade plutonium. It wasn't a proper nuclear bomb, you see, they say. Just a nuclear device. And it wasn't fired by a missile or dropped, it was planted.'

Now David couldn't believe what he was hearing. 'A device? They can split hairs like that? What the hell difference does it make? Don't they see that a city is dead? That thousands and thousands of people are dead, burnt, mutilated, poisoned, that ... that ...'

'Hey, hey, hey!' Bilquis held up her hands. 'I agree, David! But it's important. If it were a bomb then the chances are it would have been another country ... get my meaning?'

David took a deep breath. 'I get your meaning,' he said. 'But do they have any idea who ...?'

His visitor took a breath and he thought he detected reluctance. 'Various groups have claimed responsibility and ... the most likely contenders seem to be the Crimson Jihad.' The last sentence came out in a matter-of-fact rush.

'Muslims,' said David.

'Hey! Do you have a problem with Muslims?' Bilquis demanded, and David could tell even through the mask that she wasn't joking.

'Oh, I'm sorry! I'm sorry. No, of course I don't. Some of my best-' He stopped. Bilquis had her hands on her hips and was looking at him, waiting. 'That's even more patronising, isn't it?' he said. 'To say, "some of my best friends are ... Muslims, Jews, homosexuals, women, all of the above, other, fill in where applicable." I'm sorry, Bilquis.'

From her stance, Bilquis seemed to be relaxing, slowly. 'For what it's worth,' she said, 'every Islamic group and organisation in this country, and several abroad, including several Islamic governments, have condemned the act. And some of my best friends are Christian, but I don't hold it against them.' He *thought* she might be smiling behind the mask, until she added: 'despite the gangs of Christians who've been firebombing mosques ever since this happened.'

He bit his tongue on his immediate reaction: to deny that they were Christian. He had learnt the hard way that pat explanations tended not to wash and might not be true anyway. 'Do you think I'm that sort of Christian?' he said.

'Do you think I'm the sort of Muslim who nukes cities?'

'No. Could we rewind and start again?'

The mask's unblinking gaze held him for a moment. 'I think it would be best. You were asking about the outside.'

'Um, yes, I was. How are people taking all this? Apart from, I'm sorry, firebombing mosques?' he said.

'How do you think? Shock, outrage, why didn't the government do something. Seems it tried. They got a

CATHEDRAL NO. 3

warning that a Midlands city would be destroyed and everyone thought it would be Birmingham, so they pumped security agents into the place, each with a surreptitious Geiger counter-'

'-and they missed out on Coventry completely,' David said. 'I wonder if it was deliberate or just fluke?'

'What was?'

'Look,' David said, springing to his feet. He staggered and clutched his chest, and at once Bilquis was by his side holding him up again. He brushed her off.

'Look,' he repeated. 'This is what I called you for.' He pointed out of the south end of the building. 'What do you see?'

Bilquis looked. 'The old cathedral.'

'Correct! Now, what do you know of Coventry's history?'

'I know it was bombed before.'

'It certainly was. November 1940. The Luftwaffe flattened it. The cathedral was burned out, only the walls and the spire still standing, and the rest of the city was just rubble. They got to us long before we got to Dresden.

'And then, after the war, Coventry rose again. They built a new cathedral, this one, full of symbolism about love and forgiveness. German volunteers helped rebuild it. This cathedral stood as proof that the devil can never win. God's love is greater. Through Christ they could forgive. They could embrace the Germans as brothers and sisters in-'

'Supposing you don't believe in God?' His wife had called it sermon mode, and Bilquis interrupted him just as he was slipping into it. 'All this becomes meaningless.'

'Yes, yes, yes, but don't you see it?' David said, irritated. 'This cathedral, a sign of hope. A mighty monument to love. Love! Love, love, love. We must never hate. Never. The Nazis hated, but through love their evil works were defeated.'

'The invasion of Normandy and the Eastern Front helped, but that's one way of looking at it,' Bilquis conceded. 'And ...?'

'Come here, come here.' David beckoned and scuttled further into the cathedral, feeling like some shy little boy showing off a secret.

Bilquis

You're just not for real, Bilquis thought, but she followed him. David Stapleton stopped at the edge of the clear area where he had been working. 'Look,' he said with pride, pointing at some wavery charcoal designs on the floor. 'The future.'

Bilquis looked and tried to make sense of them. 'Um ...'

'I'll show you.' Again he pointed out at the old cathedral. 'The old.' He waved a hand around him. 'The new. This one was designed, you know, in a special way. As I said, full of symbolism. Now Coventry needs a new one again. Here.' He pointed at the sketches on the floor and described his grand scheme for the third cathedral, the greatest of the three.

At first he had pictured a giant dome over the hulks of both cathedrals. The time for humility was past; this new one would not be lower than the other two. It would stand out above them, above the whole devastated city, a proud statement to the glory of God.

CATHEDRAL NO. 3

Eventually he had realised that the floor plan of a building which already contained two cathedrals would be too ridiculous. He had abandoned that idea reluctantly for the final plan, the pyramid that now lay sketched out in the nave. The third cathedral would stand at the north end of the second. Future visitors to the complex would go from the first cathedral, to the second, and finally to the mighty third.

'A far greater monument even than this one, Bilquis. I can see the three cathedrals now, in a row. A new, rebuilt, Coventry around them, dominated by this pyramid at the end. The cross at its peak, towering over the whole city ...'

'David,' Bilquis said, 'Coventry is radioactive and it won't be rebuilt for years, if at all. Not until it's clean and safe to live in.'

'I know!' David snapped. 'Listen, Bilquis, I know I'm a deluded old man who will die soon.' He straightened up as best he could. 'But I am the Dean of this cathedral. I believe Coventry has a message for the world and I must see that someone takes this message to it.'

'Is that my job?' she said.

'Yes.' His assurance fled him just as quickly as it had come. 'If you could,' he added, almost as a plea.

'How?'

'Tell the world about this,' he said, pointing at the floor. 'Don't let them forget. I know I'll be long dead, but you can write. I know how the press can take one small incident and blow it out of all proportion.'

'Thank you.'

David ignored the comment, or didn't hear it. 'You can write a sob story. "My talk with last Dean of Coventry." "Tragic Dean's hope for the future." Aren't the politicians always saying the church should give a more definite lead? Here's a definite statement for them. Tell the world, make them listen, make them know. Tell them that I forgive whoever did this. Tell them that Our Lord forgives.'

'That's very good of him,' she said. 'What gives him the right?'

David looked puzzled. 'What?'

'David, you can forgive the bombers if you want, but you don't have the right to do that on behalf of the people of Coventry. That's their problem. And unless we missed the headline of the millennium, Jesus wasn't in Coventry at the time, so how can he forgive either?'

David grimaced. 'I won't go into the theology of your last statement. To answer your first point, I don't claim to forgive on behalf of Coventry, just myself, but I hope my example will move Coventry to do likewise and they must have a new cathedral to tell them this. Tell them, Bilquis. Even if you don't believe it, tell them, I beg you.'

'No,' said Bilquis. It took a moment for David to realise what she had said. He staggered back as though she had hit him. 'What did you say?' he whispered.

'No,' Bilquis said again. 'There's no story. I'm sorry, David.'

'What do you mean, there's no story? This isn't a story?'

'No, it isn't. Coventry's been here before, David, you said it yourself. All those living saints who built this cathedral and forgave the Germans – that was when the story was. And you're a very saintly man yourself, but "Dean of cathedral forgives bombers" is no longer a headline. I'm sorry. I'm really am.'

CATHEDRAL NO. 3

David slumped down onto a chair and looked at the markings on the floor. Bilquis wondered if he was finally seeing them as they really were. Pathetic, childish, a futile gesture in the face of Coventry's tragedy. Soon David Stapleton would die and just one good fall of rain through the holes in the roof would wash the charcoal markings away for ever.

'That's not it,' he said.

'What's not it?' said Bilquis.

David looked up at her. 'It's not this lack of a story. You've got another reason. Go on, say it.' He gave a bitter laugh. 'I've been through worse.'

'If you insist.' Bilquis pulled up another chair and sat down across it, with the chair back facing him. 'You're enjoying this.'

'How can you say that?'

'Because you are. This cathedral-' She waved a hand at the floor '-you've always wanted to build, and now you've got your chance. And I think you've always wanted something really big and nasty to happen to you so that you could have a really good forgiveness binge, and now it's happened. Deep down, I don't think you do forgive them, but you've convinced yourself that you do. So what do you do? Naturally, you build a pyramid. That was irony, by the way.'

David Stapleton sat in silence for several minutes, looking blankly at the floor, and Bilquis began to wonder if she should just leave. She glanced at the indicator on her wrist that showed her suit's working life; she still had half an hour or so, allowing an hour on top of that to walk back to a checkpoint ...

Then David stood slowly and his gaze drilled through Bilquis' visor. 'I see,' he said. He bent down and picked up a kneeler which he tossed to her. She flinched, but it was only a gentle pitch and she managed to catch it. 'Give me a hand, will you?' he said and, with a kneeler of his own, he began methodically to erase the charcoal pyramid on the floor. A quarter of the way through he stopped and looked at her. 'I said, will you give me a hand?'

So together, they rubbed the floor clean.

If you're trying to make me feel guilty, Bilquis thought, *it ain't gonna work.*

'Now, we'll try again,' said David. 'Crimson Jihad, you say?'

Bilquis hadn't said Crimson Jihad any time in the last ten minutes and it took her a moment to work out what he was on about. 'Um, yes, that's right,' she said.

David didn't answer for a moment. He had his charcoal lump in his hand and he was down on the floor again, sketching. Bilquis frowned. What he was drawing looked familiar but she couldn't place it.

'I'll try and make it a traditional shape,' he said. 'Easier to identify.'

That was when Bilquis saw it. 'Good grief,' she murmured. He sketched away for another ten minutes and even then the design wasn't as complete as the former pyramid, but it was obvious what he was getting at. He stood up, wincing, and Bilquis helped him.

'Coventry's new cathedral,' he said. 'Now, is there a story?'

'There could be,' she said, 'There could be.' She couldn't take her eyes off the drawings.

'I mean, the shape of the building isn't important, is it?' he said. 'Anyone can still worship in it. This is based on the Dome of the Rock in Jerusalem, with embellishments.'

'Of course, of course ...' Her time in the suit was running out and soon she would have to leave, but for the time being she was careful to drink in every detail – the carvings, the dome, the minarets – of the mosque that was sketched out on the cathedral floor.

About CATHEDRAL NO. 3

Well, technically David's new cathedral would be cathedral no. 4. The original Coventry cathedral only exists as a few ruins, even more so than the cathedral that the Luftwaffe destroyed. I hadn't twigged that in the three years I was a university student near Coventry.

That aside, I'd wanted to write a story about Coventry cathedral – by which I mean, the story of the two twentieth century cathedrals – ever since I first saw them standing side by side, ruin and big proud modern barn. And so I bit the bullet and wrote one, thrumming with love and Christianity and general goodness, and for sheer ickiness it broke all known records. Fortunately I could tell it icked and sat on it.

Eventually one of the stalwarts of my writers' group, Gus Smith (who writes as Gus Grenfell) suggested a way it could be de-icked, at least a little, and I'm eternally grateful to him for the suggestion. David takes his suggestion up in the last few paragraphs.

This came 46th= in the *Interzone* readers' poll, but what do they know? Still, if you want a much better, and funnier, treatment of the Coventry cathedral story, see Connie Willis's wonderful time travel novel *To Say Nothing of the Dog*.

JACQUI THE GIANTKILLER

Parking her buggy in the close, Jacqui Dunmore – salesperson *extraordinaire*, company troubleshooter – noticed the man because he smiled at her.

'Good morning,' he said, and carried on walking. He appeared to be out for a stroll.

'Good morning,' she said back with her best dazzling smile, and promptly forgot him.

All she had seen of the estate so far was spotless, and so it should be. The guard at the gate had scowled at the two-year-old registration on the buggy, as if to demand what she thought she was doing, taking that heap of junk through the wall (thirty feet tall, sloping outward, topped with razor-wire) into the sacred environs of Warren Court estate. But her pass was beyond reproach; her presence was approved by the Residents' Committee and she was licensed to sell.

She gave herself a quick once-over. Non-stick coat (for the water, paint or worse): check. Non-permanent humane dog dazer: check. Sunny disposition: check. Time to go. The potentially lucrative Warren Court franchise was making no progress despite the best predictions of the Marketing Department and she was going to find out why.

The street pattern of the estate resembled a giant, fern-like fractal, each frond a close holding ten or twenty deluxe residences. She walked up the nearest, spotless garden path; past the immaculate, even grass and up to the pristine front door. This was Number One. She rang the bell.

'Hello?' said a disembodied voice. Jacqui looked up at the camera over the door, smiled and held up her ID.

'Hello! My name is Jacqui Dunmore and I'm an agent for Custom Homes-'

Bzzzz.

She rang the bell again.

'What?' The voice verged on irritated.

'I assure you, I've been accredited by the Residents' Committee, so you really have nothing to fear. I'm not one of those-'

Bzzzz.

'But you are,' Jacqui muttered, and left for Number Two.

'You can answer this question with a simple yes or no,' said the intercom. 'Are you selling something?'

'Um-'

Bzzzz.

By the time she had gone all around the close to Number Fifteen and ended up back where she started, Jacqui was beginning to feel discouraged.

And then she saw the man again.

She noticed something she hadn't noticed before. His clothes were ... well, not bad, not ragged or anything, but ... like her buggy. A couple of years old, which was well past the use-by date for Warren Court.

In other words, he probably wasn't a resident either.

'You look down,' he said. She had let her professional smile slip and she fixed it firmly in place again.

'They're cagey, aren't they?' she said.

'Who?'

He also *sounded* out-of-place. There was a hint of Irish there, which was not at all the estate's intended catchment area and appeared only rarely in her own social circle.

'The people who live here,' she said.

'You're in the wrong place if you want people,' he said with a beam. 'You'll find people in the next close, but this one's too new, you see. They just finished the houses here and the first residents move in next week.'

Okay, she had met Warren Court's resident loon.

'Look,' she said, 'I have just spoken to the intercoms of fifteen-'

There was something in the way he was looking at her. Let her work it out, it was saying.

'Rich people,' he said.

'Yes, and I've-'

'Minimum required income, two hundred grand.'

'And-'

'Can afford the best.'

'Listen-'

'Of everything.'

'See-'

It began to sink in.

'Everything?' she said.

'I thought only big companies used them,' Jacqui said. She was grateful for the coffee that the man, Joseph, had served back at his apartment. He was a resident after all: he had one of the smallest places, not much more than a studio, on the edge of the estate, up against the wall.

'They're moving into the private home, now,' he said. 'Another year and everyone will have them. It's still only the really expensive models that can hold a conversation.'

'So what was I holding with them?' Jacqui asked.

'That was just some basic neural networks either stonewalling you or taking what you said and throwing it straight back at you. Imagine a bright parrot and you have those things. Artificial, but not what we'd call intelligent.'

'You know a lot about them?'

'My job.'

'Yes, your job!' It dawned on Jacqui that, apart from being the first person to act with any kind of decency that she had met on the estate, she didn't know his job yet. 'What is that?'

'Father Joseph Loughlin, of the Catholic Alliance Mission.'

Father ...

Childhood associations from a convent education welled up inside her, but she remembered her training. *You may meet people with all sorts of strange attitudes, opinions and obsessions. But they're the customers, so be polite.* And she hadn't come top of the training class for nothing. Manners took over.

'Jacqui Dunmore, of Custom Homes.'

'Ah, yes.' He nodded. 'The holographic wallpaper people.'

'You've heard of us?' She was pleased.

'Wall hangings, pictures, other fixtures and furniture available through add-on modules.' He smiled. 'I've seen your ads, but you're a bit out of my wage group.'

When he said 'wage group', the words 'minimum required income, two hundred grand' floated up from the back of her mind.

'Can I ask, very nicely and with no offence intended, what you're doing here, then?' she said.

'Do you know what the Church gets each year? It earns the pants off these people. No, Warren Court has been dubbed an area of Extreme Spiritual Need by my superiors, so here I am. The apartment is owned by the Holy Father, through one means or another.'

'I thought the inner cities had the Extreme Spiritual Need.'

'Lady, where have you been? They hit the bottom long ago and are bouncing back nicely. But this place ... Now, I can't believe a swish outfit like yours' still uses door-to-dooring, so what are *you* doing here?'

Jacqui had no reason to hide anything.

'We've tried several sales campaigns here at Warren Court already,' she said. 'Direct mail, phone, fax, e-mail, and not one of them has made a sale. Not one!'

'That's terrible,' Joseph said, with a completely straight face.

'So, I'm here to see why not, and to drum up some business. I don't normally door-to-door but this morning was by way of reconnaissance.'

'And now you know the problem.'

'I do indeed.' She put down her cup. 'Thanks for the chat, Joseph, I did need it, but I've got to-'

'-go and talk to a bunch of moronic artificial intelligences who won't give you the time of day, let alone open the door for you.'

He was right, but she didn't want to admit it. Technology moved too fast. When she had done her training there had been no question of being bamboozled by AIs. Buckets of water, Rottweiler's, feigned deafness – she could deal with all of those. But AIs?

'So what would you suggest?' she asked. He shrugged.

'You and I have the same basic aims. Get past the front doors, plug the product. We could join up.'

She was certain that the sincerity of her smile could not be doubted as she contemplated the thought of having a priest breathing down her neck.

'That's very kind of you-'

'-but you would just love to make use of the complete database that I have of every AI on the Warren Court estate,' he said. It wasn't quite how Jacqui had planned to finish her sentence but it did change her mind quite nicely.

'Show me,' she said.

* * *

'Door-to-dooring is outmoded,' Joseph said. They stood outside Number Twenty, Pineview Drive. This road, Joseph promised, did have human inhabitants. 'So are most forms of direct marketing, but door-to-dooring especially. Imagine us back in the nineteenth century, when anyone who was anyone had servants to answer the door. Can you imagine door-to-dooring then? You might talk to a lot of butlers but you would never get past them to the master of the house.'

'No one has a butler nowadays,' Jacqui protested.

'No, but they have the next best thing.' Joseph consulted his pocket infocard, a wafer of flexible liquid crystal. 'Ah, yes. The Harrisons, and a Syn-Science Personality Simulator, version five, between us and them. Slightly behind in the latest developments, these people. Observe.'

Joseph pressed the intercom button.

'Yes?'

'Hello, my name is Joseph. I work for the Catholic Alliance Mission on-'

That hateful buzz! It would haunt Jacqui's nightmares. Joseph winked and pressed the button again.

'Yes?' It was exactly the same disinterested tone as the last time.

'I have an urgent delivery of blood plasma for the occupant requiring his signature,' said Joseph, poker faced. The door slid open.

The door slid open! Through it Jacqui saw a lobby. Nicely decorated, Mondrians hanging on the wall, other doors leading off it-

She took a step forward and a hand on her shoulder pulled her back.

'Sorry, wrong number,' said Joseph. The door slid shut again and Jacqui felt like Moses, granted only a look at the Promised Land. She wanted to scream.

'In case you hadn't noticed, I just told a porky,' Joseph said. 'I'm not going to gain false entry into anyone's home.'

'But ... but ...'

'Even if you don't care about your immortal soul, Jacqui, it's slightly illegal. Let's see what Number Eighteen has to offer.'

Joseph led her to yet another door and again consulted his infocard.

'Ha-hum,' he said.

The usual ritual. Press button, wait ...

'Yes?'

'Excuse me, are you a human?' said Joseph.

'What an odd question! Of course I am. Are you?' said the voice.

Joseph grinned at Jacqui.

'A fairly simple back-propagation algorithm,' he murmured. 'It can understand an extended natural language vocabulary and devise an answer to anything you say. Keep you nattering for hours on everything but what you want to talk about. Let's try a simple verbal Turing test.'

He turned back to the intercom.

'Please repeat after me, "I'm not a pheasant plucker I'm a pheasant plucker's son and I'll keep on plucking pheasants 'til the pheasant plucking's done."'

The voice repeated his words flawlessly; the AI, Jacqui realised, was so mindless it didn't even have the gumption to ask why it should. Joseph asked it to repeat itself faster, and faster still, until it was gabbling the rhyme out in less than a second and still pronouncing everything perfectly.

Joseph led Jacqui away without comment, to Number Sixteen.

'This is good for a laugh,' he said. 'The most basic of all.'

He pressed the bell and said, 'An important message for the occupant. A matter of life and death.'

'Go on.'

'Esusjay oveslay ouyay, otherbray.'

'Failure thirteen. Syntax error in input,' said the intercom. They turned away, then Jacqui turned back and rang again.

'What time is it?' she asked.

'Eleven forty three and seventeen seconds,' the voice said.

'Okay, point taken,' Joseph said. 'They *will* give you the time of day.'

Back at his place again, they debriefed.

'They all have 'em,' said Joseph. 'You have to remember what kind of people live here. People with so much that they can afford to closet themselves away from the real world.'

'I can understand that,' Jacqui said. 'The real world isn't very nice.' She remembered the cardboard city built in the lee of Warren Court's wall. She thought of the numerous locks and alarms in her own apartment the other side of town. She mused how nice it would be to be able to take a walk outside her front door without checking her bag for defence items first. For a brief moment, her perception of Warren Court wavered suspiciously close to sympathy for the dwellers.

'Irrelevant,' Joseph said, his flat dismissal knocking her daydream aside. 'It's there and it won't go away. These people, now, they don't *need* other people about them any more. They work from home by virtual reality to earn their daily bread and the home supplies their every need. Of course they can afford a simple AI or two to repel unwanted visitors. Anything from Outside that impinges on their cosy little worldview is a threat, but I expect religious callers are Public Enemy Number One and you lot are Number Two. You see, Jacqui, there is one problem with people like you and me that has always been the case, since long before AIs were heard of.'

'What's that?' Jacqui said eagerly. Joseph's smile was apologetic.

'We're irritating.'

'We are not!'

'We damn well are. You're sitting comfortably, looking at the news, or going about your job, or making love to your partner, and ... ding-dong!' He put an inane grin on his face. '"Good morning, sir, I represent-"'

'But we're trained to deal with situations like that. We know what to say-'

'Okay, you have defused my annoyance at your intrusion with your silken words. You describe your wares. I say no thank you and shut the door. Do you leave it at that?'

'Of course not! I return-'

'Exactly, and that is why we're irritating. Irritating! My organisation has a history of bullying people into giving the right answer and we're still trying to live it down. Our job is to present the information that we're trying to impart in such a way that they can take it in without being threatened.'

'That's door-to-dooring dealt with, then,' Jacqui said, 'but that's scut work and I've told you I don't normally do it. There are other ways-'

'The same principle applies. Don't you dare take it upon yourself to tell others what to think, Jacqui. Suggest but don't tell, don't coerce.'

'But-' Jacqui said, aghast. Joseph held up a finger.

'Exactly, but. But, these people won't even go that far. They won't even give us the chance to present the info. Quite apart from being totally unacceptable to any good missionary, there's a far more sinister aspect. I'll show you a sociological profile I had the computer work out. Jacqui, these people run the country! They make all the decisions that affect us. Not politicians, but businessmen, bankers, people of influence. And they can't believe that other people really matter! They deal with you, me, everybody as theoretical entities, figures in a column of statistics. They've forgotten how to treat people as *people*, which is pretty well why the world is in the mess it is now, and as long as they hibernate their lives away here the situation will get worse. We don't just have to reach them for their own sakes but for everyone's.'

He turned back to the computer and called up a map.

'You would do well to study this, Jacqui. I've got my own programs in the estate's network, probing the opposition. Every home is protected in all directions but I can tell you the makes, model and efficiency of every single AI.'

'Why are you telling me all this?' Jacqui asked. The missionary glow in his eyes burned even brighter for a moment.

'Because, although my dream is for each and every one to turn to the Holy Mother Church, I'll be happy just to see them treat other human beings as human beings, and that even includes salespersons for Custom Homes. Sit down and I'll show you around the system.'

Jacqui sat.

'Everyone,' Joseph said, 'has a bulletin board of their own. And, anyone can leave a message on it! E-mail evangelism! Or selling. Or whatever. All of them have AIs filtering the messages that get through to their masters, but the AI hasn't been invented yet that can distinguish between physical and spiritual well being. They have to let any message to do with physical life and death through, so as long as you phrase your messages in terms of spiritual life and death they get through as well, and you haven't misrepresented yourself at all. Of course, how you're going to apply spiritual life and death to holographic wallpaper remains to be seen. And if you're too heavy handed they report you for threatening behaviour.'

'What kind of messages do you send?' Jacqui asked.

'Thoughts for the day. Bible passages.' He shrugged and the glow seemed to dim. 'That sort of thing.'

Jacqui looked at him. For the first time Joseph was looking worried; tired, even.

'Do you make many converts?' she asked gently.

'Not many. Not many at all.'

Then he convulsed in his seat. Something was blinking on the screen in front of him.

'Good Lord, Jacqui, a message! *A message!*'

It was, indeed, a message. It was from the Bishop, informing Joseph that he was being transferred to the high-priority mission area of South Kensington. The Bishop warmly congratulated Joseph on his successes so far and trusted he would do as good a job in the new area to which the Lord had called him.

Joseph swore.

Joseph had a fortnight's grace, and in that time they settled into a coffee-break routine. Jacqui was free to use his computing facilities; she had put in a request to Custom Homes for equipment of her own, but it was such a departure from Approved Routine that it had probably blown a fuse somewhere in their own system.

First came Jacqui's introduction to virtual reality. The medium for interfacing with the Other Side of computers had come on a lot since her school days and she had never been into a proper net before. She put on Joseph's goggles with a tingle of trepidation and excitement.

Warren Court had its own estate network and it was like the streets of the estate itself – gapingly empty. Every now and then a service AI would flash by on some mission but otherwise it was like wandering on her own around a maze of pipes and tunnels.

Until she discovered the main conduit into the global Net. Icons representing human users buzzed to and fro like ants on a trail. These were the inhabitants of Warren Court: the faceless people behind all those gleaming, polished, oak-imitation front doors that she had come to loathe so much.

The first time, she tried to talk to one of them. It wasn't moving as fast as some of the others, so she had her icon match pace with it on a parallel course.

'Good morning,' she said.

'*Yes?*' said the other brusquely. It was a man's voice that spoke in her earphones, but of course that didn't mean anything in VR.

'I have some information that might be of interest,' she said.

'*Go on.*'

'I work for Custom Homes-'

'*One moment.*' The icon was silent, presumably checking information elsewhere. '*I don't have them on the Stock Exchange listing. Are they a subsidiary? Who's their parent?*'

'Um- they're a private firm-'

'For sale?'

'I don't believe so-'

'So why bother me?' the icon said angrily and moved off at double time.

Jacqui selected an incoming icon at random and trailed it. As far as she could tell, it didn't notice that she was following it. It headed for a memory patch that she knew in the real world was a nicely exclusive cul-de-sac. *Big* money.

The icon's destination hove into view – the input port of a domestic net. It passed through without any effort. No traps, no passwords. She moved in after it, preparing her spiel. Why didn't Joseph try-

Shapes materialised in front of her, blocking her way. Not humans but AIs, natives of the land. They were black and shiny and their form alone suggested *menace*. The icon of the closest one merged boundaries with her.

'Password', said a toneless voice in her ear.

'Um-'

'Incorrect,' it said, and threw her away.

She yelled as the net spun around her with dizzying speed. She was vaguely aware of angry voices in her ear that seemed to flash by her and, when she had got herself under control, she saw why. She had been flung clear across the net, regardless of who or what she passed through to get there. She hadn't known they could do that.

'Wow,' she said.

'Nice try,' Joseph said when she took her goggles off.

So, it was back to pleasing the AIs.

'Remember I talked about butlers in the nineteenth century?' Joseph said conversationally over coffee.

'Mmm,' Jacqui said vaguely, not looking up from her notes.

'Learnt an interesting fact the other day. They weren't a complete barrier to salesmen, apparently. The trick was to sell to the butlers.'

Inspiration struck.

Copywriting wasn't meant to be her job, but, as Joseph put it, she had been given this area to conquer and she had to do it herself. With Joseph as referee of grammar and spelling, Jacqui prepared a number of promotional electronic flyers and left them on bulletin boards, where it would be the AIs' job to scan for new info and bring it home to their human masters if it was deemed suitable.

She followed her mentor's example carefully. Be truthful, Joseph had said. Avoid hype. AIs have algorithms to recognise that. So, out with 'I'm sure you've heard the sad case of Mr X of Doncaster who ordered holograms from an inferior competitor!!' In with 'Market research has shown that 82% of AB bracket home owners are Custom Homes customers ... shouldn't you be too?' And she had to make damn sure that market research *had* shown what she said it had: AIs would check.

Back at her terminal, she prepared different kinds of letters to the people in the estate's different sociological categories, and she personalised each one. Since Father Joseph Loughlin, SJ, Catholic Alliance Mission had just received a letter to Father Sjcam, she carefully checked that each name was correct and that she didn't make reference to wives for widowers, families for single people ...

Then it was back into the net again. Her computer could have delivered everything in a blink, but she wanted to impress with the personal touch. She went from mailbox to mailbox and dropped her letters off, taking care to stay a discreet distance from each input port so that she wouldn't intrude on the occupant's space. Don't annoy, don't annoy.

She was doing nicely until she realised where she was: the port from which she had been hurled across the net. She still reeled at the memory and had already conceived a serious dislike of the resident (56 Chestnut Close, in the real world) and his guards, which she had mentally christened Dobermans. She posted her letter and drew back quickly when one of the guard dogs came out to investigate.

It showed no interest in her, this time; she was far enough away to pose no threat. It approached the letter as though it were an interesting stick, or perhaps a trap. Feelers were sent out to confirm that the file was data only; no viruses, no hidden AIs likely to hijack the house's control systems. Then the AI scanned the data and ran it through its parameters. It took in the sense of what was said; assessed its relevance to its owners; judged whether or not it would be welcome in the home that it was protecting ...

... and accepted the message. Jacqui blinked. Public Arsehole Number One had accepted a message! No, surely the AI was taking it in to destroy it, surely ...

But no. If it was to be destroyed, that could be done in the net. The fact was, this message had been received.

It occurred to her to check on the other messages. If King Snot's AIs were receiving, surely the others were too? Every one had been taken in.

Jacqui tore off the goggles and threw them in the air.

'Ye-es!' she yelled.

Joseph was off into the spiritual wilds of darkest Kensington where, he said, the Spirit of Mammon roamed abroad and God's honest people trembled in their beds at night. He bequeathed her his network password. Custom Homes had finally come up with the goods and Jacqui had a terminal of her own. She sat in her own apartment, awaiting the surge in demand for Custom Homes products.

She could have waited a long time if she hadn't got the hint earlier. She looked up some of the statistics on direct marketing and compared them with the results.

'It's impossible!' she exclaimed. She double-checked and the answer was still the same: for a maildrop of this size, it should be statistically impossible to get exactly zero answers. Yet that was what she had.

'They're sitting on them,' she said to herself. 'They took them in but they're sitting on them.'

The AIs still didn't trust her. They were just as cagey as they always were.

'Oh, God,' she said, and buried her face in her hands.

In that moment, she hated Warren Court estate. It was like a vast, malevolent being. It was an alien mind; each AI in it was a separate neuron and the sum of the whole was an intelligence that was dedicated to keeping her, Jacqui Dunmore, away.

'What do you mean, we don't have sentient AIs yet?' she demanded of the air and the spirit of Joseph. 'They're here now, they just don't realise what they are. Warren Court is sentient and it loathes me. So there.'

Joseph's answer, she mused bitterly, would be to love them all to death. Love AIs? Who could love impulses of energy?

But it was a challenge.

'You're big and powerful and you hate me,' she said out loud, not sure who it was she was addressing. The spirit of Warren Court, perhaps; the embodiment of the 'sod-you-I'm-rich-and-all-right' attitude that dwelt in every household. *That* was the real problem. The AIs couldn't be blamed for being programmed like that – they were doing their job, which was to prop up the creature that was Warren Court.

She would take on this giant and kill it.

'But I know who you are, now,' she said to the screen, 'and I will bring you down.'

It wasn't bribery, she consoled herself as she moved through the net with her packages. Bribes were ... well, different. No, this was an investment: a dedication of existing resources towards an unspecified future goal.

The upgrades she carried with her had cut into her savings, but she assured herself that just a couple of commissions would cover them. Perhaps she could find a way of getting Custom Homes to foot the bill. Not bribes, she emphasised again silently, imagining the invoice passing through Accounts at Custom Homes HQ ('To: five hundred bribes ...'). *Not* bribes.

Expenses. Overheads.

She began to drop off her load as she had dropped off her flyers, though these were not messages for the perusal of the human occupants or anything that might conceivably be found threatening. These were for the AIs themselves. Presents. Sweeteners. Upgrades to the memory that would make them better thinkers, quicker to go about their jobs. Like giving a perfectly functioning dog a set of bionic legs. Something that the AIs would recognise as good and make them identify her as a source of good things.

Suddenly she was at the Gloomy Portal again. 56 Chestnut Close. One of the Dobermans was there; perhaps waiting for her – had her reputation preceded her? – perhaps not.

She treated it carefully, remembering what it could do.

'Hello,' she said. 'I've got something for you.'

It continued to observe her, apparently passively, though there was no way of knowing what was going on inside its tiny mind. Was it about to pounce? Would it send her flying again?

She dropped the upgrade (a generic model, should fit all types) and retreated. The Doberman stayed put.

'Not taking, huh?' Jacqui said. 'Well, I'm not moving it. I guess I'll just have to wait for a service AI to get it instead. That would be a shame, wouldn't it? A nice upgrade like this going to a bog-standard slug-brain instead of a beautiful thing like you.'

She moved off, carefully not looking back. A slave to its functioning, she was sure that the semi-sentient thing would have to take it. Or, at least, study it, go through the routines of assessing its threat ... and find none. And it should have enough self-interest to want it for itself.

She looked back just before she was out of sight: Doberman and upgrade were gone. Moving back to the apartment, she saw that all the upgrades were taken and that several AIs were wearing them.

She got back to see a request for a sample-viewing appointment flashing on her console. An AI had studied her flyer and requested a meeting on behalf of its patron.

* * *

The man walked in through the door and stopped dead. Like his wife, he was stocky, middle aged and well groomed. One look at him told Jacqui that this man had one foot firmly in the twentieth century, where men were unconditional masters of their homes and wives did as they were told.

His eyes flicked around the walls of the main living room, taking in the flowing colours that ran across them.

'What ... what ...' He looked at the two women standing in the middle of the room. 'Explain, dear.'

His wife, Mrs Wilson (Jacqui hadn't yet discovered her first name), hurried forward.

'Alistair, this is from Jacqui from Custom Homes.' She waved a hand at the laser displays covering the walls. 'Isn't it lovely? See, here's her brochure-'

'Wait. Wait a moment.' The man, whose name Jacqui felt she could reasonably guess to be Alistair Wilson, put a hand to his forehead. 'I'm sorry, Miss ...'

'Dunmore,' said Jacqui.

'-Dunmore, I'd forgotten we had an appointment-'

'We didn't when you went to work, dear,' said Mrs Wilson. 'The Household made it this morning. It saw some of her literature and-'

'*What?*' Wilson's face turned red, and in two strides he crossed to the desk terminal.

'Household. Display junk mail items received this a.m. and action taken.' Images appeared on the monitor and he ran his gaze over them, lips moving silently. Then he spun round on Jacqui.

'What did you do? Did you subvert my systems?' He advanced on her. 'Well?'

'Alistair-' Mrs Wilson began.

'Quiet, Irene.'

Irene. Okay, Jacqui thought.

Wilson stood in front of Jacqui, waving a finger.

'I want your name and the name of your employers, Miss Dunmore. I intend to make a formal complaint-'

'About what?' Jacqui asked, her first words other than her surname that she had uttered since he had come into the room and interrupted her sales pitch.

'About what? About what?' Wilson stammered, clearly trying to think of what. 'Assault against private property! In the form of my household AI – a very classy model, let me tell you, dear, well outside your price range, and designed to get rid of people like you!'

'I-'

'It's subversion!' he raged. 'What did you use? Because let me tell you, dear, there are very, very tight rules on what we at Warren Court allow in our net. Oh yes! Was it a virus? Did you get at its code in some way? I demand to know!'

Jacqui seized the chance as he took a breath to squeeze in a reply.

'I gave your AI a memory upgrade,' she said, and watched as his face now turned from red to purple.

'So!' he exclaimed eventually. 'You tampered with-'

'I tampered with nothing,' Jacqui said. 'The upgrade was a gift and I simply left it there. I didn't say I wanted anything in return and I didn't change your AI in any way that would interfere with it doing its job. If I had been a genuine threat to your household systems, your Dober- your AI would have been just as capable of dealing with me. In fact, it will now be slightly better at dealing with such threats.'

She didn't say that the point was, beforehand, his AI had viewed *everything* out in the net with blanket paranoia. Now it could get on with dealing with genuine dangers, because she had been nice to it and it knew she wasn't a risk.

'But I bought that AI specifically to keep people like you out! I want to live in peace!'

'Then if you don't want marketing flyers, tell your AI not to let them through. I can't stop that and I wouldn't want to.' She remembered Joseph: he would be proud of her, even if she did have her fingers crossed as she said: 'You naturally have a right to make up your own mind, having considered the information available.'

'Well, I choose not to buy your rubbish! I-'

'What does Mrs Wilson think?' Jacqui said sweetly, turning to the other woman. What she thought about the wallpaper, Jacqui didn't know, but body language told her that even docile Irene Wilson was getting annoyed by her husband's attitude.

'I think it's very nice,' she said. 'Payments are very reasonable, dear, and-'

'I don't care about the payments! I'm not making any! I'm not letting this ... this ... pirate into my account!'

'You don't have to, dear,' Mrs Wilson said. 'It's my treat to myself and it'll come out of my allowance.' She looked Jacqui squarely in the eye. 'I accept your offer, Jacqui. Now, remind me, thirty-six monthly payments ...?'

When Jacqui got home there were over twenty new appointments logged on her terminal.

* * *

There was a stranger in the Warren Court net; something in the way the icon moved told Jacqui, a veteran after a month's familiarity with the environment, that the user wasn't used to being here. It was an odd icon, a bit like a chess rook.

Sales were piling up; she had just about handed over to the sales team who would be handling the franchise from now on. Custom Homes' confidence in her had been justified and her reputation had soared no end. She was in a good mood and had time to kill, so she went up to the stranger.

'Hello,' she said.

'Hello!' it said. 'Do you live here?'

'No, I just work here.'

'Oh, what a shame! Listen, you've heard about the trouble they're having in the former CIS? I'm here to talk to people about-'

Now Jacqui could place the routine, and the icon. It was a watchtower.

'Thanks, but no thanks,' she said. 'I'm just passing through.'

So, she thought as she moved off, others were getting the hang of using the net to proselytise. The people of Warren Court were going to be annoyed. The outside world was imposing on their tranquil haven and she couldn't really blame them for being irked. Had her victory been worth it?

Yes, it had. If the people here didn't want to talk to door-to-door missionaries, they just had to tell their AIs to block them. AIs would obey a direct order like that; that was the privilege of the owners.

But the AIs had learnt not to fear. They had learnt trust. Joseph had wanted to teach their human patrons human values; the start had been to teach them to the AIs themselves.

A moment later, the watchtower icon flew past her, spinning out of control, and Jacqui suppressed a smile. Someone had a lot to learn.

About JACQUI THE GIANTKILLER

This story won an accolade in a letter to *Interzone*: it was a 'technical success' as it presented that impossible thing, a sympathetic salesperson. The writer suggested I apply my talents to the ultimate challenge and write about a sympathetic telemarketer. I decided to quit while I was ahead.

This was the last AI story I wrote, and like 'The Data Class' it was an older story that I dusted off and rewrote for the AI universe. It was originally published as just 'Giantkiller'; believe it or not, it was only after it was published that I realised the unintentional pun in calling the protagonist Jacqui. So in my mind, ever since, it's been renamed.

I have to admit to writing this story with my fingers mentally crossed. Joseph is eloquent about the rights and wrongs of door-to-doorers. They can quite reasonably claim the right to present the information, as long as they let the householders claim the right to say 'no thank you', whereupon the salesperson should simply walk away. I might possibly believe this – it's a philosophy based on an unhappy experience at the age of 18 when I was a Kleeneze door-to-door salesman for a couple of months, back in the days when I believed there was such a thing as easy money – but I certainly don't feel it.

Salespeople are a pain in the butt, period; and yet, they too have to earn a living. And they do stop our lives from getting too cosy.

'Giantkiller' came 12th in that year's *Interzone* readers' poll.

THE GREY PEOPLE

There was a breeze at the top of the tower, of course. Even when the day below was still and warm, up here the air would always move, gentle and cool.

Malcolm Lloyd squinted up at the deep blue sky that vaulted the top of the tower where he and the rest of the tour party stood. The cathedral spire, the tallest in Britain, sprouted from the top of the tower and soared up towards heaven. The recent restoration work had left it gleaming new.

Malcolm looked down, very carefully, over the parapet at the roof of the west transept of Salisbury Cathedral below. It was a long way down. He was suspended between heaven and Earth on a platform of medieval stone. He put out a hand and felt its comforting solidity. The platform was well-anchored in reality.

'Just look at these carvings,' said a voice in his ear. He slid an arm round Caroline's waist; she snuggled up to him in a reflex that had become automatic over the last thirty years.

'Aren't there a lot of them?' she said. There were the usual gargoyles at the corners of the tower: elsewhere the stonework was covered with vague forms that could have been saints or sinners, blurred by the centuries of weathering.

'Frightens off the evil dark,' Malcolm said. 'The church didn't have a lot of faith in its own ability to ward off wickedness so it called in outside help.'

'It must have taken ages to do.'

'The guide will know how long,' said Malcolm.

'Why did they go to all this trouble? No one ever came up here to see them.'

'Ah, but God could see them.' Malcolm knew he was slipping into his lecture theatre tone again, but it was an old habit. 'God would know there weren't any carvings up here and the stonemasons would know that God would know.' He looked at the carvings thoughtfully. Kindred souls, those long-dead masons. Kindred souls. They knew that the cathedral wouldn't be complete without these carvings. They understood.

'Whatever you say.' Caroline could tell that her husband was sinking into a philosophical mood. She turned her attention back to the guide, who was talking about Christopher Wren's modifications to the building.

Malcolm shut his ears to the guide's professional rambling and studied the stone again. He had been too intent on the vaunted view to notice the carvings at first; they were so much part of the cathedral, they were what you expected. He reached out a hand and caressed one, savouring the love and attention that the man who had carved it had put in to it.

He was all alone. The quiet suddenly pressed in on him and he looked around quickly. The party had vanished and he was completely on his own up here. Then he saw the guide lurking just inside the door to the staircase, and he sighed. Silly to get so worked up ...

THE GREY PEOPLE

He hurried to join the rest of the party shuffling down the narrow spiral staircase that led into the heart of the tower.

'Come on,' Caroline said. 'Let's see how the Menial's doing.'

* * *

The Menial was a student from the technical college named Ted, who shared the bibliophilia of his employers. He sat in front of a computer in one corner of The Agora, a converted shoe shop in Salisbury's New Canal. Its purchase had been lubricated by the golden handshake that had been Malcolm Lloyd's reward for three decades of academic service and now it was halfway through its transformation into the literary and academic emporium that Malcolm and Caroline dreamed of. 'Blackwells of Oxford, Heffers of Cambridge, stand back. Here comes The Agora of Salisbury,' Malcolm had joked. The grand opening was a month away.

'Hi y'all,' Ted said affably as they let themselves in. His eyes didn't stray from the computer screen as he finished adding the details of the book on the table next to him. The database files would not only help keep track of stock but would eventually be loaded into the desktop publisher so Ted could set the shop's first catalogue. 'So, did you like it?'

'Very much, yes,' said Caroline.

'Quite excellent,' Malcolm conceded. One of Ted's other titles was the Native Guide, born and bred in deepest Wiltshire. He had recommended that they go and see the cathedral in the first place, to take a break from setting the shop up. He himself had cheerfully spent a hot Saturday afternoon putting book titles onto the computer.

'Should think so too,' Ted said with a grin. He put the now-classified book on top of the pile on his right and picked up another from the pile on his left. He began to tap away at the keyboard again.

Malcolm sidled his way across to look over Ted's shoulder. He had been less than happy about purchasing the machine, but had reluctantly agreed that nowadays any small business needed one. He had also been less than happy about hiring a student to help out – his opinion of the breed had never been high even when he had been paid to lecture them – but Ted was intelligent and friendly and hard working. Even better, he was ready to work for peanuts, willing to work Saturdays and knew more about making the machine work than Malcolm and Caroline put together. He had helped with its purchase and had bullied the various salesmen without mercy on the Lloyds' behalf.

Malcolm just about had the hang of data entry. It was almost self-explanatory. He watched Ted work to convince himself that he had it right. Type the title, press RETURN. Type the author, press RETURN. Type-

He blinked. 'Hey!'

Ted looked innocently up at him. 'Hey?'

'Hey. What happened? It ... well ...'

Ted had touched one key and words had appeared in half the fields on the screen. The hard disk had whirred and the computer was waiting for the next book to be entered.

'Oh, that's easy, Mr Lloyd. All the books in this pile have the same category details, see; I enter title, author, price and ISBN but the rest of the fields all have exactly the same stuff in them. So, I set this key here to type it all out in the right places, automatically. It's very easy. It's called a macro.'

Malcolm swallowed hard and hoped that Ted would not see him sweating. 'No effort at all, really,' he said.

Ted was impervious to the forced levity. 'No, not really.'

'Frightening,' Malcolm muttered.

They made a pot of tea and, when Ted joined them, Malcolm took the opportunity to study him covertly. The speed with which they had acquired the Menial discomfited Malcolm. They had been at a drinks party to introduce them to Salisbury society; one of the guests had mentioned to Caroline that another guest had a son very keen on getting in to the book trade, what did she think, come and be introduced ... Ted had turned up on their doorstep the next day. So far it had been Caroline who had dealt with him the most and Malcolm trusted in her judgement, but, well ...

Malcolm finally decided he liked what he saw. Ted reminded him of their own two children. He was young, inexperienced, naive, but a good lad with his heart in the right place. Give him another forty years, Malcolm mused, and there's hope for the boy.

Ted, though he would never know it and Malcolm could never hope to be understood if he voiced the idea out loud, was like Salisbury Cathedral. He had that look which Malcolm had come to recognise. Everything about him spoke of singularity. His spiky hair, trainers, T-shirt bearing the logo of a Tolkeinesque pop group – Ted was a whole entity, a being with a place in the universe. Everything he did had the unique stamp of *Tedness* about it.

Everyone is special to themselves, of course, but Ted knew it. A million other teenagers might dress that way, but not necessarily because that was who they were. They were the followers; Ted was a leader. Ted knew where he stood in relation to himself and where he stood in relation to the world. He had his life worked out.

Good for you, boy, Malcolm thought. We're going to get on.

'Sorry?' He jerked his head round, guilty because he hadn't been listening. Caroline had said something and he knew she knew he had been elsewhere.

'Keys, dear, keys' she said. 'You were going to get some duplicates cut. For Ted.'

'Oh ...' Yes, he had been. He had said so, several times. He finished his tea in one gulp and rose to his feet. 'I'll do it now. Where can I go, Ted?'

'Ah-' The boy thought. 'There's a while-you-wait place in the mall, you know? Down on the left.'

'See you soon, then.'

* * *

His heart swelled as he walked out into New Canal. The Saturday crowds, at this time of year mostly awestruck Americans gaping at buildings older than their country, were thinning and his way was unimpeded. This was it! His eye took in the architecture: a range of styles from Stuart to Victorian, even with some black-and- white Tudor fronts thrown in as well. A town with history, with individuality, dominated by the bulk of the cathedral that nestled at the centre and which cast its aura over the community around it. Safety.

He turned into the mall. It was a modern thing and he assumed it was an old Salisbury street or alley way, entirely refurbished for pedestrians only. It had recently been post-modernised from its original sixties concrete. Different coloured stone, a cobbled effect, refacing of the shops along it – a medley of Italianate styles, architectural frills, bells and whistles serving no useful purpose whatsoever. He squared his shoulders and walked down it, trying not to wince at the computerised techno-music blaring out from a shop on his right, looking for the key shop. In the corner of his eye a flash of grey-

He stopped, so suddenly that a woman close behind him bumped into him. He apologised, watched her walk away, and looked again at-

-a slab of concrete. Grey concrete that had escaped the facelift. What else? He half- smiled and carried on walking. Then he saw the grey flash again.

As usual, it was in the corner of his eye but never there when he turned his head. The Grey People had always been there, just an infinitesimal unit of measurement away from reality, eager to renew their acquaintance. He hadn't seen them since coming to Salisbury, until now. It had been too good to last.

He shut his eyes and thought hard of the cathedral, the carvings there, the wealth of particularity that made it-

The grey blur vanished but he could sense the protest of its denizens. They would be back: he knew the pattern of behaviour too well. Whenever they found an opening they took full advantage and, if beaten once, they mustered all their strength to return.

They left him alone while he was in the shop. They rarely confronted him when he was with someone, preferring the times when he was on his own – though he could often see them even when he was with others, lurking, waiting. Caroline was the safest guard against them. She embodied a full, happy marriage; a life together – countless memories, facts, events that the two had shared. Caroline had never seen the Grey People but she could banish them by her presence alone.

The keys were cut, the money parted with. There is only so long you can linger in a key-cutting shop. Malcolm reluctantly stepped out into the mall.

So far, so good. He was fiddling with his wallet, trying to fit his credit card into its place and keep the receipt from fluttering away, and not looking ahead. Then some instinct made him look up.

A fuzzy cloud of nothing was swooping down on him, eating up everything before it. The mall was gone already and the passers-by walked blindly into its oblivion. And there, at the front, were the Grey People, eagerly reaching out, delighted to welcome their old friend back.

He turned and broke into a run, round the corner of the mall towards the far end, and just beat them into the High Street. This was still old Salisbury, Olde Worlde, everything the Grey People hated, and they balked at the invisible barrier between them. They gestured angrily. Breathing heavily, Malcolm started at a quick walk the long way round back to The Agora and stopped in his tracks as grey began to spill out in front of him. It was moving along a line of sloppily-laid tarmac. The workman who had put that down hadn't thought about it, hadn't cared, and the Grey People were using his lack of spiritual commitment for their own gain. Now they lay between him and The Agora. They radiated glee at having him trapped.

Don't panic, think straight, don't panic, think straight. The grey haze lay across the street, but it wasn't moving. The Grey People were uncomfortable in the High Street. Then, slowly, the greyness began to move towards him again.

Malcolm turned about and his heart leapt. Ahead lay the gates into the cathedral close. That would show them. He began to walk, occasionally glancing behind him. The Grey People were approaching and stepping up speed; they could sense his plan and they were angry. Malcolm began to bump into people again, at first muttering 'sorry' and then not bothering.

The greyness was spreading down the sides of the street and he had to walk in the gutter as a compromise between avoiding his enemy and avoiding the oncoming traffic. The side streets, too, were tinged with nothingness.

Then he was approaching the gates. By now he was walking straight down the middle of the street, ignoring the cars, noticing with satisfaction how the Grey People were suffering from the closeness of the cathedral. Now the greyness was too insubstantial for a Grey Person to come close to him: its tendrils reached out for him from either side of the street but turned transparent, then disappeared entirely as the gates came closer. Then he was through the gates and into the cathedral close, and the vast building's stone bulk was ahead of him. He shut his eyes and luxuriated in its glow of detail, of workmanship, then turned round and looked behind him. The Grey People had vanished.

Feeling weak at the knees, Malcolm found a telephone box and dialled The Agora's number.

'Agora Bookshop?'

'Hello, love, it's me. I'm holed up in the Close. Can you come and get me?'

There was silence. Then, 'Oh, dear, it's not-' Malcolm smiled as Caroline stopped, knowing that Ted was in earshot.

'Yes, it's them,' he said. 'They were in the mall. Ted wasn't to know.'

'All right,' said Caroline, 'I'm on my way. Give me five minutes.'

* * *

They had to wait for Ted to leave to discuss it, but the lad only had another hour to go that day. He seemed to sense their tension and when he bade them goodnight he appeared quite glad to go.

Malcolm insisted on making another cup of tea. Caroline couldn't wait that long.

'I thought we'd left them,' she said as Malcolm filled the kettle. Malcolm deliberately turned the tap off and plugged the kettle in before answering.

'We can't leave them, my love,' he said gently. 'They go where I go.'

'But-'

'I was over confident,' he said. 'That's all.' The Grey People had at least had to try to break in to the mall. Even though hundreds like it were popping up all over the country, it was impossible for the process to be done carelessly. The architects would have spent considerable time on the job; people would have spent time and attention on the aesthetics of the place; the whole thing was an effort by the city of Salisbury to smarten itself, to take pride in its appearance. What had let the Grey People in had been what was in the mall itself. No doubt the shops there also spent time and attention on their image, on their goods, on how to present themselves to the public, but the trap lay in the tools they used. He remembered the thumping bass that had pulsated out into the mall. The shops chose to make themselves special by turning to mediocrity.

'How can you ever be confident when you never know where they'll turn up?' she raged, whether at him, or at the Grey People who she had never seen, or at life in general, he didn't know. 'Why can't they be consistent?'

She had never seen them, but she had seen their effect on him. It had been on a field trip from Cambridge.

He had met and fallen in love with her as a postgraduate student, and she had interpreted his defences against the Grey People – his love for old things, good workmanship, attention to detail – as endearing eccentricities. He hadn't mentioned his enemies and the two had had a comparatively normal relationship. After a year or so they began to drift apart and then, on a field trip, he had been careless and the Grey People had struck him down.

His skin still crawled at the memory. First, the cold, slick nothingness that enveloped him. Then, advancing out of the fog with joy on their faces, came the Grey People and they *ate* him – took away his thoughts, his memories, his identity.

Caroline had found and rescued him and nursed him back to normality. It wasn't immediately obvious how the Grey People had damaged him; it was only every now and then that gaps in his memory became apparent. Like when she had had to drive them back to Cambridge – he could remember the way but he had forgotten how to drive.

It was better than the first time they had got him, when he was just six. His distraught parents had picked him up from the hospital where the policeman who had found the wandering, dazed child had taken him. It was months before he was as back to normal as he ever came. But he had been hurt. He knew his name, he could walk and talk – other than that, his first six years of life had vanished forever.

But he remembered the Grey People. From then on, they had been his enemies. He hated them as only a six-year-old can.

They had stayed with him, all through his adolescence and teens and even in university, though they had had to fight hard to break into Cambridge. That being so, he had stayed there, knowing when he was on to a good thing. The academic life had suited him and he was offered a fellowship. He celebrated by marrying Caroline.

There were other attacks but they had only been close shaves – the Grey People had never again been able to get at him personally. He had a family – Caroline and the children, Diana and Gordon. His friends and colleagues (and Malcolm took care to associate with the kind of people who could keep the Grey People away). And a life full of a million little carefully wrought idiosyncrasies and habits.

But time passed, nothing stood still. Gordon and Diana had left home to start their own adult lives, friends had moved on and it had been time for a change. After thirty years, even Cambridge was becoming cosy and untenable, so the decision was made to up sticks and move themselves. Somewhere they would enjoy, yet somewhere sufficiently new to present a challenge, to keep them on their toes – to prevent them from letting down their guard.

'Look,' Malcolm said, 'you know what the Grey People are like-'

'I just know what you've found out and you admit you've made mistakes,' said Caroline. 'Supposing you're wrong this time? How do you know they won't find another loophole to get at you-'

'They won't, I promise, love,' Malcolm said. 'Now, I've thought about it, and I know how to make safeguards. For a start there's the shop layout ...'

* * *

A magician used to warding off demons with occult signs and symbols might have recognised the layout of The Agora. Every area was guarded by carefully-positioned clusters of books that Malcolm Lloyd was certain would be anathema to the Grey People. They covered all subjects; Malcolm felt they added to the slightly *ad hoc* atmosphere that any good bookshop should have. What they had in common was their manufacture. They were the leather-bound volumes, hand- manufactured, printed on thick vellum. New or second-hand, relevant or completely out-of-date, Malcolm didn't care. They worked.

They were more than enough to balance the effect of the mass-produced paperbacks that actually brought in the money. Malcolm winced inwardly when he saw the rows of gleaming uncreased book spines in the paperback section. To counter them he had decided to open up a section for second-hand paperbacks as well, sensing that these would offer more resistance to the Grey People than copies fresh off the presses – books barely touched by human hand, never having had the love or commitment given to them by a reader that would invest them with that quality of *bookness*.

Opening day was approaching and Ted was working even harder on the computer, this time at a crateload of second-hands that had just come in. Malcolm had expected the computer to be a channel for the Grey People and had kept the area around it well protected with books, trusting in them and in Ted's precision and care to keep the Grey People well away from the machine; then Ted, quite of his own accord, had described software compilation to him. Thousands of lines of code, each one exactly right and in the proper place. The Grey People, Malcolm had decided, would come nowhere near something so carefully wrought as a computer program.

'You haven't half got some rubbish here, Mr Lloyd,' Ted said cheerfully.

'It pays the bills, Ted.' Malcolm came over to see what there was and had to agree. Lurid covers with implausible spaceships, dragons fighting it out with sultry and scantily-clad maidens. He peered further into the box and his heart pounded at a flash of grey.

'Maybe we should get rid of it all,' he said quickly. Ted frowned up at him.

'You've got some good stuff too, Mr Lloyd,' he said. Malcolm blinked again at the greyness and smiled to himself. Like a mouse in a cage, it was running around in the box but could not break out into the shop. There was nowhere near enough for a Grey Person to appear. The protection worked.

'Read a lot of it, do you?' he asked.

'Yeah, a bit.'

'Show me. Make a couple of piles, the good stuff and the bad.'

Malcolm came back some minutes later to inspect the results. One pile was significantly larger than the other and feelers of grey danced up and down it.

'That's the bad pile,' Ted said. Malcolm leaned casually against a shelf of rare first editions to earth himself.

'Pass me the one on top, will you?' Ted was too polite to register surprise at the request and passed up a title. Malcolm took it, ready to drop it immediately if the grey in it got out of control.

''Book Seven in the Epic Saga of the Cycle of ...'' he murmured, studying the cover, then glanced at the back. ''The Evil God is slain and the King is restored to his throne, but now the Dark is rising once more and a young farm boy from the furthest corner of the Empire must face ...' No wonder the last owner got rid of it.' He tossed it back on to the pile. 'Right, Ted, this lot can go straight out the back.'

Ted stared. 'You won't even try to sell it?'

'I wouldn't inflict it on anyone.' Malcolm could see the doubt in the boy's face and resorted to bribery. 'And, Ted, I appoint you Agora monitor for this kind of stuff. You get to approve every order we make and I only want to stock the good stuff. Agreed?'

'Hey, right!'

* * *

It was finished on a Friday. Caroline was out on some task and Malcolm was in the back room going through publishers' catalogues when he heard a cry of triumph from the front.

'The last one! That's the last one!'

Ted was dancing a jig around the piles of books; he stumbled and stopped with a foolish grin when his employer came through.

'Finished?' Malcolm said.

'Every last one, Mr Lloyd! Every last one! Aristotle to Zola. Arts to ... Zoology. Um ... Annuals to ...'

'All right, all right. Let's see.'

Ted, still flushed with pride, looked on while Malcolm sat down at the computer and called up a few titles at random, just to show that he could. 'You've put a lot of work into this, Ted. Well done.'

'Thanks, Mr Lloyd.'

'In fact, I think a celebration is in order.' Malcolm pulled out his wallet and handed Ted a five pound note. 'You're over eighteen, aren't you? And there's an off-licence just round the corner, I think. I'll trust your judgement, and remember to get a receipt.'

'I'll be right back, Mr Lloyd.' Ted hurried out with the money and left Malcolm alone with the computer ... the shop ... the sanctuary.

He looked lovingly about him. Yes, it really was going to be all right. All the care and attention he and Caroline and Ted had put in ... this was it.

He turned back to the computer and his fingers played over the keyboard at random. He glanced up at the screen and screamed as the Grey People welled out and took him.

* * *

Grey covered him and he floated in its vileness while they came at him, ecstatic at having him in their grasp once more. They touched his clothes and his clothes rotted away. Their hands played over him and his skin began to dissolve. They reached through him, through his blood vessels, through the layers of muscle and fat, deep, deep down into the heart of Malcolm Lloyd.

They reached into his brain and started work on who he was, peeling away his identity like layers of an onion. Biting down the panic that made him want to give up and give in, he recited what he knew, anything at all, keeping it active in his mind where they couldn't get at it.

'I'm ... Malcolm Lloyd. M-Malcolm ... *Arthur* Lloyd. B- born ... born ... September ...'

It vanquished Descartes. *Cogito ergo sum* had no meaning here because, though he might indeed think, his thoughts were as a baby's. Meaningless, uncomprehending. Unimportant. Insignificant.

He felt the cold start at his extremities and work inwards and, like Socrates with his hemlock, he knew that when the cold reached his heart he would be nothing. Malcolm Lloyd would be gone.

It cleared in patches, like mist. Vision returned through rapidly shrinking patches of grey.

('Malcolm!')

He saw whiteness. Dirty whiteness. He stared up at the ceiling, aware of something nearer his eyes.

A face. A person. Love. Warmth. Familiar.

('*Malcolm!*')

His lips moved.

'C ... Ca-'

She helped him up. He was lying flat on the floor, his feet still up on the chair. He had fallen over backwards as the Grey People rushed out at him. There were tears in her eyes.

'It was them again, wasn't it?' she said. He nodded. 'They got in, didn't they? But how ...'

''S'okay,' he mumbled. He felt strength returning as he drew on Caroline's own energy.

'It is not okay! We ... we sell everything, we buy this place, we come for sanctuary, somewhere we can be at peace and yet they're still here ...'

She trailed off and looked up. Malcolm gingerly moved his head and saw a young man standing in the doorway, staring at them with round eyes. A bottle wrapped in green tissue paper dangled from one hand.

The boy was in his late teens or early twenties, of average height. His hair was gelled and he wore a T-shirt and jeans and trainers. All this Malcolm took in at once. He had no idea who the newcomer actually was.

'What's happening?' the boy asked.

'Malcolm's had a kind of turn,' Caroline said, 'but he's better now.'

He knows my first name, Malcolm thought. I should know him.

'Oh no! Can I help? I'll call an ambulance or-'

'No, no,' Malcolm croaked. He held up a hand. 'Help me up, that's all.'

Together they got him into a chair. 'Are you sure you're all right, Mr Lloyd?' the boy asked.

'Take the rest of the day off, um ...' Malcolm gave up trying to remember the name. 'Yes, take the rest of the day off and I'll be fine in the morning. I promise.'

'Ted,' Malcolm said. The name rang no bells at all.

'He's done so much for us, dear,' said Caroline. 'We met his parents at that drinks party.'

'Drinks party?'

'Oh, Malcolm ...'

Malcolm shrugged. 'I'm sorry.' He stood up and paced around the room. Then he went out into the front room of the shop and looked about him. Caroline followed. 'You'll be glad to know I remember all this,' Malcolm said. 'It's The Agora, and I remember thinking how safe it was from the Grey People. So, why isn't it?' He walked back to the computer. 'It's this bloody machine, isn't it?' he said. 'It-'

'No, not that,' Caroline said. 'You told me you'd decided it was safe. Something to do with software.'

'Really?' Malcolm looked surprised. 'Okay, it's not the computer. It's not you or me. It's not the books. Ergo, it must be-'

'Malcolm, no!'

'-Ted.'

'*No!*' Caroline said. 'Malcolm, he can't be! You've always said how pleased you are with him. You said he was careful, and ... and meticulous, and ... and everything the Grey People aren't.'

'I liked him?'

'You liked him a lot. He's ... he's a *good boy*, Malcolm. Malcolm, I'm sorry, but it was you.'

'It was not!'

'Shut up and listen, Malcolm Lloyd. Malcolm, for the last thirty years you've been surrounded by ... by a kind of unofficial bodyguard, you know who I mean, and now it's just me. You know that-' She tapped her head '-up here but you don't feel it. You're still living as if all the others were around you, and they aren't.

You got careless. You were so convinced you were safe, you let your mental guard down, and look what happened.'

Malcolm said nothing.

'Malcolm, we need to start recruiting a new bodyguard, now, and Ted should be the first.'

'Ted?' Malcolm said. 'Darling, he's ... he's young. He may be a good boy, maybe I liked him, but ...'

'But?' Caroline said.

'He's ... he's ... *young*.' Malcolm still couldn't think of a word that better conveyed his objections.

'You were young once.' The argument didn't seem to impress Caroline. 'I've seen your birth certificate.'

'Okay, put it this way.' Malcolm was collecting his thoughts. 'Our friends back home – sorry, back in Cambridge – they were ... they were our sort of people, Caroline. And our sort of age. They'd been through life, they knew its ups and downs and slings and arrows, they'd been knocked about a bit. They knew life and they savoured it and they enjoyed it-'

'And Ted doesn't?'

'They had experience, darling. They were on their guard, they didn't let things past them, they-' Malcolm waved a hand in frustration. It was so clear to him. 'They'd grown up. Ted has plenty of potential but he still has some growing to do.'

'I see.' It looked as if he was finally getting through to her. Caroline stood with her arms folded, gazing at the floor. 'Well, dear, Ted's the only one we have, and if he needs to do some growing, if he needs to be knocked about a bit, we've got to start now.'

Malcolm held her gaze for a moment, then looked away. 'Oh, no,' he murmured.

* * *

There were tears in Ted's eyes too, the next morning. 'But ... have I done anything, Mr Lloyd? Is it something wrong-'

'Ted, Ted, you've done nothing wrong, nothing at all,' Malcolm said. It helped that he didn't remember the boy, but he could see it was hurting and he knew the pain that Caroline was feeling, and both those things stung him. 'You'd have to go soon, anyway, when term starts,' he said. 'We're just letting you go a month early. You're young and you should have a life, not be stuck here all the time. You should be out with your friends and your girlfriend. Look, you won't lose out.' He held up a cheque. 'A month's extra pay, and a bonus on top of that, for all the great help you've given us. And, next holidays, there's bound to be a job for you here.'

'If you're sure ...'

'I'm sure, Ted, really.'

'I mean, I could at least finish the day ...' Ted was beginning to sound desperate. 'There's the catalogue to set, and ...'

'It's okay, Ted.' Malcolm tried to spare him the humility of pleading and used the tone which he had used on students to indicate that no further argument was needed or wanted. He saw Ted bite his lip as the realisation finally sank in: he really wasn't wanted any more. Just like that.

'Right,' Ted said. A pause. 'I'll ... I'll be off, then.' He tried to be cheerful, disastrously. 'I'll see you.'

'Remember your cheque, Ted.'

'Oh. Yes. Thanks.' They looked at each other for a long moment. 'Well, 'bye,' Ted said, and left. Malcolm turned and went slowly into the back room. Caroline stood and put her arms round him and they held each other, tight.

'God, that hurt,' Malcolm said.

He could see it from Ted's point of view, but he could see further ahead as well. Two people that the young man had come to regard as friends, who he trusted and who were clearly fond of him in return, had abruptly turned round and slapped him in the face; but he had always regarded them as slightly cracked and perhaps, in the boy's mind, that explained it all. It would add to his character, as pain and hurt always did; it would help him develop and mature and grow as a bulwark against the Grey People. If he came through this then he would be fit for Malcolm's bodyguard.

'It won't last,' Caroline said.

'Doesn't make it any easier.'

That evening, Caroline would go round to Ted's house. She would explain that Malcolm was still affected by his 'turn'. He wasn't thinking straight or behaving normally. But they did want him, they did value his services, and Caroline had talked Malcolm back to reason. So, would he come back? And then it would be up to Ted. If he could swallow his pride, if he could forgive the hurt, wonderful. And after what had happened today, he would always be on his guard. He would always be careful.

If not-

Que sera. Either way, Malcolm would win. If he came back, that was one more for the bodyguard. If he didn't, then the pain of the sacrifice Malcolm had made would hurt the Grey People. They certainly wouldn't be expecting that.

He looked out of the window at New Canal. This was the new battleground. 'I'm going to get you, you bastards,' he murmured. 'Watch me come.'

About THE GREY PEOPLE

'The Grey People' was the seed for my novel *The Teen, the Witch & the Thief*. I can still remember the incident that inspired the story, though it would be several years before I actually wrote it: going up the tower of Salisbury cathedral and having the guide explain about the carvings we found up there. They were every bit as intricate and ornate as the rest of the building, even though no one could possibly see them, because God could see them and the craftsmen couldn't possibly let shoddy work go just because mortal eyes weren't aware of it.

There is a lot of Orson Scott Card's Unmaker in the Grey People, though they are a lot less personal. The Unmaker of Card's *Tales of Alvin Maker* series is more than the Devil: he is entropy, destruction, the obliteration of detail and identity. He is often pictured as water (or else water is his agent) because water is fluid and unfixed, and given time it will wash away anything. It's an effective picture of blankness, and what scares it away is making something: bringing order to chaos, in however small an amount.

This was the second story bought by Paul Beardsley for *Substance* – the one he definitely did read.

And Ted's understanding of computers really was spot on. For the time it was written.

JEAPES JAPES

WINGÈD CHARIOT

The funeral was straight out of a Gothic novel. The wind blew through the churchyard in gusts, up the valley from the sea; the sky was overcast and every surface was damp and slick from the drizzle.

The dead child's family stood around the grave, sheltered by the crowd of fellow villagers. Funerals here were communal events. Two men supported the mother as she wept and the funeral crowd held her in their hearts, but most eyes were on the vicar of St Mary's church who stood at the head of the grave. *See how he shares her pain*, they were thinking. *Listen to his voice catch. Dr Morgan's a good man.*

Dr Morgan knew this and could happily have done without it. He was in Porthperron because the place was all but cut off from civilisation, but as a corollary even people from the village over the hill were as foreign as the French, and almost as distrusted. Napoleon's Grande Armée could ravage Europe and these people would only hear rumours, and suspect anyone from outside the village all the more.

Naturally they were distrustful of their new rector. He was *educated*, they would say, as though explaining a physical deformity that polite people did not comment on. His strange way of speaking was explained, in their broadest West Country, as *city*.

Now they know I'm one of them, Morgan thought, as he buried himself in the final section of the service. *I heard a voice from heaven, saying unto me ...* It would take something like this to make them accept me and my life will be easier from now on. But, of all the things to bring us together, did it have to be a funeral?

'A tragic thing, Dr Morgan. Poor little Anne. A tragic thing,' muttered the verger as he removed his parson's cloak and hung it up to dry.

'Indeed it is, Mr Cole,' Morgan said with the degree of distraction he tended to use towards subordinates who were making conversation. He rubbed his hands. 'Fire lit?'

The vicarage was cold and draughty and Morgan dreaded to think of the damp problems, but it was a sturdy edifice that stood up to the worst the sea wind and the salt spray could throw at it. Once the fire in the study was blazing away the damp was banished and a man could feel quite civilised in the snug, warm atmosphere. Cole had run on ahead to see that the fire was well established in the grate.

'Still, as it says, "I am the resurrection and the life," eh, Dr Morgan?'

'It certainly does, Mr Cole,' Morgan agreed, thinking of the small body lying white and cold on its bed and the obscenely hard mass beneath the soft skin-

'Brandy?' he said. He wished Cole would leave but he felt the man deserved the offer of hospitality. Cole was reasonably bright and had what passed for an education, though his intelligence had been blighted by years of isolation in Porthperron.

'Oh, thank you, Dr Morgan,' Cole said. 'Don't mind if I do.'

The two men sipped their drinks together. Morgan hoped it would take Cole's one-track mind off the subject.

'Poor little mite,' Cole mused, gazing into the depths of the glass. 'Younger than usual, you know. I really respect you for coming to Porthperron, Dr Morgan, knowing our reputation, and your predecessor leaving because he couldn't stand it, and all that. And there'll be more, believe me.'

Of course there will be. Closed community, interbreeding, Morgan thought. No opportunities, no need to move on, to spread the gene pool. A freak mutation, a tendency towards cancer, probably developed within the last century or so and consequently reinforced by said breeding. Not helped by your ancestors siting your village on top of a naturally radioactive pile of granite.

'But there's no fighting it, is there, Dr Morgan?' Cole added.

A shot of carcinophages straight into the heart of the tumour? Not much else. Morgan had to remind himself, once again, of his role in the village. 'Only prayer, Mr Cole, only prayer,' he said.

'Of course, of course, Dr Morgan' Cole said at once. 'Still, I've heard of people cutting lumps out-'

Ye Gods! Morgan thought. In this day and age, before Lister, before anaesthetic? I'd rather die.

'Very probably, Mr Cole,' he said, draining his glass in one go. 'Now, if you'll excuse me-'

'Oh ... ah ... yes.' Cole looked at his glass, still barely touched, perhaps wondering where the vicar learnt to drain a glass of brandy like that. 'Well ... thank you, Dr

Morgan. See you at Evensong. I'll ask Mrs Pentreath to show me out.'

'Goodbye, Mr Cole.'

Morgan woke with a shout echoing in his ears. For a moment he lay, staring into the darkness. The house creaked and breathed around him, but he had grown used to it and it no longer kept him awake at night. He had been dreaming, with a vividness that he had never known in his previous life but was getting used to now. He had been back at his seat at the great black table. All his friends from the Board had sat around him. Poulsen, Carradine, Siedle, all deferring to the figure who sat at the end.

He had known that his guilt was evident to them all. He fairly radiated it. It was unnecessary for the Director to look directly at him, but look at him the Director did. And point.

'Traitor!' Eyes turned on him ...

... and now he felt a sense of devastating loss, a vast emptiness inside him. The Director thought him a traitor, he had lost the goodwill of the man he had worshipped-

No! Reason pushed its way up through the haze of fuddled and sleepy thought that clouded his mind. He had parted with the Director on the best of terms and had never seen the man again. The guilt had come later, with the knowledge that probably none of the others had escaped. Except, perhaps, Carradine ...

His heart slowed and a flood of relief poured over him. A dream, that was all. A dream.

* * *

It was curious that he had ended up in Cornwall again. One of life's little ironies, of the kind that he was getting tired of.

They had honeymooned in Cornwall – his first time in the West Country, land of Jamaica Inn and King Arthur and tin mines. They took a small, self-catering chalet north of the Lizard.

Halcyon days. Pre-Director, pre-pain, pre-guilt. Exploring the coves and bays, trekking on the coastal paths, letting their love blossom. Free, alone, together, long before the days when Security would have known exactly where they were and would have had several agents in the vicinity, just in case.

And, somewhere in that fortnight of bliss, Peggy got started. The child they had wanted, a little earlier than planned but what of it?

Carradine was the first outside the family to be called and he could barely hide his grin. They had last seen each other when Carradine was in a morning suit and white carnation, managing the guests as though to the Best Man's manner born.

'Already?' he said. 'That's what I call fast work! Say, you know that organisation I was telling you about ...'

* * *

Barbara Pentreath was white as a sheet, but fear didn't overcome her natural modesty.

'I couldn't, Dr Morgan!' she protested. 'It ... it wouldn't be right, no, no, it's just a small thing, nothing to worry you with-'

'Mrs Pentreath!' Morgan soothed his housekeeper. He had never been good at keeping his temper in the face of ignorance and unreason, and the practice he had gained in Porthperron was wearing thin. 'Mrs Pentreath, I know about these things. You must let me see, or at least feel.' He knew what it was and so did she, but he had to know how bad.

'Oh, Dr Morgan–' Mrs Pentreath wailed. Morgan's temper snapped.

'Listen, woman, pretend I'm your husband and trust me, right?' Before she could answer he had slipped his hand inside her bodice. She froze, uncertain whether to scream or faint, but he only kept it there a second. It was long enough. A lump where no lump should be, but not yet a large lump.

'Thank you, Mrs Pentreath,' he said, stiff and unbending as he walked back to his desk. Oh God, it followed him everywhere. She stood quaking in front of his desk like a guilty schoolgirl. 'How long?' he asked.

'Oh – two or three days, Dr Morgan,' she said, still not sure whether or not her rector had just assaulted her. Morgan calculated two or three days, plus the days she would have subtracted for fear of being thought to exaggerate, plus the time it would have taken her to pluck up the courage to come and see him, plus the time the lump had taken to become noticeable in the first place ...

'Does Mr Pentreath know?'

'He – it was he who suggested I come to you, Dr Morgan. I don't know why, I just ...' She trailed off in misery.

Why? Morgan thought. Because I'm the vicar, I'm *educated*, I can solve everything. Why can't you people solve your own problems?

He came to a decision and drew pen and paper towards him. 'Thank you, Mrs Pentreath,' he said. 'Send Mr Pentreath in, would you?'

He carefully wrote his name and address at the top of the paper. Then he sat and thought.

You can't do this. Lie low, don't involve yourself ...

... but he was fond of the couple who kept the vicarage for him, as he was fond of all the villagers in his charge. He started writing.

He had no notes or records on him; everything he wrote had to come from memory. He had to think down to the best level that this society could provide, remembering his basic training and extrapolating backwards. He would never get anything of the quality that he was used to; he would have to make do with the merely adequate. The barely adequate.

He looked up at the end of the letter and only then realised that Arthur Pentreath had been standing there for several minutes, patiently waiting for the rector to finish. Morgan neatly folded and sealed the missal without saying anything, and handed the man the finished article. The look in Pentreath's eyes was accusing – perhaps his wife had told him that the rector wasn't doing anything.

'I want this sent to London urgently,' said Morgan. 'Can you do it?'

Pentreath really did look sullen. 'I'll need a cart to get to town,' he said.

Morgan unlocked the safe, careful that Pentreath didn't see precisely how much he had in it, and took out some coins. 'Will this cover it?'

'It will.'

'Then do it.'

***

It was the parting of the ways. The Director's jet had taken off and the rest of the Board had dispersed. He and Carradine were together, as they always had been. They had a pack of supplies, food and medicines, and they took turns carrying it as they picked their way through the ruins and stayed away from the sound of fighting.

'Think he'll make it?' Carradine asked.

'Should do.' They ducked as rockets soared overhead. 'Think *we'll* make it?'

'Should do.' The Sub-Director for Science looked in the direction in which their leader's aircraft had flown. 'You realise that after him, you and I are next on the wanted list?'

'We didn't start the fighting.' A formation of fighters flashed by on the horizon, fortunately in the opposite direction to the Director. 'God, I wish I knew who they were.'

Carradine looked at him askance. 'Never did believe in responsibility, did you? Never did believe in the "all-for-one, one-for-all" principle, hey?'

'Which is why the Director has just fled, leaving us behind!'

'That's a lie!' Carradine roared. 'The Directorate survives for as long as he is alive, and-'

'My God, he's taken you in, hasn't he? You really believe he cares-'

Carradine's fist smashed into his mouth, sending him reeling backwards to trip over a pile of rubble. 'Don't ever, *ever* begin to doubt, you hear me? You think you can stand alone? You ungrateful bastard. He saved us, remember? He gave us all our dreams.

Would you ever have had your clinics to play with without him, hey? It was him who made it all possible! One day, one day, this miserable world will realise what a great man he was, but only if we stick together. Got that? *Got that?*'

He gazed up at his oldest friend. The friend who had got him onto the Board, introduced him to the Director. Blood trickled down his chin. 'We mustn't fight,' he mumbled. 'We mustn't fight.'

They spent the night in a hollow in the ruins. One of them slept.

The other could not. He had his escape planned and he intended to use it. Let Carradine cling to the dream of the Directorate. The Directorate was dead. When Carradine awoke in the morning, the Sub-Director for Health would be gone, taking the pack with him.

* * *

Who could he trust? Very few, very few. Once he would have had an entire hospital staff to draw on. He would have been in an operating room, the most modern, the best. Trained nurses, trained doctors.

Now he was reduced to Pentreath and Cole. One had a vested interest in the matter; the other was loyal to his rector and had seen enough of the world outside Porthperron to take on the new concepts that Morgan introduced.

Against all the odds, he had made them understand the need for chloroform and antisepsis. No one could argue with the need for a patient oblivious to pain, but the idea of tiny little creatures making wounds septic was harder to accept. They simply took his word for it until Morgan removed the lump from Mrs Pentreath and the wound, cleaned with the chemicals that had arrived from London, healed within days. Then they truly *believed*.

Anatomy was different.

Mrs Pentreath's lump had been a simple subcutaneous tumour: other tumours in the village might not be so easy. They would come in all the shapes, sizes and forms that cancer could throw at them. They might require lengthy operations. The tendency, for which Morgan thanked God, was for the tumours to appear in tissue, not organs ... until they metastasised. *That* was usually when people complained of them.

The vicarage study was a poor substitute for a lecture hall but it sufficed. Diagrams, hand drawn by Morgan, hung on the walls. Morgan was pointing to a map of the major blood vessels.

'You can feel your pulse in several places,' he said. 'Wrist, neck. What you feel is the blood pumping through the arteries there. It is vital to remember exactly where the arteries are. Blood spurts out of a severed artery in a stream that could reach across this room. We don't have the equipment to deal with such a situation, so the patient would die.' He put the marker down and unbuttoned his shirt. 'Mr Cole. You'll be doing most of the cutting. Show me the course my aorta takes.'

Cole was wrong by about two inches. Morgan suppressed a groan.

'Wrong, Mr Cole. Wrong, wrong, wrong. It's here. *Here.* You'll go merrily cutting away where you think is safe and there will be yet another funeral!'

Finally he decided he had taught them enough for one night. 'But I must say one more thing, Mr Cole, and you, Mr Pentreath. No one must be told where you learnt these skills. I want the operations performed in the utmost secrecy. The village will know but no outsider must be told, no one who was not born and bred in Porthperron. And the operations must only be performed on tumours, as and when they develop. Now, please, give me your word that this will be so.'

They gave it, reluctantly.

'You're making it sound like you won't be here, Dr Morgan,' Pentreath said, looking him in the eye.

Morgan returned the gaze. *Mr Pentreath, I'm about to introduce an enormous anachronism into this area and you think I intend to hang around?* 'Consider all possibilities, Mr Pentreath.'

'Well, I hope you're staying, Dr Morgan,' Cole said, "cos it's all very well pointing at where your ay-orter should be, but the only way I'm ever really going to learn is by cutting someone up, properly.'

Morgan looked at him for a moment. Then: 'The lesson is over, gentlemen. Thank you for your time. Mr Cole, will you stay behind?'

* * *

'Sir,' Carradine said, 'this is ...'

'Of course, of course!' The Director was a small man, as Napoleon was small, but glowing with an inner energy. The Director took his hand and shook it firmly. It was not the frantic pumping that he was expecting; somehow it was all the more sincere in its brevity.

Their host sat them down. It was the kind of apartment he was expecting – large, comfortable and with a panoramic view of the city lights below.

'Carradine has told me a lot about you,' the Director said. 'You two go back to university days, don't you?'

'Further than that, sir.' *Sir! Was he calling the man Sir already?*

'And I've studied you, ever since Carradine told me you might be interested in joining us. Are you?'

'I am, sir! You've accomplished-' He didn't usually gush but for the first time now could be quite sincere. 'You've accomplished such marvels, such wonders-'

The Director waved a hand in modest self-deprecation. 'One day I'll tell you how,' he said. 'But let's start with you. You are ... um ... is *unorthodox* the right word? Yes, unorthodox in your outlook.'

The blood rushed to his face. He blurted out, he could not help it: 'I'm unorthodox, sir, because I tell the truth! I can save lives, I can help like no other surgeon has done! Hippocrates never even knew about genetics, so why should some archaic oath in his name prevent us from doing what is needed to study the subject? Don't they realise the good that ...'

He saw the cool amusement on the Director's face and the horror on Carradine's, and he bit his tongue in mid-rant. He lowered his voice back to its more usual tones. 'I tell them that and they disagree, sir,' he muttered. 'That's all.'

The Director was nodding, slowly, wisely. 'Let me tell you about a man in torment,' he said. 'A noble, clever man who is prevented from doing what he knows he must. He knows the pain of cutting someone open, looking at the damage, then quietly sewing the patient back up and giving him a pat on the head and telling him that chemotherapy can do wonderful things nowadays.

'And then a blow is struck right into the heart of his family. He diagnoses his own daughter's condition and is powerless to help-'

'Stop it!'

'-his marriage crumbles-'

'Shut up!'

The Director's eyes were shrewd. 'You know this man?'

'You know I do! You know-'

'Yes, I know. I told you I studied you.' The Director was up and pacing about. 'Listen. I want to make you an offer. A place on the Board. Sub-Director for Health. Complete charge of our medical research programme, all our resources at your disposal and no ethical committees to fuss over you. Interested?'

He felt the ground giving way under him. His heart pounded, his head swam. 'Sir!' he said. 'If you ... if you think I could ...'

'Good!' The Director moved over to the drinks cabinet and retrieved three glasses. Already filled – the Director had known he would take the offer. 'You're on the Board as of now. Congratulations.'

They drank to the future.

'I got you just in time, to tell the truth,' the Director said, swirling the wine in its glass. 'I wanted all the Sub-Directorships filled in time for the next move.'

'Sir?' Both he and Carradine were attentive now. The Director stood with his back to them, to gaze out of the large studio window at the lights of the city.

'At present,' he said, 'we have money and influence but little else. It's time to expand.

'I'll tell this to the Board tomorrow, so keep it quiet until then. In three days time I will make an offer to the western governments. "Let me help you. The

Directorate will run your economies for you."' He turned back to them and gave a crooked smile. 'We couldn't do it worse than them. I think they'll accept.'

* * *

Cole had gone pale.

'Dr Morgan, really?'

'You said it yourself, Mr Cole. The only way to learn.'

'Yes, but ...' The verger stared at Morgan. Morgan's knowledge had inspired a hero-worship in the man and now Morgan wondered if he had gone too far in depending on it.

'Mr Cole, I genuinely want you to learn how to fight the cancer,' he said. 'Don't you want to be part of this healing process? Don't you?'

'But ... dead ...'

'Dead, and of natural causes. An unmutilated body, and we've only just buried her. She won't have decayed yet. Once you have been properly tutored, we will have her reburied. The thought is distasteful, but if you think this is the only way you can learn, we must do it.

'I-'

'Mr Cole, you yourself said it was a tragic thing, her dying. This way it can have some use for all the people who loved her!'

Cole looked miserably at Morgan. 'When?'

'This evening. We can put her in the crypt. No one will see.'

Anne Tresidder, died aged 7 years and two months, beloved daughter and so forth. The two men soon found the grave in the dark. It was only two days old and easily re-excavated.

Morgan pried the coffin lid off and managed to stand it upright. He had been holding his breath and now he breathed experimentally through his nose to test the air. It was as fresh as it was going to be.

'Shouldn't you wear a mask, sir?' came a whisper from above. Cole was remembering his hygiene lecture. 'Stop you catching the same thing off her.'

'You can't get cancer that way,' Morgan snapped. He stooped to pick up the light, wasted body and passed it up. 'Here, take her.'

Anne Tresidder was transferred to a slab in the crypt and the two ran quickly out to refill the grave. Cole applied the final touches to make the mound seem natural, then went back to the crypt to start with a ghoulish eagerness on his first practical anatomy lesson.

He was a natural surgeon, Morgan realised with a grudging admiration. His methods would never be approved by the Royal College of Surgeons but they were sufficient for the task in hand. His patients would be scarred for life but they would be alive.

Cole sliced through the layers of skin and muscle like a natural, gaily using just the right strength to expose each successive layer – the trapezius, the deltoid, the pectoralis major; merrily delving into the depths of Anne Tresidder's body to reveal the secrets that he had never known existed. He saw the vital organs: the liver and the stomach, nestling side by side below the lungs; behind them, the heart and the kidneys. Morgan told him what they did and where they went, and kept an eye on what he was doing, making sure that he was never so heavy-handed as to kill a live patient from shock. The purpose, he had to remind his verger, was to save lives, not to cut people for the fun of it.

Cole would never be able to handle more than the simplest cases with any guarantee of success, and heaven help any patient with a lump in a major organ, but it would do. Another few lessons and Morgan would have an apprentice as prepared as could be hoped. Someone who would eventually take his place.

'Enough,' he said. 'Come back to the vicarage.'

* * *

All who convert to, or become apostates from, a cause have a moment of epiphany. In this case, it had been the discovery that the Director was, after all, fallible. The man had thought that he could fool his benefactors.

The Directorate had always been advanced scientifically, but after it took control the lid was taken off to a select few – the Board – and knowledge really started pouring out, a cornucopia for every Sub-Director. For the Sub-Director for Health: a complete map of the human genome; the artificial synthesis of any form of DNA; strict algorithms determining the placement of chromosomes ... If all the other Sub-Directors were getting this level of stuff for their own departments, he had reasoned; if this treasure-trove of data was coming in, then surely, *surely* the Director would not dare throw it all away again. Surely he would not antagonise his patrons. They had all been there at that meeting of the Board when the Director finally revealed exactly what was happening, and they had all heard the warnings.

But no. The Director was greedy, his former protectors had decided that the Directorate had to be stopped and the Directorate's enemies had been happy to oblige.

Hence the war. And so, he had created the AI. A tiny little searcher, barely distinguishable from the myriad that roamed the Net. It was innocuous enough to brave even the portion of the Net controlled by the enemy.

It took time but after weeks of patient search it came up with the best of all the possible options. W. Morgan, D.D. (Oxon.); a clergyman who took over the parish of Porthperron and who made no further impact on the world. He might have died thirty years later, he might have died the next day. That information had been lost. Dr Morgan was a man of utter historical inconsequence, a man with a minimal impact on time and space. No sign of any marriage, not even a recorded death. An open-ended future. So if a man were to masquerade as Morgan, he could keep his head down, do nothing and never have to worry about conforming to predetermined events. Morgan was one of history's nonentities. Perfect.

He tucked the information away in one corner of his mind and quietly made plans.

* * *

Reaction set in, back in the sane surroundings of the vicarage. Cole's hands shook. He was high on adrenaline and fatigue.

'I can't believe it, Dr Morgan,' he kept repeating. 'I can't believe it. We ... we cut her, we-'

Morgan soothed him, placing a large glass of brandy in the man's hands and sitting him down. 'There's a book you won't have read, Mr Cole,' Morgan said. *'Claudius the God.'*

Cole looked blank. 'The Emperor Claudius?'

'The same. He asks about his personal surgeon. Where did the man learn his skills? "From your brother, Caesar," he is told. "My brother wasn't a surgeon," Claudius protests. "No, Caesar," he is told, "your brother was a successful general, who fought many campaigns and left many bodies." Or words to that effect. The Emperor's own surgeon learnt his trade by cutting up corpses on the battlefield. How else did anyone ever get to learn about surgery? And you did so well!'

'I did, didn't I?' Cole looked down at his glass, then back at Morgan. His mouth twitched into a smile. 'It – it's wonderful, really, isn't it? Like the powers of a god.'

'The human body is a wonderful thing, Mr Cole, and it's a privilege to help it.' (Listen, Cole, I've looked at the building blocks of life. I've played with them, rearranged them. I could never take human beings seriously again. And now you've got it too.)

'Why are you leaving, Dr Morgan?' Cole asked suddenly. The brandy was giving him a confidence he didn't usually have. 'You could stay here and do the operations. The folk would love you, you know.'

'What gives you the idea I'm leaving, Mr Cole?' Morgan said quietly.

'Oh, everything! You're always talking like you won't be here.'

'Mr Cole, I'm just urging you to secrecy.'

'But why, Dr Morgan? If you know these things you should ... you should tell others!'

'I know, but my fame would spread and people would hear of me, and that would be bad. There are other people who want to find me and kill me.'

'But why?' Cole persisted. 'You're a saint, Dr Morgan. The things you could do. What did you do to these people?'

'I cured their cancer and I did ... other things.' He bit his lip to shut himself up.

'Other things? What things?'

'I worked for a man who asked me to help him.' Morgan found himself seduced by the mixture of brandy and a warm, attentive audience for the first time in years. 'Would you believe, people who can breath underwater?' Virtually undetectable by sonar. 'Or live in a vacuum?' Ideal for satellite work. 'All that.'

'Oh, you're having me on, Dr Morgan.' Cole waved his hands about vaguely. 'But whatever you did, all those clever things, they must have really loved you! You've come from heaven, Dr Morgan. You're a saint.'

'Yes, well, they didn't want to do those things. That was the problem.'

'I don't understand you, Dr Morgan. I really don't.'

Morgan gave a wan smile. 'Do you know how to make God laugh, Mr Cole?'

'Er ... can't say I do, Dr Morgan.'

'Tell him your plans, Mr Cole. Tell him your plans.'

Cole sat absorbing this wisdom in silence, until Morgan yawned. 'Two hours to dawn, Mr Cole. We should get some sleep.'

'Of course, Dr Morgan.'

* * *

It was the *way* that they were defeated that hurt so much. He wasn't much involved in the actual strategy so he only picked up rumours, but what rumours!

Captured prisoners who had never heard of the Directorate and were convinced they were fighting someone else ...

... who spoke no language known on Earth ...

... who had never heard of *other captured prisoners* either ...

Then there was the way that the enemy were never where they were supposed to be; or a strike would be launched against a division said to be in such-and-such a place, verified by satellite, but which suddenly *wasn't*; or a whole new army would appear out of nowhere, again usually with only the vaguest idea of who it was fighting.

Every conceivable enemy that the Directorate might have had, it did have. One day, he found out why.

* * *

He had thought long and hard about it. He had agonised over every point in his argument.

He liked it in Porthperron. It was good for him. A man with his knowledge and experience could help these honest, unsophisticated people in a thousand small, unimportant ways that all added up. He liked having his self-respect back.

Yet at his back, he always heard ... *them.* What could they do with time? He had no idea, but he could imagine. He could picture shock waves from his actions in Porthperron rippling up and down the timelines. He could imagine *them* sensing it and coming for him.

He had to leave. Cole was coming on fine – Morgan had set him some exercises on a couple of fresh bodies, pretending that there were growths on the lungs, on the stomach, in the neck. The man could cope, just, and should improve with practice.

An unexplained disappearance would be careless. It would cause ripples. People would hear of it and it would certainly find its way into written records. What Morgan planned was far better. A sudden killing, perfectly explicable and entirely unmysterious. And the best of it was, his conscience need not groan under yet another death for no one need actually die.

He steered his cart along one of the twisty, narrow lanes that held this far-flung county together. As far as Porthperron was concerned he was riding into St Austell for a day or two. What little he could plausibly take with him was in the back; mostly clothes, but also a spade and some lamp oil. And, of course, the gold that he had brought with him from the Directorate. Without that he was nothing, in any time.

He came to the right place, about five miles out of the village. He tied the horse up and left the cart by the wayside. The spot he wanted was a short distance from the road. The charred patch where he had burnt his clothes had disappeared, washed away in the rain. The mound was still there, under a gorse bush.

He thought again of Anne Tresidder as he dug the body up. It was only a few feet down. The real Dr Morgan emerged into the daylight again and his replacement began to clothe the body in his own garments. They were an imperfect fit but the oil would make that incidental. Decomposition and the total lack of facial similarity would also become a small matter in the blaze.

He had regretted the killing at the time, but what else could he do? One more death, just one more, and that would be all. No one else need die at his hands, ever again. The device that Carradine and his team had covertly assembled and which had brought doom on the Directorate had worked well; it had dumped him almost at this spot, close to the road that his research showed Morgan would have taken as he arrived in Porthperron. He had waved the man and his horse down ...

Anyone finding the anonymous body would have blamed it on robbers, and that part of the plan still held. Poor Dr Morgan, waylaid by highwaymen and burnt in an attempt to get rid of the evidence.

He pulled on his stout walking boots and stood, reaching for the oil. A clap of thunder blew him to the ground again.

Groggily he looked up and shook his head. A dazed figure ten feet away from him was also climbing to his feet. Whoever the man was, he had been through hard times, to judge by the grime on his face and his tattered suit-

'Carradine!' Morgan blurted. The figure blinked at him.

'Hi.' The voice was harsher than he remembered. 'Didn't get very far, did you?' Carradine, once Sub-Director for Science, looked down at the body. 'Who's this poor sod, then? Someone else you ran out on?'

'Carradine, what-'

'Oh, don't bother.' Carradine sat down and looked immensely tired. 'I've gone through the stage of wanting to kill you. I'd have done the same in your place.' He shook his head. 'The time displacer! Why didn't I think of that?' He looked almost admiring. 'I designed the thing, didn't I? The perfect escape. Well, maybe not perfect. They tracked you down and sent me after you.'

'They?'

'The Home Time people, you cretin! They said charges would- ... oh, hell. Look. Apparently we had already surrendered, that night you ran out. It would only have been a matter of time before we were found. Well, I was found and I was identified. They'd already captured the Institute – you must have been just ahead of them when you got there. The coordinates on the displacer were still set for the nineteenth century, so they knew someone had used it, and they could guess who. And they sent me after you, because I could identify you. Which I have done. And now, old buddy, we are returning to the ex-Directorate, where *you* will face the music and all charges against *me* will be dropped.'

Slowly, Carradine drew a gun from out of his jacket. His tone had been jocular but there was no sign of their old friendship in his eyes.

Morgan swallowed but for some reason felt no urge to flee or fight. This seemed strangely right to him. 'How do we get back?' he said.

'These coordinates will be swamped with a recall field every 24 hours until we turn up. Since I don't fancy spending 24 hours in this hole, I suggest you take us somewhere. Where's the nearest town?'

'Porthperron is thirty minutes in that direction, but I've just left-'

'Take us there, then.'

'I said, I've just left-'

The gun whirred ominously as Carradine touched the cocking stud. A bullet had fed into the launch chamber and was pointing directly down the barrel at Morgan's heart.

'I'll take you,' Morgan said quickly. 'Just don't wave that thing about where it can be seen,' he added.

* * *

'I thought you were chief god botherer here,' Carradine said as they came into the village. Morgan hauled up the cart and frowned. A funeral procession was heading slowly down the main street. There hadn't been one of those scheduled.

Then his eyes widened in horror. A priest waited at the entrance to St Mary's; a man who he had last seen lying decomposed, five miles outside Porthperron.

'It can't be!' he yelped, jumping down from the cart and running towards the column. He caught up with them just as they entered the churchyard. 'Cole! Mr Cole! What the hell is this?'

Cole didn't look at him, didn't even blink.

'Pentreath! Arthur Pentreath!' His housekeeper's husband was carrying the coffin and showed the same lack of reaction. The man's eyes were red and wet, and Morgan felt a suspicion inside him like a lump of lead.

'No, not-'

The procession reached the gate to the graveyard and passed through it. He followed them in and saw the gravestone. Barbara Pentreath, beloved-

'Oh God, no!' he screamed.

'Look,' he heard Carradine say. The man was pointing at the gate. It had been opened for the procession and still stood open, *and shut*. Carradine opened the gate and it merged with the gate that stood open. Carradine shut it and again there were two gates.

Morgan crouched and pulled up a handful of grass. It was there in his hand, and yet still in the ground.

'They can't see us,' said a familiar voice in his ear. Carradine had followed him and his face was ashen. 'Those ... those two-timing bastards! They've diddled with time, they've cut us both off, they've stranded us ...'

'Correct,' said a voice behind them. 'We did warn you.'

They turned round. A hawk-faced woman, age indeterminate, stood a few feet away from them. They had seen her before because it had been she that far-off day who told the Board, while the Director sat back with a broad smile on his face and basked in their awe, that her people were sponsoring the Directorate. A woman of the Home Time, the place where all the lines of probability converged, where causality collapsed. That was how she had described it. Her distaste had been clear and she had made no bones about it, yet the probability stream that they were in was apparently notoriously unstable and the Directorate was the best way of keeping it steady. So much easier than removing them from the stream altogether. But there were conditions ...

Now a man stood just behind her, weapon raised in both hands, covering them both. Carradine took the hint and put his gun down, slowly.

'Did you forget so easily?' the woman said. She walked forward, hands behind her back. She stopped and looked into Carradine's face. 'We told you we could not tolerate your playing with time. Weren't you happy with all the other information we gave you? Weren't you? Why couldn't you leave it alone? Why did you have to meddle?'

She stepped back and looked at both of them. 'The Directorate is dead and gone, gentleman. We twisted and braided and platted the streams, we brought in opposition from other streams and we cut the Directorate off from history. Like a tumour deprived of its blood supply, it withered and died. All that remains is you two.'

Morgan found his voice. 'What happens?' he said.

'There is a large movement in the Home Time pressing for war crime trials. Carradine disobeyed us but that is not really a war crime. However, what you did with your prisoners ...' She looked at him with loathing. 'You will both remain here. That is your punishment. You have a probability slightly out of phase with the indigents. You will witness but you will not be able to affect events. Suitable, would you not say?' She tossed them two small plastic containers the size of cigar boxes. 'Food synths, so you don't starve. They'll last indefinitely.' Then she snapped her fingers and both the Home Timers were gone.

Morgan spun on Carradine. 'It's your fault!' he shrieked. 'You've done it! You had to be greedy, didn't you? You had to make that time machine. You had to spoil things, you had to, to ...' He fell to his knees, weeping. The familiar *click-whirr* of the gun made him look up again.

Carradine stood over him, his eyes hard and the gun raised. Morgan looked at it with a whole new hope.

About WINGÈD CHARIOT

Such an obvious title for a time travel story, I couldn't believe no one had ever used it. And yet, as far as I know, no one has. It is also the title of my second novel: similar subject, different story. The novel was reissued as *Time's Chariot*, on the grounds (said my publisher) that no one knew how to pronounce the original.

Oh, all right, for the benefit of those who still don't get it:

"But at my back I always hear
Time's wingèd chariot hurrying near,
And yonder all before us lie
Vast deserts of eternity."
– Andrew Marvell, *To His Coy Mistresse*

It has Cornwall and it has time travel: who could ask for anything more? I had no idea when I wrote it that I would one day actually honeymoon in Cornwall – but there all similarity to Morgan ends.

It also – I hope – challenges the reader over the question: when does medical research stop being ethical? I vaguely remember the discussion-cum-argument with a friend on just that issue that started the story off. Experimentation on human embryos offends many sensibilities; and yet, modern anatomical knowledge wouldn't have been possible without graverobbing to supply the necessary anatomies. Posit: the

Nazi experiments on human subjects during WW2 had no medical value and bore us no new knowledge; but imagine that they had? Supposing a cure for something terrible – AIDS or Alzheimers – had come about as a result of Mengele's work? Would we be honour bound to ignore it, or would we quietly accept it, while publicly deploring the atrocities committed?

I don't offer answers, but the story arose from a desire at least to put the case for either side.

'Wingèd Chariot' was voted 27th= in the *Interzone* readers' poll.

THE FIREWORKER

The fire was not one of Cegario's best but it had been made by more conventional means than he was used to and he did not dare make it any brighter. He pulled his cloak closer around him and concentrated on feeling warm. Every now and again he looked up, but beyond the orange light the trees were a black wall. He shivered again and waited. The horse tethered across the clearing snorted.

He heard the movement behind him: for the last couple of minutes he had been tracking its progress as it moved slowly around the fire, while staying in the dark. A hand touched his shoulder.

'Sit down,' he said impatiently.

'You were meant to jump,' said the hand's owner. Shan, a painfully thin blond boy, was older than his height gave him credit for, but as far as Cegario was concerned he had a lot of maturing to do, starting with his sense of humour.

'You're as subtle as a rutting bear,' Cegario said. Shan shrugged and sat down, holding out his hands to the flames.

'Phew! Call this a fire?' He rubbed his hands together, then held them out again. Cegario held out a hand toward him; the boy shrugged again and passed over a small pouch.

'What about the town?' Cegario growled. He took a far larger leather bag out from under his cloak and carefully poured in the contents of the pouch – small crystals that sparkled gold in the fire light. A thrill ran through his mind, as though he had just been reunited with an old and dear friend. That was how the crystals felt about him.

He performed the task with care for this was his sole supply and though there was a man in the High Republic who could have provided him with more, that same man had been sorely aggrieved by the loss of the crystals in the first place. This was one reason why, wherever he was (even if it was sitting and shivering in a glade in a forest in the Principality of Laranala), Cegario tried to be always a few days' journey from the ever-expanding territory of the High Republic. Now the High Republic was on the move again and had reached the western border of Laranala, and for the last few days he and Shan had been heading for the border to the east.

'Eh? Oh, yeah, the town.' He wasn't much good in forests, but put Shan amongst buildings and he could have been invisible. It was his greatest asset. 'Small little concern, name of Dound. Less'n a town, more'n a village, if you follow.'

'Sounding good.'

'Sure. And it was dip ... deppo ...'

'Depopulated?'

'That, by the war, like you said. Just peasants and a mayor, really. Country folk.' Shan added the last description with all the scorn of a true city-bred urchin.

'Magicians?'

'Not even a palm reader,' Shan said smugly.

A slow grin spread across Cegario's face. 'And you planted the crystals?' He jiggled the bag.

'Market square.'

'It's looking like a warm bath and bed tomorrow night, m'boy.'

'Yup,' Shan agreed.

The pair who entered Dound were very different to the pair who had camped half a mile away the night before. Instead of their usual travelling garb they wore smart clothes which spent most of their time carefully folded in Cegario's saddle bags. He usually wanted to travel quietly and unnoticed, which the vivid reds and oranges of his present attire precluded.

People in the square stopped to look as the two arrived; obviously a man of some nobility astride his mount, with his page boy on foot leading the horse.

The two headed for the nearest inhabitant, who stood and frankly gawped.

'My master, Dr Cegarius, asks where we may obtain hos ... host ... a roof and food,' Shan said. Above him, Cegario stared into the distance.

'An inn?' the man said.

''S'what I meant,' Shan said.

'That building there, young master,' the man said, pointing. 'Davo Tallen will put you up.' Shan swelled visibly at being called 'young master' and Cegario continued to ignore them.

'Thank you, good man. This way, sire.' Shan led the horse over to the inn.

'The crystals?' Cegario murmured, his lips not moving.

'There, by those steps,' Shan replied in kind.
Dound was looking promising.

Word soon spread around that someone grand had turned up in Dound and was lodging with the Tallens. Shan had, at a nod from Cegario, produced a bulging bag, delved thoughtfully about in it and eventually extracted a large gold piece that would have bought them a month's accommodation in a far grander establishment. The implication was clearly that the bag held many more coins of the type, not just pieces of iron that gave their weight and shape and nothing else to the illusion.

'Must be half an hour by now,' Shan muttered in disgust, once they had settled into their room. 'Maybe we should announce ourselves.'

'Give them time,' Cegario said. 'They're nervous.'

'Bumpkins.'

Snotty brat, Cegario thought. Shan was useful, but theirs was a partnership, never a friendship. Cegario had put up with it for three years now in their wanderings. His dream was that Shan would soon be old enough to get a girl pregnant – even if Cegario had to procure her himself – and be forced to settle down. The noble Dr Cegarius, outraged by his apprentice's shameful conduct, would publicly dismiss him from his service and that would be that. One day.

Someone was coming up the stairs. More than one person.

''Bout time,' Shan murmured as the visitors knocked politely on the door. Cegario stayed in his chair and opened a large book somewhere in the middle. He kept his eyes firmly on the page as Shan opened the door.

Two men stood outside. One, a middle aged fellow, had a cap and was actually twisting it in his hands. Cegario, whose peripheral vision was excellent, noticed that the other, a tall and muscular man of a similar age, was looking at Shan in a thoughtful way that Shan plainly didn't like. Fortunately it was the cap-twister who spoke.

'Ah ... greetings, ah ... young sir.' The man spoke to the boy but was pointedly looking over Shan's head at Cegario.

'How might my master, Dr Cegarius, help you?' Shan asked.

'I am Lee Shercek,' the man said, 'the mayor of Dound. This is Pawl Drinil, our blacksmith and my deputy. I wonder if your master would care to lunch with me? My home is the tiled building across the square and I offer hospitality far more in keeping with your master's station.'

Which was convenient: Shan had identified that building as the most important in the town and it was outside that building that he had planted a pinch of crystals.

'Wait here.' Shan went over to Cegario, knelt and repeated the request. The mayor and his companion fidgeted in the doorway as the charade ran its course. Cegario looked up from his book at the visitors, then at Shan; he nodded once and returned to his reading. Shan stood up again.

'We will be there at noon,' Shan translated.

JEAPES JAPES

The company at lunch was Mr Shercek and his wife, Mr Drinil and *his* wife, and a couple of other worthies of Dound. Shan was bundled off to the kitchen to eat with the servants, to Cegario's relief. Keeping up the appearance of aloofness was strain enough without the added irritation of Shan's over-acting.

Shan's analysis of Dound the previous evening seemed to be quite accurate. A village on the outskirts of the Principality, miles from anywhere, full of credulous country folk. Only a couple of those who sat around the table had even visited the capital, but the visit seemed to have reinforced the idea that folk from the city were by their very nature grander and wiser than folk from a place like Dound.

Mr Drinil, the blacksmith, on the other hand, had been a sergeant in the army, invalided out before the war; he had taken a bad fall from a horse and still walked with a limp. But he had seen more of the world than just the capital: he had even gone outside the Principality. He was the best travelled of all the townsfolk and he made Cegario uneasy.

'But, Dr Cegarius, may we humbly ask as to your business in our poor village?' Shercek finally asked. At last!

Cegario took a sip of wine before answering.

'My business, Mr Shercek, is fire,' he said, endowing the simple statement with such meaning that the others were impressed despite themselves.

'... ah?' Shercek said.

'I work with fire. I travel through the kingdoms with my acolyte, bringing the secrets of fire to those who have not been initiated.' Cegario wondered who would make the usual, obvious reply. No, on second thoughts, he could guess.

'Dr Cegarius, we have fire, even in Dound.' Drinil, the former soldier, spoke with a tone that was nine-tenths respectful. 'I use it every day.'

Cegario deigned to nod.

'Everywhere has fire, Mr Drinil,' he agreed kindly, 'and I do not doubt that it is a most useful feature of your smithy. But do you know the *secrets* of fire? Fire, gentlemen, is a window between worlds. Have you never looked into the flames and felt the other world calling out to you?' Cegario held Drinil's gaze and leaned forward ever so slightly. He was conscious of the full attention of everyone at the table. 'Within fire, the enquiring and perceptive mind will discover many strange things.'

Even Drinil looked thoughtful. Cegario had realised very early on that even quite unmagical people could stare into a good blaze and lose themselves in it, and he had traded on that fact ever since. Now, as silence followed his remark, Cegario looked around the table.

'But I am among sceptics,' he said sadly.

'No, no, Dr Cegarius,' Shercek said hastily, with a look at Drinil that was like a kick under the table. 'We have no doubts, but ... it is just that ...'

'Sceptics,' Cegario repeated. 'Even if you were to see, you would not believe ...'

And, inevitably, they ended up out in the town square again. The news had spread around that the stranger was to do a demonstration and a remarkable number of casual passers-by were in the area. *By the steps*, Shan had said ... Cegario caught Shan in the corner of his eye and followed the boy's surreptitious hand signals which guided him to where Shan had planted the crystals the previous night. A few grains, invisible to the naked eye; that was all, and all that was needed.

Now that he was near, Cegario could *feel* the crystals, primed as they were for him and him alone. They sensed that he was close by and needed them and they started their usual clamour in his mind.

Free us! Free us! Let us go!

He held up his hands for silence, though the noise in his mind stayed.

'People of Dound!' he called. 'I am Dr Cegarius, the fireworker. My mission is to reach through the fire, between the worlds, and to bring knowledge to those who would have it. You think you have seen fire before?'

Cegario took a deep breath and tensed himself. This was like releasing a taut spring and in the same movement catching it before it had fully expanded.

'Behold, fire!'

He *thought* at the crystals in the special way and they heard him – with a cry of joy they returned to their natural state of flame. A column of fire blazed up in front of him, shot through with flickers of bright purple, green and gold. The townsfolk stepped back.

Stop! Cegario commanded, his hands held high in the air, and the crystals complained bitterly.

You freed us! You said we could go!

In a moment.

Cegario could see Shan grinning from ear to ear but he kept his own expression stern, despite the thrill that always went through him when the crystals responded to his commands.

'Come close, you who would have knowledge!' he cried. 'Behold, the gate between worlds is open!'

THE FIREWORKER

A shuffle, a murmur at the edge of the square ... a middle aged woman was coming forward. Cegario's heart sang. Would it be love, health, a bereavement ...?

A bereavement; he could see it in her eyes.

'You have lost a dear one, daughter,' he said gently. She nodded quickly.

'My son, sir, died as an infant-'

'His name?'

'I had no time to name him, sir.'

'Then your name?' Cegario asked patiently.

'Vanera, sir.'

'And how long ago did he die, Vanera?'

'Fifteen years, sir.'

Cegario turned back to the fire and thought quickly. Shan was too young and would be recognised ... but it had to be a real memory: products of his imagination as interpreted by the crystals were far too hazy. The first boy of fifteen to come to mind was a boy he had hated, a couple of years older than him ... he would be in his thirties, now, but the face of the youth who had tormented Cegario as a child in the palace kitchens was engrained on Cegario's mind forever. And the boy had been good-looking; very popular with the girls and just the type to warm a mother's heart.

If you would be free, show me this, he commanded and *thought* of the boy, at the same time crying, 'Son of Vanera, where are you?' For a moment – a brief moment – the face of a handsome young man appeared in the flames and Vanera gasped.

'Your son, Vanera,' Cegario said quietly. 'He has grown and prospered in the world beyond but he still remembers you with love, the woman who gave him his first life.'

You promised! You promised!

Be free.

In a final burst of exultation the crystals blazed whitely into extinction and the fire vanished.

Vanera's eyes flooded with tears and she gazed up in thankful awe at the gentle countenance of the fireworker. Dr Cegarius had begun his work in Dound.

* * *

Drinil's smithy was black against the stars. A small shadow detached itself from the trees behind it and silently crossed the open ground to the building. Nothing more happened.

Some minutes later, the shadow crept around the edge of the building to the front and in through the door.

A flash of white in the shadow was Shan's teeth. The boy was grinning. He had had his eye on the smithy all the week that he and Cegario had been in Dound and he shared Cegario's dislike of the former soldier. But Cegario, Shan was certain, was actually *frightened* of Drinil and Shan would admit to being frightened of no one.

Between them they had long ago discovered that most people, even in places like Dound, had something secreted away as insurance against the future, and Shan's instinct for locating such hiding places was unmatched. He would visit the houses he had selected like a shadow in the middle of the night and the inhabitants would awaken unknowingly slightly poorer. It was rare for them actually to check on their nest egg from day to day.

That was by night. By day, when Shan was too sleepy to be of use, Cegario did his own bit towards the impoverishment of Dound, making fire and giving the people who came to him what they wanted. He never charged for his services but gifts of gratitude came in regularly. He and Shan were now housed in an empty cottage all to themselves, for instance, and the separate rooms were a luxury that they both appreciated. Shan had even been persuaded, with the threat of a broken arm, to have a bath.

A man named Cault, a dour fogey who kept pigs, had been Shan's latest victim. Shan's instincts had told him that there was something worthwhile hidden behind the sty, just where Cault thought no one would think of looking. But Shan had thought of it. And now Mr Drinil ... Drinil had been dropping hints of spoils brought back from war for far too long and Shan intended to do something about it. Thieving was fun; thieving from people Shan disliked was best of all.

Now, where ...?

Silently he moved around the room, feeling here, probing there in the red glow of the smithy's fire.

Nothing. And yet he was sure ... he was *sure*...

The anvil was a dark, solid mass, tinged with red light from the fire. Of course! Shan knelt down beside it and probed the earth floor with his fingers. Yup. The crafty old sod kept his loot underneath the anvil, where he was probably the only man in Dound strong enough to get at it. But there were ways.

Shan cast around for a suitable implement and began to scrape away at the floor besides the anvil. He would dig down, then across ...

An enormous hand wound its fingers into his hair and pulled him to his feet. Another hand with the strength of iron seized his wrist and bent it back behind him to touch his shoulder. Shan shrieked.

'Gotcha,' Drinil murmured into his ear.

* * *

Cegario was hauled out of bed, literally, by the blacksmith's free hand: the other still held Shan by his hair. Shan's eyes were watering with the pain. As Drinil recited the facts of the case, Cegario began to hope. This was his chance-

'I didn't mean to get caught, boss,' Shan whined. Cegario looked at him through narrowed eyes. So, the brat had decided that if they were to go down, they would go down together.

There was still a chance of disowning the boy, but ...

'I want the truth about you two,' Drinil said. He pushed Shan over into one corner where the boy crouched down and rubbed his arm, glaring at them both like a sullen trapped rat. Drinil backed into another corner, where he could see them both without having to switch his gaze from one to the other. 'One little lie and ... well, just say Mr Shercek will believe my story over yours.'

Cegario never believed in fighting what was inevitable. Going along with it was a far better idea. He sat down on the edge of the bed.

'Where should we start?' he said.

'For beginners, why does a man of your undoubted intelligence travel with this obnoxious little snot? Apart from the obvious answer, for which the penalty is castration, even in Dound.'

'Huh,' Shan mumbled and despite everything Cegario smiled.

'There was a man took a fancy to him a couple of months back,' Cegario said. 'Shan has sharp knees and isn't fussy about what he bites.'

Drinil looked thoughtfully at Shan. 'So he's a *vicious* obnoxious little snot.' His gaze turned back to Cegario. 'And you? What's your game?'

'We both irritated the same gentleman in the High Republic,' Cegario said after a pause. 'We felt it was time to leave and we ended up together.'

Drinil nodded. 'I knew you were pulling some scam. I've seen too many holy men, real and otherwise, but I couldn't tell what you were up to. That fire of yours – that's real. How do you do it?'

So, Cegario told him all about the crystals. Almost all.

'They were a toy, devised for a young Lady of the High Republic by ... by the gentleman we irritated, whose name it is wisest not to mention out loud.' Drinil's eyes widened; the implications were all too obvious. Even in Dound they had heard of *him*. Cegario went on, 'The crystals become fire at the owner's command, and if they can be held, they can be made to show images from the owner's mind. It takes discipline and practice but anyone can do it.'

The crystals were fire elementals, captured and compressed into crystal form and once one human had got hold of them, that human stayed their master forever. But Cegario saw no reason to tell everything.

'So how did you come by them?' Drinil said.

'I was a palace brat, from a long line of retainers. I worked my way up onto milady's staff. I was bored with my position and ... well, I thought I could use the crystals to my own advantage.'

'Very dangerous, crossing ... this gentleman like that.'

'At the time I thought he was just another court magician. Everyone thought it.' Cegario shrugged. 'Then he began to flex his muscles and now I try to keep at least one country between him and us.'

Drinil nodded again. 'And the snot?' Shan glowered at him.

'He – his whole family – were in one of the High Republic's gangs,' Cegario said. 'The gentleman is not unconnected with the organisation of crime where we come from and Shan's chief failed to pay the gang's dues. I saw what happened to them.'

As had Shan; the boy had gone pale and was trembling. Drinil seemed impressed.

'How much have you lifted from Dound, snot?' Drinil asked.

'Dunno,' Shan mumbled. Drinil made a sudden move towards him.

''Bout twenty, thirty gold crowns and other bits'n'bobs,' Shan said quickly.

'Where?'

'Outside the town. I can show you, if-' [Shan suddenly turned ingratiating] '-you want a cut, sir.'

It was the wrong thing to say. Cegario shut his eyes and groaned silently; Drinil's jaw jutted and he spoke with a quiet, intense fury.

'Listen to me, you filth. Both of you. I don't want a cut. You're going to take me to where you've hidden your stuff and you're going to hand over everything you've taken. And then you're going to get out of Dound. I was going to hand you over to Mr Shercek and the townsfolk, but if you're in trouble with ...*him*, I just want you gone from here. Got that? And you leave now.'

* * *

'It could have been worse,' Shan said hopefully, some hours later, as the horse trudged along the road away from Dound with its two passengers. It was the first thing he had dared say since they had parted with Drinil: the smith had scooped up the stolen riches and they had gone their separate ways.

Cegario rarely lost his temper on the spot. Instead he dwelt on what had upset him and let his anger build up inside him. He had been quietly furious with Shan since he had been woken and now it peaked.

'Shut up!' he shouted. He twisted round in his saddle and clouted Shan, hard enough to knock him off the horse. Shan wriggled in mid air but still landed, painfully, on his side. He writhed breathlessly, all the wind knocked out of him. Cegario dismounted and stood over him. Shan cowered.

'We were settling,' Cegario said. Now his voice was low and his expression murderous. He jabbed a finger at Shan. 'We were making a home. Dound had accepted us. We could have stayed there for a couple of months at least. But now? Do you think Drinil will keep quiet? He'll tell them all about us, and Shercek will feel it his duty to spread the word for miles around, and everyone will know that Dr Cegarius and Shan are nothing but a fraud and a thief!'

'Cegario-' Shan was still winded and could only wheeze the name.

'And every traveller who passes through Dound will be told, and in turn they'll tell everyone in every new town they come to, and before long the whole region will have heard of us, we'll have to be on the road for weeks now to get well ahead of the gossip, and it's *your fault!*'

'Boss-'

'*Shut up!*' Cegario bellowed. 'I'm just going to get back on the horse and leave you here to make your own way-'

'Look, please!' Shan wailed. There was open fear on the boy's face and Cegario finally realised it wasn't of him. Slowly he turned around.

From around the bend that lay just down the road a group of riders had appeared, trotting towards them with a characteristic brisk sense of purpose that he recognised.

'Cavalry,' he said. 'So what-'

A gust of wind unfurled the banner that one of them carried and, with horror, Cegario saw the emblem on it. The device of Laranala was intertwined with the swords of the High Republic.

'Oh, no,' he breathed.

How? The High Republic was behind them, to the west. How had it got *ahead*?

'We've got to run,' Shan whined.

'Why? We're innocent travellers, Shan. Don't say a word. And get up.'

The cavalry drew up to them: a group of thirty grim-looking men, guarding a train of wagons. The first few wagons held a crowd of sullen men and boys and the last two were empty.

Shan was standing by now and had dusted himself off. Cegario smiled ingratiatingly and went forward to greet the soldiers. He took great care to limp, as he had seen Drinil doing.

THE FIREWORKER

'Good day, good sirs.'

The lead soldier looked down at him. 'Are you a local?'

'I? Oh, no, sir, I am but a traveller, a singer.'

The sergeant looked at him, at Shan, at the horse, then back at Cegario. 'Where's your instrument?'

'My boy's pipes are in the bag,' Cegario said, mentally preparing a performance of Outraged Traveller Whose Pipes Have Been Stolen should the man actually want to look. He did have a good singing voice, which helped.

As it was, the next question was, 'Are we on the road to Dound?'

'Dound, sir? Why, yes, two hours in the direction you're going.'

The soldier nodded slowly, looking at Shan. 'Travel a lot, do you?' he said.

'Oh, yes, here, there and everywhere, sir,' Shan piped brightly.

Ten seconds alone with him and a sharp knife, Cegario thought bitterly, to any god that might be listening. *Please, it's all I need.*

The soldier was grinning. 'We're recruiting,' he explained, with a gesture at the wagons, 'but with that limp you'll be no good.' He looked thoughtfully down at Shan. 'How old are you, boy?'

'Nine, sir,' Shan lied, for once grateful for his size and unbroken voice.

The man nodded and looked back to Cegario. His words implied an option: his tone belied it. 'However, we could do with a guide to this area, if you would care to join us.'

JEAPES JAPES

And so, Cegario and Shan found themselves heading back into Dound. People were up and about by now, and they looked warily at the newcomers. Those who recognised their accomplices looked confused, not sure what was going on.

The soldiers rode into the village square and waited while the sergeant strode up to the mayor's door. Shercek came out to meet them. Cegario and Shan had casually dismounted and were standing with the horse between them and the mayor. They heard the conversation: the sergeant brusque in his usual way and Shercek plainly frightened.

'Are you the mayor?'

'I am, sir.'

'Good. We are recruiting for our lord's campaign against Neress and will require your assistance.'

'I – I wasn't aware that our lord was at war with Neress, sir.'

'Ah.' They could *hear* the sergeant's grin. 'We are plainly not talking about the same our lord. The prince died in a tragic riding accident and a lord of the High Republic was invited to act as an impartial Regent until the matter of the succession could be sorted out. It is quite complicated.'

Shan groaned quietly. Cegario shushed him. So that was how it was. Under *him*, the High Republic controlled three states directly and its citizens could come and go as they pleased in two more. And now, without a fight, without a whisper, without even any warning, Laranala had been added to their repertoire.

'Tragic!' Shercek exclaimed. 'But we in Dound had not heard, sir, we have not had time to mourn adequately for-'

'No matter. Now, where can I billet my men?'

THE FIREWORKER

Shercek reluctantly gave directions to a field where tents could be pitched and the soldiers were ordered to remount. Cegario could delay it no longer: he had to get on the horse and Shan had to climb up behind him. Shercek saw them and his mouth dropped open. For want of anything better, Cegario winked and saw uncertainty cross the mayor's face. Like the others, Shercek was wondering what was going on, but at the wink he held his peace. Clearly Drinil had not yet talked to him.

Then the command was given to ride on and the party headed off to the field.

Drinil and Shercek came for them later that day. The soldiers had split up, leaving a hard core to guard the conscripts while the rest of them scouted around the area. Already a further fourteen males of various ages had been added to the wagon train. Cegario and Shan could do nothing but fret.

Cegario saw the two approaching and assumed that they were going to speak to the man in charge. To his surprise, Shercek quite clearly beckoned to him. He walked over to them uncomfortably; he had slipped a pebble into his shoe to help his limp lest he accidentally forgot it, or which foot it was meant to be. Shan, to Cegario's annoyance, trailed behind him. The four of them stood together with empty space around them – the best protection against eavesdroppers.

'The High Republic has caught up with you, Dr Cegarius,' Drinil said. Shercek was glaring at the former fireworker with the hurt of betrayed trust and the anger of realising he had been taken in. 'I told Shercek all about you,' Drinil added.

Cegario beamed pleasantly. 'You would have denounced me to the soldiers by now if you were ever going to,' he said. 'Now, smile, as if we were friends. They may be watching.'

'Do as-' Shan said.

'Shut up,' Cegario said, not taking his gaze from the two men. 'Well, what is it?'

Shercek spoke, his tone wavering from angry to pleading. 'Dr Cegarius, whatever your name is, Dound cannot afford to lose its men to the army. The harvest is coming. We lost enough men in the last war and we have just been able to make good. The few boys who were left to us have grown up and we need every one of them here.'

'Smile,' Cegario reminded him. Shercek did so, painfully.

'I am going to talk treason,' the mayor continued, 'but I have no reason to believe that the High Republic lord who now rules us deserves any loyalty from Dound.'

'He has a large army and the backing of the High Republic, which in turn is supported by the most powerful magician in the world, but apart from that, no, I see no reason to be loyal to him,' Cegario said.

'You are in no position to be flippant, Dr Cegarius,' Drinil said. 'I expect you still have those crystals, which belong to the gentleman you just mentioned.'

'Dr Cegarius, I doubt that the prince's accident was an accident,' Shercek said.

'*Really*?'

'I believe that the High Republic has committed war against us by murdering our lord. It is our right to

THE FIREWORKER

fight against their soldiers. Can you use your crystals against them? Lay a trap, perhaps, burn them? You know their properties better than I but there must be something you can do.'

'There had better be something you can do,' Drinil said, 'or in our disappointment we will be forced to denounce you.'

'If these soldiers are killed,' Cegario said, 'more will come.'

'By which time Dound will be empty!' Shercek said. 'It's twenty miles to the border and Neress. We will evacuate the village tonight and throw ourselves on the mercy of the Neressoi.'

Cegario thought it unlikely the Neressoi would be so generous, even if the entire village managed to get that far, but it was none of his concern. What was his concern was that these two just had to have a few words with the officer in charge and he and Shan would be walking corpses. Probably literally.

Cegario pondered. 'I will see,' he promised.

By sunset, the soldiers were back in their camp and the evening watch was patrolling the borders of the field. Even in the daylight the sentry could not have seen the thin trail of crystals that ran all along one side of the field.

Cegario and Shan sat by their small natural fire.
'Sun's almost down,' Shan said. He was facing west.
'Tell me the moment it's down below the horizon.'
'Right-o.'
A few moments later, Shan said, 'Now.'

Cegario stood up and stretched casually, setting his mind to the crystal trail.

Free us! Free us!

I will not hold you back. Burn, with my blessing.

A sheet of fire twenty feet tall shot up along the camp's edge. Horses screamed and men shouted. Cegario waited until the confusion was at its peak and *thought* again, and with whoops of joy the clumps of crystals that Shan had planted here and there amidst the tents exploded into flame. No one had been able to tell the conscripts the plan but if they had any sense, now was the time to escape.

'Now,' Cegario said, swinging up onto the horse. He dug his feet in and the horse bolted, with Shan clinging onto it for dear life.

'Hang on! Trying to lose me?' he said, pulling himself up into the saddle behind Cegario.

Bright lad, Cegario thought. A soldier loomed up ahead in the flickering light, sword half-drawn.

'Oi! Get back to-'

Cegario rode him down.

A safe distance away, Cegario pulled the horse round and looked back the way they had come. The fires were still burning brightly and the soldiers should all have been concentrated into one spot by now, fighting against the fire. It was time for the final touch. A few crystals, a pinch, could produce that much flame and Shan had hidden a substantial pouch-full in the centre of the camp. Cegario *thought*...

He closed his eyes against the ball of pure white flame that erupted in the camp, immolating the tents, the soldiers, the horses ... Cegario heard the shouts turn to screams. He could dimly see the shapes of men, charred and scorched, staggering against the fire and burning brightly. He also saw the men of Dound rushing in, swords out, taking advantage of the confusion to dispatch the survivors. The screams died out, leaving just fire. He let the fire blaze until the crystals were consumed and the flames dwindled into nothing, leaving bright green scars scorched across his sight.

'Hope they escaped,' Shan murmured, thinking of the conscripts.

'Their fault if they didn't,' said Cegario, whose main worry was for the crystals. His supply had been badly depleted.

They trotted down the main street of Dound into the square, which was packed. Old and young, men and women and children, were jostling about with as much of their worldly goods as they could carry.

'Dr Cegarius!' Shercek was standing on the steps of his residence.

'Look, the fireworker!' someone called. He was cheered and the crowd parted as he rode over to the mayor. Drinil was standing by him: they and the village elders had been trying to arrange some kind of order in the crowd prior to their escape to Neress.

Shercek grinned up at him. 'Thank you, Dr Cegarius. We're in your debt.'

But don't trade on it, Drinil's look plainly added. *Play your part*.

'My pleasure, Mr Shercek,' Cegario said loudly, as arranged. 'The least I could do for all your kindness. And now I must leave you.'

There were cries from the crowd and entreaties to stay with them. Cegario held up a hand for silence. 'No, I must continue my travels. But I can leave you something.'

This was a departure from the plot, though the people didn't know it and they cheered. The smiles of the mayor and his deputy froze.

'Here,' Cegario said, 'for your noble leaders.' He threw two small pouches down to them; they caught them and stared up at him. Cegario drew the horse near and bent down to murmur for their hearing only.

'They're crystals,' he confirmed, so quietly that not even Shan could hear. 'They're all I can spare, but I've treated them so that you can use them. Only you two, so don't let anyone else get at them. Keep them to yourselves.' He pressed a piece of parchment into Shercek's hands. 'Here are instructions as to how to use them. Good luck!'

He turned to face Shan, looked the boy straight in the eyes and raised his voice once more. 'And I leave you with a final present, good folk. My apprentice, Shan!'

Shan's jaw dropped. He looked at Cegario, at Drinil and then back at Cegario, horror-struck amongst the cheers. Cegario grinned and clapped a friendly hand on the boy's shoulder.

'It's stay with them or get a knife between your ribs from me, brat,' he murmured, 'but either way, our partnership is dissolved.'

'Dr Cegarius.' Shercek spoke from by his knee. 'We couldn't possibly take your apprentice.'

'You could find uses for him.' Cegario turned back to look not at Shercek but at Drinil, holding the blacksmith's gaze.

Drinil nodded, slowly. He and Cegario understood each other. 'I think we could, Mr Shercek,' he said.

THE FIREWORKER

'Very well,' Shercek said with reluctance. Shan gave Cegario one last, pleading look, which was returned with indifference. Then he swallowed and dismounted.

'Keep him close to you,' Cegario said. He ignored the glare of pure hate that was coming from Shan.

'We will, Dr Cegarius,' Drinil promised. 'We will.'

And Dr Cegarius rode out of Dound.

* * *

'For being a brat!' Cegario shouted into the night as he galloped. Free! Never again having to wake up to face another day of Shan's company! Never again having to listen to that piping whine! 'For complaining, moaning, grumbling, snivelling, for being unbearable, for getting us hooked by those soldiers in the first place!'

He knew exactly what was going through Drinil's mind. A compromise between two men of the world: I give you your freedom, you take this brat off my hands and work him to the bone. No doubt Drinil was even now thinking of all the uses Shan could be put to.

It was almost a pity.

Cegario stopped and dismounted. He rummaged in the saddle bags and found the orange and red robes of Dr Cegarius the fireworker. These he left under some bushes. The fireworker was dead: he would find another identity.

Then he turned to face the way he had come, reaching out in his mind for the familiar touch of the crystals.

* * *

Shan groaned as the last pack was slung over his back. Drinil must have given him at least half his own weight again to carry.

'How far?' he said.

'Only twenty miles to the border,' Drinil said. 'But we'll stop at daybreak.'

'Twenty-'

'Shut up and walk, snot.'

Shan staggered on, along with the rest of Dound. Drinil strolled by his side with Shercek not far away. They were taking Cegario's advice literally.

Shan noticed, hanging from Drinil's belt, the small pouch that Cegario had given him. It looked offensively small and light.

'Sure you don't want me to carry that too?' he sneered. Drinil clipped his ear.

'One more word, snot, and you get another pack, right? And if you think I'm letting you get your hands on my crystals you've got another think coming.'

Shan trudged in sulky silence, until what Drinil had said connected in his mind. 'Crystals? But ... but you can't use the crystals!' he said.

'He gave me instructions.'

'No! No one else can use them! I know!' Shan insisted.

Drinil frowned and looked down at the pouch. 'Then what-' Their eyes met and he saw the dawning horror in the boy's face. 'No!' he shouted.

Drinil fumbled at his side and tore the pouch from his belt. He flung it as far off the road as he could, at the same time shouting for Shercek. Shercek turned, puzzled, to see the blacksmith bearing down on him. Then Drinil had the mayor's pouch and had flung it after the first.

'Drinil, whatever-'

Twin shafts of fire blazed up from the field by the road, knocking the villagers flat.

Shan couldn't get up with the packs weighing him down. He shrugged out of them and slowly stood up. Dogs were barking, children were crying and being comforted, people were shouting at the tops of their voices.

'What ... what ...' Shercek was gabbling. All of a sudden, Shan was fed up with the stupid rustic peasants and he let his impatience show.

'You're going to the same place he is and you know about him,' he shouted. 'What do you think?' *And he told you to keep me close to you*, he thought, suddenly going cold.

Drinil turned round and beckoned. 'C'mere, snot.'

Because Drinil could easily outrun him, Shan obeyed. To his surprise, the hand that fell on his shoulder was almost paternal.

'You know the kind of man he is, snot,' Drinil said. 'When we get to Neress, d'you think you could find him again?'

'Reckon I could,' Shan agreed. He looked thoughtfully out into the darkness. 'Yeah, I reckon I could.'

About THE FIREWORKER

Many years ago an anthology was announced called *Villains*, which would present heroic fantasy as it really would be if it actually happened – decidedly unheroic with grime, dirt, disease and general nastiness. So I did what I don't usually do and wrote a sword-and-sorcery(ish), anti-heroic type of story. Cegario is a not particularly likeable thief, conman and (in the original draft) murderer. Yes, in the original draft he got away with it, leaving the people of Dound to get on with their business, sticking a knife between Shan's ribs and dumping him in a ditch. When I do anti-heroic, I do it properly.

I didn't actually finish it in time for *Villains* so I've no idea if they would have accepted it or not. The gaming magazine *Dragon* requested a rewrite as the initial version was just a bit too dark for them (the editor did say that parents of teenagers would probably sympathise with the ending, but ...) but still turned down the second draft because of its reference to castration – 'above the line for *Dragon* readers', apparently. Such sensitive souls, these D&D types.

But at long last it found a home in the debut issue of the Australian magazine *Altair*. And I'm happy.

CORRESPONDENTS

He was going to be late. He had come so far and he was going to be late ...

As the correspondent entered the city, he began instinctively to compile his report. He scanned the streets and the crowds, taking in the dirt and the smell and the squalor. He recorded the contrast between the magnificent stone churches and colleges and the ramshackle common buildings; he noted the great, blank walls that so cleanly divided Oxford between town and gown with the profane real world on one side and the sacred world of scholarship on the other. The jumble of ideas and themes would all be sorted out in his report, when he had a moment.

He really ought to be getting on. A thought called up a street map of Oxford in the sixteenth century and he saw that he was almost there.

He was, indeed, too late, at least for the preliminaries. St Mary's church loomed up ahead and a crowd was coming out of it. Some people looked at the correspondent, but then they looked away again without curiosity; Oxford was big enough for strangers to be unremarkable, and who would pass up this chance for free entertainment? The correspondent was unnoticed as he followed with the crowd after the centre of attraction – Thomas Cranmer, former

Archbishop of Canterbury, due to be burnt at the stake for his Protestantism. It was March 21st, 1556.

The crowd reached the area outside the walls where the pile was waiting for Cranmer, who had resigned himself to his fate. He stood placidly in the middle of a crowd of angry, gesticulating men, each one presenting his own view of why Cranmer should recant, even at this last minute. The correspondent continued his report.

'Cranmer is surrounded by worthies talking to him, hoping for a final recantation that will spare him the flames. The mayor is on the verge of tears. The man in scholarly robes and cap on the right must be the bachelor of divinity that the records call Elye, and he is looking more and more put out by Cranmer's stubbornness. The two friars with him also appear to be losing their patience rapidly. I will try and hear their exact words ...'

The Archbishop began to undress, eventually to stand in just a shirt. He was trussed up to the stake and a cry went up from the crowd as the torch was applied. The correspondent applied his skills to the pile; a measuring rule appeared in his vision against it and he saw that it was twenty feet across at the base and ten feet high. It must have been well-oiled as it caught quickly, though putting out more smoke than flame. The correspondent stood, an island of calm detachment in the seething crowd, recording Cranmer's last act of defiance as the flames rose:

'He has managed to work a hand free and has thrust it into the fire ... he has for the last time renounced his former recantation, which resulted in his watching his colleagues Ridley and Latimer go to the stake, and declared that this hand that wrote it shall be the first part of him to be burnt ... his face shows the pain, yet he has made no further noise.'

He looked around him to gauge the crowd's reactions. Some were openly weeping, whether for a lost friend or for a soul consigned to their Hell he had no idea, but he recorded it anyway.

Others were less upset.

'Good riddance!' a voice yelled; a chorus of cheers showed that at least some of the crowd agreed. The correspondent looked over at the speaker who was himself looking around, apparently pleased by the reaction to his words.

'The heretic had it coming!' he shouted, to more cheers. 'God bless the Queen, dragging this country of ours back to the true faith, never mind that German monk's ramblings ...'

The correspondent was struck by the sheer tide of emotion around him, the currents of hate and anger that buffeted him. As he looked away he inadvertently caught the eye of a man standing by him. He had a feeling the man had been looking at *him*.

'An oaf,' the man said, quietly. He was well-dressed and sported a neatly trimmed beard. The skin around his eyes was crinkled, which gave him a friendly and trustworthy look; the eyes themselves also seemed friendly, but every now and then flashed with a hardness that indicated he maybe did not concur with everything the other man was saying.

'His name is Morris,' the man continued in the same quiet, conversational way. 'He is not entirely uneducated; he studied for the priesthood and failed. Do his words disturb you, friend?'

'There was a trial and Cranmer was judged guilty,' said the correspondent, his first words spoken out loud since arriving in this time. 'His fate is no more than the law.'

The man laughed.

'Ah, you give a safe reply! Friend, do I detect that you have travelled far to be here?'

'I have this day arrived in Oxford,' the correspondent said. 'I am come from-' (From where? Where would be a good place?)

To his surprise the man clapped a hand on his shoulder.

'The inns hereabouts will cost you a pretty penny, friend. I invite you to my humble abode. For, as the Greek proverb says-'

-but it was not Greek that the man spoke. The man dropped, instead, into the language of the Home Time.

'Welcome to this era, friend.'

The correspondent's eyes widened, but he smiled and said, in English:

'I accept your most kind invitation, sir. But first I must finish here.'

They waited a bit longer. The pile of wood was allowed to burn its course; the dead Archbishop sagged limply from his stake in the middle and the stench of burning flesh added itself to the clean, pungent wood smoke. The correspondent added the detail to the report.

He and his new friend stayed until the crowd began to drift away. Cranmer's charred body was taken down and quickly taken away by a group of people: friends or enemies, the correspondent didn't know. He considered following them but decided against it.

Cranmer was dead and it was his execution, not his burial, that had had the effect on history.

'You are ready?' the other man said. The correspondent nodded.

'My coach is this way,' the man said, leading the correspondent away from the crowd. 'The driver is a servant of this time, so until we are alone we must speak only of inconsequentialities.'

'Of course,' the correspondent agreed.

The coach took them to a well-appointed house, black and white in the manner of the time, in Headington, on the outskirts of Oxford. The house was large enough to have a hall; a large, muscular man lounged here, apparently chatting up a woman. They both jumped to their feet expectantly when the two came in; the correspondent studied them in a glance and decided they must be servants.

'Carry on with your work, Rachel,' his new friend said. The woman bustled out through a door. 'Wilf is my factotum and a most loyal man to have around. But be about your duties whilst I entertain my friend, Wilf.'

'Yes, Mr Taylor.' The man left, but with a curious glance at the visitor.

'As I said, I have servants of this time. Now, in here,' the man said, leading the correspondent through to the main room. He sat his guest down and called for beer from the housekeeper. Eventually they were alone.

'We can use the language of the Home Time, if such would make you more comfortable,' the man said.

'Please.'

'Fine.' The man easily slid into his native tongue. He sat and lounged in a chair. 'You know, I saw you from a mile off. Oh! We haven't been introduced. My name's Richard Taylor. At least, that's the name I use most of the time.'

'I'm ...' The correspondent hadn't thought of what name to adopt. 'John Smith?'

Taylor winced.

'Terrible. At least call yourself ... Edward. A good name for this time, after the late King, Queen Mary's brother.'

'Edward Smith?'

'It will do.' Taylor grinned. 'Ah, it's good to see someone I can have an intelligent conversation with!'

'How did you spot me?' Edward said.

'Oh, not from anything you were doing. From what you were not doing, Edward. Everyone's face showed something, but you just stood there, taking it all in. And you have the look that we all have. I've seen it before-'

'How?' Edward said, surprised. There was no actual rule against correspondents mixing, so far as he knew, but they were meant to be few and far apart enough not to bump into each other.

'Well, I've been around for a long time and I know the kind of thing that correspondents go for.'

'But aren't you-'

'I was,' Taylor said gently. 'I've retired.' He waved a hand around him to indicate the house and servants, while Edward's mind wrestled with the idea of a retired correspondent. 'I'm a merchant of some success. Knowing what the market will do is a major advantage. I'll have to move on eventually but I'm comfortable for now.' He changed the subject. 'So, how did you end up as a correspondent?'

'I don't really know,' Edward said. He tapped his head. 'I only arrived this morning ...'

Taylor nodded, a trifle knowingly.

' ... and your memory's still a bit jumbled. I understand.' They had to play with the memory of a correspondent. They already knew every detail of his career – what articles he would file, whether he would survive or not – but so that he could act as a free agent, they could not let *him* know. 'Five hours down, five hundred years to go ... do you think you'll make it?'

The Home Time could transmit someone as far back as they liked. They would not send the recall equipment further back than the twenty-first century, where it was just the right side of anachronism. If you were sent further back than that, you walked home.

'I hope so,' Edward said. 'It shouldn't be too difficult, should it? How long have you been here?'

'Me? Well, just say my first big report was an interview with Alfred the Great.'

'That's a long time!'

'You manage,' Taylor said with a shrug. 'I've lost count of the lurgies I've caught. I've had cholera, malaria, the Black Death and-' [he grinned] '-some unmentionable kinds of pox, but we always recover. No, keep your head low, always cheer for the winning side and you get along just fine. I'm thinking of taking a ship to America, you know. Head out west, where the white man won't end up for another couple of centuries and staying alive will be a whole lot easier.'

'That's a thought,' Edward said. 'And in the Home Time they'll love to read stories about North America developing.'

'Yes, well,' Taylor said with another shrug. 'That too.'

'You don't sound too enthusiastic.'

'I've grown fond of being alive, mate!' Taylor laughed. 'I can't blame you, your conditioning's still fresh in your mind, but you do remind me of Roger. Roger Woods, your predecessor.'

'My predecessor?'

'The one I imagine they sent you to replace. He died yesterday, mugged in a back alley, massive trauma, killed immediately. The damage was too much at one time for his body to cope with.' Taylor held up a finger. 'Remember that – we're not completely immortal. Anyway, that's how I guessed you would turn up. They were bound to send someone to cover Cranmer's execution – it's just the kind of thing to appeal to them and Roger covered Latimer and Ridley last year. Point is, he was keen on the job too. He would report on his latest meal if nothing better showed up.'

'But not you?' Edward asked.

'After seven centuries, mate, you get independent-minded.' Taylor jabbed a finger at him. 'Edward, the people who sent us here are the biggest, smuggest, most amoral bunch of hypocrites that the world will ever see! Think about it. What kind of researcher just reads second-hand reports? The best kind goes out there in the field and gets his own hands dirty, but how many correspondents do you think are academics from the Home Time? Oh no, far too dangerous! They send us suckers back, give us blithe assurances about how dandy it will all be with these organic survival machines that we call bodies, see you in the Home Time, chaps, and they sit comfortably in their offices and read our reports. How much loyalty could you ever feel to a crowd like that?'

Edward sat with his mouth open. This was heresy, this was ...

Taylor checked himself and shrugged.

'At least, that's what I think,' he said. 'Do you know what the last report I filed was? 'Sod off, you bastards, I'm my own boss now." He grinned lazily. 'That was in 1473. Now I just hang about, doing a bit of this and that ... sometimes it gets boring, but I'm happy.'

Edward explored the back of his mind again, just to remind himself it was there. The black, closed-off bit.

'There's always the Death Sentence,' he said uncertainly. The solution for those correspondents who couldn't face the thought of living as long as the twenty-first century; a collection of nonsense words that lurked at the back of the brain, behind several mental guards, impossible to activate by chance, but which would if desired simply switch the brain and body off. For ever.

'There is, but it's not for me,' Taylor said flatly. 'Listen, Edward, you're welcome to put up here for as long as you like, but not if you're going to start preaching, got that?'

'I wouldn't dream of it!' Edward said hastily. 'You're the boss.' He thought quickly about the best way of proving his good will towards his host. 'Um – tell me about this time.'

'This time?' Taylor laughed. 'This morning's affair was a good sample of this time. Mary Tudor is determined to bring this country back to the Roman way and will tolerate no opposition. Concepts like 'consensus' have yet to be invented. People will suffer endless agonies, even death, over their right to say their prayers their way. Ordinary, decent folk will happily see their neighbours tortured unspeakably for not using Latin on the right occasions. It's considered that the suffering of the flames at the stake purges you of sin and makes you ready for heaven. Certain kinds of execution are seen as a privilege!'

'And no one stops to ask why?'

'No, of course not! Get it into your head, Edward, that people here don't think like we do. Rational thought counts for nothing and emotion counts for everything. Love thy neighbour and then slaughter him – that's the locals for you.'

'That man at the stake-' Edward said. Taylor laughed.

'Ah, yes, friend Morris! He's a bitter man. He caught the priesthood bug in King Edward's reign but he was too Roman in his ways and was sent down from his college. The country now follows the Pope again, but they still prefer their priests to be motivated by something more than sheer hatred of Protestants. So, now Morris haunts the town with his cronies, looking out for the smallest sign of heresy. You heard him talk. He's a bore and a bigot, but I'd love to get him into debate. He should be able to provide some reasons for his beliefs, rather than spout what the priests tell him. But not in these times, I think.'

'You wouldn't get very far.'

'Indeed.'

Edward digested this all.

'Thank you. I'll remember that.' He wanted to like Richard Taylor but his conditioning cried out against this man, this renegade correspondent. Maybe he should leave. 'Richard, I'm grateful for your help, but I will have to go ...'

Taylor held up a hand.

'Of course. But ...' He smiled. 'I said I like the company. Can't you just stay a while? A couple of days?'

***

Edward lay in his bed. His eyes stared blankly towards the ceiling and though it was dark he could easily see the plaster above him. He had turned all his senses to maximum while he prepared his report – a habit that Taylor had said it would be useful to acquire, should anyone at some future date come by and find the correspondent apparently in a coma.

Images flickered through his mind and he separated them into two files: one that was his actual report on the execution and one that would be a discourse on life in the sixteenth century in general, once he had sufficient supplementary data.

Into the former he put the straightforward sensory data of the day. The first thing he had noticed after arriving was the purity of the air he breathed. He had arrived in the countryside; when he had got close to town he had known it because the wind changed and the air he was breathing had been the air that blew out of Oxford. It was the air of a society where the horse was the main form of transport and the populace believed that baths transmitted disease.

There was more in this vein. Oxford in the rain; the people; the *zeitgeist*. To it he added those things which had impacted on his emotions – the aura of the crowd around the stake; the hatred; the bigotry. The sheer animal unreason of it all.

He valiantly resisted the temptation to include mention of Taylor. Taylor had been good to him and had committed no crime, but still Edward doubted his masters would approve.

When the report was finished, he breathed a sigh. His first! Now it just needed filing. The Moon was up, so-

He *thought*, and a tone that only he could hear sounded in his head.

'AL/1556, stand by,' said a voice. Then, 'AL/1556, transmit.' He *thought* again and in a couple of seconds it was over.

'Report received, AL/1556,' said the voice.

His report was filed. A big moment! Perhaps tomorrow he would celebrate with Taylor. Taylor had gone sour on the correspondents, but he could probably still recall the elation of his own first report and would understand what it meant to Edward.

Edward got out of bed and strolled over to the window to look at the Moon. Somewhere up there was the station, awaiting retrieval by those who had put it there, centuries from now. The thought was comforting. He had no doubt that sooner or later in his career he would feel mighty lonely and it would be good to know that up there was something else from the far future. A link to the Home Time.

Edward turned back to the bed in preparation for sleep – and turned back to the window again, for within the last second he had heard voices outside in the street. He would never have detected them without his correspondent's abilities. One was Taylor's.

There was no reason why Taylor should not wish to leave his house late at night – but after supper that night Taylor had gone out of his way to say that he was having an early night in preparation for a busy day tomorrow.

Edward was barely responsible for his actions in slipping out of the house and tailing his host. He was a correspondent.

Taylor was not alone – he was accompanied by Wilf, the man that Edward had seen on first entering Taylor's house that day. For his servant's benefit – on his own he could have managed without, as Edward was doing – Taylor carried a lamp. It did not give much light.

They came within sight of a pub in St Clements, across the river from the main town, and the two men stopped, waiting in shadow. It was closing time and the clientele was leaving. A crowd of men came out all together and at the centre Edward saw the loud-mouthed man from the stake – the failed priest, Morris. Taylor and Wilf followed after him at a safe distance, themselves now acting like men who had just left the pub. Morris and his friends took no notice. One by one Morris's friends peeled off until Morris was on his own.

Morris didn't notice them until it was too late. When they jumped on him he bellowed and lashed out and if one of his blows had connected it would have hurt, but he had not been trained as Taylor had. Before anyone around had plucked up the courage to investigate the disturbance, the two men and their unconscious captive had vanished into the night.

Edward watched through a crack in the planks that formed the wall of a barn outside Oxford.

Morris woke up slowly. There was a flickering light from a lantern nearby, surrounded by a red glow from a brazier next to it. Irons stuck out of the glowing coals. He lay on a pile of straw.

He squinted groggily up at the two men who stood over him; Wilf smirked and Taylor had an expression of mild curiosity. He wriggled; he was stripped naked and the straw seemed to irritate his back and buttocks.

Then his mind cleared and he lunged up, to find that he was tied down with high-quality hemp.

'What d'you want? Where is this?'

'Where no one will hear you, Morris,' Taylor said.

'What do you want?' Morris shouted again.

'You are a good Catholic, are you not, Morris?' Taylor said. 'A loyal subject of the Bishop of Rome?'

'What's it to you?' Morris asked cautiously.

'Are you?'

'I am,' Morris said. His voice trembled and Taylor smiled. The word had not yet been invented for that smile; it made Morris shiver. Perhaps it was then that Morris knew he was dead.

'Good. Wilf, fetch the tools.'

Wilf walked over to Morris's left. The captive strained to see what he was doing but the man was too far behind him.

'You were heard,' Taylor said, 'at the stake today, expressing approval for the execution of Archbishop Cranmer.'

Sweat broke out on Morris's forehead. Edward took in the dilated eyes and the flared nostrils and diagnosed the symptoms of terror.

'D-did I?' Morris said.

"The heretic had it coming. God bless the Queen, dragging this country of ours back to the true faith, never mind that German monk's ramblings," Taylor said. 'My memory never fails me.'

Wilf walked back into Morris' view, laden down with tools. Taylor took a blacksmith's pliers off him and held them out, looking at them thoughtfully.

'Those were your words,' he said. 'You condone the burning of heretics.'

'Ave Maria, gratia plena, dominus tecum, benedicta tuum ...' Morris had made up his mind that he was about to be a martyr to the faith. Taylor nodded at Wilf.

'Dominus tecum, do what you want with 'em,' he said. He handed the pliers back. 'Begin.'

Morris's gabbling rattle of Latin got faster and higher as the pliers closed around his left big toe, then turned into a scream as Wilf closed the handles and bone crunched.

Wilf released the pliers and Morris gulped air in huge sobbing breaths while the pain died down to a throb. Then he vomited.

'I'll not recant,' Morris vowed as his chest heaved. 'I'll not turn to that pagan devil Luther.'

'I don't want you to turn to Luther, Morris. I want you to justify your faith to me. Why should Cranmer have been executed?'

'He was a traitor! He renounced the true faith-'

'He wrote a prayer book in the English tongue. Where was the treason in that?'

'It was a blasphemy! It-'
'Why?'
'The Latin tongue is the tongue of the true-'
'Why?'

'I'll not answer your damn questions! Rot in the hell that is waiting for you!'

'Wilf,' Taylor said. Wilf came forward with the pliers again. 'The other toe.'

Edward Smith recorded it all.

At first he had intended to march straight in. Wilf he could handle and he should be well matched for Taylor as well.

But a voice inside him had said, *watch*.

Then he had seen the torture begin and the voice inside him had said, *report*. After all, it was only his sense of propriety that was outraged. He felt – could feel – no sympathy for a man of this time.

By chance and by instinct, he was compiling a report in his mind. Provisional title: *Anatomy of a torture session*.

> 'The subject's faith is firmly lodged in his mind and he will consider no alternatives. He was asked if he believes in Jesus Christ, the Prince of Peace. He does. He was asked if he believes in loving his enemies, as Jesus commanded. He does. He was asked if he believes that heretics should be tortured and put to death. He does. Asked why, he stated that torture will speed them on their way to heaven. He was asked, does he believe he will go to heaven after this evening? At this point he invariably lapses into Ave Marias or Pater Nosters.
>
> 'The man named Wilf applied the pliers to his other big toe and he would only

repeat the same points. After that Taylor instructed Wilf to move on to the branding irons. These were applied to his chest, his stomach and his genitals. Wilf then applied the thumb screws. It appears that torture instruments should be applied singly: if applied two or more at a time they are less effective, as the subject's concentration is divided between two sources of pain ...'

There was more, much more, and Edward took it all in. He was trembling and sweating: it was like being tied down and made to watch. He *wanted* to feel Morris's pain – he knew that he should and he despised himself for the great nothingness inside him where, as a human being, his sympathy for Morris should have been.

Yet he could only report. He found himself already planning ahead: he would reopen the file later and flesh it out a bit to turn it into a report for transmission. Who would be interested? Perhaps he should make several versions. A dry, factual one for the historians; a more chatty version for the general readership ...

Eventually Wilf said, 'People will soon be about, Mr Taylor.'

Taylor checked his inner clock.

'True,' he said. 'I doubt we will get any more out of Morris.' He looked down at the broken, twisted body, which they had been careful to keep alive. Two tortured, animal eyes stared back up at him.

'You have been a great help, Morris,' he said. He shook his head, genuinely baffled. 'Amazing. You really do believe it, don't you? And you don't see any contradiction, any conflict ... mad. Quite, quite mad.'

He turned to Wilf.

'He will soon be dead. Come, Wilf.'

Wilf was already heading for the door. With a calm, smooth motion Taylor pulled out a knife from his cloak and plunged it into Wilf's back, piercing his heart. Wilf arched backwards and cried out, once. Then he toppled over rigidly, like a falling plank. Taylor casually stepped over the body. He stopped when he saw Edward standing in the entrance to the barn.

The correspondent was pale and trembling. His instinct when Taylor called a halt to the session had been to walk back to Oxford, now that the report was over. Walking instead into the barn to confront Taylor had been like walking through treacle.

'Hello, Edward,' Taylor said.

'Kill him,' Edward said.

'Why?'

'Kill him!'

'You kill him.'

Edward paused, then unsteadily walked forward, keeping an eye on Taylor. Taylor's hands were both free, but he might have had another knife hidden away.

Edward stopped by the brazier and studied Morris carefully.

'I'm sorry,' he said, 'but you wouldn't want to live. Sixteenth century medicine will never make you whole again.' He put a hand to Morris' neck, spreading his fingers out over the throat. Morris whimpered weakly. 'I'm sorry,' Edward said again, and squeezed. Once Morris was dead, Edward kicked the brazier so that it toppled over and its coals spilled out onto the straw. The fire caught and spread around the body.

'He is doing you a favour, Morris,' Taylor said. 'The flames will speed you to heaven.' He turned to go.

Edward took one last look at Morris, and followed. As they left the barn, the flames were catching hold of the walls.

They walked for a minute without saying anything. Then Taylor stopped and looked back.

'Quite a sight, isn't it?' Taylor said in the Home Time tongue. Edward carefully positioned himself so that he could see Taylor and the barn. It was burning merrily and the flickering light lit up the countryside all around.

'Why did you do it?' Edward said.

'You don't know what to think, do you, Edward?' Taylor said. 'You know you ought to be feeling horror and revulsion towards me, and you want to, but you can't. Your conditioning won't let you. Morris and Wilf were both of this time, you think, so why should their fate bother you?'

'Why did you do it?'

'Why? Curiosity, really. I wanted to see what makes a man like that tick. I don't file reports any more, but I still have this urge to find things out. I can't help it.'

'Wilf?'

'Wilf was just as bad as Morris, but a Protestant. I'd already had a long conversation with him about his faith and I couldn't hang on to him after tonight, could I? He may not have known the exact word for blackmail, but he would have understood the concept. So, Edward! What are you going to do with the report you've been compiling? Will you be transmitting it? Of course, that will make you seem like an accomplice to the Home Time, especially after killing Morris—'

'The report is over,' Edward said, in a voice that was not his own.

'Sorry?'

Edward swung round to look at him.

'The report is over,' he said, then, in a more normal but frightened voice, 'Richard, there's something inside me-'

Edward was looking out of his own eyes as if his body belonged to someone else. From the back of his mind, the sealed off bit, something had come forward and taken over. The words that came out of Edward's mouth were not of his own volition. He heard himself say something that was almost, but not quite, the words that triggered the Death Sentence. They did not trigger his-

-they triggered Taylor's. He heard the correspondent gasp, once, and then the man collapsed.

Edward stared down at him for a moment. He knelt to check the vital signs. Taylor was dead.

'What-' Edward murmured.

'His conditioning had broken down,' said the stranger in his mind. 'Our correspondents must move unnoticed among the natives, but he took a delight in causing them pain and using them for his own ends. We were aware from correspondent TW/1329, Roger Woods, that an aberrant correspondent was operating in the sixteenth century. We suspect Taylor killed him.'

'He killed a correspondent?'

'He reverted to type.'

'But ... but-'

'We needed to gather evidence against Taylor, Correspondent AL/1556. No charges are held against you and your report will make most interesting reading.'

'But ... if you wanted the report anyway ...' Edward said helplessly.

'It is unimportant.'

'But am I really a correspondent? Or am I just a machine–'

'You are a correspondent who was needed for this one mission. I shall now erase myself and you will be a free agent again.'

The thing was there for a second longer, then was gone, its mission fulfilled. Edward wondered how many other programs he had lodged in the back of his mind.

He began to walk back towards Oxford, his mind already busy polishing up his report.

Reverted to type?

He could not put Taylor out of his mind. Things were whirling about in his mind and falling into place – a whole series of deductions from a small amount of data.

Reverted to type. Taylor's conditioning broke down and he reverted to type. What kind of man had Taylor been in the Home Time? The same as he was here?

What would be the punishment for similar activity in the Home Time? A brain wipe? A life sentence?

(Several life sentences ... ?)

Was this how they got correspondents to volunteer? Edward stopped in his tracks at the thought. Were they all like Taylor, given the chance to redeem themselves by going into the past and living several lifetimes over – or not – to make it back home again?

What kind of a man had he, Edward Smith, been in the Home Time? Was this why his memory was so fuzzy?

He forced these thoughts to the back of his mind. He was a correspondent first and foremost. He knew his duty and it lay with his masters, centuries hence.

Taylor's conditioning had taken seven centuries to crack and Edward only had five centuries to go until he could transfer back. He could last that long.

Surely ...

About CORRESPONDENTS

'Correspondents' was the real genesis of my novel *Wingèd Chariot*, (which became *Time's Chariot*), much more than the story of that name was, but the genesis of the story – other than a trip to Oxford and a glimpse of the Martyr's Memorial – was a strange desire to write a story about torture.

We humans are capable of the most unimaginably brutal acts towards each other, and as a hang-over from my idealistic teen days I still catch myself thinking that if only the people inflicting the treatment could have the same thing done to them, they would realise how wicked they were and stop. In actual fact, of course, this ain't so at all. It's only in bad fiction that the baddies are enlightened enough to see the error of their ways and repent: real life is rarely so obliging. Writing stories like this is my way of keeping my feet on the ground. I say to myself 'wouldn't it be nice if ...', and by the end I'm telling myself, 'no, it wouldn't.'

This was published in the American magazine *Aboriginal SF*, who took five years to publish it, but I forgive them. It had a tendency to come and go according to the finances available to it, but I left the story with them because it was a good magazine and I believed in it. Sadly *Aboriginal* is no longer with us.

'Correspondents' was also my first American sale.

TRIAL BY ALIEN

Rachel was dead. Hugo was dead. Every human on board *Pathfinder* was dead except for him and he was under cabin arrest for no reason he could discern: the one human left alive while the ship drifted in space with the nearest help a thousand light years away.

Neil Cardoso was lying in his bunk while the wedge-shaped face of a Rustie loomed over him.

'Do not move,' Press Minor said. The voice coming from the translator unit around the alien's neck was bland and expressionless. 'You probably still need rest.'

'Probably?' Neil said.

'Our species breathe the same mix of atmospheric components. It is likely we share the same reaction to smoke inhalation. One of us in your position would need rest.'

'Look, I'm fine.' But two hundred pounds of Rustie was pinning him down, a three-toed foreleg on either side of him, so there was nothing Neil could do while the two grasper tentacles either side of Press Minor's mouth extended and depressed his tongue, pulled down his eyelids, felt his temperature. The flakes of brown-orange flesh that gave the species their nickname dangled in front of his eyes and its breath hissed gently through the ring of nostrils around the crown of its head.

'You are probably well,' said Press Minor. It swung itself back to stand on all fours next to his bunk and became a stumpy quadruped the size of a Shetland pony again.

'Does that mean I can get out of this cabin?' said Neil.

Press Minor paused.

'Well?' Neil said.

'No.'

'But why not? If I'm well-'

'Every other human on board is dead-' Press Minor said.

Neil thumped the wall. 'I know!' he shouted. 'And I want to make my farewells. I want to make funeral arrangements. I want-'

'-and we think you did it,' Press Minor said, sounding almost apologetic.

They let him out the next morning and a troop of four Rusties escorted him, accompanied by Press Minor, to the ship's canteen. It was the largest open space on board and the survivors of the Pride, the fifty or so Rusties that were the other half of *Pathfinder*'s crew, were there waiting.

'Mr Cardoso. Thank you for coming.' The speaker was Flesh Several, Senior and undisputed leader of the Pride. As it spoke the other Rusties immediately adopted the attitude of junior-to-senior.

'Flesh Several,' Neil said, I've been confined to my cabin, my friends are dead, I-'

TRIAL BY ALIEN

'All in good time, Mr Cardoso.' Flesh Several's voice had the perpetual translator unit-induced lack of interest about it. 'Our investigations have shown that the explosion was deliberately caused and you must admit that your sole survival from the human contingent raises interesting possibilities.'

'But I'm not a mass murderer!' Neil said. He looked at the Rustie at Flesh Several's side. 'Run Knowledge, tell him-'

'Can't, sorry.' Run Knowledge said. It sounded almost laid back: Neil half expected it to add a 'Man' or 'Dude' after it spoke. Run Knowledge had been Rachel's counterpart as ship's xenologist and one of the jobs they had been working on together was reprogramming the translators, making their wearers seem more individual and more colloquial to humans. Run Knowledge was using an altered unit now.

As ship's reporter, Neil had spent a lot of time with Run Knowledge: the Rustie had even read bits of the novels he tried to write and surely, Neil thought, had a fair idea of his character.

'Why not?' Neil said, baffled.

'Mr Cardoso, please understand,' Flesh Several said. 'We are in a difficult situation here. We are the first joint crew of our two species since our respective governments made their agreement to go into space together, so the situation is highly experimental and we have a responsibility to make it work.

'There can be no doubt that a crime has been committed, whether by you or someone else we cannot yet tell. There is evidence, however circumstantial, which suggests you may have had something to do with the matter. It is important for everyone that this matter be cleared beyond all reasonable doubt. It is especially important bearing in mind that we may be here in space for a long time, until someone finds us. We need to know.'

Neil swallowed. 'I understand that.'

'However, our species and yours have very different systems of justice. If one of us errs then that one is dealt with by the Pride. That is not practicable in your case and I therefore propose to hold a trial in the manner by which your own government would try a human. I have witnessed such proceedings and I believe I have grasped the concept. There will be a judge, and counsels for the prosecution and defence, and a jury. Mr Cardoso, do you agree?'

'I think it's an excellent idea,' said Neil, with complete sincerity. He had finally begun to think ahead: he could already imagine returning home as the sole survivor of a human crew wiped out by sabotage, who just happened to have been somewhere else at the crucial moment, and not having any proof of his innocence.

'Then we are agreed,' Flesh Several said. 'I will act as judge, Run Knowledge has agreed to act as the prosecuting counsel and you may select any one of us as your defence counsel if you so desire. A jury will be selected at random from among the crew. At 09:00 tomorrow morning the prosecution will present its case. For the duration of the trial you are confined to your cabin, having no contact with members of the crew save Press Minor, who will tend to any remaining medical requirements, and your counsel. Before we adjourn, do you have any questions?'

'Um, yes,' Neil said. If he was to have a trial as Flesh Several proposed, this must now be the arraignment, so: 'if we're going to have a human-style trial then you've got to tell me what I'm charged with, and take my plea.'

'Of course. Run Knowledge?'

Run Knowledge spoke. 'Neil Cardoso, you are charged with inadvertently causing the deaths of 28 members of this ship's crew and deliberately plotting the death of one member, Hugo Jorden. How do you plead?'

'What'? Neil was on his feet. 'That's ridiculous!' *Hugo?* Why would he want to kill *Hugo?* 'You can't be-'

'How do you plead?' Flesh Several said.

'Not guilty!'

'Thank you,' said Flesh Several. 'We are adjourned.'

'What do you think?' Neil said as Press Minor ran the scanner over him.

'Yeah, I think you're probably innocent,' Press Minor said. He gazed at the instrument. ''Course, I'm less sure about these readings-'

'Oh, give me that.' Neil snatched it out of Press Minor's grasper and ran his gaze over the readings. Then he looked up at the Rustie. 'Oh no, not you too!'

'Hey, I got my translator reprogrammed to Rachel's specifications,' Press Minor said, sounding wounded. 'Just about everyone has by now.'

'You sound like a neo-hippy.'

''S'my way of paying tribute to her work, you know? Anyway, what does the scanner say?'

'Hmm? Oh, yeah.' Neil looked at the display. He knew the basic Rustie medical and numeral glyphs, so-

'My god, I'm burning up!' he said.

'Your temperature is optimal for your species,' Press Minor said, and then Neil realised and deliberately rapped his own forehead.

'*Duh*. Base 12. Yeah, in base 10 I'm fine.'

'You know, Dr Xu was fond of a saying: "a doctor who prescribes for himself-"'

'Yeah, I've heard it. You can say the same for ...' Neil trailed off, gazing thoughtfully at the cabin wall.

'Yes?' said Press Minor.

'I've been thinking. Press Minor, I-' Neil swallowed. 'I didn't cause that explosion. I didn't.'

'Yes?' said Press Minor again.

'But if there's going to be a trial, and it's going to be done properly, it'll be Run Knowledge's job to believe I did it, and he'll use every ounce of his intellect and will power to convince the jury that I'm guilty.' He grimaced. Interest in human fiction aside he had never really got on with Run Knowledge, though the Rustie and Rachel had been very friendly. 'I think he thinks I did anyway.'

And Neil knew how it was with a Rustie Pride. Verbal communication played only a small part. Body language, pheromones, all manner of subtle emphases gave them a depth of understanding and communication that humans could only dream about. He had been planning to defend himself, in the pure and certain knowledge of his innocence, but faced with a Rustie playing to a gallery of Rusties- 'I need one of you to be my counsel,' he said. 'Will you do that, Press Minor?'

'You know I don't anything about your legal system?'

'Then I'll tell you.'

Press Minor looked at the floor, then back at Neil. 'Okay. What are my duties?'

Neil felt relief wash over him. 'Well, first, you no longer think I'm probably innocent. You know it.'

'You've got it.'

'And your next step is to get every scrap of evidence that Run Knowledge intends to present against me.'

'Does he have to tell me?'

'Yes he does. It's called disclosure.'

'You know, that must save confusion.'

'And third,' said Neil, 'you've got to know that people who keep saying 'you know' can be really, really annoying.'

The night before the trial began, Neil dreamed of Rachel. He turned over to face her, savouring the warmth of her body pressed against him, the feel of her hair on his face.

Hugo loomed over them. 'My God, Neil, if you knew where she's been-'

'Piss off,' Neil mumbled. 'It's only a dream and you're dead.' With a smile on his face he stretched out an arm to cover what turned out to be an empty stretch of mattress. Then he remembered, the memory pushing through the clouds of sleep, and he sobbed quietly into his pillow.

The trial was convened in the canteen. Neil, Press Minor and Run Knowledge sat facing Flesh Several. To their right, twelve Rusties sat on their haunches in two rows of six. Neil had been allowed to retrieve his aide, a portable artificial intelligence device that sat on the tabletop next to him and recorded the proceedings. The aides of the other humans on board had all been gathered together, a sad pile of anonymous electronics, along with their owners' personal effects.

Flesh Several addressed the jury, its words translated for Neil's benefit. 'I have explained the procedure. I must impress on you again the need for the utmost impartiality in this matter. Where Mr Cardoso comes from it is the custom that jurors and other court officials have no prior knowledge of the defendant or of the crimes for which he is charged, but that is not possible in this case. I therefore instruct you to put aside all prior knowledge, theories or preconceptions and to base your judgement solely on what transpires in this court.'

The amazing thing, Neil thought, was that was exactly what the Rusties would do. It was their way. Tell a human not to think of pink elephants and what was the first thing to come to mind? But if a Senior told a Rustie to forget something then it would, just like that.

'Run Knowledge,' Flesh Several said, 'it is now your duty to convince this court that Mr Cardoso is guilty. Proceed.'

'Thank you,' said Run Knowledge, rising to all fours. 'I'm going to show this court that Mr Cardoso, on the 14th of this month, acquired elements of thruster fuel-'

Run Knowledge went on, laying out the case that Neil had known he would. His disclosed evidence had been a vague jumble of facts with some witnesses thrown in for good measure. Every word was circumstantial, as Run Knowledge freely admitted, and Neil felt a warm glow in his heart. That, and the minor matter of a complete lack of motive-

'But why should he do this?' said Run Knowledge. 'What was his motive? Well, I'll explain that too-'

* * *

Rachel was waiting for him as he stepped down to the floor of *Pathfinder*'s boat bay. He grinned and dropped his bags and pulled her into a long kiss. All the months of hassle and hustling, all the favours given and called in to convince the authorities that *Pathfinder*'s maiden survey voyage needed a reporter to cover it, and that he was that man ... it was all suddenly worth it. After a moment – far too short a time, suspiciously short – she gently pushed him away.

'Neil,' she said, 'this is Run Knowledge. He's my opposite number in xenology.'

'Hello,' said Neil, glancing down at the Rustie who stood patiently nearby.

'A pleasure to meet you,' said the Rustie xenologist. 'You two are acquainted?'

'Yeah, you could say that,' Neil said. Now he could tell Rachel was keeping her distance and he wondered why.

'Neil,' she said, 'you should know-'

'Rach?' Hugo Jorden's tall figure had appeared in the hatchway. 'Is that reporter here yet-' He stopped dead when he saw Neil. Neil looked back in horror.

'What's he doing here?' they said together.

* * *

Run Knowledge's first witnesses presented no surprises: they were the engineers who had reconstructed the explosion and fire, and produced the forensic evidence that everyone already knew but had to pretend for the trial that they didn't.

An explosion had wrecked the optical storage banks of *Pathfinder*'s main computer. The data was held in backup but as the banks themselves had been destroyed there was nowhere for that backed-up data to go. It did not take a forensic genius to work out that the explosion had been caused by the detonation of a pack of thruster fuel from a spacesuit.

At this point the chief Rustie engineer was required by Flesh Several to explain how thrusters worked.

'The fuel is made to be inert, see?' it said. It too was using one of Rachel's reprogrammed translators. 'It basically just lies there until it's needed. There's a reactant that needs to be added to make it react at all, and even then it needs an electric charge from the triggering device. High voltage.'

'And do all thrusters deliver the same thrust?' Run Knowledge asked.

'No, no. I mean, you don't want suit thrusters to take off like a fusion booster, so the fuel there only has a small amount of reactant. The ship's attitude thrusters need more kick so they have more reactant-'

'Thank you,' Run Knowledge said, 'we get the picture.' And it carried on with presenting the forensic results to the court.

The remains of the pack had been carefully patched back together by Rustie engineers, together with the triggering device. Which made it sabotage, because there no way either the fuel pack or the trigger could have been carefully placed against the optical banks by accident.

The initial explosion had been bad enough. The Rusties who had then opened the safety bulkhead hadn't known, or hadn't checked, that the compartment was still combustibly hot but deprived of oxygen – conditions ideal for backdraft. As the bulkhead opened a fireball swept out of it and into the next compartment, the human quarters, where the human contingent was sleeping. Safeties that should have gone into operation to prevent the spread of smoke and flame had been knocked out when the computer went down. By the time everything was under control, seven Rusties and 21 humans were dead.

The one human exception being Neil, ship's journalist and aspiring novelist, who was walking in hydroponics at the time, in the throes of insomnia as he worked out a further convoluted plot point.

Press Minor rose to cross examine each witness. 'But was there evidence of Mr Cardoso's involvement? DNA? Body hair? Finger prints?' This last was a concept that had to be explained to the jury but the answer in each case was 'no'.

The engineers added that they were still piecing together the wreckage: scraps of optical cabling from the remains of the storage banks, fragments of shattered instrumentation, bits of tubing. Debris had also been found down the air ducts that lead away from the computer room and towards the human quarters, somehow flung there by the blast. Run Knowledge asked the jury to note that point.

Run Knowledge thanked and dismissed the engineers, and announced: 'for my next witness I call Mr Cardoso.'

Neil and Press Minor had both known he would be called. Flesh Several spoke to him as he stood up.

'Mr Cardoso, it is my understanding that under your system, no one may be induced to testify against himself. Is this correct?'

'Um, yes, I think so,' Neil said.

'Then you do not have to answer Run Knowledge's questions if you do not so wish.'

'Oh, I wish, I wish,' Neil said with feeling. The sooner this nonsense was cleared up, the better.

He sat in the chair that had been provided as a witness stand. 'Um,' he said, 'isn't there an oath or something?'

It took another five minutes to resolve. A Rustie ordered by its Senior to tell the truth would do so but all parties conceded that the same could not be said of humans.

'The witness should swear on his sacred scriptures,' Run Knowledge said.

'Why?' said Neil.

'Well, because you believe that if you lie you'll suffer eternally in hell, don't you?'

'Actually, no,' said Neil, 'but if it pleases you-'

It pleased Flesh Several, so Neil used his aide to interface with the other aides on board and sure enough, one of them had the text of the Bible stored in its memory. He displayed the opening chapters of Genesis, held his hand over the display and swore to tell the truth, the whole truth and nothing but the truth.

Run Knowledge was able finally to begin its examination and it fixed him with what was probably a beady Rustie look. 'So, Mr Cardoso, what was the nature of your relationship with the human Rachel Payne?'

* * *

'Any regrets?' Neil whispered in the dark. He felt Rachel turning towards him, felt her arms slide round him and pull him close.

'No,' she said.

They lay together silently.

'I'm sorry about-' he said after a while.

'Neil,' she said, with *that note* which told him to be quiet.

'When I saw-'

'Shut up.'

'Sorry.'

'Good.' A pause, then, 'I thought you were going to hit him again.' He could tell from her tone she was smiling.

Neil grinned. 'Me too.'

'If you went to such trouble to get on this ship just to see me, you really should have checked who else was on board.'

It had been the sheer shock of seeing Hugo standing there, though Hugo had been just as surprised – if he had thought of Neil at all it was still as a failed medic on Earth rather than the successful freelancer that Neil had become. Just as Neil always thought of Hugo, that moment at the party, frozen in time forever. The newly appointed Dr Rachel Payne, Institute of Xenology, calmly telling him that it was over, that she had made her decision – the shock alone had him teetering on the brink – and then the arm going around her waist, which he had watched with the same dread as if it had been a deadly snake. His eyes had followed the arm up to the shoulder, then to the face of its owner. A smugly smiling, equally newly appointed Dr Hugo Jorden.

And Neil had gone over the brink and his fist had smashed out. End result: Hugo pressed charges for assault, Neil was bound over to keep the peace.

At least Rachel stayed in touch. They saw each other occasionally and sometimes slept together for old time's sake – she and Hugo hadn't lasted. Why she consented, he never knew: loneliness, pity ... Each time Neil had hoped it would be *the* time: the time he finally broke through whatever barrier there was between her and the rest of the human race and she would accept him as her lifetime love. But it never was.

* * *

'Will you explain to this court,' said Run Knowledge, 'the nature of human reproduction?'

Oh God, Neil thought. 'The, um, mechanics are pretty similar to your own,' he said.

He had seen Rustie matings – quickenings, they called them. They weren't at all shy about it: an invitation to witness was a sign of friendship. Whenever the Pride wanted a new addition it decided who the lucky pair should be – any Rustie could play either role – and the whole lot of them clustered around to watch. The act, the sharing, the witnessing bound the whole Pride together in mutual love.

'Yes, but your motivations are different, aren't they?' said Run Knowledge. 'I mean, you don't engage in reproduction simply to procreate?'

'No, no, we don't.'

'Then why?'

'I object!' Press Minor said. 'Mr Cardoso can't possibly speak for the entire human race.'

'No, but he can speak for himself and that's the motivation we're interested in,' said Run Knowledge.

'Please answer the question,' Flesh Several said after a moment's thought.

'Why do we have sex?' Neil said eventually. 'Because ... because it's fun. It's pleasurable. And it ... it seals love. It seals a relationship. It's as intimate as two people can get. It's the best thing you can give the person you love.'

'That's the human way?'

'Not necessarily.' Neil looked Run Knowledge in the eye. 'But it's my way, and that's what you want, isn't it?'

'I suppose. And this was your motivation for your activities with Rachel Payne?'

'Yes,' Neil whispered.

'Was it her motivation?'

'No. No, I don't think so.'

'And did she share your views on this matter?'

Neil couldn't speak. He looked at his shoes.

'I repeat the question,' Run Knowledge said.

'No, she didn't.' Neil looked up. 'But she wouldn't have done it if ... if she hadn't been, I don't know, fond of me.'

'Fond?' Run Knowledge said. 'That's not quite the same as love, is it?'

'No.'

Press Minor interrupted again. 'Flesh Several, these questions aren't relevant to the matter and water leaking from the eyes is a sign of human distress.'

'Run Knowledge, do these questions have relevance?' Flesh Several said.

'They do,' Run Knowledge said. 'Mr Cardoso, I'm really sorry to cause you grief but it's unavoidable.

Now, will you explain to the court the concept of a crime of passion?'

* * *

'It's not you,' Rachel said. She was sitting up in the bunk, hugging her knees. Neil lay next to her, looking up.

'Then what? Who?' he said. He braced himself for the hated name. 'Hugo?'

'Oh, for Christ's sake,' Rachel snapped. 'Look, I've said I want to be alone. Can't you just take that at face value without dragging in third parties? You or Hugo. Him or me. Black or white. Don't flatter yourself! Don't be so ... so *binary*.'

It was the first time Neil had heard the word *binary* used abusively.

'Yes, I've slept with Hugo,' she said. 'Several times, and if you like I'll describe each and every occasion with time, place and duration, since you enjoy torturing yourself so much. But not lately. In fact, not for years.'

Years? 'But I thought-'

She swung round to face him. 'What?'

'Nothing,' he mumbled.

'No, go on.' Her glare verged on hatred.

'I thought ... you and him ... together all that time ...'

'You thought because we did research together we were lovers, didn't you? You thought that all those co-authored papers meant we must be doing it on the side? Neil, you're pathetic. You can't stand the man and I once, *once* dumped you for him, so we're lovers. I can't believe it! What does ... I mean, what does that say about *me*? About how you see me? I'm incapable of keeping my clothes on for a decently good looking man? I can't handle my own life? I can't make my own choices? You ... you're ...*oh!*'

She made a cutting gesture which did more to express her contempt than any words. Neil lay in silence, not daring to move. He felt like a stranger in his own bunk.

When Rachel spoke again he jumped.

'Hugo, for your information, is a professional who can detach his brain from his balls and concentrate on the job. We've worked together because ... well, we're a team, him and me and Run Knowledge. We can bring our different perspectives to the job and we're finding out so much. So much! About the species we discover, about each other. Reprogramming the translators is just the start of it. We understand the Rusties like never before and they ... well, Run Knowledge could almost be human, some of the things he says and does. We're getting so much from each other ... we *work*. We're a team that works, and we're not going to split up because you've got the emotional maturity of a thirteen-year-old with his first crush. Now go to sleep.'

* * *

'So, like you're saying, humans can be driven to murder through jealousy of a loved one?' Run Knowledge said.

'Yes,' said Neil. 'I've never met any myself but yes, I believe so.' And then it struck him and he gazed into the distance. *Humans can be driven to murder through jealousy of a loved one...*

Hugo. Hugo had been the jealous one. Just because Rachel wasn't sleeping with him didn't mean Hugo didn't want her. Neil could empathise with that. Hugo

... but even though Neil couldn't stand the man, could he accuse him of murder?

Yes, he could. Okay. Hugo tried to kill Rachel ... or maybe, tried to kill Neil? But why cause the explosion? Because something went badly wrong. So what was he trying to do that had gone wrong ...

'Mr Cardoso?' Run Knowledge said loudly. Neil jumped. 'I repeat: it's something outside your experience?'

'Um, yes.' Neil brought his thoughts back to the present.

'Thank you.' Run Knowledge turned to Flesh Several. 'Now, I'd like to submit as evidence the personal aide of Mr Cardoso.'

'I object!' said Press Minor. 'Surely, using Mr Cardoso's aide will be tantamount to his giving evidence against himself?'

Flesh Several considered the matter. 'Mr Cardoso should give his consent and no inference may be drawn if he does not. Mr Cardoso, may Run Knowledge submit your aide as evidence?'

Neil shrugged. Run Knowledge had said he would do this and there wasn't a thing there that could incriminate him.

'Sure,' he said.

* * *

It was a quiet spell and Neil had time to himself. He looked at the words floating on his aide's display and for the first time in far too long they had nothing to do with the reports he would be submitting when they got back home.

'I cannot marry you, Peter,' she whispered.

He stared at her through a howling whirlwind of confusion. 'But why not?' he stammered. 'I thought we agreed-'

'Selena?' They both turned towards the new figure to enter the ship's lounge. Metal-shod boots rang out on the deckplates. The figure that came into the light strutted arrogantly, one hand on its hip and the other held out to claim her. The brow was high and noble, the moustache immaculate, the expression of unutterable arrogance.

'The launch is ready,' declared the man. He condescended to notice Peter and inclined his head slightly.

'Good day, De Montfort,' he sneered. Selena's hands flew to her mouth.

'X!' she exclaimed.

Neil scowled at the last line. X. X? X! X had to be a name that said everything. X was a despoiler of virgins, a cad, a bounder, an arch-seducer who-

'Hi,' said an unenthusiastic voice. Neil looked up: Hugo was in the doorway.

Professional, he thought. *Brains from balls*. 'Can I help you?' he said.

'Yeah.' Hugo held out a data crystal. 'Thought you might like this. That last but one planet? Evidence of some weird symbiotic relationships among the lower life forms. Thought it might make good copy, that's all. I wrote it down to your level.'

Neil took the crystal. 'Thanks-' Hugo was looking at his aide's display and he quickly blanked it.

Hugo grinned and the old smugness was back. 'Still writing that stuff, are you?'

'Yes.'

'Anything published yet?'

'No,' Neil said. Hugo's silence was eloquent. 'It's a hobby. Just a hobby.'

'Right.' Hugo turned away. 'See you.'

He left and Neil called up the novel again. 'For character X,' he dictated to the aide, 'universal rename *Hugo*'.

* * *

'And so the plot of this novel is that whilst on this cruise Peter De Montfort kills the Duke Hugo for love of the Lady Selena?' said Run Knowledge.

'Yes,' said Neil. *Come on, Press Minor, do your job* -

'This is absurd,' said Press Minor, right on time. 'Mr Cardoso writes fiction as a hobby. The operative word is *fiction*.'

'Sure, it's fiction,' said Run Knowledge. 'Mr Cardoso, did you invent this genre of fiction?'

'No, it's centuries old.'

'Centuries old? So humans have been practising this way of life for centuries?'

'No! I mean, look, not all humans go about murdering for love-'

'Not all? You mean, some do?'

'So what?' Neil said. 'So what? 'Some' can be any number, any tiny, infinitesimal little fraction-'

'But surely your plot would be recognised by any human, no? You wouldn't have written this story if you hadn't expected your readers to understand it.'

'I suppose-'

'Then surely any human would potentially be capable of committing a crime like this! Now, Mr Cardoso, I don't suggest that all humans are latent murderers: I mean, you say yourself that in your novel, Peter De Montfort isn't thinking clearly when he commits his crime. He isn't his normal self. When you came on board *Pathfinder* you were your normal self and, sure, murder was the furthest thing from your mind but were you thinking clearly, were you your normal self when you plotted to kill Hugo Jorden?'

'I did not plot to kill him!' Neil shouted.

'Okay,' said Run Knowledge. 'For the information of this court, will you describe how in your novel the murder is carried out?'

* * *

A tube led from the exhaust manifold of the sleeping ship's thousand horsepower engines. It led into the air conditioning ducts.

Peter had already climbed through them, carefully blocking off the junctions. Now the only open passage was to Hugo's cabin – a cabin where even now the sleeping Duke's lungs were drawing in the carbon monoxide being pumped there from the engines. Quick, quiet and unfortunately painless.

Another couple of minutes, Peter pondered. Then he would disconnect the tube, go up into the ducts again and remove the blocks he had put in to prevent the deadly fumes from spreading throughout the system and killing

> *the wrong people, and retire to bed, perchance to dream-*

* * *

'And you don't see the similarity?' Run Knowledge said.

'No, frankly.'

'Then I'll explain it to you. The explosion was caused by the discharge of a triggering device into a pack of thruster fuel, check?'

'Um, yes, apparently.'

'And we learnt earlier that thruster fuel reacts to this charge according to the amount of reactant in it. A large amount will deliver enough punch to manoeuvre a ship?'

'So I gather,' said Neil. 'I'm not an expert.'

'Of course, and that was your downfall. What would be the effect if only a small amount of reactant was added?'

Neil shrugged. 'I don't know much about the chemistry. I suppose it depends on how much smaller. I mean, it could have any range of effects, from detonating the whole lot of fuel, through making it bubble a lot, to making it break down gently.'

'And if it broke down gently, what would be the effect?'

'Well, it would split. It would give off-' Neil's widened in horror. 'Oh, shit.'

And Run Knowledge filled in the missing pieces of the prosecution's case. The computer room was the last room in its compartment: the next compartment held the human quarters. A line of individual cabins along one corridor, the first of which was Hugo's, with a shared air duct that ran along them all.

Neil had gone into the computer room because the air duct linked directly to Hugo's cabin. The tubing that the engineers had found had led from the fuel pack to the duct. The trigger should have caused the fuel to bubble gently, releasing fumes which would have been picked up by the tube and carried to Hugo's room.

But for some reason – perhaps nerves, perhaps because he was hurrying – Neil had added too much reactant to the fuel. The result: instead of bubbling, explosion; the deaths of Hugo Jorden, Rachel Payne, the other humans and seven Rusties; and the crippling of the ship.

'This case is ludicrous,' Neil said in his cabin. 'Any jury of humans would see it's just too coincidental, my novel and the facts – the alleged facts of this case. They wouldn't be taken in for a second.'

'Shame it isn't a jury of humans,' said Press Minor.

'Yeah.' Neil sat with his chin on one hand, until he realised he looked liked Rodin's Thinker and sat up. 'Hypothesis,' he said. 'Hugo wanted to kill either Rachel or me. He set up everything as Run Knowledge says I did. The tube didn't lead to Hugo's cabin, it led to mine. Or Rachel's. I mean, after the explosion some of it was just lying on the floor and some of it was flung down the duct, so it could have led anywhere. You see? It's every bit as circumstantial as Run Knowledge's forensic evidence.'

'And the fact that the attempted murder matches the fictitious one so closely?' said Press Minor.

'I'm working on it. I'm working on it,' Neil said gloomily.

'Remember, we don't have to prove anything,' Press Minor said, 'we just have to cast reasonable doubt on the prosecution's story. How many others have read your novel?'

'No one. But I've discussed it with some of the others-'

'You see?' Press Minor said. 'Reasonable doubt! All we need to do is show that the gist of your plot could have reached other people on this ship.'

'You're the counsel,' Neil said. 'You do the arguing.'

'I'll do that. I'm also going to go through as many personal records and notes as I can to see who else might have had the motive. And so are you.'

'I just want to go to sleep,' Neil muttered.

'I'm trying to defend you,' Press Minor said. 'Kindly help me. Your aide can do the linking up. I'll start with Hugo, you start with Rachel and we'll take it from there.'

Ten minutes later, Neil had to explain to Press Minor what 'bingo' meant.

Neil took the stand the next day.

'I was looking through Rachel's personal notes,' he said. 'I wanted to show that others might have had the motives that Run Knowledge ascribes to me. And I found this.'

'We wish,' said Press Minor, 'to submit the last log entry of Rachel Payne.'

'I object!' said Run Knowledge. 'That information was protected on Rachel Payne's aide and I was unable to gain access to it. How has the witness managed?'

'I lived with her for God knows how long,' Neil said. 'Of course I could get into it.'

'And we will be glad to make this information available to the prosecution,' Press Minor added. 'May we proceed with our submission?'

'Please do,' said Flesh Several.

The lights dimmed and Neil set Rachel's aide to public playback. Her image appeared in front of the witness stand.

'Please note the time and date,' said Press Minor. 'Fifteen minutes before the explosion.'

Rachel began to speak. 'Whoa! Major balls-up. I just realised the latest translator update program has a minor glitch. Okay, a major glitch. This is embarrassing. Numbers are being translated literally, without taking into account the fact that humans think in base 10 and Rusties in base 12. If I say, oh, I don't know, 'twenty two' to a Rustie then the translator won't translate it into base 12 for the Rustie's benefit, though the Rustie will think it does. Result: the Rustie will think it hears a higher number. On a scientific expedition, this could be awkward.

'Fortunately no one's going to fly the ship into a star or anything because the nav systems are completely separate. Still, I've corrected the error and the central computer has just delivered an update to all the translators. First thing tomorrow I'll put out an announcement that any calculations made involving a translator in the last 12 hours or so are wrong-' Neil paused the transmission and the lights came up again.

He blinked, hoping the tears wouldn't show. Seeing her again, hearing her voice-

'Flesh Several, the prosecution would ask the defence its point,' said Run Knowledge.

'The translators were not translating between base 10 and base 12 figures,' said Press Minor. 'The prosecution says that the explosion was caused by too much reactant being added to the thruster fuel. The thruster pack in question came from a human style spacesuit. Now, if whoever set the bomb wasn't a skilled space mechanic then that individual would have received verbal instructions from the suit's computer. Because it was a human suit, the instructions would have been given in Standard. The computer would have given the desired quantity of reactant in base 10, but if one of us thought the figure was base 12, it would have put in a higher amount.'

For the first time Flesh Several had to call for order in the court as the Rustics broke into a babble amongst themselves. The strong, sweet smell of Rustie got stronger, which was always a sign of powerful feeling. Press Minor had got through to them.

Press Minor rounded off its submission. 'We don't contest the forensic evidence presented by Run Knowledge, just its interpretation. Mr Cardoso wouldn't have made the errors that were committed by the perpetrator of this crime: no human would. We ask this court to dismiss the charges against Mr Cardoso and to concentrate its efforts on finding the member of our Pride who is so aberrant in its behaviour as to do what has been done and to have concealed it from us. That ends my submission.'

Neil sat back with a happy sigh. Surely, surely. And a smart move from Press Minor, ending on that note. It was a Rustie whodunnit, it would be dealt with in the Rustie way, he was exonerated and he would no longer be required to explain the finer points of heterosexual love and passion to a group of extraterrestrial hermaphrodites-

'Run Knowledge,' said Flesh Several, 'how do you respond to this submission?'

'Like Press Minor,' said Run Knowledge, 'we agree on the details but differ on the interpretation.' *Oh, what is your problem*? Neil groaned silently. 'If the translators can get that fact wrong, what else can they be misinterpreting? What might Mr Cardoso have said that we've misheard? We ask that a mistrial be declared, a full diagnostic run of the reprogrammed translators and a new trial opened as soon as is convenient, to be conducted using only translators with their original programming.'

'And how will this diagnostic be run?' Press Minor demanded. 'There's only one person on board who can speak Standard naturally. Will you have the translators go through every word in their vocabulary with him?'

'Enough,' said Flesh Several, rising to its feet. 'You have both made valid points which I must take into consideration. We adjourn until 09:00 tomorrow when I will give my decision.'

* * *

'Don't take it personally,' said Rachel, 'but I'm giving up men.'

'Oh,' said Neil.

She smiled and kissed him lightly on the cheek. 'Well, not just men. People. I've decided I'm just not cut out for romantic love. I'm not one for short term relationships and the thought of waking up next to the same person for the rest of my life is terrifying, and there's no comfortable middle ground that I've been able to find, though God knows I've tried.'

'So ... what are you going to do?' Neil said.

'I'm going to be a Rustie.'

'*What?*'

'Oh, not really.' She waved a hand. 'I've got several million years of evolution telling me I'm human and I'm not going to fight them. But their philosophy, the oneness of the Pride, that's what appeals to me, and to do that I'm going to have to become as much like them as I can.'

'But ...' Neil said. 'But ... I mean, Rach, you're a loner. You've never been happy with other people crowding in. How'll you manage in a Pride, for Christ's sake?'

'You're right. I've never been happy with other people crowding in,' Rachel said, with an emphasis on *people*, 'because people never know when to lay off. But Rusties do, Neil. There's that constant undercurrent of communication and you can tune in or tune out at will. I've found this, like very faint glimmerings, on this ship, and now I want to study and learn and, who knows, maybe I'll find things out that will help both our races understand each other more.' She grinned. 'I've got insights already, I've learned things on this voyage that'll blow your socks off. I can't wait to get back home and publish. This'll be my monument, Neil.'

'Right.' Neil looked down at the floor and let her words sink in. She'd made her decision and if he was going to respect it, and her, he should feel good. He wanted to feel good about it, he really did.

But he didn't. 'Right,' he said again.

'Oh, Neil.' She sounded annoyed but still she leaned forward and hugged him. 'If it's any help, if I was going to stay with men, it'd be someone like you.' He didn't answer and they stood with their arms round each other for a long time.

The door opened. 'I don't believe it. Just can't get enough, can you Rachel?' Hugo stood there, amazement on his face. 'My God, Neil, if you knew where she's been-'

'Piss off, Jorden,' Rachel mumbled into Neil's shoulder.

'Piss off. Fine. Fine. Piss off. Sure. Okay.' Hugo turned to go, then glanced back. 'Enjoy it while you can, Neil. That woman's going to ruin us all.'

Neil spared one finger to deliver a non-verbal response and Hugo slammed the door as he left.

* * *

If you knew where she's been -
-ruin us all -

Neil's eyes opened and he stared through the darkness at the ceiling, trying to catch the fleeing fragments of what his subconscious had just told him. He sat up.

'Lights on. Aide on,' he said.

The lights came up and his aide spoke from his bunkside table. 'Awaiting input.'

'Interface with the aide of Rachel Payne again. Access all the xenology related files you can.' *Insights*... If what he was after in Rachel's files was coded then he was stuck but-

Three hours later Press Minor found him sitting at the table, head resting in his arms, fast asleep with his aide on stand-by on the tabletop in front of him.

'I've got it, Press Minor,' he said when the Rustie woke him. 'I know what happened.'

'Good. Now dress,' Press Minor said. 'Flesh Several delivers his decision in 10 minutes.'

'Press Minor,' Flesh Several said to the court, 'has made a good case for its contention that one of us caused the explosion that crippled this ship and killed 28 of its crew. The fact that, for a short while, the reprogrammed translators mistranslated any figure that they heard cannot be disputed.

'However, what has not been proved is that the murderer intended anything less. For all we know the bomber, who might have been Mr Cardoso or another human, had noticed the flaw in the translators and had planned to make it appear as if one of us caused the explosion.

'Run Knowledge has made the point that if the translators are wrong on this, what other errors might they have made? However, an inconsistency like this would have come out before long anyway, and I feel that other inconsistencies would have also have emerged by now.

'This trial will therefore proceed along its original grounds, and I have already directed that all members of the crew are to use old-style translators until further notice. The defence will now present its case.'

'Flesh Several,' said Press Minor, rising to his feet, 'I must announce that Mr Cardoso has seen fit to dismiss me as his representative and asks leave to represent himself.'

'That is a strange move, Mr Cardoso,' said Flesh Several. 'You originally chose to have Press Minor represent you because you did not feel you could hold your own in a debate with our species. Has that changed?'

'What I have to say will speak for itself,' Neil said.

'Very well.' Flesh Several gave the head wiggle that was a Rustie shrug. 'It is noted that you now defend yourself and we ask you to present your first witness.'

'May I approach the bench?' Neil said.

'There is no need. I can hear you perfectly well from there.'

'I meant, can I have a word in private, with you and Run Knowledge?'

'Very well. Approach.'

Neil and Run Knowledge converged on Flesh Several.

'I only have one witness I want to call,' Neil said quietly, 'and that's Run Knowledge.'

'Quite ridiculous!' Run Knowledge declared.

'Certainly unusual,' Flesh Several said. 'Mr Cardoso, this was not in your original submission of evidence and even by human standards, a request to cross examine the prosecuting counsel is surely unorthodox.'

'It is,' said Neil. 'I'll ask only three questions, and if it's agreeable to the court, Run Knowledge can still function as the prosecuting counsel while it answers. I mean, it can raise all the normal objections and so on. Its answers can be simple yeses or nos.'

'Agreed,' said Flesh Several, after a moment's thought.

'Flesh Several, I still object-' said Run Knowledge.

'Nonetheless,' said Flesh Several. 'Run Knowledge, you will take the witness stand now. Mr Cardoso, this is on the condition that you ask your three questions and no more.'

'Understood,' said Neil. He went back to his desk while Run Knowledge took the stand and was instructed by Flesh Several to speak only the truth.

'My evidence,' said Neil, 'comes from the aide of the late Rachel Payne. It will be relayed through my aide and displayed for the benefit of the court.' He set the aide to display one of the images he had found in her files at full magnification in the centre of the room. It was a frozen image of a Rustie: and more than that, it was of a Rustie at full sexual arousal. The flap of skin between its front legs was drawn back to reveal its male and female genitalia, side by side.

'My first question,' said Neil. 'Is that you, Run Knowledge? Remember, yes or no.'

'Yes,' said Run Knowledge. 'In my capacity as counsel, I must point out that I have taken part in quickenings that have been witnessed by humans. It is not surprising that an image of one should be on a human's aide.'

'Then I'll ask my second question,' said Neil. He took a breath – he knew what was coming but it was still painful – and the image expanded to show the other partner in the coupling, also frozen and poised for action. He pressed the play button and uproar broke out as the scene commenced. For once Flesh Several had to call for order more than once. Neil waited until the noise had died down, then: 'are you engaged in sexual congress with Rachel Payne?'

Run Knowledge was silent for so long that Neil almost repeated the question. Then: 'I decline to answer.'

'Well, like I said, it speaks for itself,' said Neil. He shut the image off: it was too distracting, too painful. 'My third question, Run Knowledge. When I first saw this, I couldn't believe it. I was shocked. My mind just couldn't take it in. It disgusted me. It's perversion. Any human would think so-' [Apart, he thought, from the various sects and cults that had wanted to have sex with the Rusties five minutes after first contact, but he didn't mention them to save confusion] '-and I think most of your species would call it perversion too. Am I right?'

Run Knowledge said nothing.

'You are directed to answer the question,' Flesh Several said, over the noise of the crowd. Still Run Knowledge said nothing and Neil knew that the Rustie had just become as alien to the rest of its Pride as a human.

'Flesh Several', said Neil, having to raise his voice, 'the defence wishes to make another submission-'

* * *

'Run Knowledge confessed everything,' said Press Minor. They were in the canteen, which had reverted to its normal function. Flesh Several had accepted Neil's submission that there was sufficient evidence to cast reasonable doubt on the prosecution's case and the matter had become subject to Rustie custom. With the entire Pride around it, willing it to confess all, Run Knowledge wouldn't have had a chance, even though it had previously put itself so far outside the Pride that it could disobey a direct order from its Senior. 'It was engaged in sexual activity with her, and with Hugo Jorden, at first in the interests of science and discovery but later simply for enjoyment.'

If you knew where she's been - Neil thought. 'I know the rest,' he said. This was what had come to him out of his subconscious that morning. 'Rachel was going to publish, which would ruin their careers, so they conspired to do her in, and the plan backfired.'

'No,' Press Minor said. Neil put his drink down and stared at the Rustie.

'Then what?' he said.

'At first Hugo Jordan was averse to her publishing but Rachel had talked him into accepting it. They and Run Knowledge would co-author the paper.'

'Then what-' Neil said again.

'The process worked both ways,' Press Minor said. 'She was becoming like us but Run Knowledge was becoming like you. Run Knowledge was jealous of Hugo and wanted him dead. It was inspired by your novel.'

'The bastard,' Neil whispered. 'The bastard.' Part of his mind noted that he was only now feeling sorry for the late Hugo, on whom he had earlier been quite ready to try and pin the crime. 'But Rachel wasn't sleeping with Hugo. She told me.'

'Sleep was not part of their activity,' Press Minor agreed.

'That wasn't what I meant.'

'Of course. No, they were not intimate, but they had been and Run Knowledge feared they might be again. Be grateful: if it had succeeded with the first murder, it would have come for you next.'

'So, what happens now?' Neil said after a moment.

The head wiggle shrug. 'The Pride will try to reintegrate Run Knowledge,' Press Minor said. 'If the psychological and neurological damage of its perversion runs too deep for healing, it will be put to death. My hopes are not high. It could ignore a command from Flesh Several and it had been able to hide its crime from us.'

'Oh.' Neil winced but had to admit he felt very little pity. 'That's not what Rachel would have wanted. She loved life, life in all its forms.'

'If she wanted to be like us then she would accept our ways.'

'Yeah, yeah, but she told me her work would help us understand each other better, get along more ... it's just a pity that- what's that?'

Several Rusties had run into the canteen, gasping together in their own language. Press Minor spoke to one of them, then turned quickly to Neil. 'It is *Explorer*, just showed up on radar. They have responded to our hails. We are rescued.'

Neil shut his eyes. 'Thank God.'

'*Explorer* will want a full report of the human aspects of this mission,' said Press Minor. 'Will you-'

'You bet,' said Neil. He put the glass down firmly and stood up. 'Every last byte.' Rachel had wanted a monument – he would build it.

A monument ... for a moment he had a brief mental image of a statue of Rachel on the job with a Rustie, but he pushed the thought away.

About TRIAL BY ALIEN

I love good legal dramas and I'd wanted to write one for a long time, with a human being put on trial by aliens in a human-style court but with the aliens doing the trying. I wanted the plot to revolve around something aliens could do but we couldn't, or vice versa, which would be the final clue.

When I'd finished my first novel *His Majesty's Starship*, I realised I had the aliens ready-made, and it saved the trouble of inventing yet another race. There was also a vague hope that this story would take the world by storm and cause everyone who read it to go and pick up the book. So, this story is set a few years after the events of the novel: anyone who reads the story and wants to know what Rusties and humans were doing on the same ship, you can guess what to do.

A HOLIDAY ON LAKE MOSKVA

'Come to Moscow.'

Paula extended the invitation one summer evening. We were in her university room at Heidelberg, sitting side by side at the window, wrapped in our robes and each other and watching the world go by.

'Moscow?' I said.

'For your project.'

'Oh, yes. That.' For my project I wanted something novel, something few others would be doing, and something that would keep us together over the summer vacation. The thought of doing something in the conquered Reich territories had not, until then, occurred to me.

We had met at the beginning of the year when I arrived at Heidelberg for a year's study from Cambridge. I called it going abroad, Dad called it going home. We met through the Goethe Society; she was a year older than me, then twenty to my then-nineteen, and just starting her final year. She was an aristocratic, blue-blooded Prussian by birth, if not choice, which made her relationship with middle-class, half-English, half-German me, Robert Miller, all the more unusual.

She had already anticipated my main fear. 'The killings are down for the third year running,' she said, with what would have been irony if she were English.

So for all sorts of reasons it was too good a chance to miss, and I just had to make a couple of phone calls home. Mum and Dad, it turned out, were quite happy for me to make the trip to Ostland and, more important, were ready to pay the air fare.

'That's that, then,' Paula said, and made her own telephone call to break the news to her parents in Moscow, where Paula's father just happened to be General Officer Commanding Muscovy Province.

* * *

Paula met me at Moscow airport. Going through customs was a cold-sweat-inducing experience as we filed through the metal detectors and were patted down for hidden weapons while sniffer dogs went over our luggage. But then I was pushing my trolley through the arrivals hall, smugly not feeling part of the crowd of package holiday makers that had come in on the same flight, and there she was. She wore a light, one-piece flowery dress in keeping with the broiling Moscow summer and the soft material was moulded by the gentle breeze to her form underneath it. Her blonde hair glowed and I had never seen her looking more beautiful than when she came forward to meet me. It wasn't falling into each other's arms, it was just that we kept walking towards each other until that was where we happened to be and the centres of our respective universes were in the same place. I was a couple of days later than planned, held up by

A HOLIDAY ON LAKE MOSKVA

unexpected business in Cambridge and London, and this hadn't happened for far too long.

'Wait until you see our transport, my darling,' said Paula with a twinkle in her eye as we walked out into the sunshine, she hanging on my arm.

'Is it a tank?' I said.

'A tank in disguise. There it is.'

It was a sleek black army Mercedes, parked carelessly on no-parking lines. It sat low on its wheels and pennants flew above the headlamps: the family crest of the von Bitterfelds on the right and the Wehrmacht eagle on the left. A corporal stood by the open rear door and he stepped forward to take my bags. I climbed into the spacious rear seat and Paula slid in next to me. The car pulled away, blithely cutting in front of the package tour bus, with the corporal at the wheel.

'Does it have machine guns under the hood?' I said. The powerful engine was a background whisper in the air conditioned interior. Paula took my arm and snuggled up close.

'Just armour plating,' Paula said. 'Don't worry, my love. It's more dangerous to cross the road. East of the Urals they are utter bastards but they know their place in the Western provinces. Some of the Russians even like us. Take Corporal Erhardt here. Engaged to a Kiev girl, aren't you, Corporal?'

'That's right, ma'am.' Erhardt never took his eyes off the road. The patch on his arm said that he belonged to the Ostland Regiment; he was the son, or even grandson, of German immigrants to the conquered territories.

'Kiev's in Ukraine,' I pointed out.

'Ukraine, Russia, who cares? Why not look at the view, my love?'

I thought the Russians or the Ukrainians might care, but I did as I was told, and the view was worth admiring. I couldn't believe we were going through the suburbs of a city that had once been gutted by war. I had been expecting the stark Wagnerian grandeur of Berlin all around me, but Hitler's influence had been diluted in Ostland and a modicum of taste had triumphed. A lot of white stone and red brick, nothing over three storeys, with lines that suggested delicacy and elegance. Gardens and bushes and trees provided shade and variety.

'We'll spend a week here and then I've got us travel warrants for Petersburg,' Paula said. She waggled her eyebrows up and down and moved her head closer to mine. 'No parents!' she whispered. In the driver's mirror I could see Corporal Erhardt grinning. Cheeky sod.

I kissed her. 'I can't wait to see it,' I said.

Her smile spread across her whole face.

'But Petersburg can wait. Wait until you see the lake.'

* * *

Lake Moskva stretched away into the distance, a steel blue sheen that beckoned us to plunge in and wallow beneath the heat of Moscow's July sun. The waterfront was a clear-cut edge, marking out the limits of the enormous crater that Todt's engineers had gouged from the centre of the city. I stood on the quayside with an arm round Paula's hips, her body pressing into the

A HOLIDAY ON LAKE MOSKVA

natural groove that seemed to run down my side fitted specially for her, and I marvelled.

It was a wonder of the world, sculpted and designed with its sluice gates and pumps to keep it where no natural lake was meant to exist. It was an engineer's dream, even a layman would pause for thought, and it lay over a city razed as a monument to a madman's hate and pride. Nature shouldn't allow such contradictions.

The gentle strains of "Ere we go' from behind told me that the tour bus had finally arrived. We ignored it.

'Amazing,' I breathed. Oh, I knew it well at second hand. One of my bags was crammed with every book and article and paper on the lake that I had managed to find. I had seen the pictures, watched the television reports, but now, actually being there ...

On this site the Wehrmacht and the Red Army had fought the final, decisive battle. Moscow had been devastated and millions had died. Stalin's armies had been ready to fight to the last man, only breaking when their leader's corpse was paraded in front of them. And now: a city, vanished, obliterated, drowned!

'Thank God we never fought you,' I said. All that time I had spent in Germany and only now was the sheer, casual brutality of Operation Barbarossa coming home to me.

Paula laughed and hugged me closer.

'Robert, why would we ever want to fight you? And we only did this to make a gesture, you know, make sure Bolshevism was utterly destroyed. But don't you think the lake is beautiful?'

That was my girlfriend. She renounced the army and all its works, and she only lived here because it was where her parents were and she had nowhere else ... but she talked casually about destroying cities to make gestures. I turned my thoughts away from this troubling track.

At least they had kept the Kremlin. I saw it now for the first time: it was the only island in the lake that actually had something of the old Moscow on it. The waters of the lake lapped below the red walls, low in the summer heat, and I could just see how the island had been shored up below the waterline. In the bright, warm sunlight and with Paula pressed close to me – that dress really wasn't very thick – I found that maybe I could enter into the required spirit.

'Today,' Paula said, 'we rest and relax. You get over the journey. Tomorrow I thought we would take a picnic out to one of the other islands. Papa's got a new boat he wants to try out. Sound good?'

I smiled. Yes, I had work to do, but I could forget about it for a while. 'Sure,' I said.

The launch carried us over to Kremlin Island, a five minute journey, where we tied up and entered the fortress through the Trinity Gate. A small town lay inside the walls and I began to realise just how big the place was. It was a unique blend of traditional Russian architecture and more European influences, all done on a huge scale.

'We live in the Grand Palace,' said Paula. 'The Gauleiter uses the rooms the Tsar once had. Our apartments are far more modest.' She looked left and right. 'You, um, remember that little matter we were discussing ...?'

I remembered, and I laughed when she showed me my room. The sleeping arrangements suggested a compromise made by parents who try to be open-minded but don't want to think about their children growing up: single beds in two rooms with a connecting door, and no further comment.

But then, our rooms at university also had single beds, and part of being an engineer is about overcoming the physical limitations of your environment.

* * *

'Adolf Hitler,' said the General over dinner, 'was a great statesman. But he made mistakes and it's probably as well that he had his stroke when he did.' Paula's father was a large, friendly man and unmistakably Prussian. An old military family, the von Bitterfelds had galloped back into uniform as soon as the Führer waived Hitler's prohibition on the aristocracy joining the armed forces. The General had finally grasped that he didn't have to speak slowly for me to understand him.

Frau von Bitterfeld raised her eyes to the ceiling. Paula had warned me that one of the General's favourite pastimes was making contentious statements to sound out his daughter's boyfriends.

'By mistakes, do you mean the Jews, Herr General?' I asked cautiously.

'Mmm.' The General nodded and swallowed his mouthful. 'And the Slavs. Genocide was an insane idea, but of course Hitler needed a scapegoat and the man was staring mad besides. Führer Bormann, unpleasant little opportunist that he was, was wise to call a halt when he did. We had already handed Einstein over to the Americans on a plate. All that talent, lost forever!

'But you have to admire Hitler's achievements. He built the Reich up out of the chaos of the old republic. He united the German peoples, and that took some doing. Even I might have been tempted to join the Party in those days.'

I decided to test his irony levels. 'And he won you Ostland,' I said.

'Exactly! I don't think you young people realise just what a threat Stalin and his Bolsheviks posed to the world. Even the British had an active communist party. Would you like to live in a communist state, Robert? Can you imagine your royal family brutally murdered?'

'Papa ...' Paula murmured.

'Oh, I'm sorry, is this offending your young liberal attitudes?' the General asked with a laugh, and the friendliness in his eyes showed that he meant no offence. He took a sip from his wine glass. 'I will change the subject. Tell me about yourself. I like to know the company my daughter keeps.' Like he hadn't already had me vetted six ways from Sunday. He was looking me in the eyes as he said it and I saw his gaze harden for a moment: I know exactly how you two keep company and if you do one thing to hurt her, you little shit, you'll wish you'd never been born. It's amazing how much data you can compress into a glance. 'How did you meet?'

I grinned in fond remembrance and glanced at Paula. 'On a coach to Weimar.'

'It was a Goethe Society outing, papa,' Paula said.

'Ah!' I saw the gleam in his eye, the approval, the revised assessment: only half German, morality questionable but taste, good.

'My grandfather gave me his copy of the Complete Works,' I said. 'I've still got it.' Back then I had been unequivocally English and Germans were humourless automatons the other side of the English Channel, unfortunately related to the Royal Family but what could you do? Then Granddad gave me that collection. Can anyone read Goethe and imagine that Germans don't have humanity? A love of freedom, of beauty, of the rights of the individual over the rights of powers that try to control him? I couldn't think of anyone less Nazi than old Johann.

'Your grandfather, yes,' the General said, still friendly. 'Your grandparents came from the Reich?'

'That's right, sir.'

'And you? You don't see any problem being back here?'

'They didn't like what was happening to the Jews.' Granddad, a lawyer, had tried to bring charges against the authorities after Kristalnacht and my grandparents left the Reich one step ahead of the Gestapo. 'Now that's no longer happening ...'

'Quite, quite. And you're an engineer? What will you do with your degree?'

I smiled. 'Whatever I can do. I just want to be of service.'

'Mmm. Perhaps you should speak to my daughter. She keeps telling me that Küche, Kinder, Kirche is dead and women can make their own choices about how they work, and then she makes herself unemployable with a sociology degree. I keep trying to get her to emigrate out here, you know. Ostland has vast empty spaces, so we may as well fill them up.'

'I can't see Paula as a farmer,' I said, trying to laugh the subject off, and the General chuckled.

'Not everyone is a horny handed son of the earth,' he said. 'We need thinking people as well. Administrators and governors, even sociologists. And engineers! You could get a job here, Robert! You're German enough, you've been to a German university and you speak the language better than half my men. A lot of firms just want people with the right experience. Ostland needs talented people of all kinds. Out here you could make your own opportunities. Be whatever you wanted to be.'

Interesting man, the General. He despised Adolf Hitler, and admired him. He was appalled at the aborted Final Solution and the whole concept of Lebensraum, yet he sat here and commanded the army that had conquered this territory, and encouraged his guests to emigrate here, to fill the vast empty land with little Ostlanders.

And so dinner continued, and eventually we got off the subject of what either of us wanted to do with our lives. But the General hung back as we left the table, put a friendly hand on my shoulder.

'Seriously, Robert,' he said quietly. 'There are opportunities for young people like you, ways you can be of service. We'll find the time for a chat before you head off to Petersburg.'

* * *

The bed just wasn't comfortable and what had seemed a brilliant solution to the problem of distributed, limited resources – make love in one bed, sleep in the other – was showing its limitations. Tomorrow night, I had decided, we'd put both mattresses together on the floor. Meanwhile, much as I enjoyed the feeling

A HOLIDAY ON LAKE MOSKVA

of Paula's naked body close to mine in a tangle of limbs, my outraged subconscious was catching up on a day's worth of repression. Confused impressions were running through my mind and I was resigned to a couple of hours of insomnia.

Paula, and the General. Two quite different characters, two very similar people. Friendly, amiable and both quite ruthless in their own way. People were too complex.

Paula aside, that trip to Weimar had had long-lasting effects on me. We'd visited the Goethe Oak with its plaque, Hier ruhte Goethe auf seine Wanderungen in diesem Walde: 'Here Goethe rested on his wanderings in these woods.' In fact, he happened to write the Wanderer's Night Song there. And why is that remarkable? Because a hundred years later the oak had been enclosed by the grounds of the now-dismantled Buchenwald camp where once thousands had died. The guides didn't talk about what Buchenwald had been and I wondered if some of the schoolkids on a nearby tour even knew. Goethe and the Nazis: the best and the worst of what Germany had to offer …

… side by …
… side …

A distant bang woke me up. Then more bangs, and the rapid pop-pop-popping of machine guns.

I unwound from Paula and got up. My heart was pounding as I peered out of the window. The sound was carrying unobstructed across the still water from the shore of the lake.

An exercise? Possibly. There were bound to be gunnery ranges nearby ... but at (I checked the bedside clock) half past two in the morning? Unlikely.

The popping died down and I heard alarm bells and sirens. Then there was a flash of light – the bang came a couple of seconds later. I stared in fascination at the flickering of distant flames, somewhere on the shore. I was just beginning to realise that this wasn't a film, wasn't TV. What was happening over there was real life. Another little skirmish in the battle between Russians and Germans that had been going on for forty years, ever since the people of Ostland stopped fighting the Germans face-to-face and set about reclaiming their land by more covert methods.

I heard the sound of a body moving. 'Darling?'

'Something happening,' I said.

Paula got up and padded over to join me. She put both arms round me and looked out of the window. 'My God!' she said when she saw the fire.

We stood silently for a long time, watching. Paula rested her head on my shoulder. The fire dwindled until eventually it was out.

'And Papa wonders why I don't want to settle out here,' Paula said.

'I'm told it's more dangerous to cross the road.' I couldn't resist that dig.

'Statistically it is, but you know statisticians. Ostland is fine for brief visits, but a lifetime? I'll take my chances with the roads back in Germany.'

I yawned. 'I think it's over,' I said.

'Me too.'

We waited a moment longer, then she took my hand and led me back to bed. The gentle sheen of moonlight on her bare skin subtly highlighted the curves of breast and buttock that I knew so well. It began to have its inevitable effect on me and as we snuggled together back under the sheet, our bodies fitting neatly together in the way we had become so used to, the thought did pass through my mind that now we were awake we could put the time to good use.

But people might have died out there just now. This really wasn't the time, or the place.

* * *

The next day, a Sunday, was as sunny and glorious as the one before it and Lake Moskva was a blue mirrored apron around Kremlin Island. I woke at six, which was two in the morning by my body clock, but the sun shone so bright through the curtains that I wasn't going to get back to sleep. I got up instead.

It's a wonderful feeling to get out of bed not wearing anything, and to realise you're already exactly as warm as you want to be for the rest of the day. I pulled on sandals, T-shirt and shorts, and went for a walk.

I strolled along the waterfront below the Kremlin. Pure quiet; the lapping of the water, the occasional bird and very distant sound of a motor. The lake was so tranquil, so peaceful, it could almost be forgiven for being the grave of a city. I grinned at the remembered promise of a sail on it. The noises of last night were no more than a dream.

I lay down on my front at the water's edge and leaned out as far as I safely could. I wanted to know more about what lay below the waterline. I had a project so I might as well get started. It's not enough just to dig a hole if you want a lake, especially one with islands. The islands have to be reinforced. And the plumbing!

The Kremlin was a town in its own right; all that waste couldn't just pour into the lake, so there must have been special pipes laid to take it to a treatment plant, which implied pumping stations as well as gravity ...

'That's the spirit,' said an English voice. 'Investigating already. The secret submarine entrance is down there somewhere.'

I rolled onto my back. 'Have we met?'

The man wore a grey tracksuit, stained with sweat. He looked just like a normal guy going out for an early morning jog, red-faced and panting. In shape, demeanour and accent he could only be one of the package tour. 'Of course we have,' he said. 'You can call me Mr Harrison and if anyone asks, I'm a friend of your parents. And you, incidentally, are in trouble.'

'I've no idea what you're talking about,' I said.

'Oh, all right, play it by the book. Have you heard the latest Test results?'

'I'm not a cricket man,' I said slowly. 'Rugby's my game.'

'What did you think of that last minute try by New Zealand?'

'Amazing.' My heart was pounding as I sat up. He sat down next to me. 'Why am I in trouble?'

'Why didn't you tell us you were shagging Miss Bitterfeld?'

I flushed. 'It was your business? And, um, how did you know, anyway?'

'She's the daughter of GOC Moscow! Of course it was our business. And you went through Customs with about a hundredweight of rubber johnnies.' He stretched and grunted. 'Still, it shows you're not homosexual. So, what news?'

A HOLIDAY ON LAKE MOSKVA

'I think the General wants to recruit me,' I said. At least, that was my interpretation of those closing words last night. I'd been told it might happen. I'd have been vetted and come up smelling of roses. Flawless German, semi-Aryan ancestry (dissident grandparents, but ideology was no longer considered genetic), access via my Cambridge education to Britain's ruling classes.

The General wasn't going to pimp his daughter to lure me into the clutches of the Abwehr but he doubtless knew some people who always had one eye on recruitment possibilities.

'Excellent!'

'I suppose.'

When Six had first approached me, the thought of being a double agent would have made me proud, but that had been pre-Paula. Things really were much more complicated than Mr Harrison seemed to realise. Or maybe he did realise and couldn't see a problem.

'Well, no rush,' he said. 'What's on the agenda for today?'

'We help the General try out his new boat.'

'Then I won't stop you.' He jumped up and down a couple of times, puffed heavily and carried on with his jog. I went slowly back up to the Kremlin.

After breakfast I slung the picnic bag on my back and Paula and I went out through the Saviour Gate, then down to the pier that jutted into the lake below St Basil's Cathedral.

Paula's father was waiting by the boat. 'Here it is!' he called. He waved a hand at the dinghy. 'Isn't she lovely?'

I had no nautical eye and she looked like a boat to me – sharp end, blunt end and mast in between. While Paula and the General set about making her ready, the tour party rolled up at the quayside wielding their cameras and ice boxes and 'My parents went to Moscow ...' T-shirts, and started to clamber on board a motor launch. One of them waved at us. I had no desire to be associated with anyone in that party and I turned my back.

Eventually the Bitterfelds were ready and I could climb in without getting in the way. I took the bow seat. The General pushed us off and jumped in, then hauled on ropes attached to the boom. The dinghy slowly began to pick up speed away from the island and the mob, with Paula at the tiller and me enjoying the ride.

We passed by the bright red walls and golden minarets of the Kremlin's long south-east side.

'The Kremlin cathedrals,' Paula said, pointing. 'I must show you round them. Would you have expected three cathedrals in Stalin's capital? Some of the Tsars are buried in the one on the right ... Oh, Papa, you speak English, do you understand this joke Robert made? Um, 'Was Boris sufficiently' ... Oh, my love, what was it?'

I groaned and took a breath. 'The question is, was Boris good enough?' I said in English. I hoped Paula wouldn't try my other one – how do you catch a turian?

The General looked at me blankly.

'It's a joke,' I said feebly. 'Boris Godunov, it doesn't really translate ...'

'Don't bother, Robert,' the General said. 'Relax, enjoy the day!'

A HOLIDAY ON LAKE MOSKVA

And the day was worth enjoying. The weather was superb and the breeze nicely took the bite off the sun's heat. From the shore I heard the distant buzz of a speedboat ('Philistine,' the General muttered), which barely penetrated the soporific haze that was slowly enveloping me. I found myself trailing my fingers idly in the water. Had Kenneth Grahame reached the Reich, I wondered? Because Ratty had it absolutely right. There really was nothing half so much worth doing as simply messing about in boats.

'They want you, Papa,' Paula said, half-joking. The speedboat was heading right towards us.

'It's not an army boat. It's some bloody idiots who want to spoil a sailor's day,' her father growled. I agreed. In the last half hour I'd become a born-again dinghy sailor, and this dirty great thing burning petrol really didn't belong here.

I can still remember every detail of that boat. It was a light sports model, the type used for water skiing or just for zipping around at speed. It was painted blue and white and there were two men in it, one steering and one …

'Scheisse!' Paula shouted, and the boat swerved under me as she thrust the tiller over and went about, at the same time as the second man raised a machine gun to his shoulder and opened fire. Someone in our boat – maybe me, maybe not – screamed. All I could hear was the rattle of the gun, a good long burst, and all I could see were the muzzle flashes.

The bullets tore into the water and then the boat shot by us and the dinghy bucked in its wake. It was already leaning hard over and now it fell onto its side and tipped us out. It slowly righted itself again and wallowed, half full of water. The speedboat had slowed and was turning round.

'Duck!' the General shouted and he pushed Paula and me under with a hand on each head. I just had time to take a breath.

Under water the noise of the engines surrounded me. The loud, bass throb grated in my guts. It was impossible to tell where the speedboat was, or how near. I didn't have a lot of faith in the shielding properties of a few inches of water, but I didn't want to dive deeper because my legs would stick out of the water and they would see where I was, and my lungs were bursting and I couldn't see more than a blue blur and I was scared shitless ...

A distant chattering must have been the machine gun again. The roar of the engines peaked and then, amazingly, began to grow fainter.

I surfaced in a shower of water, gasping for breath and yelling. 'Paula! Oh God, Paula, where are you ...'

The first thing I saw was the red that stained the surface. The General was clutching onto the dinghy with one hand. His teeth were clenched and his face was white, screwed up in agony. His other arm hung limply in the water but I couldn't tell how bad the damage was. Paula was supporting him and sobbing, 'Papa, Papa ...' Then she saw me. I waited for her face to light up now that her beloved was safe.

'Get the flare gun!' she shouted.

'What? Where?' I was still dazed.

'The fucking flare gun!' Paula bellowed. 'There, in the stern locker.'

I swam around to the back of the boat. The flare gun was big and heavy and ugly. My hands were shaking but I managed to follow the instructions on the tag tied to the grip and insert a flare into its chamber. I pointed the gun at the sky and fired.

* * *

It was a waste of time because three hydrofoils full of Waffen-SS had been on their way from Kremlin Island within a minute of hearing the shots. One stopped to pick us up and the other two sped by without a glance.

We heard shooting as we arrived back at the Kremlin. Long, angry bursts of machine gun fire. We were listening to an execution.

I looked at Paula. Paula looked at me. There was a quiet, deadly fury in her eyes.

'Idiots.' The General's arm was shattered and had been roughly bandaged and splinted. He could walk, but he was leaning on an SS guard. 'They should take them alive. They could tell us useful things. This area is meant to be secure. How did they get in?' He glanced at me. 'I'm sorry your day was spoilt, Robert.'

* * *

'I don't understand you,' Paula said. We were at the window in my room, looking out at the lake. I stood behind her with my arms round her and we were both ready for bed, but we'd already reached the unspoken decision that it would be separate rooms that night. Romance was on hold after the day we had had.

The penalty of being a liberal. Having to see all sides of the argument.

'Look at it from their point of view,' I said. 'Can you blame them?'

Paula looked round at me with eyebrows raised lazily. 'Yes, as a matter of fact I can. They complain that we oppress them. All they have to do is not murder innocent civilians and we'll stop the oppression.'

'It is their country.'

Paula rolled her eyes.

'It was their grandparent's country,' she corrected gently. 'Nothing we can do will change that. If – and it will never happen – Führer Ahlberg withdraws all Germans from Ostland ... where will they go?'

'Home?' I suggested.

'But this is home!' Paula insisted. 'What's got into you? Men like Corporal Erhardt were born here. There are thousands and thousands of Ostlanders like him. Native Ostlanders. If you want to take it up with someone then get a time machine and go back to 1940.'

'I can see why you don't want to stay, though,' I said, with an attempt at lightening things.

'Whatever gave you that idea?' Paula said. I looked at her in surprise. 'You think I'd give those bastards the satisfaction?' She ran a hand through her hair and looked embarrassed, but underneath that her face was hard. 'Robert, my love, my darling, you of all people should know the best way of making me want to do something is to try and force me not to.'

'You mean, you're going to stay in Ostland?' I said, while the world fell away beneath my feet and the skies caved in.

'I'm going to stay in Ostland,' Paula said.

* * *

Dawn found me sitting below the Kremlin at the edge of the island, dangling my feet in the water and watching the sun come up over the lake.

'Mr Miller?' said a voice. I didn't look round.

A HOLIDAY ON LAKE MOSKVA

'Couldn't sleep either, Mr Harrison?' I said.

'I always go for a jog in the morning. And you try and sleep when two hundred young Brits are drinking and screwing the night away all around you.' He sat down next to me again.

I laughed without mirth. 'Someone once warned me that a good agent has to put up with all kinds of conditions.'

'So,' he said. 'Two nights in the enemy camp. Anything to report?'

'I nearly got killed yesterday.'

'Ah, yes. I heard about that. It was unfortunate but I gather it wasn't fatal, and certainly none of our doing. And?'

I looked at him for the first time. I wasn't trying to look miserable, but ...

'Ah ...' he said, in the trailing-off tone of a man reaching enlightenment. We looked out at the lake together for a while in silence. 'There's no easy way to tell you this, but splitting up with your girlfriend on the third day of a fortnight's holiday with her isn't really wise.'

'We haven't split up,' I said. The unspoken yet seemed to echo off the Kremlin walls.

'But ...?' he said.

'Paula's staying in Ostland.'

'I see,' he said. A pause. 'And this is bad because ...?'

I didn't answer. I wanted to spend the rest of my life with Paula, share my every day and night ... but not in Ostland. I didn't agree with Ostland. Ostland was wrong, and all her rationales about how it was all a long time ago, where else would the Ostlanders go, and all that, didn't change it.

But then, I had been living in the middle of Adolf Hitler's deranged fantasies ever since I stepped off the plane. Decent, rational people ruled a territory that their grandparents had seized, ten million of whose population they had murdered, and unblushingly called it their own. Ostland was a vast treasure house of land and materials, owned exclusively by the Reich and making Führer Ahlberg the most powerful man in the world.

And it was to the world's benefit! There was the rub. Here the Reich had based its space programme, with its many spin-off technologies which were exported to the rest of the world. Here were the vast power plants that exported energy to all of Europe and half of Asia Minor. Here was grown the grain which for the third year running now had held off the famine in Africa. Imagine if all those people were starving instead. Would they be saying 'ah, well, at least ten million Slavs weren't murdered' as they clutched their bloated, empty stomachs? I doubted it.

There was too much uncertainty, too much ambiguity. I couldn't keep my mind on it. It was painful and I shied away.

I wondered if I would be forever shying.

'You know,' he said, 'if you stayed with her then it would be the perfect cover ...'

'If I stayed,' I snapped, 'I'd ask her to marry me, so you could forget it.'

'Then maybe it's as well,' he said. 'It's funny, I distinctly remember you telling us at Six you wanted to be of service. Your exact words. When you set off for Heidelberg, you couldn't start work soon enough. I almost felt embarrassed that we didn't have anything for you to do.'

A HOLIDAY ON LAKE MOSKVA

'Yeah,' I muttered. I'd said the same thing about service to the General, of course, but the first time, the time I'd said it to Mr Harrison's friends, had been before I met Paula.

'Well, the first lesson to learn is that you can't serve two masters. The second is that you don't get to pick and choose your assignments. The third is that you keep your two lives separate. Compartmentalise. When you're on a mission, you put your private life aside, and vice versa.'

He paused, then his voice went up slightly. 'And the fourth thing, if you find yourself headed out into enemy territory, for God's sake let us know well in advance so your control doesn't have to book himself on the next package club holiday at a moment's notice.'

'I didn't think you'd want to come,' I said pitifully.

'Of course I wanted to come! On your first mission I have to be nearby, to give advice, take your reports, get you out of trouble if you get into it ... we don't just send you into the blue yonder without back-up, you know.'

'I know.' I felt wretched for many reasons. 'But I didn't think that this would turn into a mission until you got in touch at the last minute.'

'Oh, for Christ's sake! You go to stay under the roof of GOC Moscow, you're boffing his daughter and you didn't think it would turn into a mission? What did you think Six wanted you for, boy? An agent in Never-never Land?'

Again, I didn't answer. Working for Six was business. Anything to do with Paula was personal. This visit was to do with Paula, ergo and QED, none of Six's business. It had all made such perfect sense, at the time.

'Mr Miller,' Harrison said after a pause, 'you impressed us by agreeing to work for Six. You impressed us with your zeal when you went off to Germany. You don't impress us by throwing it all away for lurv. If you really want to be of service to your country then commit to us, because if we ever go to war again, it will be with the Reich.'

He stood up and patted me on the shoulder, not unfriendly. 'If we start getting signals, we'll take that as a yes. If not, we'll take it as a no, and we won't bother you again,' he said. 'In the meantime, clichés like 'there's plenty more fish in the sea' and reminders that you've signed the Official Secrets Act will never pass my lips.' And he jogged off, leaving me to the sunrise and my thoughts.

After a while I got up and trudged back up to the Kremlin, my room, my suitcase, my wash bag. I took out the electric razor. Then I got my penknife, opened out the screwdriver blade and took the cover off the nearest wall plug.

I still had the diagram I'd studied in London fresh in my mind. I unscrewed the head from the razor, dismantled it into various bits of plastic and metal, and inserted them into the electrical fittings in front of me. Then I screwed the cover back on and put the razor back in the bag, and headed off to the bathroom for a shower and a proper, wet shave.

They hadn't told me what it did and it was bad form to ask. I might have turned the apartment's electrical system into a coded transmitter, sensitised to the operation of any electrical equipment – say, a typewriter, a computer – that ran off it. Or I might have just inserted one element of many more which were to be inserted by other agents. Or maybe, of course, it served no useful purpose at all beyond showing my resolve. I didn't need to know. Twenty-year-olds aren't given life-or-death missions to run, but they are given test runs that let them show willing and indicate their suitability for future employment.

I'd shown willing.

* * *

Paula and I exchange birthday and Christmas cards, and the odd letter. She got a job as PA to the managing director of a farming tools business and is now head of an agricultural feed operation in Petersburg with a turnover of several million Reichmarks. Somewhere along the line she met her husband.

The bastard irony of it all is that though I stayed with Six, I never worked in the Reich again. Oh, I was still willing, but maybe the equipment, or myself, didn't send Mr Harrison the right signals.

There's a need for engineers all over the world and I've been here in Africa for the last ten years, designing and implementing irrigation systems for a former colony. Tensions flared in the Nineties when certain factions within the Reich declared their intention of regaining the territories that Germany lost in 1919. I observed troop movements, counted the number of Me-9000s that screeched overhead, let Six know when a new German showed up in town; all on top of the day job of helping Africans stay alive in the wake of colonial ineptitude. Maybe my reports helped, maybe they just went into a bin somewhere in Whitehall. But I like to think I did my bit, and the crisis went away.

And now I don't think our countries will go to war. The key is Ostland. Paula and her generation are taking charge there by simple dint of growing up and working up. They don't want war, they won't fight one for the Reich, and the Reich can't fight one without them. But they're not going to give Ostland back either.

Settlers still die there; the Russians still fight their underground war. They can be as creatively lethal as the Nazis ever were in their heyday. Shootings, bombings, lynchings even – they target military and civilians, adults and children. I hate it when it's the children; otherwise I just check the report for Paula's name – not there yet – and move on. I really can't find it in me to blame the Resistance.

Lake Moskva is still there, of course; a sheet of water covering the ruins of old Moscow. Tourists love it and a daytrip around the islands will cost you fifteen Reichmarks.

Down below, the lake bed dips and rises with the ruins of buildings and streets, but the water fills it all in to provide a smooth surface. But here and there an island breaks free of the surface, and your choices are to run aground and sink, or float around it and just keep going.

About A HOLIDAY ON LAKE MOSKVA

I once heard that one of Hitler's plans for Moscow, if Barbarossa succeeded, was indeed to turn it into a lake. I also understand that he never wanted a war with western Europe. To his vile little mind the true enemy lay in the east where he hoped to build his living room extension, or something like that.

And if it had all turned out as per the Führer's plans ... what would we have done? We can't know but I think there's a clue. Here in the real world, how much longer and harder would we have thought about ousting Saddam if he had an army of equal size, strength and skill looking back at us?

Exactly.

Thinking about it, this is the second story in this collection based upon the notion that we could just accept Nazi crimes rather than have gone to war about them. I'm very glad we did go to war about them, but how much of that is down to how I was brought up and what I learned at school? I honestly have no idea what I would think now if my grandparents' generation had looked the other way and western Europe now lived in a quiet accommodation with the Reich.

Our prehistory is a non-stop story of mass migrations, often to the detriment of whoever was there first. There are very few original

Britons about. The English have been in Virginia longer than they've been in Ulster. What Native Americans make of having Andrew Jackson on the $20 bill is anyone's guess.

At some point historical atrocity stops being quite so painful, and at some point after that it stops really mattering. I don't know where either of those points lie. I hope never to pass either of them in my lifetime.

GO WITH THE FLOW

'Why, 'To Gran'?' I asked.

The professor had been about to pass me a cup of coffee. His book, the cause of the interview at his house, lay on the table between us.

'I beg your pardon?' he said.

'Why is your book dedicated, 'To Gran'?' I said. I was deliberately keeping my voice casual but the matter had been bothering me all afternoon.

We'd got on well in this interview, gathering material for a feature profile I was producing, and he had really opened up. We had gone through his career, from undergrad to PhD whose work in fluid dynamics was being applied by the European government to social mechanisms, with astounding success. He had commented on the rumours that the 2036 Nobel was apparently sewn up. For background, we had even talked about his home life, his wife and children (to whom the book wasn't dedicated).

But …

The book that started it all off, in its paper version, was six hundred pages of small font and equations. Five pages of acknowledgements, in an even smaller font. A massive bibliography that needed a magnifying glass. A twenty page foreword by a bigwig from Princeton. And the title! *Go With The Flow: A Sociological Extrapolation Of The Effects And Applications of Transient Pressure Propagation On Human Populations*. Concision was not the author's style.

And yet, 'To Gran'.

'No sugar, wasn't it?' the professor said, putting the cup down in front of me.

'Yes, thank you.'

'Gran,' he said. 'Well, she looked after me a lot when I was a boy. My parents were constantly breaking up and she was the one secure thing I had. She had her own children quite late in life and one of them was killed in a car crash, so she really, really doted on me. In some ways she was the archetypal granny – a frail old battleaxe. She's not with us any more, died in the 'teens when I was a student-'

'That would be a dedication for your autobiography,' I interrupted, 'or your first novel. But a scholarly work like this? It just … it just jars.'

'Does it?' he said. He looked thoughtfully at the recorder, then leaned forward and turned it off.

*　*　*

I suppose it started (he said) when I'd been dumped on Gran suddenly so that Mum and Dad could Sort Things Out again over the half term break. This was happening more and more by the time I was ten but Gran never minded having me.

I was in the living room doing a jigsaw, which was the highest tech form of entertainment in her household, when I heard the phone ring and her singsong 'Hello' as she answered it. Then:

'... well, I did ask for the week off so I could look after my grandson ...'

'... oh, the poor dear, broken right through? In plaster ...'

'... well, dry slope skiing isn't really for our generation ...'

'... well, I could cover for her, but my grandson ...'

'... take him with me? Are you sure that's wise?'

One of Gran's few faults was the failure to realise her voice carried. And I was only ten feet away from her, through the wall.

'... hang on, let me write it down ...'

I heard her say goodbye and hang up, and then she popped her head around the door and beamed at me. 'Do you want to come for a drive, dear?' she said.

Gran lived in one of those little greenbelt villages within the M25 – a small, secluded place that you wouldn't have thought was only a few miles from the country's capital.

'Can you read a map, dear?' she said as we got into her Mini, parked (as it always was) outside her garage. The one time I'd opened the garage doors and peeked in, I'd seen it packed full of boxes and junk that came right up to the entrance. The next moment I was wrestling with an Ordnance Survey map about the same size as me and with a mind of its own, until she showed me how to fold it down so that I was only looking at the relevant bit. 'You can navigate.'

I couldn't navigate to save my life but I now see that involving me this way, keeping me occupied, was her way of taking my mind off the actual drive and what we were doing. Gran had me navigate her – as if she didn't know the way perfectly well herself – to the suburbs of Esher.

'There's an A-Z in the glove compartment, dear,' she said. 'Could you get it out for me?'

Now she had me navigate to a small side road that led into a larger road, packed with rush hour traffic crawling slowly to the far-off motorway. Gran came to the junction, indicating left, and I thought she would wait for a break in the traffic. Then she put her foot down, tyres screeched and she swung out into the traffic stream. Horns blared and the car behind us, a swish black Rover, flashed its lights angrily.

'Gra-an!' I protested. I had an ability to split the word into an indefinite number of syllables, depending on my degree of agitation.

'Oh, sorry, dear. I thought he was slowing down for us,' she said. She reached out and for the first time I noticed that she had a kitchen timer mounted on her dashboard: one of those stopwatch types with a digital display that count down the time and beep at the end. It was set for twenty seven minutes. I shook my head, a mature ten-year-old exasperated at the vagueness of the senior generation, and settled back into my seat, fully expecting to become very familiar with the rear of the car in front of us over the next half hour or so.

It was getting away from us. I realised after a minute that Gran was actually moving slower than this rush hour crawl of traffic. I peeked at the speedometer. The needle pointed to just below 20.

'*Gra-a-an!*'

'Don't want to cause an accident, dear,' she said, not taking her eyes off the road.

The next twenty six minutes were hell on earth. The road ahead was wide open and empty: behind us there must have been a tailback all the way into London, and I could feel the hostility and hatred emanating from it and roasting the back of my head. And the few times there was enough space in the oncoming lane for a car behind to try and overtake us, Gran would speed up slightly so that overtaking wasn't possible.

At last, at long last, the kitchen timer pinged.

'Oh, good, just in time for tea,' she said. She dropped a gear, speeded up to 50 and headed back home without once asking me for directions.

A couple of hours later I was sitting in one corner of the living room doing some homework (numbers fascinated me even then and I'd brought some stuff home from school) while Gran had the news on. After the national stories came the local stuff, which included a pile-up caused by some dickweed who had been doing 70 with one hand on the wheel and the other on his carphone, and had made the wrong choice as to which hand to free up so he could use the gear stick.

'The idiot,' Gran said, not looking up from her knitting. She had a way of always speaking in the same tone of voice but somehow modulating it anywhere between warm gooey honey (which she used for me) and rock-hard ice (like now). 'The idiot.'

Neither of us looked at the picture on the mantelpiece. A man and a boy: my grandfather and my Uncle Edward, both dead before I was born thanks to a not dissimilar road-usage attitude from a not dissimilar individual.

Then there was the screeching of tyres outside on the driveway; the sound of a powerful engine throbbing into silence and a car door slamming.

'Speaking of whom, your father's here, dear,' Gran said, still knitting and still in the same tone of voice. She and Dad had never seen eye to eye: his mobile phone had gone off during my Christening and he still hadn't forgiven her for throwing it in the font.

Yeah, Dad's here, I thought glumly. That showed me who had won the great Sorting Things Out contest back home.

The bell rang, and kept ringing.

'Go and let him in, dear.'

Yes, Dad had definitely won. 'Our Kev!' he shouted when he saw me, rubbing his hands together, grinning all over his face. The same look as when he'd made some extra big deal at work and was expecting Mum to come up with the conjugal goods by means of celebration. He was a big man – big physically, big in personality – and always left me feeling small, even for a boy of ten. 'How's my man?' He threw a couple of mock punches that left me rubbing my shoulder resentfully and bulldozed past me into the living room.

'Hello, Darren,' Gran said, still not looking up from her knitting. His smile became more fixed.

'Hello, Margaret,' he said. 'Almost hit your car again. Why don't you put it in the garage?'

'No one else almost hits it, Darren. Maybe you're driving too fast. How was the motorway?'

'Eh? Oh. All right. Yeah, it was all right, for once. Doing over ninety all the way here.'

'Oh, good.'

'Right!' Dad was rubbing his hands together as he turned to me. 'You ready to come back home, Kev?'

'Yes, Dad.'

'Hey, you're allowed to smile,' he said with a grin. Another mock punch, this time making me wince. 'Well, get upstairs and get your things, then. What's that you've got there?'

'Sums.'

'Sums?' He picked up the textbook and pulled a face. '"Which of these circles has the same area as this square.' Jesus H.! Don't make it easy, do they?'

'I've been stuck on that one for ages,' I said.

'Well, get home and we'll look it up in Wikipedia.'

'I don't want to look it up,' I said, 'I want to work it out.'

'Numbers are for nerds,' he said. It was bad enough for him that his only child wore glasses. He was still smiling but there was a warning in his eyes too. 'Numbers are for the little people in Computing, not Management like my Kev's going to be. You'll have your own people to worry about numbers-'

Dad had built up his business from nothing. And never let anyone forget it.

'What's the area of a circle, Kevin?' Gran said. She had yet to look up. Then she chanted the little rhyme she'd taught me. 'If you want a hole repaired, use the formula-'

'Pi-r-squared,' I said.

'And what's the area of a square?'

Easy. 'One side, squared.'

'So, they're both something squared, aren't they?'

After a moment, light dawned. 'Right!' I grabbed my ruler-

-but Dad was still holding the book and he wasn't going to let it go. 'Upstairs, get your things, now,' he said.

'You see, dear, a lot of things are defined by numbers,' Gran said. 'Some simple, some more complicated, if you just take the trouble to learn them. If you've got the brains to learn them. If it occurs to you that they're worth learning.'

'Now,' Dad said quietly, and he propelled me out of the room with a hand in the small of my back.

When we got home, more to get me out of the way than to make me clean I was sent upstairs to have a bath before bedtime. I had a towel round my waist as I turned the taps on, and then I leapt out onto the landing in one surprised bound as a vibration like a concrete mixer rocked the bathroom.

'Dad!'

Dad appeared at the foot of the stairs.

'What is- oh, Christ.' He came up the stairs two at a time and went into the bathroom, where he turned on the hot tap at the basin. The noise subsided.

'What was that?'

'Just waterhammer, Kev. Started while you were away.'

'What's waterhammer?' I said. It sounded silly. Water was soft. It sloshed. It didn't hammer.

Dad looked annoyed but he could never bear to show ignorance in front of me.

'It's ...' He gestured vaguely. 'A small block in the pipes, Kev, means that not all the water gets through, and some of it flows back, and that knocks more back, and so you get water vibrating all around the pipes and that reminds me, *Louise!* I thought I told you to get the plumber?'

Blaming it on Mum had safely diverted the topic away from the scientific principles of fluid dynamics. My heart sank as Dad strode out to confront Mum.

'I was going to, dear, but-' she said.

'But, but, but,' Dad shouted. 'Christ on a bike, I have to do everything round here.'

'I'll call him now-'

'No, I'll call him-'

'I can do it, Darren-'

'You'll just get it wrong, you silly cow-'

'Darren-'

Slap. There went the reconciliation.

A moment's quiet, and then I silently mouthed the inevitable mantra as Dad spoke it out loud.

'Now look what you made me do.'

* * *

> The professor was looking at me as if what he had said explained everything.

'You've mentioned your grandmother,' I said, 'and you've mentioned waterhammer, but ...'

'It's not obvious?'

'Um, no,' I confessed.

He raised his eyebrows, poured us both another coffee, and continued.

* * *

We were all going off to the Chessington World of Adventure in a proud display of what a normal family we were.

Mum and I had got used to the rhythm of Dad's driving on the M25. You sat still in a traffic jam until the car in front of you started to move, then you accelerated to cruising speed and abruptly braked as the car in front unaccountably continued to crawl. This had been going on for half an hour, punctuated by Dad's 'Jesus fucking Christ' or some variation on the same theologically contentious theme every time he had to slow down.

Finally we began to move. Properly, smoothly, not lurching. The jam was ebbing; the traffic was getting up to all of 40 mph.

'Oh, now that pisses me off. That really pisses me off,' Dad said, when we finally saw what had caused this particular blockage. An ambulance and police car were gathered around a crumpled car on the hard shoulder of the eastbound lane. We were heading west, and our own jam had been caused by nothing less than all the cars in front of us slowing down to have a gawp. 'All those fucking vultures eyeballing

GO WITH THE FLOW

the wreck and they cause a jam behind them and they don't fucking *care*.'

He slammed his foot down and the car shot forward again, this time almost making 70 before the brakes came on once more and Dad was flashing his lights at the car ahead. '*Move!*' he bellowed.

'He's going as fast as he can, Darren,' Mum said, which was the bravest thing she'd said all day.

'He's going as fast as he can,' Dad mimicked. 'Christ, you sound like your mother. Hear that, Kev? When you get a girl, check out her mum first 'cos that's who she's going to turn into.'

I wasn't listening. Something had clicked in my mind: the thought of all those cars ahead of us slowing down, which meant we had to slow down, which meant the ones behind us had to slow down ... One small effect ahead sending forces of action and reaction rippling up and down the lines of traffic, magnifying as it went, flowing back down the motorway and trickling out at the junctions and up onto the side roads. A light tap on the brakes at the right place in the right time and you could surely bring the motorway system to a halt. Or speed it up again.

I was seeing the world in a whole new way. I'd never heard of transient pressure propagation or boundary conditions of a system, but I was picturing them as clear as day. Numbers. Like Gran said, defined by numbers. I was dazzled.

'Waterhammer,' I murmured.

'Oh, Jesus, the boy's off again,' Dad said. 'Dreaming- Look out, you moron! Christ almighty, put some people behind a wheel ...'

* * *

'So,' I said, 'your grandmother put the idea of numbers affecting the real world into your head?'

'Check.'

'And the traffic jam made you see how it could work?'

'Check,' he said again. 'Numbers, in the form of fluid dynamics. I mean, I was only 10 so I can't say it all fell into place there and then, but I realise it was a defining moment. A light on the road to ... well, Chessington.'

So that was it. The explanation of 'To Gran' was a bit of an anti-climax, but it had been a long shot. My journalist's instincts weren't always right.

'Well, thank you-' I started to say.

'There's more,' he said. 'I mean, it's all very well using the principles of waterhammer in a system but how do you get the system hammering in the first place?'

* * *

A month later I was back with Gran again and this time it was for keeps. I'd missed out on the details of what started it: I was getting good at simply filtering out the raised voices as the ultimatum *du jour* from Mum collapsed. So it was quite a surprise when a weeping Mum burst into my room, yanked me from the computer and dragged me out to the car. Dad had already gone off on his post-eruption trip to the pub

GO WITH THE FLOW

so she was able to get me out of the house without obstruction.

Dad turned up at Gran's soon after us. He did his usual trick of not taking his finger off the door bell until he got an answer.

Gran went out to open the door and I heard the voices in the hall.

'My wife here, Margaret?'

'My daughter and grandson are, here, Darren, yes.'

'Right.'

The door to the living room flew open and Dad stood there, glaring at Mum in her chair in the corner.

'You stupid cow, you don't go off without telling me!'

'And what stupid cow would that be, Darren?' said a mild voice behind him. He didn't look round.

'Look,' he said, 'all I said was-'

'Darren,' said the voice again, 'my daughter has come to visit me and you will kindly not block me out of my own living room in my own home.'

Dad subsided. Slightly. He stood to one side to let Gran come into the room, and bowed a fraction of an inch.

'Margaret,' he said with forced courtesy, 'may I speak to my wife in private?'

Gran held his gaze for a moment, then shrugged. 'If you will.' She took Mum's hand gently. 'Darren wants to talk to you, dear,' she said quietly. 'Come into the hall, and don't worry, I'll be right here in the next room. Be brave.'

Mum went out like a sheep to the slaughter and Dad shut the door behind them. Raised voices started coming through the wall almost at once, and Gran put her arms round me and held me tight.

The voices were getting louder, until:

'You're not fucking leaving me, you're my wife!' Dad shouted.

'Darren-' Mum said.

'You're coming home now!'

'I'm staying, Dar-'

Slap. And that was when Gran made her move. She let go of me and slowly, deliberately went back out into the hall. Mum's quiet weeping got louder as she opened the door.

'Now look what you made me do!'

'Look what you made me do,' Gran said quietly. 'The cry of pathetic bullies who've run out of excuses.'

'Margaret, if I'm not taking my wife-'

'My daughter,' Gran said.

'-then I'm taking my son.'

'My daughter's staying here,' Gran said, 'and so is Kevin. The poor dear deserves better than you.'

'Oh, *right*.' I found the courage to peek round the door. Dad was towering over Gran, standing six inches away so that he looked right down at her, and she wasn't in the least fazed. 'Let's see what the courts say, eh? A prozac addict and an old lady looking after a ten-year-old boy.'

'Courts side with the mother,' Gran said,

'Not with my lawyers, Margaret.' Then Dad saw me. 'At last, someone who isn't snivelling and whining. C'mere, Kev. I'm taking you home.'

I was rooted to the spot.

Dad's smile fixed. 'Come here, Kevin.'

My mouth moved.

'What's that? Speak up.'

'You hit Mum,' I whispered. Mum herself was leaning against the wall, still sobbing, and hadn't joined in the conversation since the slap.

'My hand slipped, didn't it? Come on, Kev!' He engaged wheedle mode. 'Look, I'll get tickets for Wembley and we'll-'

It took several tries but I managed to say it. 'I'm staying here.'

For the first time, Dad was surprised. His eyes widened and his jaw dropped, and he took a step forward.

'You are coming with me whether you-'

Gran had also moved a step and was blocking him. The only way he could physically reach me was to push her aside, and they were both doing mental computations as to what the courts would say to a father in a custody case who beats his wife and manhandles little old ladies.

Dad ceded loss of the battle, if not the war. He took a step back.

'I'm getting Kevin,' he said quietly, 'and neither of you cows are going to stop me.'

He left, slamming the door behind him. Then the thud of the car door, the revving of the engine, the screeching of tyres and the sound of the car fading away.

'Take your mother upstairs, dear,' Gran said to me. 'This is an emergency and I've got phone calls to make.'

Mum was lying in bed, prozaced to a higher plane of existence, and I was sitting by her side, stroking her hand and trying hard not to cry. Because Dad hated 'little boys that blubbed.' Funny, the way we can still want the respect of people we can come to loathe.

Gran appeared in the doorway. 'Is Mummy sleeping?'

'Yes,' I said.

Gran sighed. 'Well, I can't leave you here with her. If we get burgled she'll never wake up anyway. Come with me.'

She led me downstairs and into the hall, and over to a tall bookcase on the far wall. She reached up and touched a book on the top shelf, beyond my reach. The bookshelf moved aside to reveal a doorway.

I gasped and Gran smiled.

'It's just the garage, dear.'

Picture this: sleek, low lines of polished black metal; a turbine whining into action; fins; gull wing doors hissing slowly open ...

That wasn't what it looked like at all but it's how I like to remember it. In fact, the car that faced the doors was a Morris Minor. Between it and the doors was the thin screen of junk that faced anyone opening the doors from outside, as I had once done. The 'junk' was like a stage set – a veil of boxes and nothing more.

I gazed around while Gran opened the passenger door for me. At the back of the garage was a truly awesome computer bank, monitors glowing with mapped-out road routes and columns of figures scrolling slowly past.

Gran followed my gaze. 'It links to the Highways Agency's mainframe, dear,' she said. 'I'll explain everything, but for now, get in and remember your seatbelt.'

We got in and I strapped myself in securely. Gran pressed a button on the dashboard which made the junk screen slide to one side and the garage doors swing open. The car lunged forward, swerved around her Mini parked outside and sped out into the night.

Now isn't the time, but if you've ever wondered what it would be like to drive a turbo charged Morris Minor, I'm the man to tell you. And the surprises weren't over yet.

'Open the glove compartment, please, dear,' Gran said. I tugged on the little door, and yelped in surprise when a small computer console slid out and a screen popped up. Another glowing road network, with two blobs clearly marked.

'We're the white blob, your father is the red one,' she said. 'I thought this day might come so I took the liberty of bugging his car a couple of weeks back.'

I gaped at her.

'When he left us he stopped off at a pub, so we should be able to catch him up. My colleagues have been keeping him within range.'

A cluster of other white blobs appeared, each with a number attached to it.

'Oh, good. The others are online,' Gran said. She unhitched a microphone from under the steering wheel. 'WH7 to all patrols, target is making for the M25. Essential that he be routed onto a B-road. WH Central, please provide instructions ...'

After a moment another voice spoke. It was another old lady's voice but it spoke like a police dispatcher off *The Bill*. 'WH3, take B2219 into Banstead, maintain patrol speed. WH12, make best speed to Epsom and await instructions. WH7, make best pursuit and good luck.'

The other WH numbers radioed in their compliance. Old ladies, and old men too: the kind of voice that said I Wear A Hat In My Car.

'Give 'em what for, eh, Mags?' one man's voice boomed.

Gran held her radio up to her mouth. 'This is WH7. Acknowledged, WH Central, and thank you. And thank you, George.'

'You're welcome, Marg- WH7.'

Gran hung up and pressed another button on the dash, and a police siren blared out. I wriggled round to look behind us and only then realised the noise was coming from our own car.

'Gran-' I said.

'Don't worry,' she said.

'The police-'

'-will check their computer and see that it says another car is on the case. They won't interfere. Now, let Gran concentrate, dear.'

We hurtled through darkest Surrey, through red lights and the wrong way round roundabouts; flashing at slower drivers until they were forced to pull over and let us by (and what I wouldn't have given to see their faces when they saw what it was that was overtaking them); always closing the gap that lay between the hunter and its prey. The drama playing itself out on the computer display was fascinating: Dad's red blob in the middle and the circle that was WH's 3, 8, 9, 12,

16, 18 and 19 tightening around it. And us, WH7, now so close that our blobs were almost touching.

The man's voice came over the radio again. 'Soon have him, Maggie, eh what?'

Was it my imagination or was Gran's voice slightly softer when she answered?

'I think so, George, yes.'

'What you doing later, Mags? How about dinner for two, candles and a chance to show these young 'uns that the old generation can still-'

'*George!* I mean, WH16, this is an open channel and ... others are listening.'

'Let 'em!' the old codger declared. 'Who cares-'

'Including children,' Gran said firmly.

WH Central spared Gran's further blushes by ordering all cars to maintain silence unless reporting on progress.

Gran turned the siren off and a few minutes later Dad's BMW hove into view ahead of us. I recognised the licence plate.

'He's got to take the next left,' Gran muttered. 'It will be very inconvenient if he doesn't.'

Dad was showing no sign of slowing down or indicating, though since he rarely did either at the best of times it was impossible to guess his intentions. And then we came round a bend and I saw two cars ahead of him, driving abreast and blocking the road: a half-timber Morris Traveller and a Hillman Avenger. Dad braked sharply and I could almost hear the 'Christ almighty' and imagine him thumping the steering wheel. But there was no getting round the two cars and Dad wasn't a man to suffer that kind of speed, so he swerved into the next left turning.

Gran thumped her own wheel. 'Yes!' she said. She unhooked the microphone again. 'Thank you, WH9, WH16. Target is mine: am proceeding alone.'

'Good luck, Ma- WH7. WH16 out and, ahem, see you later, eh?' said George.

'Oh, really, that man,' Gran murmured as she hung up the microphone again, but something told me she was pleased.

Our two cars were alone on the road now. Gran revved up towards the BMW I looked at Dad's approaching car with horror. I'd watched too much James Bond: who knew what else this Morris marvel had under its bonnet? Machine guns, missiles, lasers-

'Don't kill him, Gran!' I blurted.

Gran said nothing. Did the car speed up slightly?

'Gran!' I grabbed at the wheel but I couldn't move it.

'Don't be silly, dear,' Gran said. 'Brace yourself.'

We rammed the back of the car and I felt the belt tighten across me and hold me firmly in my seat. Then, as Dad began to slow, Gran pulled back and accelerated to overtake. I had a brief glimpse of my father's staring face before the Morris slammed into the side of the BMW. And this time there was no rebound: Gran held the wheel over, forcing Dad off the road. He hit the pavement, winged the car on a lamppost and ploughed into the bank.

'Stay here, dear,' Gran said as the car screeched to a halt. She pulled out a bag from beneath her seat and I twisted round in my seat to watch the confrontation as she strode towards the wrecked vehicle. Dad's door opened and he got out, staggering but still intact.

'You fucking lunatic!' he bellowed. 'What the fucking hell are you doing? You'll be hearing from-'

GO WITH THE FLOW

He stopped, peered forward. 'Margaret?'

Gran was fishing about in the bag. She found something and held it out towards him. Dad crumpled at the knees and fell face forward on the ground.

I screamed. '*Dad!*' I knew it. Gran had killed him. I tore out of the car and over to where she was crouching over the body. I flung myself at her, sobbing, and tried to haul her off. 'Get off him, get off him–'

'He's all right, darling!' Gran said. 'Look. Help me roll him over.'

I did and saw to my amazement that he was breathing, his eyes were flickering and there was no blood anywhere. Gran held a small aerosol in front of my eyes for my inspection.

'Knockout gas,' she said. 'He'll only be out for a couple of minutes. You didn't think I'd make my daughter a widow, did you?'

She opened the bag again and started to lay things out on the ground with swift precision. A bottle of clear liquid. A tube. An empty whisky bottle. For the first time I noticed she was wearing gloves.

'Though I admit,' she added as she attached one end of the tube to the end of the first bottle, 'it's a tempting thought. Hold this for me, will you?'

She gave me the bottle of liquid. The other end of the tube went into Dad's mouth.

'Gran!'

She winked as she rose to her feet. 'I'm not asking you to poison your father, dear. It'll just solve a little problem and leave him none the worse for wear.'

She took Dad's right hand and wrapped his fingers round the empty whisky bottle, then touched the neck of the bottle to his mouth. She turned towards Dad's car and I let my bottle, the full one, drop slightly.

'Kevin!' she said without turning round. I quickly lifted it back to its former level and watched as she tucked the whisky bottle under the driver's seat. Then she came back to me, plucked the tube from Dad's mouth and relieved me of the clear stuff. 'Let him try to pass a breathalyser test with this little lot inside him!' she said. She packed everything away into her bag and stood up, ticking points off on her fingers.

'Breath ... bottle ... fingerprints ... saliva ...' She turned to me and beamed. 'I think we've done everything, dear, and I don't think the divorce court will be very sympathetic after this little event. Least of all when he starts raving to the police about being forced off the road and knocked out by his mother-in-law. Oh, that reminds me, we'd better call them–'

Then she stopped, head cocked to one side. We could hear police sirens. Real ones. 'Quicker off the mark than I thought, dear,' she said. 'We'd better be off. Get back in the car, now.'

She paused briefly to feel under the BMW's bumper. When she came up to me she handed me a small metal and plastic disc. 'A souvenir, dear,' she said.

I finally, finally found the strength and the breath to say something.

Originally enough, it was, 'Gran–'

The sirens really were close. She put a firm hand on my shoulder 'Come on, dear, we don't want to get involved. I don't believe in telling lies to policemen.'

* * *

The professor stopped abruptly, looking thoughtful.

'You're making it up,' I said, when it became obvious he wasn't going to say anything else.

He grinned.

'I mean,' I said, 'you're telling me your grandmother and her friends were using the waterhammer effect to keep the motorways clear?'

'Clear?' the professor exclaimed. 'If you'd ever driven on a motorway in the 1990s you wouldn't ask that. No, quite the opposite. They were deliberately keeping the motorways, or at least the M25, clogged up with the traffic that would otherwise have driven through their peaceful little villages. They lived in idyllic havens and wanted to keep it that way ... of course, if you've lost your husband and son to fast drivers then holding up the boy racers would be its own reward anyway. There might have been spin-off organisations doing the same thing elsewhere in the country, but I think Gran's people were the originals.

'Remember, even back in the nineties, and earlier, authorities were already applying fluid dynamics to traffic theory. That was how traffic lights were run, for instance. But Gran and her friends took it that extra bit further. They knew it just takes a little action here and there to send shockwaves all around the system, and if you use a powerful enough computer and the right chaotic algorithms to plan your moves, you can use those shockwaves to clear the roads, or to block them. That's what that little traffic-calming cruise of hers was all about.'

'But-'

'And then came the personal flyer,' he added, 'and the cars all but vanished from our roads, so of course it's not a problem any more. Not for those of us who still drive everywhere, anyway.'

I was trying to spot a flaw in what he'd said. Any logical catch.

'Where did they get their money from?' I said. 'That equipment must have cost.'

'Life savings. They weren't rich but they weren't exactly poor either.' He looked at his watch. 'Well, it's been unexpectedly pleasant but time is pressing. Are you flying back?'

'Of course,' I said.

'Good luck.'

* * *

I sat in the cockpit of my flyer, waiting for permission to join the main southbound airstream at 500 feet. It was jammed solid up there.

A network of agents cruising the nation's highways, driving their cars in certain areas, at certain speeds, for certain times, all calculated by the big computer ...

Ridiculous.

Of course, the kind of individual who thought the entire UK road network was laid out for his personal benefit wasn't going to be compliant. A traffic jam in one place would just make him drive faster elsewhere – maybe even through the villages they were trying to keep clear. Therefore, as well as the regulars there would have to be special operatives, with special equipment, acting against persistent offenders ...

Still ridiculous.

I glanced in annoyance at my watch, then up at the airstream above me. It was packed solid with flyers and traffic clearance was a long time in coming. I could almost believe it was laid on for my own benefit.

About GO WITH THE FLOW

To date, this is my last published short story. *Interzone* published it four months after *His Majesty's Starship* appeared, and since then it's been novel writing all the way. Sadly, life is too short for both; or at least, mine is.

Have you ever been stuck behind someone who never had to worry about the car in front when he or she was learning, because it was at least ten miles away and there were only about ten in the whole country? Have you ever encountered another driver whose body may be with us but whose mind is evidently two or three planes of existence removed from our own? Have you ever wondered how it is possible for someone to drive a motorised vehicle so tooth-achingly, nerve-renderingly *slow?*

This is for you.

Acknowledgements

'Digital Cats Come Out Tonight' was first published in *Digital Dreams*, edited by David Barrett, 1990, NEL, ISBN 0-450-53150-3.

'Memoirs of a Publisher' was first published in *Interzone* 43, January 1991.

'Crush' was first published in *Interzone* 68, February 1993.

'Getting Rid of Teddy' was first published in *Interzone* 76, October 1993.

'The Data Class' was first published in *Interzone* 80, February 1994.

'Jacqui the Giantkiller' was first published as 'Giantkiller' in *Interzone* 89, November 1994.

'The Robson Strain' was first published in *Interzone* 97, July 1995.

'Spoilsport' was first published in *Substance* no. 1, Winter 1994.

'Cathedral No. 3' was first published in *Interzone* 113, November 1996.

'The Grey People' was first published in *Substance* no. 4, Winter 1996.

'Wingèd Chariot' was first published in *Interzone* 118, April 1997.

'Pages Out of Order' was first published in *Fantasy and Science Fiction*, September 1997.

'The Fireworker' was first published in *Altair*, issue 1, 1998.

'Trial by Alien' was first published in *Odyssey*, issue 3, 1998.

'Correspondents' was first published in *Aboriginal SF*, Summer 1998.

'A Holiday on Lake Moskva' appears here for the first time in print, 2008.

'Go with the Flow' was first published in *Interzone* 142, April 1999.

About Ben Jeapes

An overdose of TV science fiction as a child doomed Ben Jeapes to life as a science fiction author. He took up writing in the mistaken belief that it would be quite easy (it isn't) and save him from having to get a real job (it didn't). His novels to date are **His Majesty's Starship**, **The Xenocide Mission**, **Time's Chariot**, **The New World Order**, **Phoenicia's Worlds**, **The Teen, the Witch & the Thief**, and **The Comeback of the King**. His ambition is to live to be 101 and 7 months, so as to reach the 1000th anniversary of the Battle of Hastings and the arrival – as family lore has it – of the man responsible for his surname in the British Isles. He is English, and is as quietly proud of the fact as you would expect of the descendant of a Danish mercenary who fought for a bunch of Norsemen living in northern France.

He lives in Oxfordshire and his homepage is at www.benjeapes.com.

Made in the USA
Charleston, SC
05 March 2016